JACOB FLOYD

NIGHT
OF THE
POSSUMS

Other books by Jacob Floyd:

The Pleasure Hunt

<u>Paranormal Nonfiction with Jenny Floyd</u>

Louisville's Strange and Unusual Haunts
Kentucky's Haunted Mansions
Haunts of Hollywood Stars and Starlets
Indiana's Strange and Unusual Haunts

JACOB FLOYD

NIGHT OF THE POSSUMS

Nightmare Press
Louisville, KY

To all the opossums of the world—and possums, for that matter—I swear I mean you no harm! And yes—I do know it's actually *o*possums, and not possums. But, *Night of the Opossums* just doesn't have the same ring to it.

Most of all, thank you, reader, for picking up this book and giving me a chance to entertain you. I truly hope you enjoy. None of us writers would be anywhere without those of you who read us. There are not enough thanks to give you for that honor.

JACOB FLOYD

NIGHT OF THE POSSUMS

Thank you for reading! If you like the book, please leave a review on Amazon and Goodreads. Even if you don't like it, please still leave a review.

A QUICK WORD ABOUT THIS BOOK...

Though this novel is meant to be nothing more than a fun read, like something out of a midnight movie madness or schlock horror lineup, or some old-school pulp novel, it is a very important story to me. It was an idea I had back in 2006, twelve years back from the day I am writing this, while I was working at a fast food joint and walking everywhere I had to go.

When one has no car and has to walk everywhere they need to be, they see an assortment of odd things: creepy people lurking around houses, peeping in windows; idiots driving around dressed as Michael Myers while listening to the *Halloween* theme music; a family of deer picking through suitcases near an abandoned house in an open field; couples shamelessly "making out" (a euphemism) in Wal-Mart's parking lot, right up front by the store; drunkards walking the streets with their pants around their knees, waving their arms around and challenging people to engage them in fisticuffs; and, of course, wild animals going about their daily, and nightly routines. I'd seen them all, and then some. Not to mention the fact that there were times when I was no doubt a strange sight to those who spotted me. I recall once I was walking through the field across from the restaurant I worked at, carrying a large golf umbrella, and I scared the wits out of some stoner at the edge of the field upon exiting because he thought my umbrella was a large rifle. The town of Hillview may be small, but it is certainly interesting.

I saw possums a lot; well, to be technical, they are called opossums (part of the order, Didelphimorphia) on this side of the world, though in the south, most of us just call them possums. But, officially, the possum (an arboreal marsupial suborder also known as Phalangeriformes) resides on the other side of Earth. These creatures are, in fact, two entirely different breeds. But, the opossum, which from here on will be referred to

i

simply as 'possum,' can be seen all over Kentucky, and during my days footing it about town, I had seen several of them. One night, a friend of mine and I were walking back from work, and we saw two very large possums walking through the field, and I said, "What if they just started attacking us?"

That comment kind of died there, but over the next few days, I began thinking of a story about possums rising up and attacking people. I decided *Night of the Possums* sounded good. I thought about writing it, but I didn't have much time nor did I have the resources to write much of anything back then. Also, I thought to myself that no one would read something like that. Whether or not they will still remains to be seen, but here we are, nonetheless.

So, the story sat in my mind for more than a decade. Around that time, I started writing a really bad story called *The Man Who Imagined a Fly*, which took me about three years to complete, and it is simply atrocious. The premise is good, the title is catchy, but the end result is terrible: a 220,000 word, laborious, mundane, rambling narrative starring an unlikeable character and it's not even worth the gigabytes it occupies on my thumb drive or in my computer—yes, I still have it. I might brush it off one day. But, my intention was to tie that story to *Night of the Possums*, both of which involved characters that would appear in crime novels I planned to write (one I did start, and I'll mention that one in a second): totally stupid, novice bullshit that never would have worked. So, I scrapped all that refuse and moved on.

I went through a phase of writing crime novels (more like crime novel), which consisted of a first draft that I wrote for three years that never went anywhere. Then, I got serious about writing, sat down at a local library, since we had no computer at the time, and wrote two stories in six months. Tried pitching them, got constantly rejected, and semi-gave up.

Then, my wife and I went to see the *Goosebumps* movie in 2015, and my long-time love for horror—a love I had turned my nose up to and abandoned some time in my early twenties—came back to me. In a rushing tide, I got all these ideas for a bunch of stories to write (ideas that are slowly taking shape today). I was in the middle of writing *The Pleasure Hunt* at the time and *Night of the Possums* was still in my head, waiting to be written. But, I had a conundrum on my hands: Which direction was I to take *Night of the Possums* in? Horror? Comedy? A little bit of both? I didn't know.

Then, I discovered James Herbert and read *The Rats*. After that, I knew where to go. The book, from the onset, was already inspired by *Night of the Living Dead*. When I watched Alfred Hitchcock's *The Birds* a couple of years after having the story idea, it influenced some aspects of the development, as well. But after *The Rats*, I knew how I wanted to write *Night of the Possums*; and, as I wrote it, it began to take some minor influence from *Jurassic Park*, which I read in 2012. That bit of influence will not be so prevalent in this book, though, but will come out more in any sequels that I may or may not write. I won't say much else about it. Also, I believe that my brief stint of watching Lucio Fulci's cheesy gore fests began to show its ugly head at times in the book, too.

So, at heart, *Night of the Possums* is animal swam horror through and through. Its premise is absurd, no doubt. But, I didn't just throw it together without getting to know my subject. I did a lot of research on the opossum and its behaviors. I also went back into its history, and pre-history, as well as into the origins of the entire marsupial order. I would not call myself an expert by any means, but I did pick up some tidbits that enhanced the story, as well as some information that helped me develop a potential *Possums* series; and, I edited this sucker about eight times. So, while the foundation for this story sounds silly and wild (and it is meant to be), I did put in the effort to at least make it informed. I also wrote it to be dark and bloody, so it's not a comedy. So, while I would never call this book my magnum opus, or present it as some profound work of literary genius (which it most certainly is not), I did try to make it a semi-serious story about people trapped in horrifying situations, who use everything they've ever learned in life to survive. Basically, it's just meant to be fun.

But, to me, this book does have deep, personal meaning. It means I can accomplish something. For years, I always had ideas, and for years I never had motivation, because I never thought I could ever really pull anything off. I also never thought anyone would be interested in anything I ever wrote. My wife comes along and changes everything. She has often motivated me, and with her help, I've begun to believe I can actually do things. It was she who got us started on the paranormal writings, and because of her, I was able to type our first paranormal project up in two weeks while the publisher was waiting on it. I carried this story in my head for over ten years, thinking that it would be fun, but that I could never do it. And here it is: I did it!

I submitted it to many small press publishers, and had several rejections. But, I also had a few interested and two who were ready to publish it. But, because this novel was so important to my drive as a writer, and since it had been in my head for so long, and since it was something so personal to me (and because we wanted to start our own press, anyway), I opted to publish this story myself and open Anubis Press's horror imprint, Nightmare Press, with it. Two hopes I have, going forward, is that the story entertains people, and that there will be many more quality horror novels (both from myself and other writers) filling the Nightmare Press library right alongside it. If that were to ever happen, *Night of the Possums* will continue to tell that I can do it.

Real quick, I want to mention that the story is based in a real location: the historic town of Bardstown, KY, which was voted as the "Most Beautiful Small Town in America" in the Destination Marketing Association International's "Best of the Road" competition in 2012. There's a lot of history in Bardstown, and a few allegedly haunted mansions—check out our book *Kentucky's Haunted Mansions* if you're interested in such things. But, while the town is real, and even some of the street names are too, I took liberties with the actual geography, shop names, and the city layout to suit the purposes of my story and also not to call out any real homes. I just wanted to get that out of the way before we move on.

So, I hope you enjoy my labor of love. If you do (even if you don't), please leave me a review on Amazon and Goodreads. You might not know how much that helps us authors out. But, either way, I want to thank you from the bottom of my heart for reading this struggle of mine. It won't change your life or anything like that, or wound you, or tug your heartstrings. But, I hope it will at least make you say, "What the hell?" once or twice (preferably after you're done reading it).

Thank you deeply, sincerely,
---Jacob Floyd

Night of the Possums

CHAPTER ONE

T he night of the possums began on a chilly autumn morning around 2am in late October. Brandon Smith was driving his girlfriend home and the headlight beams from his raggedy Honda hit the misty night, sweeping shadows across the street. The bushes by the roadside looked like tiny animals skittering through the dark, so Brandon didn't see the fat possum try to cross the road until it was too late.

"Shit!" he exclaimed, pressing on the brakes.

His Civic needed work underneath: whenever he tried to stop, the whole car rattled. He stomped down so hard this time that the vehicle, barely slowing, pulled to the side and crunched the creature beneath the front passenger tire.

Rachel Owens felt the bump and cringed. Possums didn't exactly qualify as cute, cuddly creatures, but they were still living things with feelings; the thought of one getting smashed beneath the car made her sad. There was never a shortage of road kill in Bardstown, Kentucky—especially possum—but she didn't want be a party to the slaying.

"Brandon! Weren't you watching?" she snapped.

"Yeah, but the damn thing came out of nowhere."

"Do you think you killed it?"

"Probably—that was a pretty bad bump. But, those things are resilient as hell. It might have lived."

She nodded but knew he was only trying to make her feel better.

They drove on with the radio playing one of Brandon's metal CDs that Rachel didn't know. He liked so many bands but she wasn't into a lot of them. She knew some of the names, like Suicidal Tendencies, Ghost, and Wizards & Demons, but she couldn't pin a track to any of them. She didn't mind hard rock—she could name several songs by Aerosmith and Bon Jovi—but she didn't get into the heavy stuff. She was more into artists like Lady Gaga, Amy Winehouse, and Bruno Mars, anyway.

She and Brandon had been together for nearly seven years—since they were seniors in high school. Neither of them had pursued college after graduation. Brandon managed a grocery store and Rachel had worked at a local hardware store since she was sixteen. Tools and gadgets interested her. She'd considered trade school until her parents died in a hotel fire during a business trip in South Carolina. She was about to turn twenty then and it really put her life in a stasis from which she had yet to recover. Her little brother, Todd, was seven when it happened. He was twelve now and still having serious problems dealing with the loss. All he'd had since then was her, and Rachel knew she wasn't the best role model. She didn't set a bad example or anything; she just didn't have any life experience to impart. She was pretty much rolling aimlessly along, same as him.

Brandon had always been good to Todd, playing video games with him, horsing around with him, and her little brother warmed up to him. It was good to have someone help her with life. Having no idea what it was like to be a boy, she couldn't teach Todd to be a man. Brandon had taken Todd under his wing, and he was a good role model; he always tried to do the decent thing even if he came off as abrasive sometimes.

"You ever notice how many possums we have here?" Brandon asked. "They're everywhere, always getting into trash and shit, walking out into the road and getting smashed. You can't even feed a dog outside without them scrounging around."

Rachel had no response for that, so she just shrugged.

It was always dark at night on the roads through Bardstown, like traveling through an endless shadow. The only place that looked like it had much life was the west end of Stephen Foster Avenue that cut through the historic district, and then Third Street down to John Rowan Boulevard. These were the main thoroughfares, and everything beyond them was a shady side street.

Rachel and Todd lived on one of those streets: Cypress Street, in a house willed to her upon her parents' death. Getting that mess settled was a headache, but a lot of folks were willing to help her through it since they knew her and the family. But, once the smoke had cleared, most of them vanished. There were a few that still came around to see if she and Todd were okay, but their number began to dwindle not long after. Soon, it was just her, Todd, and Brandon.

As the Civic pulled onto Cypress, weariness hit her and her eyes wanted to close. The hours at the hardware store were long sometimes because of the turnover rate, and tonight she had worked almost twelve hours and wanted to die.

They pulled into her driveway and Brandon walked her to the door. As she fiddled with the lock, he put a hand on her shoulder and said, "I know you're tired. I won't keep you up. Do you need anything before I go?"

She shook her head, feeling the sharp strands of her sweaty brown hair whip around.

"Okay then." He kissed her on the cheek. "Goodnight."

"Goodnight," she replied and kissed him back.

She watched as Brandon went to his car and left. Once he was gone, she went inside.

Todd was asleep in his room. He was on fall break but didn't stay up late because he was a morning person, just like her—just like mom and dad had been.

The doors were locked, all lights were out. She made herself a light sandwich and went to her room to eat it and fall asleep watching *Night of the Living Dead* on Netflix.

Brandon drove back the way he came, a little faster than before, as he often did when he drove alone. As he drew nearer to where he had hit the possum, he wondered what became of it. He was sorry he ran it over, but he couldn't help it. He didn't have time to stop though he tried. Stupid things supposedly had good night vision, couldn't it see the headlights?

The CD in his stereo had come to an end so he turned it off for a regular station. There was an announcer talking in a really serious tone about some dead body found somewhere Brandon didn't catch. He turned up the volume so he could hear it better.

A very grisly scene indeed, the newswoman said. *It appears the young man was gouged several times all over his body, with some severe tissue damage and heavy lacerations. Authorities think he was mauled by animals. In the last two days, there have been reports of animal bodies found in similar states—a couple of dogs and even a horse—but no humans, until now.*

"Damn," Brandon said and turned the radio off.

Something's going around chewing people up?

He recalled stories about the Chupacabra he heard back in the 90s, but he'd thought that was all bullshit. People got all excited about that creature because of Art Bell and *the X-Files.* But he figured that creature was just a coyote anyway, and that's probably what had killed the person they were talking about on the radio—that or wolves.

The Honda's headlights cut once more into the rolling mist. He expected to see the bright-red splatter of the obliterated possum festering on the ground any second. No one was on the road with him so he slowed down to take a look, simply out of morbid curiosity.

He hoped he'd missed the creature altogether and that the crunch under the car was just a big tree branch, though he doubted that was the case. When he came upon the scene of the crime, he saw the carcass from more than fifteen feet away. The bright lights revealed the mangled corpse of the poor possum spread across the road. It looked like he had rolled the thing with the tire once or twice. He crept closer and saw it was pretty twisted, and he felt bad because of it.

As he pulled upon it, he thought he saw its ears twitch. The cranium, amazingly, was still intact. Suddenly, the head shot up and started looking around, causing Brandon to hit the brake hard.

"What the hell?"

The car screeched to a halt, the squeal of the tires piercing the still night. He got out and left his headlights on so he could see ahead of him as he walked towards the animal. The possum seemed to watch him approach, its white-face with light specks of blood on it looking more like a Halloween mask than the countenance of a living creature. When Brandon stopped just a few inches from it, gazing upon the scattered viscera, the dying beast peered up at him with shiny black eyes and began to growl.

Brandon sighed. "You should be dead, little buddy. Sorry, I hit you."

He decided it would be best if he got his gun and put the thing out of its misery. When he turned for the car, he heard hissing from the yards beyond the light. He looked around and saw nothing. More growling, not coming from the injured possum, joined the noise. The sounds grew like an echo in an alleyway. Dogs barked far away. Brandon started to get chills from the eerie orchestra, so he continued to his car and halted a few feet from the vehicle when he saw some small dark shapes running behind it.

"What in the hell?"

He leaned into the car, snatched the .9 millimeter from his glove box, and moved back out into the night. He walked up the road, partly to euthanize the possum, and partly to find out what was causing the strange, intense noises whispering around him.

In a few seconds, he stood above the possum. "Sorry about this," he said and then shot it, blowing its face to bits.

The gunshot rumbled through the night like thunder. No doubt that would draw the cops. When the air finally fell silent, he looked around wondering what had happened to the sibilant symphony that had been recently conducted in the dark. He didn't have to ponder long; seconds after the echo faded, more small shadows darted through the lights. The hissing resumed and the growls grew more menacing. Soft scrapes and clacks of tiny claws started to click away like the chattering of katydids in the summer. Brandon saw small glowing orbs dancing in the darkness as more shadows passed behind him. The scraping started to resound up the street in front of him.

Nervousness settled in. The presence of an unknown predator began to press upon him. The growling and skittering were on every side and the flash of shiny orbs was multiplying by the second. Brandon decided the orbs were eyes and immediately recalled the radio report about the man who was torn apart by an unidentified assailant.

Away down the road, another car was coming. Its beams were extremely bright, and even though it was many, many feet away, it cast enough light to reveal an army of small creatures gathering in the road. There seemed to be a hundred eyes reflecting the light. The car soon turned and when its headlight glow dissipated, Brandon noticed his own lights were not as bright as they had been.

He looked around and saw dozens of the creatures had emerged from the darkness and were actually blotting out the light. There was a cacophony of warning growls circling him. When he turned back around and took a closer look, he saw the band of tiny white possum faces staring back at him, their lifeless black eyes glittering in the small shafts of the headlights.

"No fucking way," he muttered as the threatening mass converged upon him.

His car was his only escape and the path to it was blocked. So, he turned and fired into the crowd, blowing away some of the possums. This seemed to make the rest of the mob angry. The growls and hisses grew even louder and Brandon rushed for his car.

He had to shoot down a couple more possums along the way. One lunged at him from out of nowhere and bit down on his shoe, driving its fangs through the material and right into his foot. He cried out, shocked that he was actually being attacked by animals such as these, then kicked at it and drove it away.

A possum was waiting for him in the driver's seat when he reached the car. It looked up at him and hissed so hard that saliva flew from its mouth. He leveled his gun and shot it, spraying blood all over the car's interior. He quickly sat down, but jumped out when he saw the inside of his car had been invaded by a horde of the creatures. They hissed and came for him, barely missing him as he got out. He then shot a few more and backed away. He looked up and saw three large possums on the roof of his car; they stared blankly at him and growled. He shot all three before filling teeth sink into the back of his right leg. After crying out, he tried to run but felt his left leg be set upon by a heavy weight. When he looked down, he saw two possums had latched onto him; they pressed their faces to his flesh and started gnawing away.

Brandon screamed as he felt the teeth begin to destroy his skin, chewing and tearing away the tissue. He tried to fire at them but couldn't get a good shot, so he started swinging the butt of his gun and connected with the skull of one possum and knocked it loose. But, it was too late: too many had gathered at his feet and were chomping down on them, climbing on one another to bite at his legs.

He stumbled in front of his car and a possum that was standing on the hood flew out and bit down on his right arm, causing him to drop the gun into the teeming pile of attackers. In the headlights, he saw before him a writhing, bustling rush of possums, flooding around him like an overflowing river. He felt the severe stings and pains of his skin being gnawed upon. His flesh was flying and his blood was squirting out. He fell onto the Honda's hood to escape them, but two more possums leapt at him, one landing on his left shoulder and the other on his arm, and they went to town flaying his skin from the bone.

Rolling off the hood, he fell to his knees, smashing possums under his weight. It didn't matter, though; there were dozens more coming at him, and the searing pain ripping through his nerves brought him to the edge of unconsciousness.

Teeth bit down onto his quads and thighs, dug through his scalp and into his skull; a possum flew onto his face and gouged his left cheek and tore out an eye before descending back into the mass of small angry beasts. Just before everything went black and he fell onto the ground, he felt something dive into his naval and rip into his guts. The last thing he saw was a bunch of anxious white faces with small sharp teeth snarling. His body soon fell down to greet them.

Brandon hit the road unconsciously and never woke up again.

CHAPTER TWO

Greta Harris stood in front of the glass door of her farmhouse on East Flaget St. near the heart of Bardstown. A light rain fell from the grey sky and splattered on the bright green grass in the front yard. One of her clients, Mrs. Barbara, was late for her appointment, which worried Greta because Mrs. Barbara was always punctual. Watching the cars on the street splash water in their passing, Greta sighed and wondered what was keeping her. Never once had she been late; normally, she showed up early. Greta couldn't help but fear that something was wrong.

Her thoughts drifted to what her husband, Tony, might be up to at the garage, and she found herself wishing he was there watching the rain with her. Many times they had enjoyed the serenity of an autumn drizzle sprinkling the town, soaking the brown and yellow leaves that had been scattered in the soft fall breeze. She always liked to watch the leaves fall in autumn, and see the rain paste them to the streets like a middle school mosaic. The sight was always comforting. But, there was no comfort today. Rainy days like this made her lonely, and watching the storm pass through only made the solitude worse. A sense of foreboding hung in the air, as if something bad was coming to town. Greta hated it when she started to feel that way because it was almost always justified. She didn't know if it was the rain or Mrs. Barbara's tardiness, or a combination of the two, but her concern turned to focus on Tony—it always did.

She decided she didn't want to watch the rain any longer, so she turned from the door to head back into the parlor where her current client, Rudy

O'Dell, was waiting for her hair to finish drying. Greta was an accomplished cosmetologist and had the only beauty parlor—outside of the one chain store in the historic district—in all of Bardstown. After managing that other establishment for a while, she decided she wanted to work for herself, but she and Tony didn't want to pay rent on an extra building. So, when they decided it was time to buy a house, they looked for one large enough to house a beauty parlor within. Tony made good money running his family's auto repair shop a few blocks over; combining that with the cheap price of real estate in Bardstown, they were able to close a deal on a large lot with a three story farmhouse where Greta could have her clients come for services. Customers used to request her at the parlor in town, so building a clientele wasn't difficult.

She liked working for herself, never having some half-wit manager breathing down her neck, telling her how to do her job; and she liked that she didn't have to leave the house to go to work. But, what she didn't like was that Tony worked long hours at the garage and she was left at home by herself—sort of—for a large portion of the day. She had her customers, but it wasn't the same. She wanted her man.

She crossed the large wooden floor of the front room, past the kitchen, down a hallway, and into the parlor at the back of the house. The TV was broadcasting some lame soap opera. She hated that stuff, but her customers liked it, along with the absurd daytime talk shows that she figured were probably more scripted than professional wrestling. Rudy was watching closely as some handsome young buck with perfect black hair made sexy eyes at his pretty blonde co-star. These scenes were often so identical that Greta almost believed they were stock footage. She liked romance and all, but she preferred quality over mush. Give her a Sandra Bullock film, or even Julia Roberts, and she was fine. Soap Operas were drivel.

She checked the clock; it was time to lift the dryer bubble off Rudy's head. A news report broke into the show so the elderly lady lost interest.

"Is it time already?" Rudy asked.

"Yes, ma'am."

Greta fiddled with Rudy's hair, making sure everything was in place. One thing she liked about the lady was that she was so predictable; she never changed anything about herself, so Greta didn't have to give her all the monotonous instructions about how to maintain the style she had asked for. Nor did she have to try and sell her hair care products. Rudy already knew what she wanted, and she was clutching it in her hand.

"Oh dear," she said suddenly. "That's terrible."

"What?"

"A young man found dead last night on North 3rd near Hart Avenue. They said it looked like he was attacked by some wild animal."

Earlier that morning, while she was preparing to open the salon, Greta saw a report about a young man found mauled under an overpass around midnight the night before. It was reported that the attack was exceptionally violent. They still hadn't identified the victim, or if they had, Greta had missed it. Hearing that another body had been found churned up that anxiety she had tried to leave at the front door. She looked at the TV and saw that the new victim they were discussing was Brandon Smith, and felt a sudden pang of sorrow because she knew his girlfriend, Rachel Owens, from the hardware store. Not only was she a very sweet young lady, but she had lost her parents not too long ago. Brandon and her brother—Todd, she believed his name was—were all Rachel had left.

"That's Rachel Owens's boyfriend," she said.

"The poor girl from the hardware store who lost her parents a few years ago?"

"Yes."

Rudy's eyes began to water. "How awful."

"Yes, it is."

Rachel was on the screen now, visibly upset. She was crying and said, "He just dropped me off and left me here after work last night. I told him I was tired and wanted to go to bed, so he went home. If I would have just asked him to stay he'd still be here right now."

Poor Rachel broke down and the segment shot away.

"Why would they even interview her about that?" Rudy snapped.

"Because that reporter is an asshole."

Rudy snorted and said, "Greta Harris!" She followed this with a laugh.

"Well, he is."

Rudy nodded. "I believe it."

Greta kept it to herself that the man conducting the interview, Chip James, was an ex-boyfriend of hers from high school, and if ever there was a spokesman for adolescent bravado and roofie use, then it was him. He had date-raped his way through high school and probably college, always getting away with it because his dad was prominent and wealthy—same old story. Every town had at least one silver-spoon-fed sociopath whose reprehensible behavior was always explained away. *Boys will be boys*—right? Only Chip James was never just *some* boy. He was a self-centered son-of-a-bitch with a nonpareil god complex.

Even though she was only a foolish teenager when she dated him, she still regretted having that black mark on her record. Greta was tall and lean and had shiny raven hair and mysterious dark eyes, so she had a lot of boys interested in her. Chip was a beautiful young man on the outside, and the most sought-after boy in school. So, the high school hierarchy pretty much dictated that they had to date. If Greta had known what a monster he was—disrespectful, demanding, self-centered, and abusive (physically and psychologically)—then she would have said fuck the rules and went with somebody else. She'd never forgotten what a scumbag he was and she would have loved to have seen him get attacked by whatever had gotten Brandon. But he got to stand there and report it, instead. It didn't matter, though. He would eventually die like everyone else; and if there was a Hell, he'd surely go there.

Rudy looked around the parlor and saw no other customers waiting.

"This is unusually slow for you, Greta."

"I know. Mrs. Barbara was supposed to be here at three. Usually she's very early. I hope she's okay."

"Oh me, too. I do like Mrs. Barbara. Such a kind young woman."

Young? Mrs. Barbara was somewhere around fifty. But, Rudy was in her mid-sixties. Being thirty-two, Greta found herself having to bite her tongue at the "young woman" remark and decided to change the subject.

"Did you hear about the other body found near the on-ramp?"

"Oh yes. Very peculiar."

"They think it might be wild animals, too."

"Yes, it could be, although we've never had many problems with such things out here. But, anything can happen."

"With the way they're always tearing up nature to build stores, it wouldn't surprise me to see any manner of beast come running out of the woods to seek revenge."

Rudy chuckled. "You have such wit. That's why I like you. That and you do such a fine job with my hair."

"Well, you have fine hair to do the job with," Greta replied.

The doorbell rang. At first, Greta thought Mrs. Barbara had arrived, but then remembered that she always came to the parlor door located around back. She looked towards the front room and said, "I wonder who that is."

"Perhaps you should go see, dear."

Greta rushed to the front door, feeling that sense of menace flaring up inside her. Tony wouldn't ring the doorbell, he's just come in. She suddenly felt chilled and wondered if the mauled bodies were actually murdered by humans, and she paused just outside the front room to consider the possibility that the murderer could be who had come ringing.

The doorbell rang again and she heard a familiar voice boom from beyond the door. "Greta, open up! It's Tommy!"

It was Tony's younger brother and he sounded panicked.

Oh God! Please don't let anything have happened to Tony!

The notion propelled her into immediate action and she rushed to the door, her skin crawling with dread. Her blonde Labrador, Tippi, rose from her slumber in the corner of the living room and ran towards the knocking, cutting Greta off and almost tripping her. Greta slammed into the thick wooden door before pulling it open. Tommy's bulky frame stood there heaving with sweat upon his darkened face. His bushy black hair was matted to his forehead as he tried to compose himself.

Greta put her hands over her mouth. "Oh God, Tommy, tell me nothing's happened to Tony."

He squinted at her and shook his head. "No, no. Tony's fine."

Tippi burst onto the porch and greeted Tommy with two paws against his stomach. Tommy backed away. "Damnit, Tippi!"

Greta closed her eyes and put her hand on her chest. "Thank God!

Tippi was all over Tony, batting her giant paws at him, trying to lick his face. Tommy tried to shove her away but she'd just push her weight forward, refusing to abandon her slobbering onslaught. "Get off of me, Tippi!" he snapped.

"Tippi, get in here!" Greta woke from her relief and pulled the dog back into the house by her collar.

"But, you still ain't gonna believe this," Tommy said stepping into the house after Tippi was well out of the way.

"What?" Greta closed the door behind him.

"Mrs. Barbara's dead."

Greta's eyes went wide. "What? Oh my God. How?"

Tommy shook his head. "It's bad. They said she was mauled by animals right in her front yard. Her daughter found her still holding her mail."

"Ingrid found her?"

"Yeah."

Greta put her hand back over her mouth and tears began to fall from her eyes. "I can't believe it. I've been waiting on her all day."

Tommy put his hand on her shoulder. "I'm sorry, Greta."

She sucked in a deep, shivering sob that caused Tippi to bark loudly and leap towards Tommy as a warning. Two black cats—a fluffy one named Hitch, and one with slick hair named Romero—wandered into the room. At Tippi's sudden outburst, Hitch turned sideways and arched his back and hissed. Romero hunkered down and stuck his butt into the air and growled at the dog. Tippi turned and barked at them both and took off after them, scattering them to the far reaches of the house.

Greta wiped her eyes and said, "She was such a sweet lady."

"Yes, she was."

"When did you hear this?"

"A little bit ago. It came in on the radio while I was at the shop. Tony was busy fixing a school bus, so I came right over to let you know."

Greta shook her head. "That's the third one."

"What?"

"That's the third person killed by an animal attack."

"Really?"

"Yes. A young man's body was found under an overpass last night and Brandon Smith was found on North 3rd. Both of them had been attacked by some animal—or animals."

"Ya' don't say? Shit, I didn't even hear about that."

Rudy wandered into the front room. "I'm sorry to disturb you dear, but I think I'm ready to go now."

Greta turned around and Rudy saw the tears in her eyes. "What's wrong, dear?"

She struggled to explain the situation; she wasn't hysterical, but the words were lodged pretty tight in her throat. Mrs. Barbara had been a client of Greta's for years, dating all the way back to her early days at the salon in town. She was the first to visit her parlor on opening day. It was a heartbreaking loss and the report was hard to say out loud. Luckily, Tommy was there to be her mouthpiece.

"Mrs. Barbara's dead, killed in her front yard."

Just like Greta, Rudy's eyes widened immediately and began to tear up. Her mouth hung agape and she used her right hand to cover it. "Oh no. How?"

"They said she was attacked by an animal."

"Another one?"

"Afraid so."

"Oh dear," Rudy said and approached Greta to embrace her. "I'm so sorry. I know you were close. She was a fine lady."

They hugged, lamenting Mrs. Barbara as Tommy stood idly by. He didn't really know the lady—met her a time or two and thought she seemed pretty nice; he just knew a lot of people in town thought she was odd—but he knew Greta was very fond of her, and it broke his heart to see her so upset. Tony didn't know, yet. Tommy knew he'd be upset, too. She was always really kind to him, telling Greta she picked a wonderful, hardworking man. Tommy wanted to be the one to tell Greta because he knew Tony might not be much comfort to her in this case.

Rudy paid Greta and left a few minutes later. Once she was gone, Tommy asked, "You okay? You need anything from me?"

"I'm fine. I just need to feed the strays."

"I'll hang out here for a few just in case you need something."

"Thank you, Tommy. But, don't you need to get back to the shop?"

"No. Three other guys besides Tony are there. It was my day off. I just went in to finish a job I started yesterday."

"Well, you know where everything is if you want anything. I'll be right back."

Greta left the front room and headed towards the parlor, which seemed like an empty place of sadness at the moment. It was like Mrs. Barbara's ghost was already haunting her home, looking out at her from the beyond. She imagined her sitting in one of the parlor chairs, smiling and telling her about her daughter, Ingrid, or the people at her job. She really loved her work. She was a social worker at the county high school and was actually well-liked by the students. It was going to be a sad day when they heard about her fate. Mrs. Barbara had helped so many of them through rough times.

Greta crossed the parlor towards a cabinet where she kept numerous bags and cans containing a variety of pet food that she fed to the dozens of dogs and cats that hung around the property. Most of the neighborhood strays visited their yard and she fed them because they kept rats, raccoons, possums, and mice at bay. They also deterred any trespassers from trying to sneak in. More than once there had been a prowler slinking about the yard, maybe just passing through or perhaps with ill-intent, and some of the dogs that hung around would alert everyone within earshot about the stranger. Tony would jump up, look out the back window, and see the pack of canines chasing off the frightened straggler. Before the first such incident, Tony hadn't been real keen on Greta feeding all those animals, but after that, he admitted it was a beneficial act.

Carrying two large bags of pet food in her hands, she kicked open the back door and stepped out onto the porch. A dull thud a few feet to her left caught her attention. One of the many metal trashcans at the edge of the driveway was wobbling, as if something moved inside of it. A white-faced possum leapt out a few seconds later, rattling the receptacle, then sprung off and vanished beneath the shed across the yard.

"That's odd," she said. "I usually only see you guys at night."

Shrugging it off, she descended the steps and walked to a small wooden shelter that Tony had built for all the pet dishes lined up along the concrete walkway. She filled five bowls with cat food and five more with dog food, then unraveled the green garden hose in the nearby garden area and filled up ten more bowls with water. Almost immediately the animals began migrating towards the buffet. They knew the sounds of the bags and the food rattling around in the tin dishes. The gurgling of the hose and the splashing of the water were familiar sounds that told them mealtime had arrived. Within a couple of minutes, numerous cats and dogs had congregated at the watering/feeding hole to begin their afternoon feast. Greta smiled, picked up the bags, and went back up the steps. For a moment, this took her mind off Mrs. Barbara.

Just before she stepped back inside the house, she looked sadly out towards the driveway leading up to the parlor. Mrs. Barbara's old Ford should be there now, like the countless times it had been before. But, it wasn't, and it never would be again. Greta couldn't believe she was dead.

She turned back to the backyard and saw two possums peeking out from under the shed. Their black eyes were staring directly at her. In her stomach, some sort of dread began to churn. For some inexplicable reason, they made her nervous. Maybe they were just observing the feeding frenzy, waiting for the animals to leave so they could scavenge the remains. Possums liked pet food and would not pass up an opportunity to steal away with as much of it as they could. But, she looked harder and could see they weren't facing the other animals—they were facing her. It was crazy, but she could feel them watching her, as if there were some unspoken menace passing between them.

Greta stepped back and closed the door, not wanting to be exposed to those creepy creatures any longer.

CHAPTER THREE

H uck Davis pulled his van into the driveway of a long, one-story brick home located at the bend on Westwind Trail. He had received a call from Selma Donaldson about fifteen minutes prior claiming that several possums had swarmed her basement. It was about four-something in the afternoon and he seriously doubted it was a group of possums causing the ruckus. Possums weren't often active during the day and this was not behavior likened to their breed. Nonetheless, the woman sounded awfully distraught, saying something about being concerned for the well-being of her father, who, as she curiously informed Huck, was a Vietnam veteran, which meant he was pretty damn old. He didn't doubt *something* was down in Selma Donaldson's basement, he just didn't think it was possums.

Huck had been drinking with his buddies, Danny and Ray—fellow owners of the wildlife control business known as the Nelson County Critter Getter—and drew the short straw on this one. Critter Getter was just three dudes (and sometimes a guy named Herbert, who helped out from time-to-time) who had been friends since high school that got together in the late 90s and decided to wipe out the squirrel problem that had been plaguing the city. They did so well that people started asking them to remove other animals from their homes: skunks, birds, raccoons, stray cats, possums, and whatever else made its way into their attics and basements. They decided to go into business together and had the market pretty much cornered ever since, covering not just Nelson County, but many of the surrounding counties, as well. Pretty good gig for just three ex-high school jocks.

Huck got out and glanced up at the blue autumn sky, wishing he was still drinking. He had heard on the radio about three people being killed by wild animals and thought maybe that whatever was in Ms. Donaldson's basement might be somehow connected. It was probably not possums, but maybe wild dogs. Perhaps coyotes had come up from the hills south of town and started mauling folks. He wouldn't be shocked if a couple of bobcats had wandered into town, neither. It had happened up in Bullitt County about twenty years ago. Nobody got hurt, but the animals had been spotted slinking around the small town of Hillview before Animal Control finally caught them. There were a lot of possibilities; Huck just didn't think a possum attack was one of them.

There was a large net attached to a telescoping pole in the back of the van, alongside a cage big enough to fit a few smaller animals in. After checking to make sure his flashlight hung from his leather tool belt, he headed towards the house with his equipment in hand. An alarmed Selma answered a few seconds after he rang the doorbell.

"Thank goodness you're here!" she said.

She swung the door open to allow Huck inside. She was thirty-five and stout with short auburn hair. Her face was ashen and fear was in her eyes. After taking a few steps further into the spacious front room, Huck knew why she was so concerned. Coming from downstairs was the loudest chorus of screeching and banging he had ever heard. It sounded like a horde of large dogs were fighting over rats that were screaming in agony. He paused midway through the living room and listened.

"Jesus," he said. "How long has this been going on?"

"Since about ten minutes before I called you."

Leaning sideways and straining to hear, Huck crinkled his face and asked, "You said those are possums?"

She swallowed and nodded.

"You sure?"

"Yeah."

"Did you get a good look at them?"

"Yes."

"Tell me what happened?"

"I went downstairs to do the laundry and heard them running across the floor. There was a loud bang followed by some squeaking sounds. I thought mice were on the loose, again. We've had rodent problems in the past. Stray cats have even gotten down there through the window before and killed a bunch of them. I'm not really worried about rats, so I went on down. When I turned on the light, I saw a big pile of possums in the corner, stacked on top each other, bouncing around and stuff, almost like they were trying to climb the wall."

"What do they look like?"

Huck was thinking these were large rats, or maybe regular rats and mice that appeared bigger due to shadows and fear. There was no way they were possums.

"Grayish, with long pink tales; some were big, some were small. When I stepped off the bottom step, several of them turned around. I saw their white faces and black eyes. I yelled upstairs to my dad and the rest of the possums stopped moving and turned around. They hissed and growled and several of them ran across the basement towards me, so I ran up the stairs."

Huck began to suspect this woman might be insane or on something. This story had delusion or hallucination written all over it. If her father really was there, he wanted to speak to him.

"Where is your father?"

Just then, an older man with broad-shoulders wheeled into the room on a black metal electric wheelchair wearing a red blanket draped across his lap. His skin was rough and his eyes were lively. The whir of his chair stopped and he said in a clear, strong voice, "I'm right here. What do you want?"

"Sir, did you see any of these creatures in the basement?"

"No god-damnit. Do you think I wheeled down the steps?"

Having heard the patronizing tone of Huck's voice, Selma's father became angry. His face was red and he gripped the arms of his chair so hard they were shaking.

"So you can't say if they are possums or not?"

"No. But, I know what you're thinking, and my daughter ain't crazy."

Huck held up his hand, not wanting to anger the old fart to the point where he had a stroke. Enough weird shit was going on in that house and he didn't need an old dead goat and his hysterical half-wit, delusional daughter to make things even stranger than they already were. "I'm not implying that, sir."

"Bullshit!" the old man snapped. "You think I'm stupid? You think we ain't ever seen possums 'round here, god-damnit? I know this isn't how these little bastards usually act, but god-damnit, there's something down there causing a ruckus and my daughter knows what a god-damned possum looks like. If she says a bunch of them came after her, then I believe her, and you'd better, too!"

"Sir, I do believe her. I just need to be sure."

"Well, if you want to be sure, god-damnit, then get your ass down there and see for yourself!"

"Dad," Selma said, putting a hand on his shoulder. "Calm down. The man is just trying to do his job."

Her dad looked at her then back at Huck and sighed. "I know, I know. I just don't like this bullshit. It sounds like a god-damn battlefield down there." He then held out a broad, weathered hand and said, "Capt. Dean Little—formerly of the U.S. Army."

Huck returned the handshake. "Huck Davis."

"Huck? Like the Mark Twain book?"

Huck nodded. "That's what I was named after," (And he hated it).

After the handshake, Huck said, "Well, I reckon I should get down there and see what I can do to put a stop to all that racket."

"I'll come with you," Selma said.

"No need, ma'am. If it's as bad as you said, then it might be dangerous. I'm used to this sort of thing."

"You ain't used to this, I promise. Besides, it's my house and I'm coming down there."

"Fair enough—just be careful and stay behind me. These animals are obviously aggressive."

The cacophony of thuds and squeals ringing out from the basement was chilling. Huck stood in the living room, inching slowly towards the basement, bending his ear and feeling the sweat run down his back. The rumble from the darkness below reverberated in his guts. Dealing with psychotic animals was his specialty, but no matter how experienced he got, a serious threat was always looming. Sometimes he could shrug it off and other times he could not—this was one of those times he couldn't. He had been chased around a small room by an angry raccoon once and it was rather unpleasant. But, a basement full of pissed off possums would be a whole new terror introduced into his life and he wasn't too sure he was ready for it.

Selma followed his slow approach through the living room and across the kitchen to the basement door with Capt. Dean rolling after them. The closer they got, the more intense the crescendo of the riot downstairs became. The jitters Huck had felt before became so intense he could feel them ripple through his skin as he stood before the door. It felt like he stood there for ages, looking down at the doorknob—the doorknob of doom—which would open the gateway into his tomb.

"Something wrong?" Selma asked.

Huck jumped lightly, causing sweat to drip from his forehead. He turned to face her and said, "No. I'm just trying to devise a plan of action if they rush us as soon as we open the door."

He thought it was a good lie, but his fear was obvious. Though he had initially dismissed Selma's story as not being wholly accurate, the possibility that it was began tugging at his mind. Considering the possibility squeezed the courage from his heart.

"If you're afraid, I can go first," she said.

"No, no—that won't be necessary." Huck chuckled and smiled. "It just sounds like there are a lot of them down there."

"That's because there are," Capt. Dean snapped. "She already told you that, god-damnit!"

"Dad," Selma turned and said. Capt. Dean waved her off.

Huck put his hand on the knob and said, "Well, let's check this out."

He yanked the door open quickly, unveiling a dark, menacing staircase stretching down into the dimly lit basement; weak streams of sunlight came through the tiny rectangular windows but had little effect. Though no sight of stray possums was seen near the steps, the noise was clearly audible; it was like a group of people pounding on a door, trying to get someone to let them out. There were also the constant growls, which made descending the steps feel like travelling down into Hell.

Huck got out his flashlight and turned it on. "Don't turn on the basement light. If they're as aggressive as you described, they might rush at us. I'll just use my flashlight."

They stepped cautiously down into the darkness with the steps creaking beneath them. Each squeak felt like an ice-pick in the ear, and Huck feared the creatures would emerge from the shadows hideously disfigured like some Lovecraftian monster. The urge to halt almost seized him, but Selma put her hand on his shoulder, reminding him she was there, and he didn't want to look like a coward in front of her, so he kept stepping.

Capt. Dean remained at the top, waving a crutch around. "If any of them little bastards come for me, I'll brain 'em with this."

The noise became more ominous the deeper they went. Huck swept his flashlight beam across the bottom as he descended the final step. When he had both feet planted on the concrete floor, the horrendous sound of the hisses and growls scratched at his ears. There was also a strange squishy sound mixed in; some offensive funk assaulted his nose. He leveled the flashlight towards the noises and stopped dead in his tracks.

Sure enough, Selma was correct: her basement was infested with possums. Not just infested, but teeming with them. There were several dozen covering one-third of the floor. They jumped over each other, writhed about in a mass pile, squeaking and bouncing and throwing themselves against the walls. Huck's mouth hung open and the flashlight trembled. Selma saw the light shaking and said, "Maybe we should go back upstairs."

He leaned his net against the wall to hold the flashlight steady. "No. I need to properly assess this situation. I might end up having to call one of the other guys to assist me."

As his light jumped from one section of the undulating mass of gray and white fur to the next, the marsupials parted, leaving holes in the crowd. They slowly scattered and he saw carcasses lying on the floor among them. The shredded bodies of many animals lay on the far side of the room, holes torn into their corpses, blood pooling around them. There was a stained bird skeleton with its head missing; there were mice with only remnants of their bodies remaining; he saw a raccoon's arms and legs twitching as several possums gorged themselves on its body. There were rats, too—bunches of them—many dead and some resisting. He watched

23

as they fought back, leaping at their attackers, only to be taken down and ripped apart. He even saw the body of a large canine with blood pouring from gashes in its chest area.

"Oh my God," he whispered.

Selma came up beside him and gasped, putting both hands over her mouth. She saw something Huck had yet to notice.

"Look over at the window, in the corner," she pointed.

Huck moved the flashlight, casting the beam along the wall and landing on a window in the far-left corner; the glass was shattered and the weak metal frame obliterated. A dark stain of some kind was smeared down the wall beneath it. He slid the beam along the smudge all the way to the floor—and almost dropped his flashlight at what he saw.

"Jesus H. Christ! It's fucking Marty Miller!"

Marty Miller, a middle-aged man who worked for the city, hadn't reported to work that day. Huck knew this because his wife, Melissa, was friends with Marty's wife, Clarissa. Both of them worked at the hair salon in town. Marty hadn't missed a day of work in over ten years. He went in no matter what: chills, fever, broken sternum, death in the family; nothing kept him from his job. So, when he hadn't shown up, and when Clarissa didn't even know where he was, it was cause for alarm, even if he had only been missing for a few hours.

It didn't take long for the Marty Miller mystery to become a scandal, and Melissa was soon calling him to ask if he had seen the missing man. Obviously, he hadn't, but he told his wife to assure Clarissa that if he saw Marty, she would be the first to know. Now, he wasn't so sure he wanted to keep that promise.

Huck might have now known where Mr. Miller was, but he could only guess how he ended up in Selma's basement. Judging by the awkward position of his body, and the stain on the wall, Marty had broken the window and fallen through, bleeding all the way down to the floor.

But why would he have done that? Was he running from the possums? Had he become so desperate to escape them that he thought busting into someone's basement was his best shot at sanctuary?

The real question was what the hell was making the possums act like this? Despite old wives' tales, possums were peaceful; they would usually faint and play dead before they would fight. When they did attack, it was only in self-defense and as a last resort. Possum attacks were not common. They certainly weren't known for eating other animals, especially humans.

At that moment, Huck had a good idea what had been tearing apart the people in town, no matter how unlikely it seemed. Half of Marty's skull was exposed, a skeletal grin stretched across his face. Flaps of flesh were dancing around where they hung off his head, possums digging greedily into it. Both eyes were gone, leaving behind bloody sockets. The little monsters crawled all over his body. He saw the ass-end of one sticking out of a gaping hole in Marty's chest. In the small dim beam of the flashlight, it was hard to see all the gruesome details, but he could see possum heads moving around, back and forth, spastically shooting up as if they had been tearing at something hard with their teeth. Marty Miller was a dead duck, eviscerated and destroyed.

"I guess we know how they all got in," he said.

Selma looked at him, angry at first, but then realized he was in shock. Though she thought of a few things she could say in response, she remained silent. He was only a small-town exterminator, not a big game hunter. This was obviously as extreme of a circumstance for him as it was for her.

For a few seconds, they both stood in horrific awe of the ghastly feast taking place before them. A banquet of flesh and blood indulged by the greedy hunger of vicious creatures created a living nightmare at their feet. The slurping and crunching sounds thrust into their ears, sending waves of revulsion from their brains to their bowels. No horror ever imagined could have prepared them for this.

Suddenly, from upstairs, Capt. Dean yelled, "What the hell is going on down there? What do you see?"

Huck jumped and dropped the flashlight. It rolled a few feet towards the sickening smorgasbord, rolling to a stop with the beam shining towards the possums. He and Selma watched as the dining ceased and the curious animals began turning their heads and bodies. Within seconds, Huck and Selma were staring at a dark wall of glittering eyes shining from the basement shadows.

Selma backed up towards the stairs. "This can't be good."

Huck was transfixed, petrified by the mass of tiny terrors now heading his way. It wasn't until a group of them engulfed the flashlight that reality checked in and he turned to follow Selma, who was already ascending the steps, shrieking at the top of her lungs.

Selma was not very fleet of foot, and neither was Huck. But, propelled by the surge of fear, she was already at the top of the stairs, but he was still a few feet from the bottom steps. He watched a wave of possums run past him and up the stairway, racing for the light. Several more banged into his feet with the force of a bowling ball. He lost his footing immediately, just as the basement door slammed shut and he was closed in the darkness. Sharp pains shot through his calves and quads as he felt the small feet travelling up his body.

He hit the floor hard, feeling numerous possums crunch beneath him. By the time he was on his back, they had swarmed him with unrelenting claws and teeth, tearing away at his skin, boring holes into his body. Something dug into his eyes, smearing them like jelly. One thought that existed inside the agony of his obliteration was the repeating of the words, *Fucking bitch!*

Fucking bitch!

Fucking bitch!

Fucking bitch!

It pissed him off that Selma had closed him down there like that. *She* had been the one to call *him*. *She* needed *his* help, and he came over to give it, and she would just abandon him to this grisly fate, simply to save herself and that crazy old coot of a father?

Fuck that fucking bitch!

All anger died away as Huck howled for mercy. He actually felt his hands be pulled from his wrists, and his stomach wrenched from his abdomen. His screams didn't last long as one possum stuck its head into his mouth and bit down on his tongue, and then ripped it out. His mouth still hung open as he tasted blood slide down his throat. Another furry head reached in; only this time, it went deep into his mouth and the neck and shoulders of the creature were soon stuffed inside, ravaging the man's throat as he gagged on the grimy, rotten flavor of the filthy animal's body.

As he lay there being torn asunder, the cool numbness of death began to set in, and he was grateful for it just before he took his final breath.

Selma slammed the door hard just before the possums had gotten her. One managed to force its head through before she could shut it all the way, but Capt. Dean kept true to his word and jammed the butt-end of the crutch right into the possum's face, splitting its skull. It fell back and Selma managed to close the door just before the rest of the gang slammed against it.

But, she was struggling to keep it shut. They were pounding at the door and it was rattling, ready to pop open. The lock had never been too strong and with the weight of all these brutes bashing against the backside of the door, she didn't think she could hold it long enough for them to give up.

Capt. Dean thrust the crutch at her. "Stick this under the doorknob. It's long enough to reach the wall."

He was correct. If she placed the arm rest under the doorknob, the crutch would stretch easily to the wall across from the basement. She took the item and stood up, quickly pushing the crutch in place. It fit in real tight, reinforcing the door so well that it didn't even shake when the possums beat against it.

"Good thinking, Dad."

"What happened to the other fella?"

"It was too late. They were coming up the stairs."

Capt. Dean nodded. "You did what you had to do."

He understood that all too well: he had to leave men to die on the battlefield before. But, as horrific as war was, at least he knew his enemy. This made no sense, and a part of him thought old age had finally seized his brain and started twisting it like a Rubik's Cube. But, he saw Selma sitting on the floor before him, scared to death. He knew his little girl: she was braver and stronger than she realized. Right now, she looked weak and fragile, and that was certainly a cause for concern. Whatever she saw down there must have been nightmarish beyond her words, and that scared him, too.

They both sat quietly and listened to Huck screaming in the dark. It ended after a few seconds. The creatures gathered on the steps and were ready to beat down the door and storm the upstairs.

CHAPTER FOUR

Over on Cypress Street, Chip James had finished his interview with Rachel. He'd asked her several questions after the live broadcast was over and that footage would be shown later on the evening news. He made sure to ask harsh questions that would touch her nerves. All the tears she cried would make for a good segment. When he asked if the death of her boyfriend brought back the same feelings she experienced when she lost her parents, it had the desired effect: she broke down. He didn't have time to get that on live TV, but it would look good on the replay. He really thought that was a dynamite question and he patted himself on the back for being so brilliant.

Now, Rachel sat on the light-yellow flower-patterned fiber couch located against the wall in her front room with the curtain open on the window behind her. The dim glow of the fading noontime outside mirrored her darkening mood. Her eyes were puffy and pink from all the crying and she was still sobbing lightly. The sadness was bad enough to begin with, but when this slimy reporter came around asking her personal questions, it stirred up all sorts of repressed agony. Try as she did, she couldn't stop the tears, and now the whole town would see her bawling like a child. Chip, the culprit, sat at the other end of the couch. When he heard her sniffle, he slid over and pulled a tissue from the box on the cushion next to her.

Dabbing her eyes, he said, "I'm sorry for your loss."

"Thanks," she said, backing away.

He inched a little closer, his solid blue eyes shining out from his tanned face. His blondish-brown hair was perfect, every little strand in place. It looked harder than a motorcycle helmet. No man should use that much hairspray, or mousse, or whatever this bozo used to plaster that junk to his head. The jerk really thought he was smooth, too. He flashed a grin of bright, perfect teeth that were probably worth a fortune as he tried to wipe the tears from her eyes like a baby reaching for a Sippy cup. He was one of those arrogant gum-chewing guys that gnawed on Wrigley like a cow does on grass. His face reminded her of the giraffes at the Louisville Zoo, smiling behind all the hay in their mouths. But giraffes were kind and cute and she had no doubt that Chip James was a complete dick.

"I'm good, Mr. James. Please."

His arm slid along the back of the couch and tried to snake its way around her neck. The smell of his deodorant combined with the cologne and gum made her want to vomit. This guy really thought he was suave, and that was so far from the truth. Rachel became even more repulsed than she was only seconds ago.

"Get away, Mr. James. You're making me uncomfortable."

With a sly smile, he moved away. "Of course, of course—I'm sorry. I was only trying to be a comfort. If you want your space, I totally understand."

The brass balls on this guy, preying on a woman in pain.

Did he really think she was stupid enough to fall for such bullshit? Did he think she'd spread her legs for him because he wiped her eyes? She wished she was Freddy Krueger so she could slash that feigned innocence right off his fake face.

But instead, she just said, "Thank you."

They sat in silence, Chip looking at his phone and Rachel bouncing her right leg, which was crossed over her left. Her arms were folded across her belly and she really just wished this asshole would go away. Todd was out back brooding. She saw the tears in his eyes when he found out about Brandon, but he had cried so much when their parents died that he didn't want to show anymore tears. In his mind, he was too old to cry.

She never did quite understand the male mentality about crying. To little boys, crying is okay if you get hurt, pissed off, or sad; but when you get older, it's as if a switchbox is implanted with a lever that says, "Tears: Only in the Case of Emergency."

Brandon's death was an emergency enough, but Todd didn't understand. He was at the cusp of adolescence, just beyond the borderline of childhood with manhood on the horizon; he didn't know what he was supposed to do and he had no man to guide him. Brandon had tried to help him out as much as possible. But, Brandon also had an arrested development of sorts having a drunk for a father who performed a better vanishing act than the greatest of magicians.

Brandon at least had his mother—someone to nurture and take care of him. Todd didn't even have that. Hell, even having an absentee father was better than having a deceased one. At least it provided an example of bad moral conduct that he would grow to realize he needed to avoid. Brandon was the closest thing Todd had to a male role model, and now he was gone, too.

So, why didn't he want to cry? Why bottle it up? Didn't that hurt more? Or did it hurt a male more to be what he perceived as weak? Maybe it wasn't really weakness. Perhaps there was some naturally embedded instinct in the male brain that somehow understood the vulnerability of tears. Rachel remembered all the crying she did when her parents died, and how all these people who never really gave a shit about her before suddenly began to flock around the tragedy, like spiritual buzzards who survived by scavenging the dead hopes of other humans. She cried and cried, and the more she cried, these imposters with feigned concern on their faces, jutted lips, creased foreheads, and intrusive outstretched arms surrounded her and lied about how sorry they were. Some people, she knew, were genuine, but most were just there to be woven into the tapestry of tragedy so they could pretend to have been close to the victims and their families, allowing them to play the role of survivors when they were nothing more than posers. None of these people stuck around long after all the sadness had lost its luster; most went right back to their lives as strangers to the broken branch of the Owens family in Bardstown.

She knew why men didn't often cry: such an expression of sorrow is a beacon to the disingenuous soul-suckers that survive off people's misery. It's a call-to-arms for those who don't have enough drama in their lives to crawl out and put on a stage play. That way they could go back to work or church or to the next family gathering and talk about those poor orphaned Owens kids and how unfortunate their lives had become. They would stand around and babble all that bullshit about how they're praying for her and Todd, wishing them well, hoping they make it through, all-the-while not even intending to lift a finger to assist—not even attempting to lie about it to make someone feel better. She and Todd had survived it alone—*all* alone. She was foolish enough to think someone would care, but no one did. They all disappeared, except for Brandon.

Now, she sat there crying once again and the vultures had come. This half-tanned asshole with his wannabe Ken Doll appearance (probably succeeded in replicating the doll's crotch area), and his circle of goons had descended, stinking up the place physically and spiritually. She sat there enduring it, thinking that talking to the news about it might make her feel better—which she was entirely incorrect about—and Todd had retreated to the backyard, holding in his tears, mulling about and avoiding the vampires.

Good for you, Todd. Maybe it's you who learned the life lesson.

Coldness swept across the room, or maybe just her soul. She sat nervously, now her left leg crossed over her right (she must have switched them without knowing), bouncing it up and down, looking over at Chip the Bastard still sitting there with his smart phone out, punching away at God-knows-what to God-knows-who (who really cares?), probably some floozy he tricked into thinking he was an adorable guy with a great personality. He didn't look at all concerned with Rachel, now. She figured that since he got his story—and she had thwarted his feeble sexual advances—his radiating interest in her had waned into a tiny sparkle.

Dumb son-of-a-bitch—turn that phone sideways and sit on it.

Truth was that she wanted *someone* to comfort her and if Chip hadn't reminded her so much of some asshole in an Alanis Morissette song, she might have been okay with his attempted reassurance. But, she knew what he really was: a slavering beast pouncing on vulnerability. Why did a good man like Brandon have to suffer such a gruesome end when a shameless predatory scumbag like Chip James got to keep kicking? Life was a fucking joke.

Chip's crew bustled about the house, pulling up cords and moving equipment out the door. Bastard Chip kept right on typing away, chuckling at little messages that popped up, not giving a damn about the woman who just lost her fiancé. She wished there was a serial killer among the news crew that would decide now was a good time to strangle the fuck-stick. She tried to imagine the many colors of coming death his face would shuffle through before croaking. No doubt it would be a pretty sight.

"Excuse me," Rachel said.

Letting his eyes slide up her legs, he replied, "Yes?"

"The interview and all that is over, isn't it?"

The Bastard nodded.

"Then you really don't need to be here anymore."

"Oh, we'll be heading out soon."

"Could you hurry up? I'd prefer to be alone right now."

Chip lowered his phone into his lap, repositioned his ass on the couch. "Are you sure? I don't mind hanging out here for a few to keep you company."

"No thank you." She couldn't hide the disdain in her voice.

Chip slid his hand over and put it on her leg, something he had obviously wanted to do for quite some time, considering the hasty movement of his arm. "Are you sure?"

Rachel knocked his hand away. "Don't touch me!"

He backed away. "I'm sorry. I was trying to be a help."

Chip went back to his phone and started typing. A tinkling tone sounded from the device, signifying a message. Chip looked at it and laughed, then began typing again. Rachel narrowed her eyes and stared at him with disgust, indignant that her misery was such a minuscule thing to him.

"I'd really appreciate it if you left now, Mr. James."

"Hold on one sec."

"This is my home, Mr. James. I have told you to leave—so leave."

Hearing the seriousness in her voice, Chip stopped typing and looked up with semi-wide eyes for a second and then scoffed. "I'm not leaving my equipment here."

"You can wait outside then," she said, cutting him off before he could say anymore. "Your crew looks to be almost done. You can wait for them in your van."

Two men were passing through the room towards the front door, hauling large cases in their arms. Chip turned and said, "How much is left?"

"Patty's bringing out the last bundle of cables," replied a man in a dark baseball cap.

"Anything else?"

"Nope."

The two men exited through the screen door, letting it bang shut, as rude as their asshole master. Chip looked back at her and tried to smile.

"You can wait outside," she said before his mouth could spew anymore diarrhea.

Rachel had a somewhat narrow face and ears so flat against her head that they almost looked like they weren't even there. Her eyes were a deep, dark brown and had a vacant, disinterested look to them. But when she got mad, they became menacing, and the hole she glared through Chip apparently drove the meaning home. He stood up and grabbed his knapsack off the couch next to him—which he had placed there without asking permission—and looked down at her.

"I'm sorry for your loss. I hope you feel better."

"Bullshit," she spat. "You got your story. You don't give a fuck."

She could feel the anger boiling over, not just at Chip, or Brandon's death, but over everything the incident drudged up from the past: the pain of losing her parents; the distance her family took afterwards; the broken promises; the callous indifference; the abandonment they inflicted on her and Todd when all was said and done. Fuck them, and fuck this newsman jerk-off. He might not have been her family and had no real reason to care, but fuck him anyway. His career flourished off the misery of others, and his goal—and the goal of all assholes in his line of work—was to be the first vulture on the scene so he could stare into a camera and delightfully vomit out someone else's suffering to the city—or the world—with a look of satisfaction on his smug fucking face. The urge to stand up and level him with a Ronda-Rousey-like barrage of punches became stronger by the second.

"Excuse me?" he asked.

"Get out of my house!"

Chip looked like he might actually challenge her, and she was daring him—pleading him—to open his scum-hole and say something inflammatory so she could leap up and claw his fucking eyes out. Patty passed by in the background, wires trailing behind her. Rachel flicked a quick glance her way. Once she was out of the house, there would be no witnesses. Maybe she could stand up right now and attack this asshole and claim he grabbed her or something. Who cares if it would be a lie? He obviously deserved it, and she was willing to bet he was secretly known as a sexual deviant among his colleagues, even if no one was brave enough to say it in front of him. She was almost resolved to attack him when their stiff moment of silent tension was shattered by a loud scream from out back.

Rachel knew Todd's voice despite his distorted wail. She sprung from the couch and sprinted for the back door, leaving Chip standing slack-jawed behind her. He didn't regain himself until she was already through the kitchen and opening the back door. He then rushed after her, curious about the commotion.

The first thing Rachel saw when stepping out onto the small porch was Todd waving a broom at something. For being only twelve, he was rather large: about 5'7'' and a-hundred-and sixty-or-so-pounds, and he swung his weapon hard, making a loud swooshing sound in the air. Rachel couldn't see what he was fending off, but even with his back to her, she could tell his face was red each time his head moved to the side, so he meant business.

"What the hell is going on?"

Todd didn't answer; he just kept thrusting and swinging the broom at something his sister couldn't see. Though she was unable to glimpse his intended target, her eyes did hone in on a dark smear of crimson on the back of his right leg. He had on shorts and the red liquid was a noticeable contrast to his pale skin. She saw it running down his leg in a thick stream pouring from a deep gash in his flesh and instantly began to descend the steps.

"Oh my God, Todd, you're bleeding!"

"I know!"

As Rachel got closer, she saw what he was locked in combat with. A few feet away from him was a possum, dodging his shots and hissing.

34

"Did that possum attack you?"

"Yes! And there are more."

Rachel glanced around the yard and saw, not too far off, three more possums standing by, watching the battle take place. Behind her, she heard Chip gasp as his feet began tapping down the concrete steps.

"What the hell?" he said, coming up behind her.

She ignored him and stood back from her brother, waiting for him to finish his fight. He jabbed three times at the creature, which growled and snapped at the bristles; Todd rammed the broom at it again and the possum jumped up and pounced on the end of it, ripping it from Todd's grip.

The broom hit the ground and the possum sprang towards Todd, who blindly kicked his foot out as Rachel squealed beside him. The blow landed and the possum was knocked to the grass, rolling several times. Todd began to limp and wobble, almost falling. Rachel rushed to his side to keep him standing.

"You okay?"

"I'll be fine, but it hurts like hell."

"We got to get you to the hospital. Why the hell did that thing attack you?"

"I don't know. I was just standing out by the shed and it suddenly came after me. It started to growl and shit, so I turned to walk away and it bit me. I kicked it away then grabbed the broom and started fighting."

"That's really bizarre," Chip said, almost sounding humored. "Possums don't just up and attack people."

Rachel shot him an angry glare. "Well, this one did."

"Did you do something to provoke it, young man?"

"No," Todd said. "And who the fuck are you to question me?"

"No reason to be nasty, son."

"I'm not your fucking son, asshole," Todd replied.

Normally, Rachel would have scolded Todd for such language, but she didn't give a rat's ass about Chip. Todd could have punched him in the balls and she would have shaken his hand for it. In fact, she was about to cuss a blue streak across Chip, but she heard a loud chorus of gurgles and strange vocalizations coming from the yard. Chip and Todd heard it too, and they all looked towards the sound. From the shade of the numerous trees and bushes lining the back of the property, they saw dozens of possums pouring side-by-side into the yard, marching and growling as one.

"What the hell?" Chip said.

"Holy shit," said Todd. "We got to get inside. If they're half as pissed as that one was, we're fucked."

The eerie sound of the possums' bodies swiping the grass as they moved through the backyard made Rachel shudder. Rows and rows of small glittering eyes danced towards the house. Keeping Todd's arm around her shoulder, she helped him limp up the porch and into the house. Chip hadn't moved: he was in awe of the spectacle, so Rachel decided to leave the screen door open for him, although it was something she briefly debated.

Rachel imagined herself standing on the back porch and ringing the triangle for the animals. *Dinner is served! A great big ole pig for your hungry bellies! Come and get it!* Even the possums would probably think Chip tasted like dog shit.

The newsman couldn't believe what he was seeing. Possums weren't pack creatures, and they weren't even vicious. They ate meat, but didn't hunt down larger creatures for it, certainly not humans; and, they were nocturnal. Yet here they were, swarming the yard in daylight, and one had just bitten the boy. As he watched them amble forward, it dawned on him that maybe they were the wild animals that killed Brandon Smith.

He took his phone from his interior coat pocket to begin filming the situation. "This is news," he said with a grin.

Once the video began recording, he started speaking. "I'm standing behind the home of Rachel Owens, girlfriend to this morning's maiming victim, Brandon Smith. After completing the interview with Rachel, my crew and I were packing up when we heard a sudden scream from out back. When I came outside, I saw Rachel's younger brother, Todd, swinging a broom at a possum that had attacked him."

He went on describing the incident to the phone—and his soon-to-be audience (so he hoped)—not really considering the closing proximity of the swarm. In just seconds they would be upon him. Once that realization finally registered, he stopped recording and headed for the house. There were only six steps on the Owens' back porch, and Chip had made it to the

36

fourth when he felt the sharp pain of angry teeth burrowing into his right leg.

The door handle was in his grasp and the door was halfway open when he screamed and fell forward, landing partially on the kitchen floor with his legs still on the steps outside. He rolled over, flipping the possum, and started slamming his leg into the concrete. The possum did not release; it just kept biting.

More were coming. The few that had been standing in the yard were almost to the porch, and the rest of the creatures would be upon the house in seconds. He had to act quickly. Rachel and Todd were nowhere in sight when he dragged himself all the way into the house. If the possum didn't break its grip, then he'd drag it in with him and deal with it once the door was closed. Chip heard the commotion of the siblings in the front room, but didn't bother calling for them because he didn't want to waste the seconds. After dragging himself into the house, he tried to close the door with his legs, but felt the scuffle of a few other possums on his feet. They began biting his shoes, scratching at the soles, but had been unable to reach the flesh beneath.

Blood poured from his leg as the other possum gnawed on it. It dug its teeth into another spot of flesh, causing Chip to scream. Even though he was in a sitting position, dragging the possum across the floor with the back of his leg, it did not let go. He managed to pull himself all the way in without the other possums squeezing inside. Just as he was backing away, the rabble collided with the screen door, bulging in the material, tearing at the mesh. It wouldn't take much for them to break through.

Chip stopped for a second and reached for the possum on his leg, grabbing at the fur on its neck, trying to wrench it free, but it dug its teeth in deeper. He sat back and tried to kick it off. As he did, he looked at the monsters outside trying to claw their way in. The smell of rot and filth rolling off of them was horrendous, but their appearance was much worse: dirty, disgusting creatures; fur matted in mud and dried blood; chunks of red and black meat clung to their chins and teeth, and dangled from their jaws. Their mouths drooled for something—probably Chip's meat—their eyes held a hellish resolve to break in and devour any living thing in their path. He had to stop them, somehow, or he would be consumed by their voracity.

The screen ripped at the corner, a small flap pushing inward. A smaller possum began to stick its head through as many more piled up behind it. The possum attached to his leg was spilling blood all over the floor; dark puddles and smears stained the light-colored kitchen linoleum. The throbbing and burning flesh was almost numb now. Chip knew he had to get that back door closed before the screen was decimated and the beasts were able to pounce and rip him to shreds.

A mop was against the wall next to him, so he reached out and grabbed it, bopped the possum that was trying to squeeze in right in the face, then slid the pole along the floor, catching the bottom of the back door, and pushed it shut. The door didn't close all the way, so he jabbed the end of the mop at the possum shredding his leg, finally making it break free. Once it was detached, he swung the mop again, nailing it in the face and knocking it aside. Swinging up on his knees and slipping on his blood, he pushed the door until it clicked shut. Seconds after doing this, he heard scratches on the wood. The attackers had broken through the screen.

The possum that had been on his leg was back on its feet, and the slight strike with the mop wasn't enough to stop it. It lunged for Chip and the reporter screamed and rolled sideways. The creature attached itself to his arm and bit down on the shoulder, making him scream some more. Chip rolled around in his own blood, trying to peel the possum off, to no avail. He felt heavy thumps on the floor coming towards him. The possum was soon torn from his body and thrown across the room.

Rachel stood in the middle of the kitchen, staring down the possum she had just flung against the stove; it stood in front of the appliance, watching her with evil intent in its dark animal eyes.

Knowing she was about to get attacked, she started launching cereal boxes from the small counter behind her at the assailant. Some landed on the possum, some struck the floor around it, and some hit the stove behind it; Frosted Flakes, Golden Grahams, Lucky Charms, Cheerios, Rice Krispies, and Cookie Crisp exploded across the kitchen, driving the animal back. Once her cereal arsenal was depleted, she quickly grabbed the wooden chair closest to her and slid it as hard as she could along the floor. It skidded a few inches and stopped, then fell forward, almost crushing the possum. But, once again, it moved quickly and avoided disaster.

Not understanding where this creature suddenly developed the acumen for sophisticated battle tactics, Rachel decided she would have to try something severe to stop it. She looked around the kitchen for something bigger—something better. There was a vacuum cleaner inches to her left, up against the wall that divided the kitchen from the living room. The plug had not been wrapped up and was lying next to an outlet. She remembered how much her old cat hated the sound of the vacuum and hoped maybe a possum would feel the same way. She looked at the cord, then at the possum—now growling and positioning itself for an attack—and moved quickly to plug the appliance into the wall.

The possum leapt, but Rachel stopped and stepped back, and the creature flew past her into the living room. She then continued forward, fell to the floor, plugged the cord into the wall, and stood up. The possum growled again; she clicked the vacuum on with her foot and turned. The animal was coming towards her, but skittered aside, changing its course to make a berth around the cleaner, and stopped at the threshold to the hallway with a look of fear now in its eyes.

"Yeah, you little shit. Don't like that, do you?" she taunted.

Chip sat against the wall near the back door, listening to the possums outside try to force their way in. Blood flowed profusely from his wounds and he searched for something to tie them up with. A couple of rags lay next to him on the floor. They looked clean; he figured they had fallen off the corner shelf when he was flailing about trying to knock himself free from the possum. Both were big enough to wrap around his leg, so he tied one around his leg and pressed the other on his shoulder. The right leg of his grey pants had been shredded, exposing the torn flesh. Blood still leaked from the wounds, so he pulled the rag, thoroughly soaked with blood now, tighter and was able to slow the flow. His shoulder was another matter; he'd need assistance dressing that wound, and he doubted Rachel would be willing to help. He'd have to go to the emergency room as soon as he got the hell out of there. Rachel was keeping the possum busy—maybe he could sneak past.

Rachel was barely fending off the possum with the vacuum. The thing was climbing the appliance, coming almost within striking distance of her hands. She was able to shake it loose each time and drive it back with the roaring machine. The possum danced from side-to-side, running back and forth, trying to juke around her movements, but Rachel kept up with each evasive maneuver, even managing to nail the creature with the vacuum head a few times.

Chip watched closely, waiting for Rachel to drive the creature down the hallway so he could make his escape. At the moment, she was blocking the entrance to the living room and he couldn't get by, but as soon as the path cleared, he was moving out. He just hoped the possums hadn't swarmed the front yard, too.

The possum backed up and rushed forward. Rachel assumed it was going to try to run up the vacuum again, so she lifted the suction plate and stopped the possum, causing it to back away. Seizing the moment, she rolled the vacuum forward, forcing her opponent further down the hall. The possum turned and rushed down the shadowed corridor and found a dead-end with closed doors. Rachel stopped a few feet from it, resolved to go for the kill. She had never killed an animal in her life, and never wanted to. But, this wasn't just an animal. This beast attacked her brother and was now trying to attack her. There was something devilish inside of it. She had encountered several possums in her day and never saw anything like this; and, all the others outside looked just as bloodthirsty. Mercy was not an option here.

Without further hesitation, she rushed forward with the machine. The cord, which had already been stretched to its limit, came loose from the wall and the vacuum died with a feeble whir. The possum had backed up as far as it could go, even having moved its back feet up the wall. But, once silence returned, it was able to collect itself. Slowly, its back feet met the floor again; its hissing turned to a growl; its lips curled to unveil its red teeth; the creature's eyes were now picking up the shimmer of the kitchen light behind Rachel, evil intentions swirling in its mind.

She watched as its fur began to ruffle and its paws dug at the carpet. Like a cat, the possum took its position and then sprung into the air, landing on the vacuum handle. Rachel shrieked and let go, allowing the vacuum to fall forward. The possum lost its grip and fell to the floor at her feet. Rachel instinctively kicked it as hard as she could, lifting it inches from the floor and propelling it against the wall. The possum fell to the floor with a thud but didn't miss a beat. It was back on its feet coming for her. She backed up, watching it waddle her way.

Chip, now to his feet, was limping towards the living room. Rachel almost backed into him, but he shoved her aside, making her stumble. The possum sprung into the air and landed on her chest and bit down, finding purchase with its teeth into the fabric of her shirt. She screamed as Chip ran through the living room and out the door.

Todd, who was up against the couch, bleeding on the floor, hearing his sister's struggle but unable to stand to help, yelled, "Where are you going, you pussy?"

Chip slammed the door behind him without a word. As he flew down the porch steps, he looked around, seeing the yard was clear. Two of his crew stood outside the van smoking. When they saw his bloody condition, they froze with their mouths hanging open.

"What the hell happened to you?" one man asked.

Chip looked nervously around the yard again as he hobbled towards them as fast as he could. "Get in the van, man. We got to go. There's some crazy shit going on out here. I'll tell you about it on the way."

Chip leapt into the van and motioned them inside. They got in and took off.

In the kitchen, Rachel had managed to wrench the possum from her shirt without getting bitten. Now, she was losing the dance. She was tapping and stomping trying to keep it from climbing her legs. She had torn down a hanging basket full of fruit, cake mixes, and other random objects, and tossed it at the critter; she kept knocking over chairs to try and squash it; but it wouldn't go away, and it eventually climbed one fallen chair and made it onto the kitchen table and started hissing at her. She grabbed the telephone book off the microwave next to her and hurled it in the possum's direction, barely missing it. It then jumped towards her, heading right for her face, but she ducked just in time. She took a sideways step, her foot landed on a banana, and she slipped and fell on her butt.

A throaty growl to her left caught her attention. She turned her head to see the possum running across the kitchen floor, eyes shining, mouth seeming to grin, knowing it was about to dine on the soft, sweet flesh of human. She turned and tried to back away, but her feet were slick from the squashed fruit. The possum jumped and everything seemed to go into slow motion.

41

It looked to Rachel like the possum grew as it flew through the air, zeroing in on her exposed throat. Small paws with sharp little claws extended outward. Jaws opened up, revealing those eager bloodstained teeth; the face stretched into something that resembled the generic mask from *Scream*. She lifted her hands to block it and began to fall backwards. Just as she was ready to take the attack, something dark invaded her line of sight, blotting out the image of the small killer gliding on the air towards her face.

It took a lot of the strength Todd had left in his leg to make it to the kitchen. But when he did, dragging that large stiff cushion off the couch, he made it count. He arrived just in time, and the impact the cushion made when it struck that vicious monster was as good as he could have hoped for. He swung the cushion like he was the Maharajah of Mash and the blow drove the possum down the hall like a furry softball on a line-drive. Todd couldn't keep his footing and the follow-through brought him spinning to the kitchen floor.

Rachel, momentarily shocked, looked at him wide-eyed. But, he waved towards the hall and said, "Trap it in the bedroom!"

The words took root and Rachel quickly stood, grabbed the cord to the vacuum, plugged it into an outlet at the front of the hall, and rushed to the machine and turned it on. The delirious possum jumped up, frightened, and looked straight ahead at the roaring, oncoming giant.

The animal rushed to the right but Rachel cut it off, lifting the suction face once again and pinning the possum to her parents' bedroom door. She leaned forward and turned the knob, then pushed the vacuum against the creature. Once the door fell open and the creature was no longer pinned, it tried to jump over the vacuum and rush to freedom. Rachel tried to fight it back, but it was soon on top the machine, about to climb away. A loud thump behind her made her jump. She turned and saw Todd coming down the hall, sliding down the wall as he leaned against it, wielding the pillow again. He slung it towards the possum as if it were an axe, letting it fly from his hand. It struck the creature again, knocking it backwards off the vacuum and into the bedroom.

"Close the door," he yelled.

Rachel flung the vacuum aside and went for the door. The possum was back on its feet, running towards her. She grabbed the knob and pulled the door shut, and it jammed on the creature's body. Todd took off his shoe and threw it at the door, hitting the floor just in front of the possum. Though it did not connect, it startled the possum enough to make it move back, and Rachel was able to close the door. The angry animal started to growl and hiss while scratching at the door. Rachel collapsed to the floor and they both sat there, silently catching their breath.

"We got to get you to a doctor," she said after a few seconds.

"I'll be okay. Just put some Hydrogen Peroxide on it and wrap it up."

"Todd, that bite is bad. We have to get you looked at."

"No—we have to do something about that crazy possum. Let's get it taken care of first, and then I'll go."

"It might have rabies. You might get infected."

"And it might get out while we're gone, and then attack us again when we come home. Let's get it out of here first."

Rachel considered his words for a second then nodded. "Okay. I'll call the cops."

"Good idea. Help me back to the couch."

Rachel stood and extended her arm to her brother, who had undoubtedly saved her life. She helped him limp to the couch, his leg trailing blood along the way. She called the police. The dispatch lady said that there were only two officers on duty and they were on other calls, but she would try to get Animal Control out there.

"Whatever. I don't care who gets the damn thing out. I just want it out of here."

The lady then repeated that she would call Animal Control and they should be over shortly. Rachel thanked her and hung up, then sighed and listened to the pest down the hall make a ruckus trying to free itself from its momentary holding cell.

CHAPTER FIVE

In the backyard of a little house on Sunset Drive, Herbert McElroy and two of his friends—Steve Curtis and Gene Randall—were making some minor repairs on Herbert's work van. They'd been working on it for a few weeks because it seemed like every time they got one problem fixed, another one arose. Everything from lights to breaks, from starter to tires, and many things in between, had been giving Herbert problems. He'd been running the van ragged for years, so it was only a matter of time before the breakdown happened, he just didn't anticipate it all happening at once.

Herbert was a local jack-of-all-trades who worked as a part-time exterminator for the Nelson County Critter Getter, a part-time mechanic, and sometimes as a wildlife trapper. These were all professions he had begun after returning from Afghanistan. He wanted to keep himself occupied and there wasn't a lot going on in Bardstown or the surrounding areas, but he didn't want to move to Louisville or Lexington and deal with the big city bustle. He liked quiet, small town life—not the country where there isn't a neighbor or store within twenty miles—but small town, where there weren't too many people, never many cars crowding the streets, and not many strangers wandering around. He didn't want to know everyone's business—a person's privacy is their own—but he liked knowing his neighbors' identities. Unfamiliar faces made him nervous and there were just too many of those in the city.

Small town life provided for his numerous professions. There were a lot of bug infestations, plenty of wildlife, and not many mechanic shops around. He did most repairs from his backyard but sometimes helped the Harris boys at their garage in town. His buddy, Steve, who was close to twenty years his junior, assisted him on his jobs a lot. Steve was a friend of one of Herbert's cousins and they were introduced about four years ago, right after Herbert started working as a paid mechanic. He was always good with vehicles, fixed his family's and friends' cars, but never really did it for money. That didn't start until he came back from the war and the town had grown in population, and the Harris boys just couldn't handle all the business. They'd asked him to do some work for them, and then he sometimes got offered paid work from random townsfolk, and that organically grew into his own side-business.

It was thought that Steve, who was quiet and had good work ethic, would provide some much-needed company to the retired veteran. At first, Herbert was distant and unreceptive; not thinking a young kid like Steve would be worth his salt. But, it turned out that Steve was a fast and ready learner eager to put his education to practice. It wasn't long before Steve was a valuable assistant to Herbert when it came to auto-mechanics.

A year or so after Herbert had warmed up to Steve, he had the kid help him start up the trapping business. Herbert got the idea to embark upon this venture when a few people on the street were experiencing severe squirrel problems (a nuisance that happened periodically in Bardstown). It seemed attics up and down the street had become colonies for the little creatures. Herbert once had the problem himself, but took care of it. When others started talking to him about it, he explained to them how he had gotten rid of the pests from his own home. This led to people offering to pay him to eradicate the squirrels from their homes. It was easy money, so he decided to make it a business and have Steve work for him.

It was actually Steve who suggested they do some work for Critter Getter. His friend, Huck, said they sometimes needed assistance. Herbert, enjoying the work he was now finding in Bardstown, liked the idea of taking on something else to keep him busy, so he agreed. When he met Huck, he thought he was a buffoon, but he had a good business going, and his friends seemed to have more sense, so he and Steve started taking assignments for Critter Getter when they were overwhelmed with calls. The war hadn't affected Herbert so bad that he felt alienated—at least, not anymore than he already had, always being a reclusive sort. But, it was good to have someone that he not only liked, but respected, hanging around.

Gene was a little different. Gene was a war buddy who came from eastern Kentucky. He and Herbert ended up in the same regiment during the latter portion of Herbert's tour, a few years before he retired. During those years, they had killed together, nearly died together, and watched comrades fall together. Gene got shot in the hip about two years after Herbert came home. He didn't have anything left back in the hills of Kentucky except for dying coal mines and deteriorating neighborhoods, so he moved to Bardstown to be around someone he knew.

Yes—Gene was Herbert's friend from the war. But, he was also an obnoxious loudmouth who always had something argumentative to say. It didn't matter if he even knew anything about the subject, he would always weigh in, and it would usually be with an opinion that differed from the majority. Herbert didn't know if the man was merely an iconoclast by nature or just a contrary asshole—not that there was a cure for either condition.

Gene could escalate a discussion into a near-brawl. He had been in shoving matches over dissenting points of view, often times over trivial matters, such as politics. He got into a shouting match with a guy during the 2016 election campaign trail because he had a Hillary bumper sticker. Gene maintained that Donald Trump was an idiot, but Hillary was the Anti-Christ and the two men almost exited their cars and came to blows.

But, despite the man's pigheadedness, he had a big heart and a heroic streak. There were times during the war when Gene ran towards the fray just to pull a man out of the fire. He might have seemed lazy and sluggish most of the day out in the field, often complaining, but when one of his fellow soldiers was pinned down, he was the first man to rush in and stand by him.

One day, two of their scouts were held up in a busted-up stone building somewhere in Iraq, and Gene was the first one to hit the ground, crawling through the dust with his rifle, ready to pick off the enemy one-by-one if need be. He got inside the building and pulled the men out, and also started a skirmish, which he faced head-on. Herbert came to his aid about halfway through the fight, fearing that Gene and the other men would be cut down, but they all survived. It was dumb, but ballsy, and though he got his ass ripped by their lieutenant for such reckless behavior, Gene gained a lot of respect from the entire platoon.

It was no surprise to Herbert that Gene was injured saving a fellow soldier. One man was trapped down in a hole and three enemies were coming to finish him off. Gene snuck around, picked off each one, and then dragged the soldier from the hole. In doing so, he was shot in the hip and nearly crippled for life. Doctors really thought he might not ever be able to use that leg again, but he did, and he was able to come home a hero.

Gene was a man full of courage and love—love for his country and love for his fellow man—but he was also full of piss and wind. While the man's noble nature was beyond reproach as far as Herbert was concerned, he was still one of the most annoying bastards he'd ever met in his life.

"Hey, turn the fucking radio up, dipshit," Gene said to Steve after having asked him to turn it up once already.

Steve turned the radio up. "Fuck you, Gene."

The newscaster was saying something about people in town being attacked by wild animals. Gene, heavyset with greasy black hair, sat on a picnic table with his mouth agape, sweat dripping from his chin onto his button-up jean shirt. Steve, with the sleeves of his white tee-shirt rolled up like he was Bruce Springsteen, put a smoke in his mouth and lit it. Herbert rose up from looking under the hood of the van and listened, feeling like a stuntman on fire in his heavy-padded work suit. He lit a cigarette, too, and listened to the story about the mauled townsfolk.

"What the hell do you think about that?" Gene asked when it was over.

"Probably coyotes," Steve said.

"No way! Coyotes don't attack people."

Steve shrugged. "Sure they do."

"Not like that—wolves, maybe, but not coyotes."

Steve shrugged again, in his typical fashion.

"What do you think, Herb?"

Gene and Steve were probably the only people Herbert let get away with calling him Herb. Tony Harris could have, but he never did because he knew Herbert didn't like it, and Tony was always respectful. Steve rarely said it, only when they were joking on each other, and Steve didn't joke a whole lot. Gene did it all the time because he was Gene and that's the kind of shit Gene did. But anyone else—except for maybe a beautiful woman—and Herbert would have given them a piece of his mind.

"It ain't coyotes," Herbert said. "Could be wolves."

Gene pointed at Steve. "Told you."

"I doubt it's wolves," Steve replied. "We don't have many of those around."

Herbert nodded. "They don't come 'round here too often. That's true."

"What if it's some psycho killer escaped from a crazy-house somewhere?" Gene proposed.

Steve rolled his eyes and Herbert chuckled. Gene looked at both of them with his brow furled. "It could be."

Herbert grinned and shook his head. "I doubt it."

"Why?"

"Because cops can tell the difference between murder and an animal attack."

Gene thought about it for a minute. "Maybe not. Maybe they just half-assed the examination."

"Sure." Herbert threw down his cigarette and stomped it out.

Herbert had a weathered face with small dark eyes that stared through a person's soul. They often made Gene feel uneasy. As they looked through him at the moment, seeming to accuse him of being foolish, he started to get a little irritated. Gene was a sensitive man beneath his unpleasant personality.

"Why you looking at me like that, Herb?"

"Because you're doing it again."

"Doing what?"

"You're letting that paranoia out: worst-case scenario bullshit."

"Hey, screw you!" Gene rose from the picnic table. "What do you mean paranoia?"

"No crazy man did that shit they were talking about on the radio. It was some animal. I'm telling you. We ain't overseas, anymore."

"Oh yeah? What if you're wrong?"

"I'm not."

"But, what if you are?"

"But, I'm not."

"How do you know?"

This was the childish banter to which most of Gene's arguments degenerated. Ultimately, Herbert couldn't really tell him he was wrong because Gene would insist that there was no proof, and he wasn't technically incorrect. But, Herbert sometimes relished getting his old friend worked up, so he kept on.

"Okay you two—knock it off," Steve said in jest.

"I know because you're an idiot and you're almost always wrong." Herbert lit another cigarette, and then blew smoke in Gene's face.

Gene, a non-smoker, didn't like that, and Herbert knew it. He also knew that Herbert didn't like being called Herb, but he did it anyway. The challenge was laid out and now Gene had to answer.

Gene gave him a light shove. "I'm an idiot, huh?"

Herbert shoved him back. "That's what I said."

"Oh yeah?"

"Yeah."

Suddenly, Gene bent over and made to tackle Herbert around the waist. Herbert held his ground and wrapped his arms around Gene's back and locked his hands at his friend's midsection. Steve quickly got into position, pretending to be a referee as the two men danced around in their lock-up.

"Don't make me go Goldberg on you," Gene said from underneath Herbert.

"If you're Goldberg, then I'm Brock Lesnar," Herbert replied, trying to drive Gene towards the ground.

"Goldberg always beats Lesnar."

"That's in the fake shit. In real life, Lesnar would beat Goldberg's ass."

"Lesnar beat Goldberg at WrestleMania, anyway," Steve interjected, counting and demanding Herbert break the hold.

"Who cares?" Gene said. "Wrestling is fake!"

"Yeah, but this ain't." Herbert then lifted Gene off the ground.

Steve stepped back, afraid of getting kicked as Gene's feet rose into the air. Kicking his legs frantically, he said, "Wait! Wait! Come on, man. You'll drop me on my head!"

Herbert let him go; Gene backed off. Herbert quickly stepped in and caught Gene from the side, wrapped his arms around him, and began to lift his bulky friend from the ground again. This time, Gene struggled but lost, and Herbert managed to lift him, turn, and drop him belly-first on the ground. Gene's feet kicked out so far that he ended up catching Steve on the side of the head, knocking him to the ground.

From his hands and knees, Gene looked at Steve and asked, "Shit man, you okay?"

"Yeah, I'm good." Steve rubbed the big red mark on the left side of his face. "I should disqualify you for striking an official."

"Whatever."

Herbert grabbed a crowbar from near the van and held it over Gene like a sword, tip pointed downward at an angle as if he would drive it into him if he moved. "Do you yield?" he asked.

"Screw you, Herbert. *Prince of Thieves* sucked."

"Say it wasn't a psycho," Herbert demanded.

"Piss off."

"Say uncle."

Gene started to get up but Herbert moved closer, brandishing the crowbar. "Say it was an animal."

Breathing heavily, Gene leaned back on his knees, looked up at Herbert, then quickly bag-tagged him lightly, causing him to double over. Gene then stood up and grabbed his own crotch and said, "I got your animal right here, Herb."

Herbert laughed and tossed down the crowbar. Gene hadn't hit him hard, and the coveralls were so thick in the crotch that he probably wouldn't have felt a solid right hook. It was as thick as one of the bite suits he used when having to remove a particularly unfriendly animal from a public area.

"I still say it's animals."

"Whatever. You don't know."

Herbert went back to working on the van and Steve joined him. Gene, still worn out from the impromptu wrestling match, sat down on a nearby lawn chair to catch his breath.

Herbert looked over at him with a smile. "You're out of shape, man."

"Kiss my ass."

"How many years did you spend running through the desert over there?" Steve asked.

"Plenty. What would you know about it? You didn't serve."

There were comments Gene would tolerate from Herbert about the war that he wouldn't from Steve, or anyone else who didn't serve. He wasn't one of those guys who thought that since he served in the war that he was entitled to opinions others were not, but he just didn't much appreciate the comments from someone who doesn't know what it was like. It was rough over there, and he knew he wasn't the toughest guy around, but he tried, and he fought, and he gave it all he could stand to give. He wasn't asking for kudos from the public, just enough respect that people didn't try to make him talk about it.

"Be glad of it," Herbert said, looking at Steve. "Sometimes I wish I wouldn't have."

Gene stared at Herbert. Herbert made that comment to him sometimes and Gene usually didn't say much about it. Though he didn't often speak of it, Herbert wasn't a fan of the politics involved with the war, and had long since felt like he wasn't fighting for anyone other than wealthy warmongers who profited off selling weapons to the military—ours *and* the enemy's. But that didn't change the fact that he and the other troops went through hell and fought bravely just to survive, nor did it change the fact that when they were under fire the only thing they thought about was making it out alive and all the politics be damned. He loved his military sisters and brothers—him and Gene both did—but he didn't love the things he had to do sometimes; and, after a while, he started to feel like the fight wasn't for freedom. Often times, when he got to thinking about it, he wished he hadn't gone.

"Do you really?" Steve asked.

He'd always admired Herbert for his wisdom, his grit, and his work ethic, but also because he was a veteran. To hear him imply he would take it back if he could was a bit of a shock.

"Of course he doesn't," Gene said.

Both men turned and looked at him and he continued. "I'm sure he has regrets about things he had to do. I know I do. I know he has the nightmares. Hell, I imagine all of us who were over there do; and, a lot of us have our doubts about what the fuck was going on. But, I know, like me, he wouldn't take it back." Gene shifted his gaze from dancing between both men to focusing straight into Herbert's eyes. "Would you, Herbert? I got shot in the fucking hip and it nearly crippled me. That injury changed my life, but I know that I did some good over there for somebody, and I wouldn't sacrifice one life I might have saved to be rid of all the horror I experienced. Would you?"

Herbert stared back for what seemed like hours, Steve hinging on his answer. Finally, Herbert shook his head. "I don't have the limp you do. I don't have the visible scars. But, I got fucked up, too."

"I know you did."

"You're right, though: I wouldn't take it back."

Gene nodded. Steve swallowed hard, and that was that. Herbert went back to working on the van and the subject was dropped. It wasn't often they spoke of it, and that was as open as it ever got. Neither man needed to say anymore.

After a few minutes, they were done replacing the water pump and a few other pieces. Herbert got in the van and fired it up; it started without pause. He banged the steering wheel and smiled. Steve slapped the hood.

"Hell yes. This is cause for celebration. I'll get us some more brews."

He went off towards the house. Herbert shut off the engine and got out, locking and closing the door behind him. Gene stood up and said, "Well, that's a load off. I was afraid it might not start."

"It's always something with this thing. At least the problems were minor."

"One day it will be the transmission."

"Don't jinx it."

Gene got a little closer to Herbert and spoke in a serious tone. "So, what do you really think killed that kid last night and that lady this morning?"

"I don't think it was a person, I'll tell you that."

"What then?"

Herbert shrugged. "Some sort of animal: wolf, rabid dogs, maybe even a bear, though I doubt it; hell, could've been a mountain lion—not likely, but maybe."

Gene nodded. "I guess. I wish they'd give us more details."

"They won't. They don't want to get the town in a panic. It's bad enough anyone got killed. They'd only make it worse if they didn't leave out the gore."

"That makes sense."

Herbert turned away from Gene and lit another cigarette, then looked up at the sky. Gene sat back down in the lawn chair and looked in the same direction. That sharp, afternoon sheen was spread across the sky, casting short shadows throughout the land. This was the prelude to twilight, just before the sun started to vanish to the other side of the world. Herbert thought of this as the midway point between the light and the dark: the limbo of the day. This is when things got quiet, or seemed to take a break, like a daylight intermission, and the sun called the moon on the walkie-talkie to remind her that it was about time to trade places.

The thought provided Herbert with the image of the Raisin Bran sun, brandishing his scoops and telling Mac Tonight he'd better get his ass over there, and then Mac flipping the sun the bird and telling him to stick those scoops where the sun doesn't shine, and the sun replying, "That would be up your ass, then," and then both of them guffawing like that was the funniest joke ever. But, Mac Tonight was a dude and Herbert always imagined if solar and lunar deities existed, the moon would be a woman because it gave light in the darkness; but, the sun gave light to the entire world, so maybe they were both women. Or maybe he was just a half-loony middle-aged man letting his mind wander again.

"Everything comes to a close," he said out loud.

"Huh?"

Herbert, almost forgetting Gene was even there, or that Steve had gone into the house, or that any of them even existed, turned to look at Gene. "Nothing—just mumbling to myself."

"You're going to be one of those old men that stand in front of grocery stores and talk to themselves, aren't you?"

"I don't know, Gene-O. That's not exactly something you make plans for. I didn't even know those guys existed."

"Sure they do. They wear sweat pants and play with themselves when cute girls walk by."

Herbert screwed up his face in disgust and said, "Where the hell are you from, anyway?"

"A really shitty town."

"Apparently."

Both men looked back to the sky for a second, not really knowing what they were looking for: glimpses of the future; where they go from here; an answer to the recent murders? Maybe they were just allowing themselves to take in the calm of the sky as it transitioned to evening. Whatever it was, it brought them a small slice of serenity for a second—a peacefulness that once existed long before they left the country; a peacefulness they had nearly forgotten; a peacefulness that was shattered when a high-pitched scream from inside the house suddenly rattled their wandering minds back to reality. They looked to the house and saw Steve stumbling back out into the yard with something attached to the side of his head and blood running down his face.

"Get it off me! Get it off me!" he cried.

The screams sent shivers up the backs of both men. Steve rarely even raised his voice, much less screamed like that, and it was a chilling sound to hear. They ran towards him as he fell to his knees about ten feet from the house. Whatever was attached to his head was furry; its white head was moving ferociously back and forth, causing more blood to spurt from Steve's face.

Steve was trying to pry the animal off, but it was latched on like a Koala, tearing and scratching at his facial flesh. As Herbert drew nearer, he could see it was a possum.

Rabies.

That was his first thought. But, possums were not known to be carriers of the disease. They were rarely aggressive, though often mistaken for being mean creatures due to their growling, so that was the only conclusion he could reach as he sprinted towards his friend.

Gene, huffing and puffing as he trundled behind Herbert, said, "It was possums that killed those people! Get it off him or it's going to kill him, too!"

He stopped beside Herbert, who had the possum by the back of the neck, pulling it away from Steve's face. His friend screamed as the creature was torn loose, teeth and claws ripping skin that hung in small flaps from his skull. Dozens of small gashes streaked down his face and large puffs of blood oozed from them, sending red waterfalls cascading down his cheeks and flowing to the ground beneath him. His left eye had been destroyed, gouged and torn, partially hanging from its socket. A huge perforation expanded on his left cheek, revealing the teeth on the side of his mouth; blood poured down from the damaged gums.

"What the fuck?" Herbert said as the possum kicked and thrashed about.

The creature managed to wiggle sideways and turn its head to clamp down on Herbert's arm. Its teeth barely penetrated the sleeve of the coveralls. He looked at the soulless black eyes, blood-caked face and matted fur, reeking of the metallic odor of spilled blood. It was spitting and growling as it gnashed its teeth along the sleeve. Confused, Herbert yanked down on its tail to try and pull it loose. The tug of war did not last long as Herbert was much too strong for the animal. It fell to the ground and went for his leg, finding the same difficulties making purchase through the pant leg that was equally as thick as the sleeve.

Gene was kneeling before his fallen friend, who was now on his side, twitching from the pain roaring through his demolished face. "Hold on buddy. Just hold on," he said.

Herbert was kicking his leg, trying to knock the possum free. "Get the fuck off me!" he yelled.

Gene looked over and saw the struggle and quickly grabbed a metal trashcan lid off a receptacle a few feet away.

"Hold still, Herb," he said, holding the lid sideways.

Herbert stopped shaking his leg and Gene swung the lid repeatedly like a discus, hammering it into the possum's body. The animal squeaked and squealed with each shot before finally releasing the leg and running off into the trees at the edge of the property.

After the possum had fled, Herbert checked his leg for any wounds; to his relief, no punctures had been made. He knelt next to Gene, who had immediately returned to Steve. The left side of the young man's face was ruined. Blood poured onto the grass, dripping in long, thick streams that pooled into dark red puddles on the ground. The eye would never work again, both men were sure of that. But, neither was sure if it would matter because they didn't think Steve was going to make it.

They breathed heavily; Steve winced and groaned on the ground, pale as the unstained sections of his tee-shirt. His hair was matted from the spray of blood, and his upper lip was ripped into a half smile. He felt at his face weakly, probing it and whimpering until his head collapsed on top of his hand.

"I can't feel my face."

"Steve, we got to get you to a hospital," Gene said.

"More," Steve whispered.

Gene and Herbert looked at each other.

"More," Steve repeated.

"More what?" Gene asked.

"Of them."

"Huh?"

Herbert looked towards the house and saw movement somewhere in the darkened interior—a lot of movement: small white spots scurrying around. Hissing and growling began to roll out of the house like a death call.

"He means there are more possums inside."

"What?" Gene looked at Herbert, who then pointed towards the house.

From the shadows inside, the animals emerged, angry black eyes searching for the blood their long snouts detected. Messy fur stained crimson glittered in the sun, their teeth red and brown with the remains of tattered flesh; they came forth, hungry for more human.

"What the hell?" Gene muttered.

The mass—must have been dozens—trundled onto the back patio, their bloody bodies banging into one another, their pink tails slithering along behind them. They took small, quick steps towards the carnage that was Steve, still several feet away from them. Herbert jumped up and grabbed Steve under the armpits and lifted his upper body, much to Steve's screaming chagrin.

"Grab his legs!"

Gene quickly grabbed Steve's legs and the two men began to run sideways.

"Where are we going?"

"To the van!"

Keeping hold of Steve with his left hand, Herbert reached for the key and dropped it.

"Shit!" he yelled.

He took a quick step forward and the key landed on his foot and was sent flying into the grass near the van. It was just a single key not attached to a ring, so it was now out of sight, and to stop and search for it meant death.

"I lost the key!"

"Now what?"

"To the shed!"

It wasn't much of a plan, but he didn't have time to think of a better one. Hell, he wasn't even sure what he thought was happening was actually taking place. Blood-covered possums in hungry pursuit of humans? That shit didn't happen. He had been trapping for years and never saw possums act like that. Some got scared and might try to fight back, but even that was rare. They certainly didn't travel in flesh-hungry packs hunting down people in their backyards. Herbert thought that maybe his sanity had finally slipped away while he was staring up at the sky, but it hadn't. These possums were real, and they were right behind him and Gene.

"These little bitches are fast," Gene said nervously.

He was right: they were gaining. Steve's bouncing body, tossing blood everywhere, was getting heavier by the second. Suddenly, as if he was shot with adrenaline, he started kicking his legs about, trying to break free, causing Herbert and Gene to misstep.

"Let me go!" he yelled.

"Just hold on, buddy," Herbert said.

A possum jumped on Steve's leg and started biting. Another ran forth and bit him on the side. Two more climbed on his torso and started tearing at his flesh. One of the attackers made for Gene's hand and bit down, only barely scraping the skin. But, it was enough to make him drop Steve's leg, and when he did, Steve's upper body twisted free from Herbert and he fell into the ferocious mass.

Gene wrested the possum free of his hand and tossed it back into the feeding frenzy where Steve was being ripped apart in shrieking agony. Gene and Herbert watched in horror as numerous possum heads burrowed into their friend. Steve cried out but his face was devoured by more possums, buried beneath their hungry onslaught. Soon, there was no sound other than their feasting.

Momentarily in a state of shock, Herbert forgot the possum trying to bite through his coveralls. The creature reminded him when it realized its fangs could not penetrate the fabric and began to climb the leg towards Herbert's exposed skin. Herbert grabbed the ascending killer by the scruff of the neck, trying to avoid its bloody mouth, and ripped it free then flung it back into the pile. When it landed, it hit a few more possums. This caused a small ripple of white faces to cease eating Steve and look towards Herbert and Gene. As if realizing there wasn't enough of Steve to go around, a small band started to break away and make for the human spectators.

"Run!" Herbert said. "We're about to become dessert!"

Gene turned and started hauling ass, passing Herbert along the way. Herbert kicked it into high gear, looking at the shed several feet away on the outskirts of the large backyard. His foot struck a tree root sticking several inches out of the ground and he fell.

The fall was only brief—just a second before he managed to pop back up and start running—but in that second, a lot happened. Three possums had taken hold of his body, clinging to the coveralls and scrambling towards his head. Gene had heard the thud of Herbert's body smack the ground and turned to help him, but saw he was back on his feet almost immediately. Gene's hesitation allowed one of the fast waddling creatures to wrap itself around his ankle and bite down, sending a shockwave of searing pain up his leg.

"God-damnit!"

Hebert moved to help Gene, but stopped when he felt the tiny feet crawling onto his head. When he reached up to grab the animal, it quickly bit down on his sleeve, still missing the exposed skin. Another possum began to crawl up towards his face, its black eyes promising pain. Herbert knew this was it. There was no way, even as he removed the other possum from atop his head and flung it away, that he would have time to stop the other from ravaging his face. After throwing the other possum away, he braced for impact as he watched the small open mouth rush upwards. It was so close he could smell what he assumed was Steve's flesh on its breath.

He waited, refusing to close his eyes, willing to meet death with defiance, gazing into the cold black orbs of this possessed possum. Just before it bit down, Gene grabbed it by its head and pulled it away. As heroic as this move was, it was misjudged. His fingers slid into the creature's mouth just before it snapped shut, like a miniature gator, and began gnashing along the fleshy tips of Gene's phalanges.

"Son of a bitch!" he cried out.

Blood gushed from the beast's mouth. Herbert stepped forward and slugged the creature so hard he felt the bones in its face shatter. Several teeth broke and the possum let go of Gene and fell to the ground, kicking a bit but unable to continue its assault.

"Let's go!"

Herbert made a move towards the shed, but was beset by three more possums. More had broken away from the feeding, as Steve's body was almost stripped to the bone. Gene looked towards the house and saw more pouring out from inside, turning the yard into a sea of possums in a sanguinary rage. It was madness—unreal. It was something worse than a nightmare; maybe worse than the horrors of the war.

Herbert struggled to run with the possums on his legs and waist; five had attached themselves to him and Gene knew he wouldn't make it. But, before he could decide what to do about it, he felt something gouge into the back of his leg and tear away the skin in a long strip down to his foot. He howled at the sky and turned to defend himself. The possum was on the ground enjoying its prize: a long, bloody chunk of the back of Gene's leg. The pain was excruciating, but the adrenaline kicked in and the pain melted into an anger that brought Gene's foot high above the possum and hard down onto the back of its neck, shattering it so badly that the head separated from the shoulders. Blood exploded from the possum's face and it died almost instantly.

Gene turned and saw more of the bastards on Herbert. The rest of the swarm was at their heels, now. As far as Gene was concerned, he had only one option at this point. Despite the large portion of his leg that had been stripped away, he ran towards Herbert and started pulling the possums off of his friend in a flurry; some were dug in so tight that their claws and teeth were actually dislodged and remained in the fabric. Both men tried to run, but the path was awkward with all the possum interference, making the pace a plodding one as they stepped and stumbled, back-and-forth and side-to-side. Once the final possum was removed, they saw the shed was only a few feet away; they put their heads down and ran as hard as they could.

But Gene didn't have much wind left in him. He had left his days of hard running overseas and had allowed himself to become incredibly out of shape. He felt the teeth biting at his feet and ankles as he ran. They would have him soon, and Herbert, too. But, there was still a chance to save one of them, and Gene wasn't about to allow these furry turds to take them both down, so as they came upon the shed, he stopped short, turned, and started kicking and stomping as hard as he could at anything that came near him. He thrashed the possums about like Sauron swinging his mace at the beginning of *The Fellowship of the Ring*, sending groups of the marsupials flying through the air. It was a mighty effort, but one still to no avail as he soon found himself overrun and at the mercy of their relentless ripping.

Herbert got the shed open quickly and turned to see Gene losing his fight against the horde. He yelled to him and made his move to help, but Gene said, "Stay back! Get in the shed! I'm fucking dead! They got me!"

"Bullshit!" Herbert moved towards the fight, intending to drag Gene away with him.

Gene saw him coming and quickly turned to meet him and, with all his might, ran towards Herbert and pushed him backwards towards the shed. Herbert resisted, but Gene had the momentum and it was too much for his old friend to surmount. Ignoring the pain and numbness tingling across his lower body, Gene pushed Herbert right into the darkness of the shed. Herbert hit the wooden floor and rolled slightly backward. Gene took the opportunity to close the doors and throw himself against them; he saw the lock on the ground and snatched it up, then put it back where it belonged. When he pushed the device shut, he turned back to face the creatures.

Gene looked down and saw the possums had fallen off of him, but his lower half was torn to parts. He saw flesh and bone; severed skin dangled from his body. His clothes were nearly eradicated and blood poured onto the grass before him, landing on some of his fallen skin. He looked up to see the mighty sea of possums stalking him. He knew this was going to hurt, but he didn't care. There was no escape now.

"Well, come and get me you little bastards."

Gene held his fists up, ready to die fighting. The first few possums that attacked him got their faces caved in and their mouths shattered. His kicks were weak because his legs had nearly lost their strength, but his punches still had it. But the defense wasn't enough. He was only able to take a few out before they took him down, screaming in both agony and anger, issuing his final war cry before his entire body fell beneath the enemy.

Inside, Herbert heard the commotion and tried to get out, pushing hard on the doors. They kept banging and banging but wouldn't open. Every time the doors would pop open just a bit, he could glimpse the possums climbing over one another to get at Gene. His friend screamed for a few seconds before falling silent. Beyond the heavy wooden doors, Hebert could hear the chilling chorus of hisses and growls, and the sounds of the creatures chewing up his old friend's body; the same friend who had risked his life in the war to save his comrades, and had now thrown his life into the mouths of mad possums just to save a friend.

Herbert stopped pounding and leaned against the doors. "Damnit, Gene."

For a moment, Herbert feared the possums would try to gain entry, but he had built that shed himself—him, Gene, and Steve. They doubled-up on the wood and reinforced the doors and locks to keep people from breaking in. He had no doubt the little shits would try, but they wouldn't succeed.

He turned the interior lock shut, pulled the chain on the overhead light and looked around. It was a rather large tool shed: 10-foot-by-10-foot with a lot of shelves and potential weaponry. He wouldn't be trapped in here forever; whether the possums moved on or not, he would exit this shed after nightfall and find his way out of this mess—or die trying. Once he got away, he'd go to town and find out what the hell was going on—or *why* the hell it was going on—and do his part to clean it up. No doubt Tony Harris would be on top of it once he heard. He'd have a crew ready in no time. Herbert's van wasn't far away. All he had to do was bust his way through the motherfuckers and get in it, as long as he could find the key—which was buried in the grass he hadn't cut in a couple of weeks; finding that would prove the biggest obstacle. He needed a good plan to get him through.

He turned on one of his brightest lanterns, sought out the lamp he had placed in there as well, plugged it in and turned it on. He knew it was a good idea running electricity to the shed with all the work he did in there. Placing the lamp on the middle shelf on the back wall, and carrying the lantern with him, he began to search the shed for the proper items with which to make a stand: a bat, a shovel, hacksaws, hammers—he had them all, and he would be sure to load himself up with enough weapons to cut a swath through the possum populace waiting on him outside.

He walked the interior of the shed, turning to allow the light to cast a glow over every corner. The shadows grew larger and loomed around him. Somewhere in the darkness, he knew he'd find something good. Then, off in the corner at the northeast end of the shed, as the shifting light drew back the curtain of blackness, he saw his old helmet and smiled.

This was going to be one hell of a fight.

CHAPTER SIX

It was a disturbing scene over on Pulliam Avenue. Mrs. Barbara Jones—the woman who never made her hair appointment with Greta Harris—lay in her front yard, horribly mauled by possums. She had been in her late-forties; she was a plump lady with graying hair and a nice smile. People always thought she was a little strange, often saying things to people that were out of place: asking them personal questions, telling them unnecessary TMI details about her personal life. Most chalked it up to her becoming a tad dissociated because of her husband dying of a heart attack at forty-two. He wasn't out of shape and he didn't smoke, so it surprised everyone. Some say he had a lot of stress at home because Barbara was a handful, but no one really knew for sure, but they figured it had been a hell of a shock to her.

Regardless of the cause, the fact was that Ray Jones had died, leaving Barbara in her late-thirties to raise their daughter, Ingrid, and their son, Jeremiah. Fortunately, Ray had the foresight to take out a very lucrative insurance plan that covered the funeral and paid off their house; there had even been money left over to save for the children's college funds, which never did much good. Ingrid went to art school for a while, but had to drop out so she could help her mom; and Jeremiah, after his father's passing, hit a downward spiral and never did well in school. He ended up learning to lay carpet and made pretty decent money doing that. Ingrid became a postal worker who did freelance artwork in the area for businesses and schools. Both did well enough to live on their own, but neither did; they stayed at home to help Barbara, who was, a lot of the times, a total mess.

Barbara became increasingly scatterbrained through the years. She lost things, got lost, forgot important events—such as paying monthly bills— and would sometimes just sit around the house thinking it was her day off when she was scheduled to be at work. Needless to say, she never kept jobs too long. Somehow, though, she never missed her hair appointments.

Neither child was bothered by remaining home to help take care of their mother. They didn't have much ambition—especially Jeremiah—and there wasn't really a whole lot to do around town, anyway—or in the entire state of Kentucky, as far as they were concerned. Jeremiah would sometimes go to the lake with his friends, and spent a lot of time with his best bud, Bobby, cruising downtown Bardstown or a few of the surrounding towns, but there wasn't a lot going on in them, either. Turkey Town—officially known as Fairfield—was nearby but only had about seventy people living in it. He used to catch some of the backyard wrestling events, and he'd been on all the bourbon tours the state had to offer.

Ingrid drank a lot, but wasn't interested in bourbon tours. She liked touring My Old Kentucky Home and Wickland Estate near the historic district, as well as visiting the Nelson County History Museum in the main square. But, one could only do all that so much before the cracked face of decayed history lost its luster. She spent a lot of time at the local gym working her frustration out on the weight machines. When she got a wild hair, she would drive up to Louisville and visit Museum Row, or an art store, or something cultured. Years ago, when she was a teenager, there were some pretty cool places to go for poets and musicians in the Highlands neighborhood, but most of that area, as well as Downtown Louisville in general, had degenerated into streets lined with over-priced bars pumping out obnoxious people and music too loud to be any good. She missed the days before shameless commercialism and gentrification had squeezed the soul from that city. That's why she mostly stayed in Bardstown, now: it was peaceful, quiet, and stuck in the past. As long as the bulldozers and bullshit stayed on the opposite side of the Nelson County line, she was content in her rural town.

Barbara Jones became her children's lives. Jeremiah had some friends and a few girlfriends through the years, but he never got serious about anything other than hanging around Bobby all the time—mainly because

Bobby lived real close and was sort of reclusive, so a friendship with him was convenient. Jeremiah wasn't a real handsome fellow: his neck was too long and his head was shaped like an Easter Island statue. The bushiness of his hair combined with his tall, thin frame made him look like a walking Cabbage Palm. But, he had just enough charm (and a reputation for having a large member after Jackie Waters gave him his first handy in eighth grade and blabbed to everyone about it) to get a girlfriend sometimes.

Most guys said Ingrid would be pretty if she didn't look so damn mean all the time. She had hard eyes and lips that seemed to be in a perpetual state of angry pouting. Her chin-length reddish-black hair was simple and lame. Her body was often complimented for its fitness, but that was usually by other women. She had thick, well-defined biceps and triceps from all her time spent at the gym, and legs to match. The perceived anger on her face was more determination than anything. Her life had been tough and she damn sure planned to make it through, no matter what ran across her path.

Jeremiah's friend, Bobby, who sat next to him at the kitchen table, where she and her brother were coming to terms with the violent death of their mother, had always been obsessed with Ingrid. She didn't know if it was some sick fetish that involved her being his best friend's sister, or if he was one of the few guys that found her attractive, or if he was just an all-out sex-nut who couldn't go five seconds without thinking of possible penile conquests. He had never been shy about making his bawdy feelings for her known. He and Jeremiah had been friends since elementary school and even then he was a deviant-in-the-making. As kids, he would try to kiss and hug her all the time. As they aged into junior high, that nonsense then turned to peeping in her window and through her door, or "inadvertently" walking in on her in the bathroom (her own dumb fault, she thought, for not locking the door). He still hit on her as they got older and stared at her as she walked across the room. She wanted to hate him for it, but she didn't. Outside of his lascivious yearnings, he was a nice guy, and he was always there for Jeremiah. He used to pick Barbara up from places and run her to the store when she and Jeremiah weren't available. Bobby went out of his way to do things for people. He even often complimented her artwork, telling her how talented she was without making lewd comments or lecherous advances. He wasn't dangerous; he was just one of those guys with sexual entitlement who thought that kind of behavior was humorous and acceptable, even after Ingrid had hit him a few times for it. He was a short, handsome guy with broad shoulders, and she might have given him a chance if he wasn't so nasty sometimes—and if she hadn't known him since they were kids. She was three years older than him and he was always around. Bobby was pretty much an honorary little brother, which is probably the only reason he got away with some of the bullshit he said and did.

Jeremiah broke Ingrid's thoughts. "What the hell do you think did that to mom?"

She shrugged and blew out smoke. "I don't know. Animals, I guess."

Both of them had already sat in each other's arms and cried their eyes out over Mrs. Barbara. Now they were in shock, coming down from the agony of unexpected parental loss. They had always joked that their mother's final chapter would be an odd one, often making up peculiar scenarios and events that would bring about her demise, all in good fun, but they never anticipated it would be so grisly. This wasn't just murder—this was vicious, as if something unnatural emerged from another plain of existence and went berserk. They could think of no motive because no one had anything against her, and nothing had been stolen from her home or person. This was just pure savagery.

"Animals didn't do that. Not anything we have around here," Jeremiah said.

"We got bobcats coming out of the woods, sometimes. Maybe they did it."

"Bobcats wouldn't do that."

"I don't know then."

Ingrid put her cigarette out and Jeremiah looked absently around the room. Bobby watched Ingrid's muscles flex as she moved her arms. She felt his eyes on her and cast him a look of disdain. It sent a warm rush of regret through him because she caught him watching her while she was grieving her mother's death. He cast his eyes down to the table in front of him, willing himself not to look at her for a while.

They sat in silence as the cops and reporters came and went. The medics would be picking up Barbara's body soon, but neither child wanted to ride to the hospital with her. They would handle everything soon enough, but not right now. They just couldn't.

"What if there's a killer in town?" Jeremiah spoke. "They did say someone else was killed last night. Right?"

"Early this morning," Bobby said.

Jeremiah looked at him. "Who cares what time? It happened though."

"Doesn't mean there's some maniac walking around butchering middle-aged women," said Ingrid. "I think it was some sort of animal, or more than one—maybe wild dogs."

"I agree," Bobby spoke up, and Jeremiah gave him another disapproving glare.

"Of course you do. You always agree with Ingrid."

Bobby got defensive and wiggled in his seat. "Hey, I'm just saying it makes more sense."

"No, it doesn't. A pack of wild dogs, or any sort of animal, is not just going to spring up and start mauling people in the middle of the neighborhood. They only do that shit when they're rabid, scared, or starving. They're not fucked in the head like people are. I think a person did this."

"It didn't look like a person. It was too vicious. It looked like animals," Bobby argued.

Ingrid snatched her pack of cigarettes from the table and lit another. "Hey, you two, I really don't want to sit here and discuss mom's violent murder. Okay?"

Both boys fell quiet, realizing the conversation was rather crass.

It was too hard to believe. Barbara had been about to head to another one of her hair appointments with Greta Harris. Ingrid liked Greta: thought she was smart and really sweet. Barbara always spoke well of her, saying how kind she was, and that meant a lot to Ingrid since not a lot of people were very kind to her mother. They thought Barbara was a simpleton and that their snide remarks went over her head, like she was Prince Myshkin from *The Idiot* or something. But she wasn't. Barbara was sharp, just forgetful. While she might not remember you taking a jab at her, she would understand it quite clearly in the moment. She was just tired enough of life to let it slide. She didn't feel the need to argue. She didn't really care what people thought; she was concerned with her children and nothing else.

Her hair appointments always made her happy, and whoever or whatever the vile monster was that took her at one of her happier moments in a life drenched with shitty days, Ingrid hoped for the most dismal end for them. They didn't have the sappy, television show mother-daughter bond, but they loved each other. There was no explanation or reason to make anything about this heinous attack okay. She didn't care if it was a madman who supposedly didn't know any better or a pack of crazed animals, she wanted the perpetrator brought down, and so did Jeremiah. He was mostly soliciting opinions from the others about the culprit because he was devising ways to kill them. He was a mama's boy by admission and didn't give a damn what anyone thought about it. His mom had been his life and now he wanted to kill in the name of her death. In the place of a mother's love now sat a son's rage and he would not stop until either he or the killer was dead.

A lot of random people had been wandering in and out of the house since the first few arrived on the scene. All Ingrid remembered was she came home and saw her mother's ravaged body in the yard, screamed, called the police, and called Jeremiah. After that, the dam broke and everything became a haze of heartache and rage.

Most of the people straggling about remained unknown to her. Jeremiah seemed to recognize a few of them—Bobby, too. But, she didn't know any of them except for a familiar face from one of the local news channels. Some little blonde lady, but she couldn't recall her name. Ingrid rarely watched the news. That was Barbara's thing. Her mom didn't really care about current affairs as much as she did gossiping with Greta during her hair appointments.

The thought of her appointment made Ingrid's stomach knot up again, so she switched to something else: Jeremiah's eyes and how the sclera in each one was light pink; how they were rimmed red, watery, and shiny. His sniffles were slight but she heard them. She looked at his nose: the tip was red and the upper lip moist just below the nostrils. He was trying to hold back the tears, maybe to be strong for her, or because he didn't want to cry in front of Bobby. He certainly didn't need to remain strong for her, because she was stronger than him. And fuck Bobby. Why give a shit if he saw Jeremiah cry? They had been friends forever, had been through all kinds of bad times together. Bobby bawled when he was fifteen after his dog got hit by a car, and he did so in front of Jeremiah, Ingrid, and several other people—and the dog didn't even die; they took her to the vet and all she had was a broken hip. What did it matter if he saw Jeremiah shed tears over his murdered mother? It's not like it would bother Bobby, anyway.

Two men with notepads made their way into the kitchen, flanked by two cops. They were talking in hushed tones to one another. The journalists were getting some statements from the officers. Ingrid, Jeremiah, and Bobby caught some of the exchange. Jeremiah's face darkened as Bobby stared at them, surprised that these four assholes could be so tactless. Ingrid turned in her seat and gave them her best death glare. At first, the men didn't notice, but after a few seconds, it was as if the heat of the three of them glowering in their direction rolled over the gathering, for they all got quiet and looked towards the table.

A shaggy-faced reporter with smudged glasses and a diminutive stature stuttered and said, "Sorry."

"The fuck you are." Jeremiah stood up but Ingrid turned her glare on him and he sat back down.

Normally, she'd have been okay with her brother giving that grimy leech a verbal lashing, but with two cops present, she didn't want to witness the inevitable outcome of Jeremiah going to jail. She hoped that they'd understand, given the circumstances, but she wasn't going to bank on her hope for human compassion. They were, after-all, standing in the kitchen coldly discussing the murder of their mother with the reporters just to give them a better story—or the story the police wanted the reporters to tell. Not a lot of class rested within people like that.

The portly female cop quickly ushered the journalists from the room. The tall male, who had a stripper's mustache, remained behind. He stalked into the room, his broad frame swaying as he approached. Jeremiah half expected him to tell Ingrid she'd been a bad girl and then rip his pants off in one quick tug. He then imagined the guy dancing around the room without his shirt, his hairy, perverted pecs bouncing wildly as he swung his junk at his sister.

Why the hell am I thinking of shit like that?

Jeremiah's mind often resorted to absurdity in the face of adversity. It was his best defense. Rationalization came after the emotions wore off. He often got too worked up in the heat of the moment and wanted to pummel all offenders in his path. Rationale was for the birds, so outlandish mockery and ridicule of all around him were his calming agents.

"Look kids, I'm sorry about that," the cop said, his mustache slithering beneath his nose.

"I'm sure," Bobby said.

He didn't usually smart-off to cops. It surprised Ingrid and made her kind of proud.

The cop looked angry at first and then breathed deeply, turning on the human switch in his brain that disengaged the robotic autopilot Ingrid imagined he mostly operated under. "I really am. Look, I wasn't just trying to give that guy a story. Sure, that's what he wanted, but I want people to be aware of what's going on."

"I thought you guys liked to keep that shit quiet, so people don't freak," Jeremiah said, his voice shaking on the edge of eruption.

"Normally, we do; and, I'm sure my boss wouldn't be happy about me telling those guys anything. But, people already know something's up. They should be able to have some idea what it is, or at least what it's doing, so they can be ready."

"What is it?" Ingrid asked.

The cop shrugged. "I don't know. But, it's pretty vicious, and it's not just an isolated incident. Reports of other attacks keep coming in from all over the city, some happening simultaneously. They almost seem strategic. At first we thought animals might be attacking people, or some escaped psycho. But, it can't be; it's too widespread and too well executed. It's baffling."

"Well, you'd better get out there and find out what the fuck's going on," Jeremiah said, the edge apparently getting thinner.

"We're going to, young man."

Ingrid looked at the officer's badge. It said Jackson. She felt his eyes on her and she wanted to meet them, but the tone in his voice had begun to sound sincere, and sincerity would be too much for her right now. Sincerity would send her over the precipice into a river of tears. She wasn't afraid to cry, she had done it enough already, but she needed to maintain right now to get through everything. She'd cry more later—she'd cry until her eyes popped like water balloons once it all was over—but for now, she had to hold back or she'd never get through this nightmarish ordeal in one emotional piece. She turned from the man and simply said, "Thank you, Officer Jackson."

"You're welcome."

Ingrid could feel that Jackson was about to say something else, but was stopped when three gunshots were fired out back. The din of panicked chattering immediately followed. The other officer who had previously been in the kitchen came running towards the back door, hand ready on her piece. Jackson backed away and followed his partner. The two sleazy journalists came sliding in behind them. They stopped out on the back patio and one said, "Holy shit!"

Men out back began screaming, and then an eerie sound invaded the house: a sound like a swarm of locusts slaughtering armies of katydids and cicadas, amplified a hundred times. The harsh hissing of something unfamiliar made the backyard beyond the door sound like the site of the apocalypse. Ingrid, Jeremiah, and Bobby all rose from their seats and went towards the door, but more gunshots made them stop and kneel.

"Get a picture of that!" one of the journalists said.

"I am! I am!" said the other.

"Holy shit! There are so many of them. I've never seen anything like this."

Ingrid started to rise, but more gunshots rang out and a wild bullet flew through the kitchen window. Two shots sounded nearby and one of the journalists was thrown back in a spray of blood. Ingrid looked and saw it was the slimebag with the shaggy face, only now he had just half a face.

"Holy shit!" Bobby screamed.

"What the fuck?" Jeremiah added.

Ingrid had her mouth covered, shocked at what she had seen. What in the hell was happening out there? She had to know. She rose from the floor and crept to the window to see why men were screaming and firing guns; to know what that awful cacophony of shrill sibilance rising into the air was. When she saw the cause, she gasped, first in horror, and then in shock.

The yard had been overrun with what looked like possums, only they weren't normal looking. They were fast, mean, covered in grime, and caked in blood. Some were much larger than any possums she'd ever seen. Their eyes shone with madness as they sped across the yard, attacking the men like wild dogs. Many were blown to pieces by the cops, but it mattered not. All around the perimeter of the yard, more possums poured in, coming over the six-foot-high privacy fence, digging their way underneath, and even burrowing through it. A horde, piled on top one another, scratched and pushed at the wood until it gave away. All Ingrid could do was stare in frightened perplexity.

"What is it?" Jeremiah asked.

When she didn't answer, he stood up and looked out the window, gaping at the horrendous sight before him.

"What the fuck?"

From the shadows of the tree branches reaching over the fence, from the darkness of the woods beyond, from the high swaying grass at the backend of the yard, they came: dozens—maybe hundreds—of fierce looking possums—hissing, growling, clicking something in the back of their throats, mouths seeming to salivate blood, lunging at the men and women with their mouths open. Some were as big as or bigger than medium-sized dogs. The officers stood no chance. They fired their guns until they ran out of bullets and never had time to reload. Six officers in all, a few other people none of them knew, and the last journalist, were now either writhing on the ground beneath the incursion of the cruel creatures, or were on their knees fighting to keep their heads above the savage swell.

Officer Jackson was the last person standing, but he didn't have much left. His left leg was torn to shreds and his right hand was almost completely severed from the wrist. Viscera protruded from his mangled uniform shirt as he hobbled back towards the house. But, he didn't make it. When Jackson was four feet from the door, one of the huge possums leapt off the roof and landed on his head and shoulders, sinking in its fangs, spilling Jackson's blood like the yoke of a fried egg.

The backyard was carnage. Mangled flesh and torn bodies lay scattered about. Agonized wails of dying men filled the air around them. The little blonde reporter lay by the gate with her chest torn open. Jeremiah was reminded of some Lucio Fulci zombie flick where ghouls rummaged around in the innards of their victims, making those disgusting squishy sounds for effect. That sound traveled from the backyard into the house; the sound of tissue and internal organs being pulled from bodies, moved about, and chewed. No way was he seeing this.

From beside them, Bobby broke the silence. "What the hell, man? Are those possums?"

"Yes," Ingrid said.

"Possums don't eat people."

"These do," said Jeremiah.

Ingrid saw many of them breaking away from the packs and heading towards the house, and she broke from her terrified shock.

"And they're coming for us!"

She ran to the back door and closed it just in time. Several small bodies banged against the other side; squealing, they were ready to bust in and tear more flesh from bone. Their angry protests at being kept out gained their allies' attention. Soon, a bunch of hungry eyes and flesh-dangling teeth turned towards the house. The small feet began to kick into high speed and charge forth. More than a hundred hellish possums bombarded the building and slammed against the door so hard that it made the blinds shake. Thumps against the window got Ingrid and Bobby's attention. They saw the small crusty forms slinging themselves against the glass with so much force small cracks began to form in the panes. The window was on the verge of collapse; when that happened, they would pour into the house in a tide of murderous hunger.

Ingrid grabbed a set of keys from the key ring holder on the wall and said, "We got to get out of here."

Bobby was already ahead of her, at the front door peering towards the cars and vans parked around the yard. "It's clear out here," he said.

"It won't be for long," she replied.

"Then let's get the fuck going!" Jeremiah said.

"Should we grab any weapons?" Bobby turned suddenly.

The back door rattled and some wood cracked; seconds later, the sound of breaking glass followed.

"We don't have time!" Ingrid headed past him and out the front door. "Come on!"

She got to her car and stuck the key in, but it didn't turn. "What the fuck?" She looked at the key chain. It wasn't hers.

"It's not mine! I have to go back in."

Bobby, still on the front porch, quickly slammed the door and said, "You can't. They've swarmed the house."

He jumped off the porch and joined Ingrid by her car. Jeremiah was a few feet away, gazing towards the back of the house. He saw a dark mass round the corner and head their way.

"Give me the key!" he yelled.

"What?" Ingrid asked.

He held out his hand. "Give me the god-damn key!"

Ingrid handed it to him and he said, "This is to my car. Come on!"

His Ford was on the other side of the yard, which was about ten feet away, and the possums were only about eight feet behind them. They ran as hard as they could towards the car. Jeremiah always left his doors unlocked—something Ingrid usually bitched at him about. Today she was glad that he never listened to her.

The driver's side was by the road, so Jeremiah had to run around the car. Bobby jumped into the passenger seat just after Ingrid leapt into the back. Jeremiah was yanking open the driver's door just after she closed hers, and a possum bit down on his foot. He screamed and stomped on its head with his other foot, breaking its skull. He kicked it away and got in the car.

Possums were all around the vehicle, clamoring to get on top of it. Jeremiah shoved the key into the ignition and started it up, then drove away as fast as he could, peeling dirt, squealing tires, and splattering possums around the roadside. The spinning tires flung gore into the air, much of it splashing against the windows. Some strange chunk of purple and crimson carcass smacked the window next to Ingrid's face and dangled on the glass for a few seconds before sliding off and dropping to the street.

"What the fuck was that, man?" Jeremiah asked.

"A bunch of pissed off possums, it looked like," Ingrid replied. "It looks like Bobby was right: animals are the killers."

Bobby looked back at her, eyes wide, mouth open, breathing heavily. He looked straight ahead again and started shaking his head, then looked at Ingrid once more.

"No fucking way! I meant dogs or coyotes or something else. Not a bunch of fucking possums! Possums don't do that shit!"

"Maybe they got rabies," Jeremiah said.

"Yeah! Maybe that's it," Bobby said and looked to Ingrid for the answer.

She shook her head. "I don't think so."

"How the hell do you know?" Jeremiah asked.

She shrugged. "I don't."

"Then that was probably it. That's the only thing I can think of.

Ingrid looked out the window and watched the trees passing. As they sped along, she saw possums coming out of the woods, many running along the road. Turning around and looking out the back window, she saw a small gathering of them pursuing the car, although unable to keep up, fading into the distance, only to see another small group emerge from the woods on one side of the road and the grass on the other.

"They're everywhere."

"Yeah, no shit! I see them," Jeremiah replied.

Bobby sat still in silent shock.

They rode on for a few minutes without a word. Ingrid then asked, "Where are we going?"

"Fuck, I don't know—far away from here."

"Go to the police," Bobby finally spoke.

Jeremiah nodded. "That's a good idea."

"Cops already know what's going on," Ingrid said. "It's been on the radio."

Bobby turned to her. "But do they know it's possums?"

"I don't know. Probably—especially after what happened back at our house. One of those cops was bound to have called it in."

The car came to a sudden turn that Jeremiah had forgotten about. He didn't often travel this way, so he had to jerk the wheel hard at the last second to avoid rolling off the road and into a field. The tires screeched as the car jerked to the left. Once the car was back in position, Ingrid looked out the back window and breathed in deep and loud.

"What?" Jeremiah asked.

"Behind us."

A glance in the rearview mirror told Jeremiah the horror story coming up the road. Bobby looked in the side-view mirror and said, "Shit!"

A dark wave of possums came forth from the field to the right of the car, and more from the woods to the left. Jeremiah stepped on the pedal. The needle on the speedometer jumped, the engine revved, and they were soon barreling down the road.

Ingrid was busy marveling in terror at the mass of white faces charging after them, coming in from all sides. How many were there? Hundreds, at least—maybe thousands. What the hell? An army of possums waging war on mankind? Not likely. Possums rarely attack. Ingrid remembered pestering one with a stick, jabbing and swatting at it, even hitting it, when she was a child, and all it did was hiss. She finally stopped after it fell down. She thought it was dead and it made her cry. Her mother later told her that possums did that as a defense mechanism to avoid a fight, and then scolded her for antagonizing such a docile creature. After that, she never bothered them again, even started leaving food out for them to make up for her previous transgression. So this had to be a bad dream. She fell asleep at the kitchen table, exhausted from the events of her mother's death, and now she dreamed some absurd scenario that somehow symbolized her current sadness. She kept trying to will herself to wake when the car came to a disastrous halt that sent her flying against the back of the front seats.

As Jeremiah had driven the car over the hill in front of them, what came into view filled him with fright and disbelief. Spread out along the road and into the field was a legion of bloodstained possums ferociously bearing their teeth at the oncoming car. Jeremiah slammed on the breaks and the bald tires were unable to get a good grip on the slick pavement. The car began to fishtail and careen sideways. Jeremiah pulled the steering wheel in a feeble attempt to regain control but the car slammed into a telephone pole so hard it rocked the light hanging from it. The front end was smashed in and the windshield slightly cracked, but thankfully it did not break. Bobby smacked the dashboard and Ingrid ended up in the floor in the back, but no one was seriously hurt—yet.

Within seconds, possums had engulfed the car. Their claws scratched along the windows, smearing the blood of their previous conquests; their bodies beat against the doors. The collage of crimson masks and small, flesh-ripping claws created a tapestry of terror that was near to maddening. As the three of them sat in the car, feeling it rock back and forth, none could speak. A combination of fear and disbelief strangled their minds and mouths for an uncountable matter of seconds.

"What the fuck do we do?" Bobby finally said.

Jeremiah tried to start the car but it wouldn't turn over. The sound of the engine trying to start sent the possums into a frenzied sense of urgency. They started darting about, beating on the roof and windows, banging against the doors.

"Stop it!" Ingrid said to Jeremiah. "You're making them more hostile."

"They can't get any more hostile, Ingrid! It's like the fucking possum apocalypse!"

Ingrid didn't hear him; her ears had picked up a strange squeaking sound from somewhere beyond the creatures shrieking in unison on the windshield. The smell of blood invaded the car and made her nauseous. She wanted to vomit, but held it back to try and pinpoint the slight noise.

"I wonder what would happen if I turned on the wipers."

Jeremiah gave it a shot. The fluid sprayed up, causing some of the creatures to jump back. When the wipers started to move, the possums actually jumped away.

A visual opening momentarily appeared on the windshield and revealed to Ingrid what the squeaking sound was. She looked up in horror as she watched the large light on top of the pole—rattled loose upon impact—dangle precariously above the car.

With a shaking finger, she pointed upwards. "Look you guys."

Bobby and Jeremiah looked up and saw the light swinging back and forth, barely hanging on by a wire.

"Oh shit," Jeremiah said.

The possums began to scramble back onto the windshield, causing the car to shake again. The light above them slipped a little lower. The car began to rattle harder, and just before the last small radius of vision on the windshield was obscured by more possum bodies, all three of them saw whatever held the wire in place snap and the light come loose.

"Fuck," Jeremiah said.

It took only a few seconds for it to fall, and its descent brought grim tidings. Like a bomb blasting a battleground, the thick, heavy glass casing crashed into the windshield, shattering glass and squashing possums. When the windshield broke, the lunatic beasts fell into the front seat, washing over Jeremiah and Bobby like a tide from the shores of Hell. The rank aroma of rancid blood and dirty fur swarmed in with them.

Ingrid screamed and pressed herself against the backseat as she watched the ruthless animals tear into her brother and his best friend. Three clamped down on Jeremiah's throat and began gnawing. Blood gushed from their attack, coating them in more thick crimson liquid. Several more fell into his lap and began dining on his torso and arms, ripping and tearing through his flesh, removing internal organs to chow upon.

Bobby's face was ravaged by two possums that were standing atop a pile of their brethren visiting a gruesome evisceration upon his body. The two possums gouged his facial flesh with claws and maws that disfigured him into a pulpy mass of serrated tissue. His left eye was pulled cruelly from its socket and chewed to bits; his tongue was ripped sideways from his mouth; blood spurted from the orifices and tumbled down onto the other creatures. The screams of their agony rattled Ingrid's brain, but the horror show of blood and body bits spurred her into action.

With two immobile humans served to the possums on a silver dish, they took no notice of her in the backseat. Though she was rendered almost numb with terror and sorrow, her instinct to survive kicked in. Knowing that soon the possums would finish with Jeremiah and Bobby, and assuming their inexplicable bloodlust was insatiable, she realized she was probably on the menu, as well. Though her brother meant the world to her, and mourning had already begun deep in her soul, hesitation would mean certain grisly death, so she had to move.

Jeremiah's car had collapsible backseats, so she turned and pressed one of the latches to drop the right seat and began to force her way into the trunk. As she burrowed her way frantically into the hot, stifling darkness, she felt something bump her leg. She yelped and scrambled in as far as she could and positioned herself to pull the seat back up and shut herself inside. When she did, she saw a possum had spotted her and was trying to follow.

It was standing on the collapsed seat, eyes shining madly from its bloody face. No hint of the white fur could be seen as all was stained dark red and black from fresh and crusted blood alike. Their eyes met and the beast growled and ambled towards her. It was only a medium-sized possum, but it was strong—too strong for its kind. It leapt at her face and, lying on her side, she was able to roll onto her back and seize it as it fell upon her. She avoided the gnashing teeth and held it by the throat, feeling the surprising strength the creature possessed as it kicked its legs and tried to force itself down upon her skin.

The backseat was still down and the hissing of her assailant grew louder. In seconds, she feared its friends would flow in and devour her. She squeezed its throat as hard as she could and rolled towards the opening in the backseat. She flung the creature forward and it hit the back of the passenger seat, catching the attention of the others. Cold black eyes took notice of her. Some simply went back to their feeding, but others began to abandon their meals for a new slab of meat. They started to climb over the seats to make their way to the back. Feeling her bladder nearly let go, she reached for the seat and tried to pull it up. Her first tug brought it up, but it slipped and fell back down. One possum put its front feet on the seat and was about to come after her, but she quickly pulled it up again just as the backseat filled with the stinking monsters.

As she pulled the seat up, she was afraid she would be unable to get a good enough grip to shut it completely. When the seat rose back into position, and the sight and smell of the merciless animals were traded in for darkness and the aroma of motor oil and gasoline, she listened for the click of the lock falling into place, but it didn't come. She held onto the side of the seat and tried, with the minute grasp her fingers had on it, to pull it shut, but it would not click. It appeared to be an act one could not perform from within the trunk. She would have no choice but to hold the seat in place for as long as she could.

She breathed heavily, holding the seat, fearful that her fingers would grow too weak and the seat would slip away, opening the door for her painful destruction. She did not want to be torn to shreds and eaten alive by possums—a possibility that would have never occurred to her in a million lifetimes that she might face. The idea almost made her laugh. But, the feel of something furry brushing against her fingers stifled all acts of mirth or madness, grounding her back into the grim reality to which she was chained.

Ingrid expected to feel sharp teeth clamp down on her fingers any second, as they had obviously found her flesh. She wiggled them backwards on the seat a little, and felt the strain of holding it in place increase dramatically. Slowly, the seat began to slip away. The opening toward the top corner revealed a little more light every few seconds. The sound of the possums hissing and scratching on the other side made her tremble. The more she shook, the more the seat slipped from her grasp. Soon, the crack had lengthened so much that she was able to see a few sets of black eyes staring in at her with what almost looked like a sense of triumph.

That's when she noticed the car had fallen still and silent. The frenzied behavior had ceased. There was still the slight sound of sucking flesh, but mostly, the horde had halted its attack, and Ingrid hoped that they were sated and would leave.

As the seat slipped further and further from her hands, she came to realize that her hope was just a torment on her spirit, for she saw something that chilled her to the core. The possums were watching her, patiently waiting for the seat to fall. They were not hissing, bumping into each other, or scrambling about. They were still and silent, sure that their victory was near.

That was all Ingrid could take. Suddenly, she screamed, "Fuck you!" long and loud, causing them to stir.

The seat began to fall away completely; with a sense of nothing to lose, she reached out for a better hold on it. If she missed, then she would be completely exposed and vulnerable to the possums' attack. Her fingertips brushed the fabric and she squeezed, pinching a piece of the seat in her hand. Quickly, she pulled back on it, clenching it as tightly as she could. Her hold was true: the seat did not fall; and when she yanked back on it, it came up towards her, closing her once again in the protection of the metallic cocoon.

An alarm must have gone off in the collective mind of the possum union, because they began their frenzy once more. Their noises reverberated across the car and she felt their weight shifting around the interior. Something heavy slammed against the seat—a large mass of them, she imagined—and shoved so hard against it that she heard the latch click in place. She pulled back, sliding her fingers from the crack so they didn't get stuck, and held her breath. She watched for many seconds, waiting for the seat to fall, but it did not. The possums scratched and screamed and slammed against it, but they could not reach her. She was safe—for now. Her new concern was that they would eventually be able to rip their way through the seat—cushion, springs, and all. She doubted it, but after seeing what they could accomplish, nothing was for certain. She had to get out.

The car had an interior trunk release, but she feared to use it in case the possum army was still surrounding the car. She found the lever in the dark anyway, wanting to chance a peek. She tugged it slightly and felt the trunk unlock. Cautiously, she pushed up on it just enough to allow her eyes a small glimpse of her surroundings, and what she saw only intensified her current state of terror. As far as she could see, the filthy creatures roamed about like rats in a New York sewer. There were hundreds of them, hissing and scavenging. She saw many of them feasting on other animals that had crossed onto their path. Carcasses she could not define, mid-sized animals, except for a larger body that looked like a deer. There was no escape. She was trapped. She lowered her head and pulled the trunk closed, fully aware of the hopelessness in which she was imprisoned.

On the other side of the seats, the possums clawed and squealed. The ripping of the fabric confirmed her fear: they would try to tunnel through to reach her. The only question she now had was if they could.

Ingrid felt around the backseat for a weapon and began to devise a plan.

CHAPTER SEVEN

Rachel cleaned and dressed Todd's wound as best she could with the hydrogen peroxide and gauze they had in their bathroom medicine cabinet. It burned and Todd rubbed at the stinging sensation for a few minutes.

"Is it okay?" she asked.

Todd pressed on it and rubbed softly. "Depends on your definition."

"Does it hurt?"

"A little, but I'll live."

"We need to get you to a doctor."

"Yeah, but I'm not real cool with the idea of going outside right now."

Rachel got up from the easy chair in the corner and walked to the front room window. Todd was stretched out on the couch. A few possums were still scattered about the front yard, but not nearly as many as before. She pressed her face against the glass and looked in all directions, squinting to be sure they weren't hiding somewhere. They had already proven to be crafty critters, so she was leaving nothing to chance. After a minute of surveying the area, she determined most had gone—she had no clue to where, but she didn't really care. All that mattered was that they were gone and that meant she could get Todd to the doctor.

She turned from the window and said, "Not so many out there, now. Maybe they've moved on."

Todd shrugged. "What if they haven't? What if it's a trap like in *Return of the Living Dead*, and they're just waiting for us to walk outside so they can attack us?"

"I don't know. We can try to go out to the car and see what happens."

Todd looked past Rachel and out the window. He could only see the pale sky, some treetops, and roofs behind her. There was no way he could tell if any possums remained roaming the yard. All he could picture was the day's earlier vicious attacks and that was enough to hold him at bay for a while.

"How about we just wait a bit?" he said. "They might not be that far away, and they might be coming back."

Rachel sighed and nodded. "Why are they doing this anyway? Attacking people like that?"

"I don't know. Who cares?"

"Just wondering. It's really strange."

"Strange? More like completely fucked up."

Rachel nodded and then turned at the sound of something grinding into the driveway. A long silver Oldsmobile from the 80s came to a stop just outside the house. That meant her cousin, Julie, and her boyfriend, Ralph (yes, Ralph), had arrived for a visit.

The few remaining possums out front scattered as the car rolled in. Ralph—a skinny, balding man in a white button-up shirt and gray slacks—rose from the driver's side, and Julie—thin with teased up blonde hair and blue top and jeans—emerged from the passenger side. Both moved quickly towards the house with a purpose. Ralph ascended the porch steps quickly with Julie right behind him. He beat on the door like the world was ending, and Rachel was already opening it after his fourth thump.

She pushed the glass exterior door open and the two barged in. "Is everything okay?" Julie asked. "I heard about Brad!"

"It's Brandon," Rachel said, trying not to taste the pain that came with speaking his name. "And everything isn't okay."

Ralph saw Todd's bleeding bandage and went straight to him.

"What the heck happened to you, buddy?" Ralph was in his mid-thirties but thought he was much older. Todd didn't appreciate his attempt at fatherly compassion.

"A fucking possum bit me."

Ralph blinked at the foul language, but let it slide due to the unusual cause of the injury. "What?"

"A possum?" Julie asked and headed to Todd. "Mean little fuckers, aren't they?"

"Actually, no," said Ralph. "All that stuff about them being aggressive is a myth. They're actually very timid creatures."

"Like Hell, they are," said Todd. "I got the bite mark to prove that's a bunch of bullshit."

"Yeah, and I have the dead boyfriend to back it up," Rachel added.

Watery-eyed Julie went to embrace Rachel. "I'm so sorry, dear. He really was a nice guy."

But you never can remember his name, can you? Bitch.

Rachel hugged Julie back, thinking her to be a disingenuous hoe-bag. This was the moment when one of her distant jerk-off relatives shows up to pretend like they care. But, Julie and Ralph really struck gold with this visit of feigned concern: they showed up thinking they were only getting the dead boyfriend; they had no idea they were getting a partially-maimed little brother to go along with it. This was their lucky day.

"Yes, he was," Rachel agreed, feeling the warm water leak through her eyes.

Ralph put his hand on Todd's knee, setting off creeper bells in the young man's head. "So son, what happened with this opossum?"

Opossum? Was this fucking biology class? Todd didn't want to hear that proper bullshit.

"A bunch of them attacked some of the reporters that were here earlier. One dickhead got bitten pretty badly on the legs. The possum that bit him got loose in the house and the guy ran like a pussy, bleeding all over our floor. We had to fight it off, then. We managed to trap it back in mom and dad's old bedroom."

"Wow!" Julie said. "See Ralph, they *are* aggressive. You don't know what you're talking about."

"I assure you, Julie, they are not. Something must have triggered the violent response in the opossum that got in the house."

"Would you stop saying *opossum*? It makes you sound like a god-damn nerd," Todd said.

"Language, Todd."

"Horse shit."

"Be nice, Todd," Rachel said.

As much as she thought Ralph was a pompous dickhead, there was no need for Todd to be so rude. If she could keep herself from telling Julie to bite the bullet, after years of enduring her condescending attitude, then he could listen to Ralph's foolishness for a few minutes.

"Whatever," Todd grumbled, but didn't get smart again.

"Look, Todd's telling the truth." Rachel then explained what had happened.

Ralph shook his head. "Impossible. We didn't see any opossums when we pulled up."

"They must have moved on," Todd said.

"To where?"

"Fuck if I know! All I know is one of them bit me!"

Julie pointed in the direction of Rachel and Todd's parents' old room. "So, you like, got one trapped in the bedroom?"

"Yes. Todd knocked it out of the air with a pillow. It was leaping towards my face."

Julie giggled. "I bet that was funny to see."

"Not really. I sure wasn't laughing." Rachel rolled her eyes.

"Can I see it?" Julie took off down the hall.

"No!" Todd said as Ralph went to join her.

He stopped at the edge of the hallway and looked back at Rachel and Todd, then back down the hall at Julie, who was already in front of the door.

"Julie! Leave it alone. It's obviously unstable," Ralph warned.

"Oh I'm sure! Is it all bloody and stuff?" Julie asked with a bizarre glint in her widened eyes.

Rachel moved to stand by Ralph at the threshold of the hallway. Julie always liked trouble, and she was almost completely dissociated with humanity most of the time. This possum madness was her kind of hullaballoo, never mind that they had killed Brandon. That didn't matter as long as Julie was entertained.

I should push you in there with it, you sleazy slut.

Rachel almost ran down the hall to carry out that desire. It took all the will within her to refrain. Julie never did anything for anybody, at least not out of kindness, but she always expected people to do stuff for her. You could be dying of the flu or having the worst day of your life, Julie still expected you to drop your pains and plans for her if she needed you. But, if you needed her for something, it always came with a price tag (gas, food, money), and if that fee couldn't be met, then she was too busy. She never paid anyone back, and she never returned any favors. She was never nice, either. Anything she said that sounded kind was really fueled by an agenda. She was no good—rotten to the core. If Bardstown got torn to shreds by these creatures, Julie would no doubt be the only survivor, like a cockroach after the nuclear holocaust, only more useless. A part of Rachel hoped the possum would get out and go directly for her bitch cousin. If not for Todd being there, Rachel would open the door for Julie herself and let the damn thing out. She might enjoy seeing how well it could entertain the heartless whore then.

Julie put her ear to the door. "Wow! It's growling."

The possum growled loudly and beat against the door so hard it made it rattle.

"You sure that's just an opossum in there?" Ralph asked, half in a trance.

"Yes."

"Stop with the *opossum* bullshit!" Todd said again.

Julie reached her right hand out for the doorknob, but stopped when Rachel yelled, "No! Don't go in there."

Julie looked at her and smiled, then laughed. "What's the big deal? It's only a possum. Ralph said they're not dangerous. Right, honey?"

Ralph's mouth opened, but before any words could come out, an impact against the bottom of the door sent shards of wood scattering outwards; a large, fat possum busted through, attaching itself to Julie's left shin. Blood began to spray out in small puffs as soon as she started screaming.

"Oh shit!" Ralph ran down the hall with Rachel screaming behind him.

"That's not the one we locked in there! That one is bigger!" she said.

As Ralph approached a frantic Julie, she yelled, "Does he look fucking timid now, you idiot? Get him off of me!"

Before Ralph could make it to the end of the hallway, a tide of possums busted through the bedroom door, washing over Julie and engulfing her in seconds. Squirts of blood shot up from her wailing form, splashing Ralph and the walls around her.

With a girlish shriek of his own, Ralph turned and ran, leaving Julie to suffer her demise. Blowing by a stunned Rachel—who was trying to decide if she felt guilty for her earlier ill-wishes on her cousin, or vindicated that Julie didn't get to survive—Ralph ran to the back door and opened it. When he did, another battalion of possums awaited him. The screen had already been obliterated and there was nothing to stop their forward surge.

Another squeal escaped his wimpy lips and he ran straight into the laundry room located to his left. Years ago, the Owenses had a second story added to the house. It was mainly just two more bedrooms and a bath and it rarely got used. After their parents died, Rachel and Todd all but abandoned that second story because they didn't want to deal with it, anymore. It was somewhat of a family project that both of them would rather have forgotten. Luckily for Ralph, *he* hadn't forgotten it. He never really helped them with it—only retrieved a couple of tools for their father—but, it was enough for him not to forget its existence in his state of panic.

The stairway leading up had been erected in the laundry room. It was the one room that would always remain unseen by guests, and was not meant to be nice and pretty, so they didn't really care if they had an unsightly stepladder-like stairway rising up in the center of it. It really was a steep climb—twelve steps leading almost straight up. It hurt Ralph's weak knees to climb it, but the possums were on his tail, so he gave it his all. The only thing that was harder than scrambling up the high-angled steps was keeping his bowels from letting loose and splattering down on his pursuers.

All the possums that came in the back door went for Ralph, ignoring Rachel. Julie was still a fresh meal to the hallway horde. Rachel thought this would be the perfect time to escape. But if there was another swarm standing by, she didn't know what they would do. Todd wouldn't be able to outrun them if they attacked, and she didn't think both of them could fight many of them off. She had to make a quick decision because they were all over her house—which was what helped her make up her mind.

I didn't see them earlier because many of them found a way into mom and dad's old bedroom—most likely through the window. Was it open? I don't know. The rest were waiting by the back door. I didn't see any out front, so most of them must be inside the house. If any had been hiding beside the house, then they would have gotten Julie and Ralph as soon as they got out of their car. Now's our chance.

She ran from her spot in the kitchen and scampered across the living room.

"Get up," she said to Todd.

He was already leaning against the couch. All the screaming gave him pretty good motivation to assume they were under siege.

"They're in the house, aren't they?"

"Yes."

"Where?"

"In the hallway and heading upstairs. We've got to go, now."

Rachel opened the front door and peered outside, moving her eyes side to side, surveying the front lawn—not a possum in sight. She pushed open the storm door and stepped cautiously onto the porch, craned her neck and looked all around. She heard a lot of faint hissing in the distance, echoing from somewhere behind the house. They were near, but they might not be heading to the front. She turned back to her bleeding brother, who was sweating and struggling to walk.

"You need to take anything with you?"

"No. You?"

"Nope."

"You got your keys?"

"In my pocket."

"Julie and Ralph?"

"Ralph's the reason the possums went upstairs. More got Julie in the hallway."

Even though Todd didn't like either of them, he felt bad for them both. To die so young and so horribly—he wouldn't wish such a fate on anyone. But, he loved his sister, and in light of the danger she was in, those two could choke on possum balls.

"Let's go," he said.

He limped towards Rachel, who reached out an arm to steady him, but he lightly pushed it away. "Just get to the car. I'll be right behind you."

She nodded, knowing he was strong enough to make it. Todd may have only been twelve, but he had been through enough to make him into a man. She was proud of him for his strength.

They dashed out the door: Rachel first, Todd limping powerfully behind her, only barely wincing at the pain in his leg. They made it to Rachel's rusty Buick without incident. She turned the key in the ignition and they drove off, leaving the house and all the pain it held behind them.

Ralph emerged from the darkness of the stairway into the shadows of the abandoned upper-floor. The hundreds of claws scraping on the wood behind him made his brain shiver with fear. He could hear them struggling up the steps, their small razor-like claws digging to find purchase and pull their squat, four-legged forms up each step one-by-one. Low, guttural growls and angry, sibilant hisses pervaded the air behind him. He glanced back to see if they had made it to the top and all he saw was a whispering blackness, threatening him with death.

The upstairs was just a short hallway running the length of the house. There was a window on both ends, both shrouded by dusty shades—much too far away for him to try either of them as an escape route. Three doorways lined the wall across from him, all spaced about six feet apart. The one directly in front of him was a bathroom. The door was open and he saw no window. The one to his left was a tad closer, since the doorway to the stairs was not centered precisely, but the door was closed and he didn't want to risk getting down there and finding the door jammed or locked from the inside. So he went for the open door to his right. As he took his first steps towards it, the first pile of possums spilled onto the upper floor.

Ralph fled down the hall quickly. There were many thuds against the walls as their bodies bounced around, having difficulty moving in unison down the narrow passage. He reached the doorway and turned into the room. Immediately, he sought out the window located on the far side. There was no shade or curtain, just a bare square of glass in the middle of the wall. The floor, too, was dusty hardwood, and he slipped slightly as he took off across it.

The window slid up easily after he turned the latch. The possums were coming; the sound of their presence had amplified dramatically. There was no screen, so Ralph leaned out and looked behind him. Two possums had just become visible. He turned back and began climbing out onto the ledge. Looking down, he discovered the reason the terrifying noises the possums made had increased so much: on the ground below him was an ocean of possums scrambling about at the base of the house. They were piling up on one another, as if trying to make a wall high enough to reach him. Hundreds of black eyes dotted into eerie white masks looked up at him, shining in the falling evening. The rancid smell of decayed flesh and tangy blood rushed up at him, making him queasy.

Ralph glanced over his shoulder and saw the scourge rushing into the room. With nowhere else to go, his mind frantically searched and could find just one solution to pull him from this horror: the roof.

He climbed on the window sill outside—which was wide and long and able to support him—and reached for the roof, but was unable to touch it. He stretched his arms, pressing himself as high on his tip-toes as he could, but his fingertips barely scraped the gutter.

Ralph was not an agile man, so he couldn't picture himself leaping onto the roof. He would have to think of something else quickly because the possums had almost reached the window. Having nowhere to go at the moment, he quickly pushed on the window from the outside and managed to force it almost all the way shut, leaving it open only about a couple of centimeters at most. He doubted the creatures could open the window, but just in case they could, he was going to think of a way out of this predicament.

The possums on the ground had gotten louder; their pile had gotten higher, bringing the possum wall ever closer. Their eyes seemed to have gotten darker, and their teeth longer, their bellies hungrier, craving the quivering human they had trapped on the second story window.

Those bastards are actually plotting this! They actually have a plan to get me!

He could hear Julie, now. *They don't look so timid now, do they, Ralph? You dumb fuck!*

Oh yeah, they're passive creatures, he heard his own voice say stupidly in his mind. What a crock of rubbish that had been.

"But you guys *are* passive!" he yelled at the swarm below.

His raised voice had no effect on them, not even when it got higher and cracked as he shrieked. None of them gave a shit. They just kept climbing, trying to get to him. They would sometimes make an inch or two of progress only to slip back down a foot. But they were determined, driven by this single-mindedness that was almost robotic, like it was programmed into their minds to slay Ralph and be damned with all else.

Loud raps on the glass behind him shook him out of his current state of fearful marveling. The possums inside were now bashing themselves against the window. The harder they banged, Ralph saw the window open a little more at the bottom, so he began forcing it back down. The bodies would then slam harder against the glass, rattling it in its frame.

Now they are reckless? Kamikaze possums from Hell that want to eat me! What a catchy title that would make for a late night drive-in schlock film. He laughed to himself in disbelief.

Glass cracked behind him, killing his silly mirth. The sharp snap of the thin material was followed by a line snaking its way through one of the panes. As the possums flung themselves against the window, the lines multiplied and extended into a spider-web, ready to shatter.

Now, Ralph was rapidly running out of ideas. The mass of possums was still trying to climb the wall. Knowing the glass was going to break any second, he looked up at the roof to formulate an approach for climbing upon it.

Reaching high for the ledge, standing on his tip-toes again, his fingertips barely brushed the bottom of the overhang. He tried this several times to no avail as the glass began to break away from the window. A small hole had been punctured through one of the lower panes and a possum nose was slowly forcing its way through, the edges of the glass peeling back fur and skin as the snout moved forward.

Knowing he had only seconds left, Ralph became frantic. He started swinging for the rooftop, waving his arms wildly, nearly sending himself off-balance and off the ledge. The small hole in the glass got wider as the weight of the possums started to make the window cave. The spider-web increased with cracks forming throughout the entire frame. As if they were fully aware they were about to break free, the possums started scratching harder and slamming themselves against the window more frequently.

With each pounding impact, more streaks appeared along the panes until the glass was near to shattering.

This was it—Ralph had to make a leap. Sucking in a deep breath, he crouched slightly and leapt for the roof as hard as he could just as the window exploded with numerous possums bursting forth, barely missing his rising feet and falling into the mass of their kindred below. Ascending toward the sky, Ralph spied the gutter getting closer, and he threw his hands up to catch it. His fingers barely wrapped around the gutter's edge and he held on in terrible fright.

The victory was only momentary as both hands could not grip the flimsy gutter, and he found himself swinging by one weak arm that could barely hold his weight. As he dangled from the gutter, floating slightly away from the brick wall, he looked down at the ocean of bloodthirsty critters below. As if it was not a harrowing enough sight as it was, his bones chilled even further when he saw that they had ceased their scramble toward the top and were gazing up at him with those nightmarish faces.

Dinner was coming and they could sense it. He pictured them all holding a knife in one paw and a fork in the other, neat white bibs tied around their necks. One of them might as well have shaken the dinner bell. How does a possum say, "Come and get it?"

He pissed in his pants, knowing he was going to die. "I got to get out of here," he whispered to himself.

Before he could make an attempt to swing his arm up and pull himself onto the roof, a sharp crack echoed through the air as the gutter broke loose from the house. The section he was hanging onto slowly began to slope downwards, dropping him towards the ground.

"No!" he screamed and tried to hold on to the end with both hands as he slid away from his only sanctuary.

One last snap and it all came loose. Ralph watched in numb horror as the house began to drift away, the window full of possums being the last thing he saw as he floated towards the ground in fear and sadness that this was to be his final moment. There would be no tomorrow, no evening, not even another hour. There was nothing left in the world for him but pain and a yard full of flesh-craving monsters.

As he fell, he wondered if Rachel and Todd had made it out. He would have traded spots with either of them in a second—let them die this wretched death instead—but, he did hope they had managed to escape. He'd always liked them both even if he had never wanted to deal with their baggage.

Ralph hit the ground and landed on a pile of the animals, breaking bones and drawing blood when his body struck. This would be no defense, however, as he was soon consumed beneath them. They wasted no time tearing away his flesh. His tormented screams rang out from beneath the mass that had engulfed him, muffled by them as they ate him alive.

Teeth and claws latched onto his flesh, puncturing it in countless places. They began to pull in different directions and Ralph cried from the torment of feeling his skin being stretched across his bones. He heard a loud rip around his midsection and looked to see the skin slowly coming apart, large streaks of red seeping out. The ripping continued until the skin was parted and ripped along his torso. Viscera spilled out; his disgusting intestines popped up from his stomach. On both sides, the possums kept pulling as more attacked the buffet of his exposed innards. He felt the skin tear along his upper back, then down his spine; when he looked down again, he saw his breastplate and ribs exposed, and the slippery beating heart within them. He was transforming into nothing more than a living skeleton, bleeding and spewing internal organs all over the grass.

As he lay there, a skinless bag of flesh and meat, he felt himself begin to slip away into coldness, the dimming glow of twilight subsiding to complete darkness as more possums climbed upon him and ate his insides. It hurt, but it was soon over as he plummeted into unconsciousness and died.

As Rachel sped down the road, she looked at Todd. His face was pale and sweaty and he was breathing ragged breaths. His leg was still bleeding, drenching the gauze. She had to do something about his injury. She doubted he would bleed to death from the wound, but he could develop a fatal infection if he was not soon treated.

"We're going into town. You need to see a doctor."

Todd turned his head and fixed her with a glossy stare and nodded. "Okay—assuming it isn't overrun with possums."

Todd laid back and drifted off to sleep.

CHAPTER EIGHT

G reta stood on the back porch looking around for Hitch and Romero. They had zipped out the door when Rudy left a few hours ago and hadn't been back since. It wasn't unusual for them to fly off like that, often chasing down birds and vermin, both of which were around the property in droves, but they were not usually gone this long. Normally, they were back before nightfall. The sun was almost down and she squinted against the spreading darkness, trying to spot their silhouettes moving somewhere outside.

"Hitch! Romero!"

No sign of them. She feared something awful might have happened. They usually got along with other animals, interacting with all the strays that usually came around, but there are always going to be territorial battles in the animal kingdom. There were also the bizarre murders that had taken place. If it had been wild animals that committed them, then they could be anywhere, and either of her cats could have crossed paths with them.

Tippi whined at the screen door so Greta let her out. Once out on the porch, she began shaking her tail, sniffing the air with her eyes intently fixed on something in the distance.

"What is it, girl? Do you see them?"

Tippi didn't look up; she was too transfixed on whatever it was she was watching. After a moment of pondering the whereabouts of her two cats, Greta decided to set some more food out. That might lure Hitch and Romero back to the house. The strays had gobbled up the last batch and

95

the little bit that was left went to the hungry birds lazing about in the trees like hippies. Watching them feast on scraps was interesting sometimes, the way they would fight and flap their wings at one another; or, how they would nibble the crumbs so fast their beaks were like a blur. Greta sometimes got really bored waiting for clients, or for Tony to get home.

She returned inside and gathered the food. Tippi growled and barked sharply three times before blasting off the porch like a bottle rocket. Greta rushed back out onto the porch to see what the fuss was about.

"Tippi! Not you, too!" she groaned.

She yelled three times and watched as the dog's golden fur vanished into the arms of the night.

"What the hell is going on?"

She went back inside and finished gathering the food. After spreading it all evenly among the empty bowls and replenishing the water, she called in vain again for her animals. When they did not appear, she then made her way back towards the porch.

Tommy came storming through the door and nearly knocked her down the steps.

"What the hell you doing out here?"

"Jesus, Tommy. I'm feeding the strays."

Tommy rolled his eyes. "I don't know why you all still do that. You're just asking for trouble."

"How?"

"One day they'll start fighting each other, or worse yet, they'll attack your animals. Or they'll attack one of you. They'll start trying to come in the house and all that. It will be chaos."

"They haven't done any of that yet."

"Doesn't matter. They will."

A long, high howl echoed from beyond the backyard, making Greta nervous. "I hope that's not Tippi."

"Why would it be Tippi?"

"She ran off into the backyard a second ago."

Tommy raised his eyebrows in surprise. "Really? That lazy thing actually left the porch?"

"She leaves the porch a lot."

Tommy ran his right hand through his hair. "I don't know. She seems pretty lazy to me. Must have been something awful spooky out there for her to run after it."

The howling ceased and Greta looked in the direction from which it had come. "Something weird is going on," she said in a low voice.

"What's that you said?" Tommy asked.

"Nothing. Let's go back inside."

The TV was still playing in the parlor when they walked in. According to the evening news, another group of people had been attacked by animals. The anchorman was saying they can't confirm if it was dogs or not, but someone said they might be raccoons. Tommy snorted.

"Raccoons? That's ridiculous. Dogs maybe—wild ones—but not raccoons."

Bodies have been found mutilated, as if by claws and teeth, but small ones...

The report trailed away as the exterior door to the front of the house opened, followed by the rattling of the doorknob. Greta recognized Tony's black hair in the small window of the door as he let himself in. She smiled as the door flew open and in came her tanned, stocky husband with three other men. She recognized each of them: Fred, wearing the red baseball cap and flannel shirt; Tyler, the blond kid with bushy hair, skinny as a rake; and Morris, the overweight loud-mouth who always wore dirty white tee-shirts and looked like a lazy slob but was probably the most knowledgeable man at the shop. They barged into the house, each man with alarm on his face. Tony was sweating and, while his composure was as calm as usual, Greta could sense the urgency underneath it.

Tommy stopped and stared at them. "What's going on? Why you guys here?"

"What's wrong, Tony?" Greta asked.

Tony sighed and looked at the three men behind him, then to Tommy, and finally to Greta, and said, "People in town are getting killed. There have been attacks all over the city."

Tommy pointed to the TV. "We just heard about another one."

"They think it's animals, but some people think there might be a madman running around town."

"The news said the bodies were mutilated by small teeth and claws. I don't think it was a man," Greta told him.

Tony nodded. "I don't either. But, there's something out there killing people, and the cops can't seem to find out what it is. I even heard that some men on the force might be dead from attacks, too. But, I don't know if that's true. It's been going on all day and we can't just sit by and let people get killed. So, we're going to go out to see if we can't figure out what's causing all this."

Greta held her breath for a second. That was typical Tony—trying to save the town. He, Tommy, and his buddies were the unofficial Bardstown militia. Whenever something major was going down—a lost kid, a rash of burglaries—Tony and the gang were always vigilant, ready to assist law enforcement. Usually, Greta was proud of that. But, they'd never dealt with killings before, and that was a task she thought should be assigned exclusively to the police.

"Tony, you need to keep out of this one. It's too dangerous."

"Which is exactly why we should help. The police force here is small enough as it is. They can use the extra eyes."

Greta sighed. There was no sense in contesting him. If Tony thought the town needed help, then he was going to do it. "Please, just be careful."

"As always. Can you make some calls to let people know that we're going out there to look around?"

Being such a fine hair stylist, Greta pretty much knew every woman in town, save for the few who didn't bother with anything more than a haircut and ponytail to get them by. Through the years, she had always been an ear for a lot of women. After just a couple of visits, her clients were often opening up their entire lives to her. She knew the pains and secrets of so many women, but she never shared them, not even with Tony—not that he would have been interested in hearing any of it, anyway; he'd always believed that a person's business was their own.

This patronage soon became her network and she became somewhat of a leader among the women in the community, much like Tony had been for the men due to his honesty and involvement in important town matters. Most everyone thought they were reliable and trustworthy. So, whenever something bad was going on or there was something newsworthy that others needed to know about, Greta became the open line, receiving the calls and sending them out.

"What do you want me to tell them, exactly?"

"Tell them about the killings, and the suspicion that it might be some swarm of animals. Let people know they need to stay indoors; and, anyone with a weapon willing to help needs to get a hold of me. Go ahead and give them my number if they don't already know it. Tell them I'm rounding up some of the guys to see if we can't put a lid on this situation."

"Okay."

Greta picked up her cell and went to the kitchen so she could make the calls in peace. She knew if her first couple of sources answered, the word would spread before she made it all the way through the list. She only hoped enough men would come out and help Tony. She didn't feel good about this at all. Her stomach was winding into knots, but she made the calls anyway. It was best to cooperate with her husband on this because he was going to do it regardless.

Back in the living room, Tony turned to the other three and said, "First, we get Clyde. It's the last Friday of the month, so he'll be hosting a bonfire out at his place. There's going to be a lot of people there, which might attract whatever in the hell is tearing people up."

"You think he'll want to help?" Fred asked.

"Absolutely—Clyde's solid. His family has lived here for generations, and he's always ready for a fight, and he's got a lot of friends. So, maybe we can get this taken care of before anyone else gets hurt."

"What do we do after we get him with us?" asked Morris.

"We're going to ride around and make sure the roads are clear—maybe pile some people in several different cars and try to cover the whole town as quickly as possible. We can then all meet at the roundabout in town and see what's going on. The police station is right there, so we can check in with them."

"What do we do if we see the animals, or whatever it is, attacking someone?"

"We take them out."

Fred and Morris smiled, but Tyler looked nervous. Tony noticed this and asked, "You sure you're up for this? You don't have to do this, you know."

With a slight shudder, Tyler shook his head and said, "I'm good. I got this."

Tony appreciated the kid's bravery, but feared that his apprehension might become a liability in the face of danger. They had all heard the speculation of what could be out there slaughtering the townspeople, but Tony imagined it was something far worse than possums. This was not the work of their kind, of that he was certain. He didn't know what was out there, and neither did his friends. It could have been anything, and he didn't want to put Tyler, himself, or anyone else at risk if the kid became too scared to swing his bat against someone's skull if it came down to it.

Tony looked for a reason to separate Tyler from the group without offending him. "Well, the reason I ask is because when I'm out there, my wife's going to be here alone, and I need someone to stay with her. I need someone I can trust to think fast in case anything bad happens."

Tyler looked at Tony and nodded. "I can do that."

"Good."

Tony didn't believe that Greta needed any sort of help at all. If any situation got out of control, Greta had a .9 millimeter she could use to perfection. Tyler had a little bit of strength, but he wasn't tough. He couldn't fight and he wasn't brave. But, he was goodhearted and came from a good family, so Tony was actually leaving Tyler with Greta so *she* could protect *him*.

"I know you got this, kid," Tony said.

"Yep. No problem."

Greta got a hold of Laney Johnson, the town gossip, on the first ring. She told her everything that Tony had asked. Laney insisted that her sons would be willing to help once they got back from a trip to Lexington. In the meantime, she promised to spread the word.

Next, Greta called Hope Davis, one of her clients. Hope was a cheerleader at Nelson County High and quite possibly the most popular girl in the history of the county. She could not keep a secret and had a mouth like a wind tunnel. More importantly, she had just about every jock in the school at her command, and she was always trying to be at the center of everything noteworthy. Greta called her on the pretense of having her warn her parents, but knew she would take it much farther than that. It was quite possible there would be a few testosterone-spewing teenage meatheads helping Tony and the gang out, just dying to impress Hope. Greta felt guilty for manipulating the situation, but justified it as being for a good cause.

The calls continued: Jessica Deville, the local alcoholics' favorite bartender; Trudy Macintosh, PTA president; Ruby Smith, City Council big mouth; Esther Martin, participant in every bridge, bunko, and bingo gathering in the five closest counties; Eleanor Dodgson, 1993 prom queen and local MILF all the young horny idiots thought about when they jacked; Mary Rogers, notorious school secretary who knew everything and everybody; and so on, so forth, until Greta had exhausted her call book. Some ladies didn't answer, so she left messages. Despite that, it had taken a little over an hour to make all the calls.

Expecting Tony and the gang to already be out on the streets, she moved to the living room. To her surprise, she found that not only was Tony, Tommy, Tyler, Fred, and Morris still there, but several other men were now standing around, swinging their weapons and gesticulating wildly. Their excited, grumbling voices melded together so well that the combined conversations sounded like nothing more than a series of unintelligible grunts. Greta had to stifle a laugh as she pictured a gathering of barbaric Neanderthals getting ready to hunt a mammoth.

Regardless of their comical appearance, she felt safe because she knew this was a serious group of men who could effectively handle a threat. Other than the five who had already been present, there was Mike Quills from up the street, a former Army soldier who fought in the Iraqi conflict of the early-90s; Gus Green, retired chief of police; "Big-as-a-House" Bill Dorsett, a massive, reclusive farmer who lived up the hill just north of town and only talked to Tony and Tommy; Jeremy O'Shea, the local tough guy, only 22 but one of the most feared fighters in the town; and Jerry Daniels, former Marine sniper who was one of the best hunters in the state. If this group of savages found the slayer, or slayers, Greta might almost feel sorry for the culprit.

"Where did these guys come from?" she asked Tony.

"We made some calls. Did you get through to everybody?"

"Not everybody, but enough. You'll probably have more men joining you."

"Good—we've already got some others waiting for us; a few others have rounded up some more people to search the town. Whatever—or whoever—is killing people won't be at it for much longer."

Greta smiled, but it was a sad gesture. She thought of those who had already fallen prey to the attacks and realized that no amount of justice visited upon the perpetrators would bring back the dead—as cliché as that sounded—nor would it repair the damage done to their loved ones. While this could save many more lives, it could not help those already affected.

Her cell phone began to vibrate in her right hand and she checked it to see who was calling: Doris Phillips—the alpha woman of the bus drivers' squad.

"I'm going back to the kitchen," she told Tony. "It's Doris."

Tony rolled his eyes. He never much cared for Doris and all her huffy, big-mouthed yammering. She started more rumor-mill drama than anyone in town. He had tried on several occasions to convince Greta to stop talking to her, but Greta insisted that staying on Doris's good side was for the best. She was right: in a small town like Bardstown, the queen hen of the gossip circle had a lot of clout. She could get people talking faster than anyone. Most of the time, that was annoying, but today he could use her dubious position: the more ears that heard what was going on, the better.

Greta answered the call and headed into the kitchen. Doris asked her why she had called and Greta went into the same story she'd told everyone else. Doris, in her hard, scratchy voice, responded mostly with grunts. She was a very serious woman and was not prone to hysterics or outbursts. She spread her gossip in a deliberate fashion, without any nonsense. While it may have sounded like she was uninterested or not listening, it was quite the opposite. She was absorbing every word and visualizing everything so she could document it all in her mental diary.

Once Greta had completed her report, Doris began to explain what she believed was going on, which would soon lead to what she intended to see done about it. Greta went to the refrigerator to remove the large bottle of Starbuck's frozen coffee and pour herself a glass when something peculiar in the backyard caught her eye.

It was now dark as the last blue twinge of evening gave way to the night. Outside of the moon and starlight, there was not much illumination to see by. As she stood gazing out the window next to the fridge, she saw several dozen small yellow balls moving through the darkness. They looked like fireflies flying low to the ground. But, she could tell by their flight patterns that they were not. They simply moved back and forth, or straight forward—and they multiplied as they drew nearer. What at first seemed to be dozens now looked like hundreds, and they piled upon one another. The window at the other end of the wall was open, and she heard the faint sounds of what she thought was hissing and growing filtering up from the night. She felt the prickles of goosebumps crawl along her arms and neck as she listened, thinking of the horde that had murdered Brandon, Mrs. Barbara, and whoever else.

There was a floodlight that hung from the back of the house, pointing out over the yard. Reluctantly, she flipped it on, fearing what she might see. When the switch popped up and the light blazed to life, she almost dropped the bottle of frozen coffee. Hurtling towards her home was a tidal wave of animalistic white and dark faces. They were not the usual stragglers come to pick the remains of the food she left for the strays; these animals approached with a purpose, looking intent on mayhem. They looked like possums—dozens of them—and she recalled the eerie look in the possums' eyes earlier when they stood in her backyard, watching her. She had known then something wasn't right. Now, in her gut, she knew *they* were the culprits of the slayings.

Even though the phone was still pressed to her ear, she hadn't heard Doris's rambling. The woman was still rattling on about her theories and what action needed to be taken when Greta interrupted her and said, "One second, Doris."

Turning from the window, she pressed the phone to her chest and fled to the living room.

She burst into the room and yelled, "They're here! They're outside!"

All the men got quiet and looked at her. Tony sensed her alarm and said, "Who?"

"The animals! The killers! They're out back, coming through the yard."

There was no hesitation as the local lynch mob stormed across the house, brandishing their weapons, ready to destroy. The walls vibrated beneath the heavy thuds of their boots and shoes; the determined strides caused glass to clink and doors to rattle. In unison they marched like soldiers intent on killing the enemy. Tony reached the back door first with

Tommy and Bill behind him. He grabbed the knob, turned it, yanked the door open, pushed open the screen door, and faced the oncoming mass of funky possums with his cavalry right behind him.

The possums leading the charge slowed, sensing the challenge before them. But, they did not stop. They did not balk. They continued to move forward, ready to maim and kill, driven by some unknown rage and lust for human flesh. Their growls intensified as they stormed the yard. When they were a few yards from the front porch, Tony leveled his shotgun and opened fire, blowing one to bits. He then took a second shot, then a third, making good with both. He stepped down off the porch to meet the monsters and his battalion followed suit.

Though they were confused by what they saw, the men knew this was the threat the town was facing, and they prepared for battle and would worry about the whys afterwards. Ten men then formed a blockade behind the house, staring down the imminent battle. Tony, Tommy, Jerry, and Bill stood with their shotguns aimed at the possums. Jeremy had a baseball bat, ready to bash in some brains. Mike had two machetes and was itching to hack some creatures up. Gus stood off to the side with his .357 leveled. Tyler had some strange wooden club with a chain wrapped around it and no one had a clue where he found it; he'd had a bat when he arrived at the house, but had mistakenly left it inside. Fred and Morris had indistinct pistols aimed at the enemy.

"What the fuck is going on?" Fred asked.

Tyler, who was shaking even more now, said, "I don't know, man. But, it's some crazy shit."

"I think we have our killers right here, boys," Tony called out.

"Then let's get rid of them," replied Tommy.

Tony squeezed off another shot and the other guns began to fire. Possums were getting blown away left and right as bullets flew into the mass. Blood was squirting and possums were squealing as the men tried to mow down the offensive. But, there were so many that they could not hold it off. Many were breaking through, but they were getting smashed and chopped by the other men's weapons. Tyler, instead of freezing up like Tony had feared he would, actually seemed to go into a frenzy, smashing and clubbing away at any possum that got near him. He was taking them down as they attacked, none seeming to make an effectual move upon him.

Fred hadn't been so lucky. As soon as his gun ran out of bullets, he didn't have time to reload and found himself sinking beneath a sea of angry possums. His screams were drowned out by the other gunshots, but his death did not go unnoticed. Morris had seen the blood squirting from Fred's throat and side; knowing that his friend was suffering, he tried to shoot him and release him from the agony. But, he only managed to get a shot off into Fred's belly as two possums assaulted him as well just before he fired: one on the left leg and the other on his right arm. Since he was standing beneath a tree, a climbing possum had dropped down just as he fired the gun, knocked his arm down, sending the bullet off its mark. The large hole it tore into Fred's flesh gave the assailing possums something to burrow into, and they did so, entering Fred's body and feasting on his guts. Morris was soon brought down as several more possums attacked his legs, causing him to collapse. A few more of the animals rained down from the tree and landed on his body, then began ripping apart his skin. He died screaming over the next couple of minutes.

Jeremy's bat did not avail him. He managed to end only a few possums before he was overrun. A swarm of them climbed upon his body and started chewing. He dropped to his knees and was accosted by several more, three of which dug into his neck. He was unconscious by the time his face bashed against the driveway.

Soon, the men decided they needed to break apart. They dispersed and began to run about the yard, causing the possums to scatter. This did not work well for Gus, who had a bum knee, and was not fast enough to escape the enemy. He soon found himself caught against the brick wall at the side of the house punching away at furry, bloodstained faces upturned and glaring their black-eyed stares at him as they gnawed on his body. There was a chain link fence a few feet in front of him, and numerous possums were climbing it just so they could jump from it and land on his torso. He soon found his punctured, bloody body on its back, dying beneath the torment of these vicious villains.

Bill had been bitten on the ankle and was out of bullets, but he was still fighting the possums off. The butt of his rifle was caving in faces and splitting skulls with savage accuracy as he fought the pests away. He was nearer to the house than everyone else when he heard the gunshots ringing out behind the curtain of darkness beyond the reach of the floodlight. He heard Tommy holler out, "Come on, man! Over here!"

Tommy emerged from the pitch and was cutting across the light, looking to his right. Jerry came running into view and was without his shotgun. Some possums ran up behind him and he began to run harder. Tommy took aim at one and pulled the trigger, but nothing happened. He was completely out of shells.

A few possums that got too close to him got swatted with the butt hard enough to send them rolling away. He then threw the rifle at one of the possums about to attack Jerry, but it came up just short, and the possum was clinging to the back of Jerry's leg the next second, digging its teeth into the meat of his calf. Jerry screamed, fell down, and became dinner for the rest of those in pursuit.

Bill was still beating several of them back, taking a couple more small bites to his body, but none seemingly fatal. His defense was fierce but there were just too many possums to contend with. They seemed to be pouring out of the shadows. More and more came upon him, and he thought he was surely going to be taken down beneath them, but Tyler suddenly came from around the house, blood splattered on his face and clothes, dripping from his club with the chain now dangling, and started swinging and clubbing the animals around Bill while screaming some mad battle cry. The club smashed bodies, and the loose chain swung about aimlessly, landing a few solid blows by accident. Bill soon joined in with the bashing, and found that he and the lad were doing a pretty fine job clearing the ground around them as the broken possum carcasses piled up at their feet.

Tommy was about to get attacked by a few possums on his heels, but Tony came into the picture and shot two of them, then flung his empty shotgun down as the brothers were soon being chased by several more.

"Where the fuck are they all coming from?" Tommy asked.

"I don't know! Just keep running. We got to get in the house!"

They ran as hard as they could with the creatures not far behind. As they came upon the house, they saw that a few were waiting for them, heading them off.

"Shit!" Tommy exclaimed.

"We're just going to have to stomp them," Tony said.

Just before they reached the creatures, Mike came dashing around the house behind Bill and Tyler, who were not far from the back door. Mike passed them and jumped upon the porch, then leaped off in the same motion, flying through the air towards the possums in front of Tony and Tommy, with his machetes raised high. He landed mere steps before the brothers, and when he did, he brought the machetes down hard, burying both in separate possums, nearly splitting them in half. This caused the other possums to scatter in surprise.

Many more now swarmed the porch, making it impossible for anyone to get to the door. Tyler began swinging his club and knocking them off the steps. Bill swung his gun hard and it slipped from his hands, swiping a few possums away. But, their efforts were not enough; Tony and Tommy had no weapons, and Mike's machetes had remained lodged in the possums' bodies before he turned to flee from where he landed. Bill decided to start breaking their necks and managed to snatch a few up and snap their heads all the way around. But this method only lasted so long before he had many of his digits removed by sharp, unforgiving teeth. Once he could no longer grab them, he started pounding on them with his arms and hand-stumps. This strategy took out a few more, but was soon thwarted as several possums took his arms, then climbed onto his chest and started digging in. As the skin and blood flew from his body, he kept fighting silently, ramming himself against the house to squash his enemies between bone and brick, until he finally fell down dead on the driveway with the last spasms of his fading life twitching through his legs.

The same surge of possums that killed Bill had driven Tyler away from the porch. Though many of them were distracted by the large meal that was Bill Dorsett, several others found Tyler to be promising prey. He swung the club furiously, shattering bones and splitting skin, keeping the attackers at bay. But the more his mouth screamed and his blows connected, the more attention he drew to himself, and many surrounding possums took notice. As they approached him, he continued to back down the driveway.

Tony, Tommy, and Mike were trying to make it to the porch but found themselves encircled. It looked pretty bleak as the possums began to close in on the men. They stood in a triangle—back-to-back-to-back—ready to take some possums with them if they were going down. Just before the snarling killers pounced, the back door swung open and Greta stood there, aiming her .9 at the creatures, and began showcasing her talents as a markswoman. Each shot, fired in rapid succession, connected perfectly, dead on the skull or in the neck. The possums dropped instantly, and the circle was cleared in seconds.

The three men looked at her, relief flooding their faces, and Greta said, "Sorry boys, but Doris just kept talking. It took forever to get her off the damn phone. Then, it took me a few minutes to find my gun."

"What about Tyler?" Tommy said and pointed towards the driveway.

Greta turned, saw Tyler with several possums around him, and began firing. She dropped a few before she ran out of ammo. She knelt on the porch, pulled out another clip, and reloaded. She then shot down the rest of the possums around the young man, not wasting one bullet. Tyler, shocked into silence by how close he came to death and how near the bullets came to him, stared up at his savior.

"Come on, Tyler. Get in the house," she said.

Tony, Tommy, and Mike had already ascended the porch. Tyler bolted towards them and bypassed the steps by leaping up the side. They filed into the house; Mike, the last one in, turned to see if there were anymore possums, and sure enough, there were—looked like another hundred charging from the woods.

After the door was closed, he said, "There are a lot more out there."

"We have to get moving," Tony said, getting another 9mm out of the living room. "I don't know why the hell a bunch of possums is attacking people, but they're doing it all over town and they're not going to stop."

"Did you see the size of some of those guys?" Tommy asked. "Some of them were bigger than any possums I've ever seen."

"He's right," Mike agreed. "I saw some that looked like they could have been thirty pounds or more. And they got teeth that can cut right into bone. That's not normal."

Tony shook his head. "I don't know and I don't care about the details. We have to get out of here. We can just take the van. I don't think a truck is wise since it would leave so many people out in the open. These things are dangerous and no one needs to be exposed. Greta?"

His wife turned around from gathering ammo. "Yeah?"

"What are you doing?"

"Gathering ammo—apparently y'all need a woman's touch," she held up the gun when she said this.

"I'll never hear the end of this," Tony said to the other men. "Is there any way you can make some calls to let these people know what we're up against?"

"Yeah, but if we're leaving, we need to do it now. I'll make the calls in the van."

"Okay, just stay behind us."

"Screw that," she said. "I'm going out first."

"I don't think so."

"I'm a better shooter than you are. I'm going out first."

"She's got a point, Tony," Tommy said.

"I know, and I'll never hear the end of that, either. At least the shooting lessons were a wise investment. Lead the way, honey."

Greta lifted her 9mm and headed towards the front door. Tony handed the keys to the van to Tommy and fell in behind her. Mike went third with Tyler behind him, and Tommy took up the rear. As soon as Greta opened the interior door, she spotted two possums in the front yard. She then opened the screen door, stepped onto the porch, and shot them both dead. She looked around the yard and took out four more. The yard was now clear so they all began walking to the van. When they reached it and stood before it, she said to Tony, "Open the door and I'll keep watch."

The van had a driver-side sliding door and two rear doors, as well as a front door on each side. Tony grabbed the sliding door and pulled it open, and two possums flew out at Mike, one attacking his neck and the other digging into his face. He tried to scream but his voice was cut short by the horrid gash torn across his throat. Blood poured from the wound as he fell to the ground. Greta quickly shot both possums dead, but it was too late to save Mike. Blood was flowing from both wounds and his eyes soon drained of life.

Tyler quickly jumped into the van as more possums came running from behind the house. Tony hopped in and Tommy closed the door behind him. Greta ran to the passenger side while Tommy climbed up behind the wheel. Tyler pointed out to the others that the rear doors were open, which they assumed is how the possums got in. He then closed them. Greta situated herself into the passenger seat; Tommy put the keys into the ignition of the raggedy old van and took off.

"Where are we going?" he asked.

"To Clyde's," Tony answered.

"Still?"

"Absolutely. We're going to need all the help we can get."

The van sped away, leaving the possums that chased it in the dust. But, even if these humans got away from them, there were still plenty more out there to shred between their teeth, and they were going to find them—*all* of them.

CHAPTER NINE

C lyde Jefferson and Susie Bergstrom were making out at the edge of a field on Virginia Avenue. Susie had on a white tank-top and basketball shorts. Clyde was shirtless, showing off his abs, muscles, and tattoos, and wore a pair of baggy blue jeans. He kissed Susie gently on the lips, loving the taste of her, and she kissed back, loving it even more. Their hands worked along each other's bodies and he wanted to take her right there, and she wanted to let him, but there were roughly thirty people milling about the area, gathered around the two large bonfires roaring against the night.

"I wish you could take me right here," she said breathlessly.

"Good things come to those who wait, baby," he replied in his deep, smooth voice.

Clyde was seven years older than Susie, who had just turned nineteen two months before. People sometimes looked at them with disdain when they were out together because Clyde was in his mid-twenties and already done with school, settled into his warehouse job on the other side of town, while Susie was fresh out of high school, ready for trade school, and seemingly uncertain of which direction she wanted to go in life. They were both at such different stages in their lives that a lot of people thought the age gap was too wide. But, it wasn't like Clyde was some perverted old man looking to bag himself a fresh one. They had actually been together for two years, after he'd met her through a mutual friend. They had similar interests—music, movies, books—but most of all, he enjoyed her sense of humor and she loved his kindness towards her and how he made her feel safe. At first, they talked to each other while they were hanging out with friends; this allowed them to get to know each other. Soon, they were talking privately, meeting up in secrecy, and soon decided they really enjoyed each other's company.

They formed a relationship without making it official. Susie was only seventeen and Clyde was twenty-four at the time, so they didn't want to stir up any small town controversy. But, they were always together and everyone just assumed something was going on. Many speculated that Clyde was just some dirty skeezer taking advantage of a young girl's crush; others thought Susie was simply a whore who wanted to get back at parents who were always too strict. But none of these people were aware that Susie and Clyde hadn't even had sex until well after Susie had turned eighteen, and only when she told Clyde she was ready for it; before she made that declaration, Clyde had never tried. He genuinely liked Susie and intended on their relationship being long-lasting, so he decided he would wait. At his age, sex was no longer a mystery, and Susie made his heart beat in ways no one else ever had. Eventually, most of the people in town began to see that what they had was real and soon found something else to fret about as they gossiped.

Clyde held a bonfire party on the last Friday of every month. His parents had a lot of acreage at the end of the street, and were pretty well-to-do. The guesthouse on the property was where Clyde's grandparents stayed for many years until they passed away. They weren't indigent by any means, just growing infirm—the grandfather was ninety-seven when he died and the grandmother was a-hundred-and-three—so when they were too decrepit to take care of themselves, Clyde's mom moved them in. The wealth they'd had was passed down by the grandparents anyway, by way of a very lucrative lumber business that his grandfather started in 1954 and his father took over in 1986.

When his grandmother passed, Clyde moved into the guesthouse, which had two bedrooms and a full bath, with a kitchen, dining room, and living area, with a storage shed out back. It was more than spacious enough for him. The warehouse he worked in was family-owned and he had quickly moved up to line supervisor. Of course, some people cried nepotism, and Clyde couldn't deny it. He had no doubt being the heir to the company afforded him advanced opportunities, but he worked his ass off—as hard or harder than anyone else there—and he had the second most productive team in the facility, behind a woman that had worked with the company since she turned eighteen, fifteen years ago. He proved his worth every day and didn't feel bad about his position.

He threw these monthly bonfires for his team and friends, and their friends or families, as well as any other employees and their brood who wanted to show up. It all came out of his pocket. Most people appreciated it, but there were a few grumblers who liked to say things like, "Well, he should do something like this, since we're making his family rich!" Or, "He owes this to us, anyway." Those statements just rolled off his back because he knew there would always be people like that; and, he didn't even think they were wrong, anyway. Knowing that a leader was nothing without his team was something that helped him run such a productive line.

Susie was going to trade school to be a welder, which was a good line of work in Nelson County and the surrounding areas. She wasn't sure what she wanted to do with her life, besides make a decent living and be with Clyde, so she was just winging existence right now. Clyde was only the fourth guy she'd been with. Some of her friends had been with thirteen or fourteen guys, and she wondered what that would be like having that much experience—and she considered finding out until she met Clyde. Now, she wanted no one else—and she didn't give a hoot about his money. She'd heard other women call her a gold-digger because the Jeffersons were among the wealthiest families in the area, but she was far from that. She rarely even let Clyde pay for things unless she was flat broke, which she hardly ever was. She just loved *him* and nothing else about him but who he was. Those ladies were just jealous they didn't have the type of love with their men that she did with hers. She'd seen how bitter those women in town got when their relationships lost the spark and their husbands worked too long and hard to come home and give a shit. She guessed just lying in their men's arms, or just simply having them home, wasn't enough for those women—too bad for them. She appreciated her man; if they didn't appreciate theirs then that was their problem, not hers.

Wrapped up in his arms, all Susie was aware of in the world was his presence: the strength of his arms; the hardness of his body; the love in his lips as they wrestled with her own. And Clyde—at that moment, all he cared about was feeling Susie's soft skin under his rough hands, and her hot breath on his face while he kissed her. The bonfire was nothing compared to their heat. They were all there was in the world—Clyde and Susie—until some joker that Clyde didn't even know—some goof with a pale smooth face and long greasy hair, looking like a Hollywood vampire—disrupted them and said, "Hey Clyde, you hear about those killings?"

The young couple disengaged their lips and Clyde turned his head so he could see this asshole and said, "Yeah man, why?"

"It's crazy isn't it?"

Though he could have gotten up and punched the dude's face inside-out, he kept his cool and replied, "Damn straight. It's messed up."

"I wonder who's doing it."

"So do the police. So, don't worry about it. I'm busy."

The idiot smiled. "Of course—sorry; I'll leave you all alone. Great party!"

The goon kept smiling while he backed away, then went back to the laughing mass of merriment near the fires and Clyde shook his head. "Dude was rude, wasn't he?"

"Isn't that Kyle's cousin?"

"Kyle who?"

"Gilbert—your dad's assistant."

"Oh, that dude? I don't know. I don't care. I'm more interested in your lips."

Susie giggled and they started kissing again.

Susie lay back with Clyde easing her down. He propped himself on his elbow next to her and continued smooching with her. Though the ruckus of the bonfire went on around them, there was nothing else in the darkness but those two. They returned to not caring about the world, just their little section of it. People around them drank, smoked weed, shot off fireworks, wrestled, screamed, cursed, snuck off to have sex, and did all other kinds of stupid shit, but none of it mattered. Clyde didn't have to concern himself with the police because they were pretty secluded on this end of the avenue, and even if someone did call, the cops wouldn't do much about it beyond asking them to keep it down. Clyde could just lay with Susie and focus on her.

That's exactly what he did for several minutes until a shrill cry from the darkness, well beyond the leaping flames, pierced the empty night air. It rang out for a few seconds, drawing everyone's attention. Once it died off, a commotion began to ripple through the crowd. Phone lights began to come on as people searched for the screamer. Clyde and Susie sat up watching the flickering glows dance like fireflies for a few seconds, and the urgent silhouettes rush back and forth around the flames.

"Oh my God, what was that?" Susie asked.

"Somebody screaming, it sounded like," he replied.

"But who? Why?"

"I don't know. I'll go check it out."

Clyde and Susie rose from their spot to join the others. Clyde went around inquiring about the origin of the scream.

After a few minutes, Susie's friend, Jessica Hatcher, ran up to them with tears in her eyes.

"What's up, Jessica?" Clyde asked.

"I can't find my sister! I think that was her screaming!"

"Shit!" Susie said.

"Was she with anybody?" Clyde asked.

"Yeah, some guy named Johnny that works at the lumberyard. They went off into the woods to make out. I'm afraid he hurt her."

"Which direction did they go?"

Jessica pointed to the east, her dark brown eyes brimming with tears. Clyde nodded and called a few guys over to him. They came running instantly. "Anybody see Johnny from the yards around here?"

Clyde didn't know Johnny's last name, but knew exactly who he was, and so did everyone else. He was a big guy, swarthy and handsome, and favored by the ladies. But no one had seen him. Everyone else at the party, save for a few towards the woods still searching, congregated near Clyde.

"What about Jaime Hatcher?"

They shook their heads again.

"Any of y'all got a flashlight?"

A short guy from the back of the crowd spoke up. "I got a lantern over by my chair."

"Then let's get that shit and look for Jaime."

Clyde followed the short guy to where he had settled in for the party, with Susie and Jessica next to him, and the rest of the crowd behind. The guy fired up the lantern and they didn't even make it a couple of feet before they heard a male voice hollering near where the first scream had come from.

"What the fuck is going on?" someone asked.

Clyde ran towards the scream. The short guy tried to keep up, but his stride could not match Clyde's and he was soon left back by many of the people in the crowd. The cry died off, but Clyde kept racing towards the trees. As he drew nearer, a man with a large spotlight shining into the trees cut him off. It was Kyle Gilbert, the tall, scrawny assistant with big ears and an odd face.

"Hey man, Kyle Gilbert," he said. "I work with your dad."

"What's up?"

"The scream came from over there," he told Clyde.

"The fuck was it?"

"I think it was Johnny and Jaime, man." Kyle threw a nervous glance at Jessica, who put her hands over her mouth and whimpered. "They went in there together a little while ago."

"Let's go check it out, then!"

Clyde strode towards the woods. Kyle fell in beside him. "Be careful. I saw some glowing eyes. I think some animals might have gotten them."

"You don't think Johnny was hurting her?" Clyde asked.

"Nah man, Johnny's not that kind of guy. He's an unfaithful man-whore, for sure, but he's not like that. He'd never force himself on a woman."

"Well, he better not."

"I'm pretty sure I saw some animals in there. I heard them, too. It sounded like a lot of them. I think they might have attacked them both."

Clyde stopped and thought about the killings that were reported on the radio. He didn't want to walk into something that savage unarmed, and he didn't want to lead people into something like that, neither.

Turning to the crowd, he asked, "Anybody got any weapons on them right now?"

A few of the men answered affirmative.

"Anybody got some in their cars?"

A few more men and a couple of women affirmed.

"Then go get them. Those of you that got them on you, follow me. For the rest of you all, hang back. We don't know what the fuck is in there."

He then pulled Susie closer to him and said, "Stay here with Jessica. If something's wrong with Jaime, she doesn't need to see it."

Many people headed to their cars to retrieve their weapons. The men who already had them followed Clyde into the woods. Kyle didn't have a weapon on him other than a pocketknife—his shotgun was in his truck—but he had the spotlight, so he walked alongside Clyde to help him see. The rest of the people hung back, waiting to see what happened.

They crept towards the woods, the ten-million-candle-power spotlight illuminating a large radius of land beyond the trees. Within that light, they saw movement. Clyde held up his hand and stepped out in front, cautiously walking forward. He saw a bunch of smaller forms moving through the grass and among the shadows of the trees. This must have been the animal's Kyle had mentioned. There did seem to be a lot of them and they definitely gave off an uneasy air.

"Keep your eyes open, y'all. Something's weird here."

They all stopped at the edge of the woods, waiting for some kind of sign. After a few idle seconds passed, a man yelled, "Help me!"

Immediately, Clyde stormed into the woods, Kyle behind him shining the spotlight, and the rest of the crowd stepping in to stand around him. They halted several feet in and started looking around.

"Johnny, is that you, man?" Clyde asked.

The response that came was labored, and filled with pain." Yes. Up here—look."

"Shine the lights in the trees, man."

Kyle cast a few sweeps around the woods with the light, waxing the shadows of the trees as they shifted in the moving light. After a few times around, he unveiled a human form sitting on a branch a few feet off the ground not far from where they stood. It was Johnny and he was naked and bleeding.

"What the hell happened to you?" Clyde asked. "Where's Jaime, man?"

"Dead. They got her."

"Who?"

"The fucking possums, man!"

"The what?"

"The possums got her, man. A bunch of big, fat, smelly-ass possums got her. They ate her and they tried to eat me."

"What the fuck are you talking about? Possums don't eat people. Man, if you hurt her, I'll fucking kill you, dude."

"No! It wasn't me! I know possums don't usually eat people, but that's what they did!"

"Where's Jaime, Johnny?"

Clyde had been walking towards the tree and was now underneath it. The story sounded like such bullshit that he was ready to pummel Johnny, thinking he had hurt Jessica's sister. His hands had involuntarily balled into fists from the growing rage. But, when he looked up at Johnny, with Kyle's ridiculously bright light blinding the guy, Clyde could see the man was clearly distraught. Johnny was a big, tough dude, and usually as stone-faced as Mt. Rushmore, but he now wore a distorted countenance of dread and disbelief. Whatever had happened must have been incredibly distressing. Clyde started to feel a tingle of paranoia creep up his spine. Susie was out there, and whatever did this—he was almost certain Johnny was innocent—might be about to attack her.

"Way back in the woods, man. We were doing our thing and we started to smell this real nasty odor, like dirty dogs covered in shit or something. Then, we heard the leaves rustling and crunching all around us. Then there were these weird hisses and growls. I was on top of her when she suddenly locked up and started to scream. I felt her blood spraying on my face, man; and I could smell it, and it went in my mouth. Then, that dirty dog smell got stronger—a lot stronger. Soon, they were all around us, and I pulled out and jumped up. In the little bit of light we had to see by, I saw a bunch of animals running around me. They piled on her and I could hear them biting and chewing on her. I started to run and some of them chased me. Before I could get away, I got bit on the leg and I screamed, but I kept running, and apparently that was enough to knock the animal off of me. I could still hear them coming and I was right by this tree, so I climbed up here. The thing fell off of me on my way up. I don't know where they all went, so I stayed up here. You guys showed up a couple minutes later."

Clyde looked around, nervous that Johnny's story wasn't a fabrication. The fear dancing in his eyes and the anguish on his face told Clyde that

Johnny wasn't making this shit up; there was something dangerous in the woods. Whatever it was, he was willing to bet that it was what had killed Brandon Smith, Barbara Jones, and whoever else they had been talking about on the news.

But, in case Johnny *was* lying, Clyde didn't want to let on that he might believe his story. He didn't want Johnny to get too comfortable if it was him that hurt Jaime.

"That's a real nice tale there, Stephen King. Why don't you write it down?"

"I ain't making it up."

"Well, if you ain't, you're a dumb motherfucker because possums climb trees."

Johnny's eyes went wide. "Shit! I didn't even think about that." His head began to move from side to side.

"I guess you didn't. Now, get the fuck down here and let's find Jaime."

"Hell no! I'm not going back there. Call the cops and get *them* to find her."

"Don't be a pussy, man. Get down here before some possum climbs that tree and gets up in your ass."

Then, almost as if on cue, a large, grey possum fell from an upper branch onto Johnny's shoulder and clamped its teeth on the bone. Johnny screamed and jumped out of the tree, taking the possum with him.

Clyde jumped back. "Oh shit! The dude ain't lying!"

He ran towards Johnny and pulled the possum off, but it did not separate easily. It held onto the skin and tore a huge chunk from Johnny's shoulder, causing blood to spill down his arm.

Clyde tossed the possum away as fast as he could, hearing it hit the leaves at a distance. He then yelled, "Kyle, shine your light over there. If one of you all motherfuckers sees that thing, blast its ass!"

Kyle's light landed right on it, and one of the men fired at it and missed. The possum then ran back towards Johnny. It moved too quickly for Clyde to do anything about it. As Johnny stood there holding his shredded shoulder, leaning back and crying, the possum ran upon him, flew from the ground with its mouth open, and shut its jaws down on his testicles.

Johnny howled and dropped to his knees, grabbing at the possum, but it was too late. His balls had already been torn away, and now the possum

119

was chewing its way up into his groin. Blood caked the ground beneath Johnny, the possum bathed in the thick crimson and feasted on Johnny as he fell to his side.

Everyone stood frozen in fright. Some of the men in the back of the crowd failed to notice that the gunshot and screaming had drawn another group—small, bloody, cruel beings with sharp teeth and the urge to kill. Those men were soon brought down as a low-lying black shade of hunger swept them off their feet and devoured them, their screams replacing the death cries of Johnny-from-the-Yard.

"Run everybody!" Clyde called and took off towards the mouth of the woods.

Everybody came pouring out seconds later, as the other group of people returned from their cars and came running to greet them. When the two ranks merged, Clyde pointed towards the trees and said, "Shoot every fucking possum that comes out of those motherfucking woods!"

Everybody looked at him like he was crazy, but when they saw the animals come rushing out, the sight was enough to convince them that Clyde was perfectly lucid. So, they took aim and started shooting in the dark, with only Kyle's light to see by; some missed their marks while others hit their targets dead-on.

"What's going on?" Jessica asked frantically. "Where's Jaime?"

"I'm sorry," Clyde said. "These little bastards killed her—Johnny, too."

Jessica's knees buckled and Susie caught her.

"What do you mean they killed her?" Susie asked in shock.

"I know it sounds crazy, but I think possums have been responsible for the attacks in town," Clyde said. "I just watched them tear Johnny apart."

Susie stared silently with her mouth open in deep confusion, trying hard to process what Clyde had just told her. Clyde gave her a quick hug and a kiss and backed away.

"Get Jessica to the car. I'll get you two after we're done taking care of this."

Susie nodded and helped her sobbing friend to her feet, then led her away. Clyde instructed the rest of the unarmed to follow them and wait in their cars. He hoped that all the gunfire would soon draw the police. They could certainly use their help.

After the unarmed were gone, Clyde yelled, "Anybody got an extra piece I can use?"

The short guy who had the lantern handed him a 9mm.

"Thank you," Clyde said and opened fire on the possums.

Gunshots echoed through the night for many minutes. People down the street came out of their homes to see what was happening. Most of them just dismissed it as another rowdy bonfire hosted by that privileged kid at the end of the street, and went back into their houses without any concern. The others just didn't care.

A lot of possums were dropping, but many more kept coming. It seemed there was an innumerable amount hidden in the woods. Kyle had the light on them and knew that sooner or later the mass would overrun the party. The ammo wouldn't last much longer. They were all as good as dead if they didn't move."

"We can't stay here," he said to Clyde.

"I know," Clyde replied and fired his last shot.

The shots were now fewer and farther between as the ammunition was slowly depleted. The few that had bullets left stepped to the front and fired what remained. The possums were still coming and were not far off. Their arrival was imminent.

"Let's go, y'all!" Clyde turned and started running, as did everyone else, with the possums in pursuit.

Ahead of them, where the cars were all parked, a symphony of screams began to play as the unarmed were cut off by another swell of possums coming in from the opposite side of the field. Those who had been armed pushed harder to help them, even though they had nothing left with which they could fight them off.

"Grab some sticks and start swinging!" Clyde called out. "Kyle, get that light on the ground!"

Kyle began shining the light around the grounds, trying to reveal anything that could be used as a weapon. There were large branches, heavy sticks used to poke the fires, random machetes and knives lying about, and even a bow rested against a tree, with a small quiver of arrows next to it. The owner, a skinny young man with no hair, snatched up the bow and slung the quiver over his shoulder and pressed forward.

121

By the time they reached the melee, it was almost hopeless. Most of the people who had headed back towards the cars initially were already being brought down by the possums. Screeches and cries filled the night as the small, sharp teeth punctured flesh and gnawed down bone.

Even in the face of this shocking carnage, the fighters swung their weapons to knock the possums away. The archer stood off to the side of the action, kneeling and firing arrows, hitting with most shots, but missing with a few. One arrow went wide and hit another man in the chest. He was then mounted by numerous possums and taken down.

Clyde, with Kyle at his side, managed to find Susie and Jessica atop Clyde's van. They were huddled in the center of the roof, looking straight ahead, not wanting to gaze upon the horror unfolding around them.

"You guys alright?" Clyde asked as they reached the van.

"Not really," Susie said.

"I mean either of you been attacked?"

"Not yet. But, it looks inevitable at this point."

"Fuck that. We got this."

The wails began to sound again behind him. Clyde turned to see the fighters falling to the four-legged fiends. Their meager weapons were no match for the far superior numbers that had rushed in from all sides of the field. Clyde couldn't help but think the attack was planned—but surely that was impossible.

Still shining his light all around them, bringing the gruesome deaths into a clear picture, Kyle said, "Look at the size of some of those bastards."

Clyde peered ahead and saw some massive possums among the normal-sized ones. "They look like dogs."

"I didn't know possums could get that big."

"Me neither."

The archer continued to fire off arrows and even sharp, skinny sticks that had fallen off the nearby trees and some possums were running around with arrows and sticks protruding from their bodies. Others lay dead from mortal wounds. As he drew his final arrow from the quiver and readied to nock it, three possums pounced on him. One attacked the leg that he was kneeling on while another ran up behind him, stood up, and then began biting at the base of his spine. One of the larger possums flew into his stomach and knocked him over. Once the archer was on his back, he was destroyed within seconds.

Clyde, Susie, Jessica, and Kyle watched in a mindless terror as the possums ate the fallen. In minutes, the warriors were all dead, reduced to gory mounds of flesh bleeding on the ground. With the possums' physical hunger sated, and only their desire to maim left to drive them, many soon turned their attention to the four remaining humans at the van.

"Oh shit!" Clyde yanked the side door open.

He rummaged through some stuff and produced a shotgun, then took aim at the possums and fired three shots, making good on each one. But, that wasn't enough. There were more possums than bullets. There was no way to fight them. If they made another stand now, they would surely die.

"Get in the van!" he said.

Both he and Kyle held up their arms and motioned for Jessica and Susie to get down, but the two young ladies hesitated, too afraid to even move. Jessica was shivering with her knees against her chest, and Susie was chewing on the tip of her right index finger and looking at her feet, pretending none of this was happening.

"Come on, Susie, you guys got to get down," Clyde said after a few more seconds.

She shook her head and said, "I can't."

"If you guys stay up there, the possums will get you," Kyle told them. "They climbed the trees and got Johnny."

There were still a few screams left in the night. A couple of people that had not been as severely mauled clung to life; they tried to get up and run, or fight, but were only more sport for the possums in the end. Susie gathered enough nerve to raise her head and look out at the killing field. She couldn't see much of anything due to the fall of night, but the moon was now casting enough of a glow to show her the innumerable small shapes moving out there in the shadows. Many of them seemed to be drawing closer. Their stink traveled on the air, growing stronger; the frightening sounds they made were getting louder. Suddenly, she realized their imminent doom. She quickly grabbed Jessica's arm and tugged hard.

"Come on," she said. "We got to go."

Jessica snapped from her daze and mindlessly followed Susie towards the edge of the van's roof. The skin of their bare legs squeaked as it slid along the metal; the heavy thumps of the roof denting in and resetting itself sounded like war drums in the night. The two of them scrambled down and jumped into the van, narrowly escaping death.

Kyle got in and Clyde behind him. Clyde slammed the door shut and waited, hoping the possums would decide to move on. But his wish would not be granted as the creatures began to mount the van and pile upon the windshield. Clyde moved into the front seat and started rummaging through his pockets frantically.

"Shit!" he cried.

"What is it?" Susie asked.

"I ain't got my god-damn keys! I left them in the house!"

"Are you serious?"

Clyde stared ahead at the windshield now darkened by the possums. He heard the claws on top of the van and felt the weight of the mass rocking the vehicle. Hard bumps now sounded against the sides. Those trapped inside—with the exception of Jessica, who was still in shock at the loss of her sister—looked around, stopping their gazes on the side windows.

"What the fuck?" Kyle said softly.

Outside, the possums were piling on one another so high that they nearly covered the windows. The rocking intensified as more and more piled on. What they could not see from inside was the wall of possums circling them, at least five feet out on each side, and many more climbing on. The roof began to indent in spots as the blanket of beasts cast the van into a shade of darkness—a darkness that issued sinister noises around them.

"Man, they're going to break through the windows!" Kyle said.

Inside, they all sat and waited, knowing there was no way out of the inevitable, unless the creatures gave up or found something better to eat. But, several minutes passed and it seemed that the shaking only got worse, and the windows began to rattle. The windshield was holding up so far, but how much longer it would, they could not tell.

Then, suddenly, the van was rattled by a huge impact that sent vibrations all through it. This snapped Jessica awake and she joined the others in sitting in stunned silence, eyes wide with terror. Whatever had caused the blow lifted the van slightly on the left side for a few seconds before it dropped back down. After a couple more seconds, the impact hit harder and the van was lifted again, only a tad higher and for just a bit longer.

"Holy shit, man," Clyde said. "They're going to flip this motherfucker."

Kyle looked at him in wide-eyed shock. "No way."

Susie gulped. "Can they actually do that?"

As if to answer the question, the third attack brought a harder impact, then a higher lift that lasted even longer. For a second, it seemed they might topple sideways.

"What the fuck is doing that?" Kyle asked.

"I don't know man! I don't know!" Clyde replied.

"It's the possums!" Susie cried.

"No way! That's impossible!" Kyle said.

Then, the final blow was struck and the van was lifted quickly on the left side, and then dumped onto its right, shattering both windows, but only cracking the windshield. As the van had fallen sideways, the possums on the left side of the van fell off, and when it hit the ground, most of them broke away from the windshield, unveiling the outside.

The fall caused Clyde to hit the brights, and when they came on, they lit the night before them. As those inside gazed out the windshield, they were shocked to see a group of possums as big as medium-sized dogs lurking around the van. Their lower jaws were much more prominent than the upper, and long, sharp teeth stuck up from them. Their snouts were stained red with blood and their horrid black and brown faces stared with the blackest eyes any of them had ever seen.

"Dude, what are those?" Kyle asked.

"Are they possums?" Susie said.

"Not like I ever seen," Clyde said.

There were more than a dozen of the monsters, and they had the rest of their crew gathered behind them. They looked almost intelligent, and seemed like they might be about to speak. One of the massive possums in the middle of the group came forward and mumbled something that was unintelligible, but still more defined than a simple hiss or growl, and then issued a sound that was almost like a bark. The larger possums then stepped aside and the rest of the horde began to make the last push towards the van.

Clyde, Susie, Jessica, and Kyle lay there in the busted up van listening to the coming of their deaths—ends that would no doubt be grisly.

Clyde shifted enough to face Susie and grab her hand. "I love you, babe."

With tears in her eyes, she replied, "I love you, too."

Clyde then struggled to move, and crawled to her and lay over her body. "They'll have to get through me, first."

Susie started to protest but he put his finger over her lips. "We got no choice, babe."

She then squinted and tried not to cry, knowing that he was correct.

Kyle looked at Jessica and said, "I'm sorry about your sister."

Jessica swallowed. "Thanks. But, I guess it doesn't really matter, now."

Kyle smiled weakly. "Sure it does."

Clyde and Susie held hands and stared at each other as the first set of possums crawled up near the driver's side window. Kyle looked up and saw a couple of heads come into view. Soon there would be more and they would all be pouring in to dine.

Kyle grabbed a wrench that was next to him and said, "It may be pointless, but I'm taking at least one with me."

Nobody else said anything. They waited silently to die. Clyde looked at Kyle and smirked, and even thought about joining him in one last fight, but he elected to protect Susie, instead. There was no winning the fight. All he could hope for was that eating him would be enough for the possums and they would walk away without touching her. It was not a likely scenario, but it was all he could think of. If nothing else, her death would be quicker—most likely a tear at the throat, and she would bleed out before feeling the agony of being devoured. If Clyde could make her death less gruesome, that would be worth it.

Possums were up on the van, now. Any second, dinner would be served. Each person inside braced themselves for the horror. But, a sudden noise outside, beyond the nightmare, shook them from their death-acceptance. Many bright lights came into view, blinding the four humans trapped in the van. Tires screeched to a halt outside followed by rapid gunfire. The possums that were by the window were blown away and their blood splattered into the van. Loud voices and the sounds of more car tires, then more gun fire, joined the fray. The four of them looked around, almost smiling.

"What the fuck is that?" Kyle asked hopefully.

Clyde smiled at one of the voices he knew so well. "That's the motherfucking cavalry, bro!"

Outside, the familiar voice barked orders. Rapid footsteps could be heard rushing around the van as heavy gunfire continued. Hisses and growls and screams mixed together as possum and man alike died in combat on Virginia Avenue.

As the fight outside raged, Susie almost started crying from relief.

"Who is that?" she asked.

Clyde smiled again. "That's my boy!"

When it was all over, they felt something rock the van again. Someone was climbing upon it. A voice then called to them.

"Clyde—you crazy bastard! Glad to see you made it out okay."

Clyde turned his head and saw Tony Harris peering down at him, blood splatters mixed with sweat on his semi-smiling face.

"Oh you know, we just thought we'd hang out for a little bit."

"What the hell happened to the van?"

"Possums dumped it," Kyle said, breathing a little easier now.

"I'm not surprised. There were enough out here to eat an army. Luckily, an army is what I found on my way over here."

"You clear them all out?" Clyde asked.

"Most of them. Some of them ran. There were some really big ones out here that looked like hogs. I got one of them, but the rest got away; they move pretty fast for fat fuckers."

"Good to know," Clyde said. "You mind getting us out of here?"

"Sure."

Tony jumped down and called for someone to help him. In a few seconds, they had the side door open. Clyde and Kyle helped the ladies out first, and then Kyle climbed out, followed by Clyde. When his feet hit the ground, he and Tony embraced.

"Man, am I glad you got here."

"Just in time, it seems."

Clyde saw the field of dead possums and humans and whistled. "Damn. What the hell is going on, Tony?"

"Possums are behind the attacks out here. I don't know what's making them do it, but they're doing it," Tony explained.

"Man, when we were in that van, I saw those big-ass possums you were talking about. I swear to you, dude, they tried to communicate—or something."

Tony smirked. "Come on, Clyde."

"Nah, man—I'm for real. There was a bunch of them looking at us, and then one walked in front of the others and made some weird noise, like it was trying to talk, then the rest jumped our van."

Tony looked at Clyde for a second and read the seriousness on his face. Clyde didn't have an inkling of hysteria in his personality, nor was he a liar or exaggerator; he was solid, all the way to the core. Tony then looked at the people behind him, then around at the field.

"You know what? I believe that, man. When we were starting to win the fight, some of those big ones squealed and ran, and the few that were left ran with them."

"That's crazy," Clyde said.

"Ain't it? This whole thing is."

"Where are they all coming from, anyway? There must be hundreds."

"Thousands," Tony corrected. "I don't know what the hell is going on, but it sure is fucked up. When we pulled up on y'all, and saw all those things engulfing your van, I didn't think we'd survive. They've been tearing through town left and right."

Greta and Tony went into a recap of everything they knew that was going on. While she and Tony and their crew had traveled over to Clyde's, they came across another group of people. They had guns and trucks and were ready to fight. Now, all but one of them was dead. The only one remaining was a young lady named Cara Hall, who was still in college but really tough. She was a volleyball player at the University of Louisville and had some pretty impressive muscles that were visible in her sleeveless tee-shirt.

Clyde, in turn, told him everything that happened out there in the field. Tony said, "We got to go into town and find out what the police are doing about this."

"They ain't got enough people to do much."

"But, we can help them," Greta said. "You all need to ride with us."

Clyde pointed at his van and said, "Can't take that. But, I got a truck around back."

"My truck's out in the field," Kyle said.

"Good—you take Jessica and Susie will ride with me. I got some more ammo inside. It ain't much, but I'll bring everything I got."

"Good idea," Tony said. "We'll need all the ammo we can get."

From the other side of the van, Tommy said, "We should take this sucker with us."

The rest of the crew walked around to see what he was looking at, and were shocked at the sight. While they had seen the bigger possums, and while Tony knew they had taken one down, none of them really had a moment to realize exactly what they were dealing with. There on the ground, with several large bullet holes in its dead body, was the largest possum any of them had ever seen.

CHAPTER TEN

Capt. Dean was in his bedroom loading a duffel bag full of weapons when Officer Jack Denton pulled into the driveway. Selma was in the kitchen making tea, trying to ignore the possums beating against the door. Ever since closing Huck down there (a move she was still remorseful about), the creatures had not given up the fight to break free. Some of the wood on the door had already cracked, so she had taken every movable chair from the front room and kitchen and created a barrier against the door, hoping it would be enough to keep them from getting loose upstairs.

Capt. Dean's bedroom window faced the front yard, and he was right in front of it when Denton arrived. He watched Denton walk up the driveway then zipped up his bag and strapped it to the back of his chair, positioning it to be accessible by his left side. If the possums in the basement stormed the upstairs and attacked, he was going to make one hell of a stand. He wasn't going to go down easily, and he damn sure wasn't going to let anything harm Selma—not a bloody chance in Hell of that.

He started up his chair and rode into the front room to let Selma know the police had arrived. The pounding against the basement door had grown heavier and much more rapid. It sounded as if dozens of creatures were firing themselves against the door nonstop, one right after the other. The weighty impact sounded like a large animal slamming its paws against the other side. The way the door shook, if Selma hadn't created the barricade of chairs, they would no doubt be overrun by now.

As he listened to the ruckus, he thought, *If you little bastards come up here, I got a bag of tricks for you.*

It wasn't the safest and most organized battle-bag he could have thrown together, but it would do. There wasn't much time to be meticulous. He had hastily grabbed some of his favorite weapons, and those he deemed most necessary should a shit-storm descend. He had his classic M67 hand grenades in the side pouch in the event of a vicious swarm. He had a Beretta M9 that a friend of his who had fought in Somalia gave to him; a Smith & Wesson M1917 Revolver that the widow of an ex-service buddy had given him; his own M1911 pistol he'd had since Nam; and his M249 light machine gun in case the situation became extremely dire. He wasn't even sure if he could still use that weapon at his age, but if it came down to it, he would not hesitate to find out. If all else failed, he was also packing his trusty Ka-Bar if the fight got really personal. Needless to say, his bag was heavy and he was glad that, despite the disapproval of his daughter and deceased wife, he had purchased the largest duffel bag known to man for an occasion such as this.

Capt. Dean rolled into the front room just as Selma walked in holding two cups of tea. They both stopped midway into the room and looked at each other before she spoke.

Holding out a small green tumbler, she said, "I made some tea—thought you might want some."

Her nerves were frayed and so her hand shook slightly. Capt. Dean was about to reach for the offering just to ease her of the burden. But then loud bumps against the basement door made her jump and drop the cup. It hit the carpet with a soft clunk, bouncing once and spilling the tea.

"Shit," she said. "I'll get you another."

He waved her off. "Never mind that nonsense. The policeman just pulled up."

As soon as he finished this announcement, Officer Denton knocked on the door.

Selma set the other cup of tea on the wicker coffee table in the middle of the room and headed towards the door.

"What's in the bag, Dad?" she asked before turning the knob.

"Just some insurance."

Selma opened the door and Officer Denton, with his tanned face and broad shoulders, said, "You called about a disturbance in your basement?"

"Why…uh...yes, yes. Come in."

Selma waved him in and stepped aside, allowed him to pass, and shut the door behind him. Officer Denton looked at Capt. Dean, with his Vietnam Veteran cap on, and saluted him. "Good afternoon, sir. How are you?"

The captain liked Denton a lot better than he had Huck—God rest his soul—though, he had felt sorry for the idiotic exterminator. That guy was a slob and it was no surprise to Capt. Dean that he'd died down there. He looked like the only fighting he'd ever seen was on one of those silly video games kids had been playing since the 80s. He recalled one of his friends had a son who played this awful game during the early days of Nintendo, or whatever, that was nothing more than two morons trying to knock each other into a manhole. These two thugs would stand on opposite ends of the sidewalk and punch each other until one of them rolled onto the next screen. If the police drove by, the fight would stop until they passed. Sometimes, some lady would throw a potted plant from her window and you had to make sure you didn't get hit on the head by it. After switching screens a couple of times, a manhole would appear behind the guy who had been knocked down the most and if he got knocked down again, he fell in and lost the fight—completely stupid shit. Poor Huck probably lost at that dumb game a lot; hell, he couldn't even survive a swarm of possums in the basement. The man was clearly not made for any sort of combat, real or imagined.

But, this Denton guy seemed like someone who could handle the matter. He looked strong and sturdy; he didn't have a goofy countenance like Huck, and he had eyes that told Capt. Dean that he was all about the business at hand. Denton was the kind of guy Capt. Dean would have wanted watching his back when he was in the bush. He began to feel more optimistic about the situation.

"Given the circumstances, I am fine, young man. Thank you for asking," Capt. Dean replied.

A good portion of Denton's family had served in some branch of the military: his great-grandfather, grandfather, great uncles, father, mother, aunts, uncles, and numerous cousins on both sides of the family had seen some action and did their time. His sister, Julianne, was killed in Afghanistan back in 2005. Denton, however, could not serve because of ulcers, which he thought was bullshit, and appealed the decision as high as he could. But, the stomach issue was so severe that he was deemed unfit for service and spent many years in an emotional funk because of it, thinking he was a disgrace. But, he soon decided to join the police and do what he could to protect the citizenship. He spent a couple of years as a state trooper, but soon found himself a job in Bardstown, which was his hometown, and he was proud to protect and assist the town and its people anytime he could. Whenever he saw a serviceman, he always showed him his due respect.

Turning to Selma, he asked, "You say there are animals in your basement and a man was killed by them?"

"Yes."

"What kind of animals?"

"They looked like possums."

"Possums?" he said in surprise.

"I know it sounds strange, and that's what the exterminator said, too. But, I know what I saw. They were possums—not rats, not raccoons, not badgers, muskrats, or anything else—possums!"

Denton nodded. He had to admit it sounded kooky, but he also had to admit he had seen a lot of oddball occurrences in his few short years on the force—including some very bizarre animal attacks. He remembered when squirrels were becoming such a nuisance. They had infested attics all over town and when people would try to remove them, they would attack. At first, it was humorous in a quirky sort of way, but it soon became dangerous as the squirrels started getting loose in homes and attacking pets and people. If they could do it, why not possums? He also couldn't deny the racket coming from the basement. He'd heard it the moment he walked through the front door. When he looked towards it, he'd noticed the chair fortress blocking the basement door. Something was trying to pound its way out, and it sounded large and numerous.

"Well, I can tell *something* is down there."

He also noticed a low growling and hissing combination coming from beyond the door. After standing silently and listening to it for a few seconds, he could definitely determine that there was more than one animal, and the noises they were making did sound like possums.

"Those definitely sound like possums," he said.

"You can tell?" Selma asked.

He nodded. "We had tons of them on our farm when I was a kid. I actually used to play with them, sometimes. I've heard them make these sounds many times. Usually they growl to warn off a threat, but I've never heard them sound so aggressive. They're not violent creatures by nature."

"Well, these certainly are. They killed the exterminator, and some guy named Marty Miller, apparently."

"Marty Miller? His wife called the station today, worried about him. How in the world did he end up down there?"

"I don't know. I think he broke out one of the basement windows and crawled in, trying to get away from the possums. When the exterminator and I were looking around down there, we saw a dead person all chewed up. The exterminator said it was some guy named Marty Miller."

"Huh," Denton grunted. "That's crazy."

"But it's true," Selma said defensively.

He nodded again. "I believe you, but that is so peculiar. I can't imagine why they'd do it."

"Me, neither. They might be rabid."

"Could be, I don't know."

"So, what are we going to do?" Capt. Dean asked.

"I'll take a look and see how bad it is."

"It's pretty bad—can't you tell?" Selma asked.

Denton watched the basement door rattle, shake, and crack. Loud heavy thumps kept vibrating the floor and even making the windows around them shake. Denton then looked at Selma and Capt. Dean in surprise.

"You sure you want to open that door, son?" Capt. Dean asked.

Denton looked at the door again. He could hear the wood stretching with small bits splintering inside of it. He shook his head.

"Not really, but I might not have to."

With fright etched on her face, Selma asked, "What do you mean?"

"How many did you say were down there?"

"I don't know—a lot—enough to kill several animals and two grown men. Why?"

"Because I don't think that door is going to hold much longer."

Selma and Capt. Dean looked at the door and watched it bounce and tremble. Each time it jumped, it pushed some of the chairs back slightly. The repeated impact eventually caused a few of the smaller chairs to fall off the pile, pushing the lower chairs aside and giving the door more leeway to spring open. The cracks were growing around the hinges and the doorknob was coming loose. The hard knocks from the other side turned into one long, powerful push that was causing the door to bulge in the middle. The creaking and cracking began to fire off rapidly, and all of them knew the door was only seconds away from bursting.

"I think you're right, son," Capt. Dean said.

A small rip at the bottom of the door began to give way, and pieces of wood started falling to the floor. A couple of bloodstained snouts snaked their way out and sniffed the air. Seconds later, the creatures started hissing. The possums behind them began pushing harder, the growls intensifying.

"We got to get out of here," Capt. Dean said.

"And go where?" Selma asked.

Denton grabbed his radio, which was on his shoulder, and said, "Dispatch, this is Officer Jack Denton. Do you copy? Over."

He waited and there was no response, so he tried again with the same result. It took a few attempts before a woman's voice crackled through the static.

"Go ahead, Officer Denton."

"We got a situation out on Westwind Trail. There seems to be a basement full of wild animals in the home of Selma Donaldson, and the residents say these animals already killed an exterminator, as well as Marty Miller. I'm requesting backup. Over."

"One second, Officer Denton."

The basement door was cracking even more and the three of them moved back towards the front door. After about a minute, the dispatcher returned. "Officer Denton?"

"Go ahead."

"I'm not getting any responses from the other officers on patrol, and no one is currently here at the station. Apparently, there have been other reports of wild animals attacking people in the city and the other officers are answering those calls."

Denton looked confused, and Selma looked frightened.

"Dispatch, can you please repeat that? I'm not sure I heard you correctly. Over."

As the dispatcher began to respond, the basement door popped and crumbled, scattering the chairs and spitting splinters across the living room floor. The possums started pushing their way out of the basement, skittering hungrily through the room in search of delicious flesh.

Selma jumped and Capt. Dean said, "Let's get the hell out of here!"

He pulled his Beretta just as Denton pulled his 9mm and they both fired at the oncoming animals, blowing a few to pieces. The report of the gunshots seemed to momentarily stall the creatures, so Denton turned and pushed the glass door open, letting Selma out first and then Capt. Dean. Just before he stepped out himself, he closed the interior door behind him, hoping this would keep the possums at bay long enough for them to escape.

As he turned to flee, he heard Selma scream just before a couple of gunshots drowned her out. He saw Capt. Dean holding his Beretta and firing at a huge mass of possums that was crawling over his patrol car and Selma's Volvo. Getting to the vehicles was now out of the question. Denton fired a few shots and joined Selma and Capt. Dean.

"We can't take the cars! We got to run!" he said.

"But where?" Selma cried.

"My house is just two blocks away. If we can make it there, we can take my car and get to the city."

"Lead the way, Officer!" Capt. Dean said and turned his wheelchair.

Many of the possums on the cars were shaken by the gunshots and had frozen in place for a moment. This gave the three of them a good head start as they took off through the yard. Officer Denton took the lead with Selma and Capt. Dean close behind. Selma gave it all she had but couldn't gain much speed, and Capt. Dean's wheelchair would only go so fast. The possums were quickly coming out of their stupor and began to move again, fast enough to overtake them. Selma knew this, so she stopped to grab the handles of her father's wheelchair and start pushing.

"What the hell are you doing?" Capt. Dean asked.

"I'm not leaving you behind!"

"Bullshit! You go on. I can take care of myself!"

"But they'll catch you!"

"Let 'em! I got a surprise for them if they do."

Denton looked back to see Selma guiding her father's chair and said, "Here! Let me push him."

"Nonsense," Capt. Dean protested. "I can manage."

Unwilling to have his request denied, Denton holstered his gun and took control of the wheelchair. He and Capt. Dean began to move fast and they passed Selma up without Denton realizing it.

"Hold on!" Capt. Dean yelled. "You're leaving Selma!"

Realizing Selma was lagging behind, Denton slowed and waited for her to catch up. The sound of the possums' claws scraping the concrete behind them sent a shudder through them all. The instinct to run as fast he could threatened to take control of Denton, but his sense of duty prevented it from prevailing.

Denton turned to see how close the possums were, and they had gained a few more feet. He knew the three of them would not survive the chase. The possums grew ever closer, so he said, "I'm going to turn and fight!"

"No! Let me!" Capt. Dean said.

"Daddy, no!"

Capt. Dean leaned his head back, looked up at Denton, and said, "You take my little girl and get her to safety. Leave me and I'll take these bastards out."

Denton looked down at him, seeing the seriousness in his eyes, and asked, "You're going to need more than that Beretta."

Capt. Dean smiled. "I got a lot more, son." He then patted his duffel bag and Denton smiled.

"She won't let me do that," he said.

"Selma will do as I tell her. Now, leave me, soldier. That's an order."

Denton smiled at the mutual respect the two men shared.

"How would you like me to leave you?"

"How far behind are they?"

Denton glanced back. "A little more than ten yards."

Capt. Dean sighed. "That's not very far, but it's far enough. Spin me around."

Denton stopped and spun the chair around. Selma stopped suddenly and said, "What the hell are you doing?"

Capt. Dean unzipped his duffel bag and pulled out two grenades. "You go on, honey."

"What?"

"I said you go on, now. There isn't a lot of time."

Capt. Dean then pulled the pin from one grenade and said, "Chew on this, you little shits!"

He threw it at the oncoming tide. The three of them held their ears as the explosion blew many of the possums to pieces.

The other possums skidded to a stop all around the road and began to fall back in a panic, frightened by this new development. They stopped about forty feet away and stared at the three humans, waiting to see if another blast would come. Once they were satisfied it would not, they began to cautiously move forward.

Selma, now with tears in her eyes, said, "I'm not leaving you, Daddy."

"Yes, you are. You're going to go with Officer Denton."

"No!"

"Yes! You're going to go with him and get in his car and get the hell away from here."

The possums continued to edge forward and had managed to creep up another fifteen feet, so Capt. Dean launched the other grenade into the densest pocket of them. When it landed, it blew many more into the air, raining down blood and small body parts; the survivors retreated again, moving as much as seventy feet away. He then retrieved two more grenades from the bag.

"I'm an old man, Selma. You're still young, and so is Officer Denton. There's no reason for you two to die because I held you back."

Selma shook her head. "Don't talk like that."

"Listen, god-damnit!" he said sharply. "I love you, dear. You are my world. If you all wait for me, you'll be dead. But, if I stop and fight, I might be able to kill all these god-damned bastards. I got enough artillery in this bag to wipe them all out."

"Then we can help!"

"No! If I fail, then I will die. If that is to happen, I want to do it alone, without you. I want you to live on, or there would be no god-damned point to my death. So, go with him."

Selma still protested, so Capt. Dean said, "Officer Denton, will you get my daughter?"

Denton grabbed Selma by the arm and said, "Let's go."

"Get the hell off of me!" she said. "Who the hell do you think you are?"

"He's an officer of the law, god-damnit!" Capt. Dean said. "He's sworn to protect the populace, as I was once sworn to protect my country. God-damnit—do as he says!"

Selma stopped, as she always did when Capt. Dean used his stern voice—his Captain's voice, as she referred to it.

"I love you, Daddy," she cried.

"I love you, too, Selma. Go with Officer Denton, get in his car, and come back to get me. When you do, I promise you every one of these sons-of-bitches will be dead."

Selma looked up and saw the possum army heading towards them. The three of them had stood idle so long that the creatures regained their nerve. The growls began to float on the air again. Selma was afraid this would be the last time she would see her father, and she wasn't ready to let him go.

Denton tugged her arm and said, "Come on. We'll come back."

"Go, my dear," Capt. Dean said. "Let Daddy protect you one last time."

Selma reached out and touched his cheek and felt a tear fall along it, and she let her own tears cascade down her face. "I love you," she said again.

"I know, dear," he said, sucking up the sorrow and looking bravely at her, just as the clouds began to pass in front of the evening sun. "I love you, too. Now go!"

Selma let Denton guide her away. He said, "Turn away and don't look back."

She did as the officer said and he fired one last shot at the possums to shake them up. After that, the two of them fled down the street and around the corner, leaving Capt. Dean to face the angry horde.

The weathered old veteran turned back to face the enemy. They were nothing like any enemy he had encountered before, but that would not intimidate him. They were inferior quadrupeds who had to sniff the dirt for their dinner. To Hell with their teeth and claws; to Hell with their cruelty and bloodlust; and to Hell with their greater numbers: he might have been one man alone, but he was armed to the teeth, and those teeth had a hell of a lot more bite than these god-damned possums did.

"Come on, you little bastards," he said. "I fought Charlie for most of my young adult life, getting shot at every day. I had friends blown up right beside me. You think anything you have can scare me?"

He threw his last two grenades at the possums, blowing more of them away. Their numbers were now considerably less, but still daunting. He fired what was left in his Beretta into the crowd, taking several more away. The possums let the dead fall to the wayside, and they kept coming. The dead were dead but those living were still hungry. Their black eyes leered eagerly at the captain, but he was unmovable.

"Come on!" he yelled. "Is that all you got?"

They pressed on towards him, unfazed by the last explosions and round of shots. They had learned that they could still fight on despite the attacks. So, Capt. Dean pulled out his Smith & Wesson and emptied it at them—in front of him, on each side of him, he did not miss—dropping one with every shot.

He threw down the empty gun and smiled. "After all these years, I'm still a fucking marksman."

But it wasn't enough. Though many were dead, many more were still coming. Capt. Dean's defense had been enough to slow them, but not to stop them. But, he wasn't finished yet.

Next, he pulled his M1911 and kept them back, splattering their brains and bones all over the street. He took out several fronts charging on him, and one possum even leapt at his chair and was blown right out of the air, splitting into three gory sections upon impact. He had enough ammunition to hold them off for a few minutes. But, once the gun was spent, he threw it down on the concrete next to him, as well.

That's when he turned off his wheelchair, locked it, and pulled out his big toy—the light machine gun—and fell to the street in front of his chair. Propped up on his elbows, Capt. Dean began putting the M249 together. While assembling the weapon in its standing position, he said, "If I laid my life on the line just for my country, what do you think I'll do for my daughter, huh? If I killed men in the name of America, what do you think I'll do to protect Selma? You might kill me tonight, right here in this cold street, but I will be *damned straight to hell* before I let you bastards take my little girl!"

He completed assembling the weapon; the possums were almost upon him. He aimed, and yelled, "Come on you motherfuckers!"

Capt. Dean then opened fire. One by one, the little creatures were obliterated and pieces of them sent flying through the air. Anytime one would get near, Capt. Dean would blow it to smithereens, but they kept coming, and they were getting bigger. Possums pushing fifteen pounds were trundling towards him, but they couldn't stand up to the machine gun. Their bodies collapsed, riddled with bullets.

More creatures came from the shadows the twilight cast along the yards. There were more than he imagined, and he kept laying waste to them. Blood painted the pavement, innards littered the yards, as Capt. Dean's onslaught punched major holes in the possums' attack.

Capt. Dean turned to the left, shot several of them down; turned to the right, blew down several more. He then aimed straight ahead and let loose a barrage of bullets that massacred dozens of the creatures. The streets around him were getting clearer as the army grew smaller. In the span of a few minutes, he had managed to slay the majority of the animals. A few more came in at him from the street, but they did not last long. Once the last bullet was spent, there were only a few possums left. So, he struggled into a seated positioned, snatched up his duffel bag, and pulled his blade from inside and said, "Come get it, fuckers!"

Five possums ran towards him. The first that reached him got a knife right through the face. The second pulled in quickly and found itself skewered between the ribs. A smaller one reached him before he was able to wrench the knife free, so he grabbed it and wrestled with it for a second before turning its head sideways and snapping its neck. He quickly pulled the knife from the dead possum and leaned back as the next one leapt at him and landed on his upturned knife. When the tip of the blade pierced its chest, Capt. Dean quickly reached behind the creature, placed his hand on its back, and pressed it all the way down onto the knife. The possum squealed and thrashed before it coughed blood onto his face and died. He soon felt the final possum crawling up his leg, so he sat up and rammed the dead possum down on top of it, driving his knife through the corpse and into the other possum's body, pressing his own hand through the dead possum's carcass, feeling its innards leak onto his flesh.

After the last five possums were dead, Capt. Dean breathed and looked around him. An entire legion of possums lay dead along the street. The massacre was horrendous—mauled, mangled, and bloody marsupial carcasses were scattered all over the area. He laughed, saluted, and said, "Mission accomplished, sir!"

The fight was over—he had won, against all odds; this was a battle he believed he had almost no chance of winning, but here he was, surrounded by the corpses of all of those who had opposed him on this day. Soon, Officer Denton would bring Selma back, and they would find out if any killer possums were left in town. If not, they would return home and clean up the mess. If there were, then they would get the hell out of there. Capt. Dean could help eradicate the possums that were left, but he'd rather make sure is daughter was safe. He would get her as far from there as he could until the problem was over. All he had to do now was sit there and wait.

Just before he began to push himself back up into his wheelchair, he heard a loud snort and growl that sounded like a failed attempt at formulating speech several yards away. When he looked towards the noise, he had to squint against the onset of the night, into that last sheet of light that drips against the horizon before the moon replaces the sun. A silhouette formed against that light—a very large, four-legged silhouette—and it was looking right at him.

The sight of the creature was disconcerting. It certainly did not look like a possum. It was much more formidable than that. Capt. Dean had nothing left now but his knife, so he could not shoot the monster before it reached him. He would have to engage it in hand-to-hand (hand-to-paw?) combat and slay it with his blade.

Despite the beast's ominous arrival, Capt. Dean Little would show no fear in the face of any threat. So, he grabbed the handle of his knife tight and yelled, "You want some, too?"

The large, dark figure stood on its hind legs and let loose four clipped barks towards the sky.

"Well, I ain't going nowhere! I'm right here waiting!"

142

The creature lowered itself back on all fours and began to run towards him. When it was close enough for him to see it, he said, "What the hell?"

He had been wrong about the animal before. Barreling down upon him now was the largest possum he'd ever seen. It looked to be over four feet long, a couple of feet tall, and maybe as much as forty or fifty pounds. Its lower jaw was long and jutted out, revealing some very formidable bottom teeth. The sound of its mighty claws scraping the street sent shivers through his hide. But, it wasn't the first time he'd faced fear. So, he pulled the knife from the dead possums and held it up, ready for the fight.

"Come on, you son-of-a-bitch."

The massive possum closed in on him. He marveled at its size; he never even knew a breed this impressive existed. The face was the most striking feature, being so abnormally large. The snout almost hit the ground as the creature bobbed its head. The eyes were mostly black, but there was a small ring of light brown inside, and the look in them was one of intelligence. The fur on its face was matted with grime and gore, and the stink emanating from the creature as it approached was of filth and blood. Capt. Dean feared he may be looking into the face of his final moment as his possible killer raced towards him at an impressive speed that belied its portly stature. He hoped Denton was getting his Selma to safety. But, if he was going to die, this abomination before him was coming with him.

The creature fell upon him quickly. The mangling mouth opened, revealing reddened teeth inside of the foul-smelling hole. A deep, gross growl rumbled from the depths of its throat as it leapt. Though it possessed a surprising swiftness, agility was not its strong suit, and that might have actually played to its advantage. It only maybe got an inch or two off the ground as it jumped on top of Capt. Dean. He thrust the knife forward, towards its exposed underside, and managed to plunge it deep into the section between its chest and belly.

Had the creature been able to jump a little higher, Capt. Dean not only could have successfully aimed the blade at its heart, but he could have avoided the monster's jaws. But, as it was, his blade definitely made an impact, sinking down into the gristle and flesh of the beast's body, barely missing anything vital enough to kill it quickly. That, however, was not the worst of the situation: as he dug the knife in, the possum's freakishly long, mighty jaws came forward and bit into Capt. Dean's right clavicle.

The flesh split like butter and the bones broke like straw; the blood from his wound mixed with the possum's own blood gushing from its mouth as Capt. Dean dug his blade in deeper and twisted. He screamed from the pain of the bite and the possum shrieked from the mortal blow it had been dealt.

The teeth of the monster pulled out, cutting more skin away from the bone, and it leaned its head back as it felt the sharp metal turning in its organs. Battling through the pain of his wound, the captain's free hand gripped his foe by the throat and squeezed, though without much strength. Feeling the tightening on its neck, the possum brought its head back down in hopes of biting another chunk out of its opponent, but Capt. Dean released the knife and used that hand to push the thing's face aside. As its head was turned to the right, Capt. Dean let go of its throat and jabbed his fingers into its left eye and pulled, rendering the eye inoperable.

The possum squealed and Capt. Dean then felt a sensation like daggers jabbing into his pelvis. His legs did not work, but he still had sensation in his lower half. He looked down and saw his body being ripped at by long, thick, sharp, black claws.

"You motherfucker!" he screamed and wrapped both hands around the possum's neck and started squeezing and turning.

The creature writhed and thrashed, still clawing at Capt. Dean. Despite the excruciating pain in his shoulder, Dean used his adrenaline to finish the fight. He knew he was as good as dead. Even if Selma and Officer Denton reached him now, they could not save him. This truly was his last stand.

When he realized he could not break the creature's neck, despite it obviously losing vitality, he reached a hand beneath its body, pulled the knife from its guts, and brought it up in a sideways arc and drove the tip into its temple, slowly pushing it in. The struggle within the creature slowly subsided as it twitched into death. Once it passed away, its body falling limp upon Capt. Dean's bloody form, he withdrew the knife and pushed the creature aside.

He could barely breathe, and when he did, it felt like pebbles were in his lungs, threatening to clog his throat with each inhalation. He looked down at the possum, into its eyes, and saw no life there. The fight was over, he had won. But, the price would be his life. But, it would not be in vain: the scourge of Bardstown lay dead around him. How many lives had he saved with his own this night? Many, he imagined; but, if Selma's was the only one, then that was all that counted. Saving the town was the duty of a hero; preserving the life of a child was the sacrifice of a father.

"My duty here is done," he said.

For a moment, he sat still and decided to wait for death. But, then he remembered that he had told Selma to come back for him, and he knew she would take that to heart. Even though he only told her that to give her hope, for he had known he would die right there in the street (his last battlefield), she would hold him to his word, and she would have Officer Denton return. Officer Denton was a good man, Capt. Dean knew that from the start, and he would do it just to ease her mind, even though he knew, too, that Capt. Dean intended to die that evening, sacrificing himself so his daughter could escape.

He backed himself towards his chair and turned to lift himself into it. It was a struggle, and there were seconds when he thought he had no chance of making it. But the chair was sturdy and he was determined; after a struggle that could have rivaled his battle with the mutant possum, he mounted the chair one final time. He looked down at his mangled lower half and decided he did not want Selma to see it. His legs were flayed to the bone in many parts. His pelvis was gouged and turned inside out, insides dangling outward. This would not be a sight for his daughter to see. Finding your parent dead is bad enough; to find the death was so ferocious would be unbearable. So, he reached into one of the pockets on the side of his chair and pulled out a cloth, unfolded it, and draped its red, white, and blue glory across his lap. He then noticed that his knife was on the ground next to the possum, and decided he wanted that with him when he died. He turned on his chair and wheeled a few feet forward, leaned over, and was able to grab the knife without toppling off.

After he was able to reposition himself properly into the chair, he looked down at the dead monster at his feet and shook his head. "You were a fine enemy. I never have seen anything like you. I want anyone who sees me to know that *I* defeated *you*."

The creature lay still with its eyes and mouth open and blood leaking from its carcass. The soldier in Capt. Dean wanted to honor the warrior that had brought him death, and so he sighed and, with a grunt, leaned over again and grabbed the thick, pale, disgusting tail and heaved the animal onto his lap, where it landed with a slap and a squirt of blood.

He moved the beast around until it was well centered, and he rested the knife across its side. Then, with one last requirement before his fading eyes saw their last bit of light, he reached into the small zipper compartment on the very front of the duffel bag—which still clung to the side of his chair—removed his wallet and opened it. Inside was a picture of Selma, taken earlier that year; he always kept the pictures of his daughter updated, unwilling to ever let her be lost in mere memories. He hated when parents displayed only old pictures of their children—school days, baby pictures, prom, graduations—even when they had long been adults. It was like they felt some kind of shame that their offspring didn't turn out exactly how they planned, or that they mourned their loss of parental control. Clinging to your child's past was a sad decision, and an indictment of one's bad parenting—at least, he thought so. There was never an ounce of shame or regret in him regarding anything his daughter had become. He loved her and was damned proud of her. She could not have turned out more perfect in his eyes. She was his everything, so he pulled out her picture and let the wallet fall to the ground.

He smiled one last smile as he looked into his daughter's eyes for the final time and said, "Get yourself far, far away from here. I don't know what the hell is going on, but you don't need to find out. You just need to go...and remember that Daddy Dean loves you until the sun shines no more." He then kissed the picture and held it to his chest.

With his fallen foe across his lap, bleeding on the flag that he believed represented all that he stood for, and his daughter's picture pressed against his chest, the rugged veteran, Capt. Dean Little, leaned his head back and looked at the last rays of the sun dropping behind the wall of the coming night. He sighed softly and closed his eyes, then let the darkness of death devour him.

CHAPTER ELEVEN

Night fell while Herbert was trapped in the shed, listening to the disgusting sounds of the possums eating Gene's corpse for God-knew-how-long. The small digital clock on one of the work shelves no longer functioned; its batteries having died at 6:08am on some anonymous day. His cell phone was somewhere in the backyard—on a table, on a chair, inside the van—wherever he had left it. Herbert wasn't real keen on carrying the cell phone, but found it helped with work purposes. Outside of business matters, he didn't use the device too often. Many times he would lay it somewhere and forget about it. Usually, he didn't care; the phone was not a top priority for him. Tonight, he wished he had given it a little more concern.

There was a small window in the back of the shed he had cut out a few months ago while renovating the structure. What was once an average-sized tool shed and had been made into a full-fledged work room. The window faced the land behind his property; he wanted to be able to see out over the field near the woods in case some idiot tried to sneak up on the shed and rob it while he was inside. As crazy at it sounded, it was not an unlikely occurrence in that section of Bardstown. There wasn't a high population of bad guys or thugs around, but there were some rowdy country boys who liked a good set of tools and weren't above stealing them off a working man's property. The window made perfect sense at the time, but god-damn he wished he'd had cut one out on the front side, too.

The countless seconds slowly turned into hours as Herbert waited for silence to reign beyond the doors. During that wait, he made constructive use of his time cleaning off his trapper helmet and rounding up artillery for his escape. He didn't have a lot of room for baggage, so he needed to carry the most effective weapons he could scrounge up. He found a good, sturdy tool belt that strapped around his shoulders and across his waist, but decided that would weigh him down. Nothing short of a brown bear could tear through his coveralls, but his hands would need to be heavily gloved, so he needed a small amount of large, heavy items that were easy to grab, hold, and swing with deadly precision. So, he found a strong, simple belt that strapped across his waist and had two large pockets on each side, three loops in the front and two in the back. He grabbed a hammer and a mallet and put them down the loops in the back, found a small hacksaw and slid it into a side-pouch, and a butane spray can and small blowtorch that he jammed down the other pouch. The largest Phillips-head screwdriver he possessed went down one of the front loops, a police Maglite went down the middle, and a twenty-two-inch weighted machete would be occupying the final front loop when it wasn't in his hand. His large black gloves were cut and burn proof and they slid up far enough on his wrists to keep the skin from being exposed. He had no concern about his ankles and shins because the coveralls would shield them. His boots were tough leather and steel-toed, so there would be no penetration at the ground level. The helmet he wore when trapping wildlife kept his entire head and neck covered. He was now ready for the fight.

The silence he had awaited came about fifteen minutes before he had finished his preparations. His plan was to make it to the van, find the key, and drive the hell out of there. If he couldn't find the key, then the next course of action would depend on one thing: how many possums were outside. If he got out there and the coast was clear, he would walk to town and see what was happening, or to get help, hopefully finding someone along the way, provided this rash of animal attacks hadn't spread through the city, which his gut (and the radio reports) told him it most likely had. If there were a bunch of possums out there and their onslaught became too much to ward off, he would duck back into his house and hole up, or return to the shed—whichever was the safest route. In the event of possums, he hoped for the house because it got him one step closer to getting out of there, even though there might be no escape from that point. But, at least once inside, he had his landline to call out on, if it was still operational, and if the lines in town weren't down. If he found his cell, then he would be in good shape; if the situation became too urgent, then he could close himself up in the van and make a call to the police. If he had to huddle in the van without his cell, then so be it. He would wing it from there.

If he had to fall back to the shed, then he could watch the field beyond. He had a spotlight inside powerful enough to light a path halfway to the woods. He could keep an eye on the field and if that remained clear, he could make a break for it and take his chances among the trees. However, it might be best to wait until morning to execute that plan. Nighttime was no time to be running through the woods from wild, nocturnal animals. Again—he would wing it.

He kept a motion-activated floodlight attached to his house, so when he opened the shed doors, if any possums moved up that way, the light would flick on and alert him of their presence. Stepping to the doors, he undid the interior chain and locks and pushed them open slightly. At first, he gave them only a soft nudge to see if Gene's corpse was still propped against the doors. They pushed out with ease, which meant the body must have either collapsed to the ground or been totally devoured. The outside lock prevented him from pushing the shed all the way open. Without Gene against the doors, he could push it hard enough to break the lock, but it would make a lot of noise. If any possums were nearby, they would surely hear it and come running.

He peeked out through the crack with one eye. The floodlight was not on, but the moon was bright, and he couldn't see any movement along the ground. He considered forcing open the doors and stepping out, but thought it too risky. He reached for his Maglite and clicked it on, flashing the beam along the yard. There was nothing out there except a ragged mound of flesh and bones near the house.

"Poor son-of-a-bitch," he said, remembering Steve's horrific end.

Recalling that brought Gene back to the forefront of his mind. He guided the beam of light towards the ground just outside the shed. There he saw the eviscerated carcass of his old friend slumped in the grass. The head was just a chipped and cracked skull with minced bits of flesh clinging to it. His body was pulpy, clothes unrecognizable. He looked like a large pile of vomit comprised of beef-chunks and raspberry jelly, but did not smell anywhere near as pleasant as that might. His hands and feet were totally gone, most of the arms up to the shoulders and the legs almost to the knees—or, at least that's what Herbert guessed from the position of Gene's gelatinous remains. It was difficult to tell.

Judging by the condition of the two bodies, the possums had fed well; and judging by the appearance of the backyard, they had since moved on. This would give him plenty of time to look for the key.

Replacing the Maglite into his belt, he took a deep breath, held it, and shoved the door as hard as he could, dislodging the exterior plate that held the lock in place. The doors flew open with a bang as they hit the shed. Herbert quickly removed his flashlight once again and shined it along the yard. No possums came to investigate the noise and none had shown in the beam, so he stepped into the yard and looked around, checking all corners and crannies with his light, finding each one empty. Feeling sure that he was now alone, he walked towards the van and knelt down, shining his light along the ground in hopes of finding the key.

He searched around the vehicle for many minutes, running his hand through the grass to hopefully catch it, without success. He remembered being near the van, but not exactly next to it, when he accidentally kicked the key away from him. He tried hard to picture the silver object sailing low along the grass, catching sparkles of sunlight as it flew before landing somewhere in the van's vicinity, but could not conjure the image. So much had been going on with them trying to get Steve and themselves to safety that his memory of the entire event was a distorted blur.

Many more minutes passed without any sight of the key. Herbert was near to surrender when the floodlight suddenly lit up behind him. He watched as the shadow of his hunched self appeared on the ground and van before him. Instinctively, he jumped, turned his body, and placed his back against the van. With both the flashlight and machete now held out in front of him, ready to slice and dice possums, he squinted against the glare in search of an imminent threat. A small, four-legged silhouette dashed into the center of the blinding radius, like a performer stepping into the spotlight, ready for the show. He turned off his Maglite and hung it back on his belt, then held the machete with both hands so he could swing with maximum force if needed. The light shut off, the yard went dark, and two eyes shone in his direction.

"You don't stand a chance alone, little guy. Your friends better not be far."

The eyes moved and the light came back on, blinding Herbert once again. He held up one hand to ward off the glare.

"One more time, huh?"

The silhouette moved in his direction and he got his machete ready for battle. A few more steps and the animal was almost upon him. When it was only a couple of feet away, he lifted the weapon and prepared to strike.

"Meow!" the creature cried.

Herbert froze, let out a breath, and looked down at the dark-colored cat at his feet. He couldn't tell if it was black or some form of dark brown or blue, but he lowered the weapon and sighed.

"You shouldn't be out here little guy. It's a bad night for the likes of you."

He knelt down and petted the cat. It was long and heavy and appeared to be pretty capable. It had some crusted blood on its right shoulder and around its mouth, and all Herbert could hope for was that it had taken out at least one damned possum that evening.

He touched the shoulder and the cat jerked its head at his hand and bit down slightly. Herbert took his flashlight back out and shined it on the cat's wound. There were definitely teeth marks there. Something had bitten the cat, and it looked like whatever had done it meant business. Looking closer at the cat's paws, he saw a lot of blood clotted there, too. Apparently, this cat had a tangle with another animal.

Smiling, Herbert asked, "Did you take one of them suckers out? I sure hope so."

The cat stuck around for a few more seconds, enjoying the petting, before darting back off across the yard from where it had come, setting the floodlight off again.

Herbert watched it go with a half-smile on his face, wishing it well on this dangerous night. After he watched it disappear into the pitch, he turned towards the front of the van and spotted something glinting in the grass. He shined his flashlight at it and saw that it was the vehicle's key.

"Well, I'll be damned. I don't know if you was a black cat or not, but you sure didn't mean bad luck."

He took a couple of steps away from the front of the van and knelt to grab it. "Yep, you're my key."

It had been a couple of feet directly in front of the driver's side headlight. All the time he spent searching, he never ventured up that far. He had kept around the side of the van because he had been sure that's where it had gone. Thankfully, ole puss had come along and literally showed him the light.

He strolled over to the van and unlocked the door, pulled it open, and prepared himself to jump in—but was stopped short by a shrieking possum staring in his face. This one looked to be over ten pounds and had a blood-soaked countenance. Its squeal was nauseating, and Herbert was glad for the helmet, not only because it muffled the sound, but because the creature bounced off the plastic face mask when it leapt at him.

He stumbled back and planted his feet, looking around anxiously for the little monster. He then felt something latch itself to his leg, so he reached back and peeled it off, then brought it around in front of him, holding it by the scruff of its neck. It thrashed about, trying to get away, and screamed in his face.

"Shut the fuck up," he said and jammed the machete into its chest, running it all the way through.

The possum died quickly and he flung it aside then headed back to the van, thanking his foresight for donning the helmet. Had he not, his eyeballs might be sliding down the possum's gullet right now.

As he reached up to lift himself into the van, he heard more scrambling from the inky space in the rear of the vehicle. Soft scratching followed by low squeaks began to run together as one noise, and many small vibrations rippled swiftly through the automobile. It intensified to a heavy hum that made the van quiver. Herbert didn't really need to guess what was causing this, but he took out the flashlight and shined it into the back anyway.

The entire back of the van—from the floor to the ceiling, from the front seats to the rear doors—was crammed with smelly, bloody, snarling possums, and they had now taken notice of his presence. Herbert stepped back and slammed the door just in time; several possums smashed themselves against the window, smearing blood and saliva while clacking their teeth against the glass.

For a moment, he watched them curiously as they battered their bodies against the window and door. They smashed their faces against the glass, smearing blood all over it. They scratched desperately to get to him, staring at him all-the-while. There was one possum in particular, a larger one with a big head, at the front of the crowd, squashed against the window. Its black eyes stared at him without blinking as it hissed and breathed heavily. Blood was crusted all around its mouth; it curled its lips back and Herbert saw that several teeth were missing. Herbert leaned forward, bringing his face closer to the glass, and returned the possum's glare.

For a second, it stopped carrying on and engaged Herbert in a staring contest. Herbert tapped the glass and said, "What's gotten into you, little buddy?"

As Herbert stared deep into the animal's eyes, he saw something intelligent. For a moment, he felt as if the two of them were somehow communicating. In that moment, he knew that there was some sinister shit at play. It wasn't as if he had really doubted it before. It was, after all, pretty damn obvious something was fucking rotten when a horde of them had eaten his two best friends and cornered him in the shed. But, the creature's eyes told of something else—something that hadn't been present in possums before (and he had trapped enough in his day to say so)—something relentless and hostile. He knew there would be no way to stop them other than eradicating them all like zombies in some trash horror film.

He stepped back and the possum banged its head against the window; then began screeching once again. It wouldn't be too much longer until the creatures found their way out of the van, or possibly called more to arms with all of that racket. It was time to go.

"Well, guess I'm walking," Herbert finally said. "See you on the flipside."

He turned from the van and walked a few feet before he heard a heavy growl that froze him where he stood. When he spun to see what was behind him, he stepped back and held his machete with both hands. About six feet in front of him was the largest possum he'd ever seen. It was nearly thirty inches long and could have easily weighed thirty-to-thirty-five pounds. Behind it, several possums were dropping from the passenger side window to join their larger mate. In a few seconds, Herbert was staring down at least twenty possums, possibly more. Knowing what they had in mind, he did not hesitate. He raised his machete and ran at them, heading straight for the largest one.

With a primal yell, he pulled the machete back over his right shoulder, preparing to slash the big one's head off. When he came within a foot of them, the big one emitted a strange squeal and fell to the ground with its mouth hanging open and tongue lolling out. Herbert stopped in his tracks and watched as the others followed suit, dropping like dominoes and emitting a foul odor. Soon, they all lay before him, arms sprawled, claws splayed, and faces looking like death masks.

Lowering the machete, Herbert chuckled. "Playing possum, huh?"

He thought about taking the blow torch and butane can out and lighting them all ablaze, but decided against it. While he'd definitely get some of them, the torch itself was not big enough to get them all, and the ones that did not burn might rush him. Even though they were playing dead, he didn't know how long it would be or how little it would take to incite them back into attack mode. He was pretty well loaded with armor and weaponry, but would have still chosen to avoid the battle if he could. This was a small blessing, and one he best not ignore.

"Until we meet again," he said, and trotted off toward town, wielding his machete like a crusader.

CHAPTER TWELVE

Selma and Denton made it to Denton's house unscathed several minutes later and jumped into his Crown Vic to attempt a rescue of Capt. Dean. They had heard the gunfire behind them as they ran, and Selma was tempted to turn back and return to her father a couple of times, but Denton had to keep her going.

The last time, she stopped at the edge of Denton's street. He stopped, too, and said, "What are you doing? We're almost there."

"We have to go back."

"We can't."

She looked at him with her eyes watering and said, "Then *I* have to go back."

Denton grabbed her gently by the elbow and said, "Selma, he stayed behind so you could get away. Don't dishonor his courage by making his efforts in vain."

The gunshots rang out again, travelling through a neighborhood that had grown hauntingly quiet. For a second, she swallowed her emotion and thought about the reality of the situation. Yes—her father had remained behind to fight for her survival—the same reason Denton had left with her and not stayed with him. The young officer was brave—he reminded her of her father—and he was correct: if she went back to her father now, it would render his efforts useless, and she could never wish to do such a thing. She then decided to continue on with Denton, as her father had wanted.

Denton had a girlfriend of about two years who left him nearly five months ago. She got tired of the long hours that his job demanded of him. That's why most of his relationships ended. Not only did women seem to not like the amount of hours he had to put in—twelve or more, most days—they also didn't like wondering if he would come back at all, not that Bardstown was a particularly dangerous place, but anything could happen. One lone nut wanders into town and robs a liquor store, Denton gets the call, walks in unprepared for a complete madman and catches a bullet to the face—not likely, but very possible. He couldn't really blame a woman for her trepidation regarding a relationship such as that, and that's why he lived alone.

The quietude of the empty street was unsettling. The last glow of the day had sunk behind the distant woods and most of the land was dark. Usually, there were scatterings of headlights traveling the shadowy country roads. People could often be seen on their porches, even in the autumn chill. Lights were usually on in windows and shining through screen doors as people left their interior doors open to cool their houses. Those who enjoyed their evening strolls could be glimpsed on the roadside, walking peacefully, taking in the last twinkle of twilight. Not tonight. None of these sights could be seen, and it wasn't even very chilly for autumn in Kentucky. Word must have spread about the attacks.

Earlier that morning, the death of Brandon Smith had rocked the town, followed by the death of Barbara Jones. The body found under the overpass prior to those two incidents had been written off as a murder. Since then, it seemed the situation had slid like an avalanche cascading down an icy slope. It had been feared a killer was walking the streets, but then people decided wild dogs or even bobcats were on the loose. Did anyone know it was actually a bunch of damn dirty possums chewing the town apart? Would anybody believe such a story if it were told to them? Denton wouldn't have—he didn't, in fact, when he'd gotten the call that Selma Donaldson had a bunch of man-eating possums in her basement. But, he had seen them and, sure enough, they were possums.

Selma didn't speak as they fled to Denton's house. She hated herself for leaving her father, but she always respected his wishes, even as an adult. Not because she felt she had to, but because she respected him, as a father and a man. He was the best man she had ever known and she looked up to him every day of her life. When her dickhead ex-husband started banging waitresses and gas station attendants around town, and even random lot lizards at the local truck stop, she feared a messy divorce. He was the kind of asshole to make life as difficult for her as possible. But, her father would not allow that.

Capt. Dean spoke to the philandering bastard himself, and let him know that Selma would be leaving him and there was nothing he was going to do about it. Her father told him that if he protested, put up a fight, or sought any sort of court action against her, then he would see to it the man either left town on his own accord, or by force. When her ex challenged her dad—mainly because he was now wheelchair-bound—Capt. Dean called a couple of old friends, who happened to be the mayor and the police chief, and had them handle the situation. The unfaithful scumbag then let her go quietly. Capt. Dean raised her to be strong, hardworking, and virtuous, and he did a damn good job. When times got tough, he still had her back, no matter how old she got. That was love, and sadly, not every person grows up to have that kind of parental love in their life, and she knew it, so she was more than grateful to have experienced it.

Now, she was almost certain that he was forever gone. There's no way he could have survived that madness. He was tough—always had been—and brave. But, now he was old and there were a lot of ferocious possums out there. They had already gnawed through the basement door. How could he, in his elderly, fragile condition, expect to fight them off? Still, she bit her thumb and hoped she was wrong as Officer Denton sped towards the spot where Capt. Dean had made a stand.

Denton didn't have much hope, either, but he held out a little bit as he turned onto the next street over from the firefight. Selma felt her heart quicken the closer they got. With each rapid turn of the wheels she felt the pressure building in her gut. Denton could feel it rolling off of her like a fever. He felt it rippling through himself. He turned the corner to the street and said a quick prayer for the old man's survival. Selma knew better. She felt it as soon as they hit the street. Her daughterly instincts told her that her daddy—the local hero, the war veteran, the man everybody loved—was dead. When they rode upon his stationary wheelchair, with the sag of his head and the slump of his immobile frame visible, she knew. The tears that had started to leak from the bottoms of her eyes finally blinded her as they flowed like hot lava.

Denton stopped the car and got out. He walked over to the chair and knew right away Capt. Dean was dead. He was covered in blood and his eyes were closed. His chest did not move, and he had the biggest damn possum Denton had ever seen lying on his lap. That, too, was dead, and bleeding all over the American flag. In his hand, held to his chest, was the photograph of Selma. Denton reached down to look at it, saw what it was, and decided it was to remain with the body.

The sight of Capt. Dean was impressive: a pale old man, clearly still as tough as nails until the last second of his life, dead in his wheelchair with the fallen enemy draped across him, the banner of the nation he once proudly defended covering his fatal wounds, and the picture of his beloved daughter held to his heart. The road around him, scattered with dozens upon dozens of dead possums, was the battlefield of his triumph: the Captain's Last Stand. The man died as he lived: a hero. But, not defending his country, defending something far more valuable to him: his world—his daughter. This was a man—a real hero. He thought that Selma should see this and understand the glory of her father's final day, but he was unsure how to approach that. Her cries were stifled, but still loud. This was her father. How could he expect anything less?

He turned to see if she was okay, but she was only three steps behind him now, her face stern and resolute like Capt. Dean's. Her anguish had not weakened her, but driven her, and Denton could guess from whom she inherited such grit.

Selma stepped up beside him, her auburn hair a mere shadow in the night, and looked at her father and smiled. Tears were still racing down her face, but she smiled because she knew what this last vision of her father stood for—courage and selflessness, things he had always represented. This would be the final image of Capt. Dean Little before he was dressed up for the grave and she could think of no better end for a man like him.

Denton cleared his throat. "He died a hero."

She looked up at him and wiped her eyes. "He *was* a hero."

"*Is*," Denton replied.

She nodded. "Yes—always."

They looked at Capt. Dean again. Denton marveled at the carnage around them. "He killed every possum that was after us. You see the size of the one on his lap?"

"He told me when we came back for him, every possum would be dead. My father always keeps his word. He was a real badass, right to the end."

She turned her head and looked at the officer. If not for the shade of night, Denton would have seen the intrepid expression she'd inherited from her beloved dad.

Denton smiled. "That he was."

"It took every possum on the street to stop him."

"That it did."

Denton broke the silence that followed over the next few seconds. "He's holding your picture in his hand. Should you take it?"

She shook her head. "No. He knew I'd come back. That is his last, 'I love you.' He always said he'd take my photograph to the grave with him. The picture stays."

"Whatever you want to do with him, I'll help you."

"Let's take him back home and put him in bed, then we'll be on our way. Hopefully, these were all the possums. But, what if they aren't?"

"I don't think they are."

"Me, neither. So, his body can stay at home until this is over. Then I'll handle the rest."

"Whatever you say."

Denton helped Selma lift her father and carry him back to the car. They kept the flag over him but had to leave the chair. Selma said he wouldn't have wanted it, anyway. They grabbed his duffel bag and gathered up what weapons they could find; he wouldn't have wanted to leave without them. They then drove towards the Donaldson home and left the giant possum dead in the street.

CHAPTER THIRTEEN

R achel's sudden exclamation woke Todd from his nap.

"Shit!" she snapped.

"What's wrong?" Todd's voice was slightly raspy and his face was sweaty.

"Gas is almost out."

The car began to slow down. Todd looked at her accusingly. "Are you fucking serious?"

The vehicle vibrated slightly before rolling to a stop on a long, forested street. Waning daylight hung slightly in the air, but it could hardly be noticed beneath the shade of the towering trees.

"Good job, Rachel," Todd said and opened the passenger side door with a sigh.

"Hey, it's not my fault."

"Well then whose fault is it? It is *your* car, isn't it? Who else is going to put gas in it if you don't?"

"How the hell was I supposed to know possums would take over the city? It's not like that's really something you prepare for. I thought I just had to worry about having enough gas to make it to work and back until payday. I didn't know I'd be on the run this week."

Todd struggled out of the car. He had dozed for a few minutes but came back around feeling real shitty. His black bangs were sticking to his clammy forehead. He kept his right leg up as he stepped out of the car, not wanting to put too much pressure on it. The bleeding had finally stopped, but the pain was getting worse. Any movement seemed to make it burn, like a great ball of fire was expanding beneath the skin of his leg, traveling through his blood all the way down to his foot. He was afraid to look under the dressing to see if it was changing colors. No doubt there was an infection of some kind coursing through him. He couldn't think about that. The car was dead in the middle of an empty road surrounded by woods during a mass possum uprising—nothing about this situation was hopeful, so he had to stay focused on surviving.

Rachel noticed her brother's struggle to stand, and she also noticed his condition seemed to be worsening. She had hoped that the brief nap might have revitalized him some, but it was plain to see that it didn't help much. He was a tough kid, but he had suffered a severe bite. Since possums didn't normally act that way, there had to be something disrupting their minds to make them so violent, and she feared whatever it was might now be in her little brother's bloodstream.

After they were both standing at the front of the car, Todd looked around and said, "This looks like a good place to become a possum feast."

"Shut up, Todd. I don't see any around."

"Doesn't mean they're not here. There are enough woods around us to hide an entire colony."

"We just have to get off this road and down to the roundabout. Once we're in town, we can figure something out. Can you walk?"

"Do I have a choice?"

"Maybe you should stay in the car while I go to town."

"And wait for the unhinged, bloody-toothed possums to pile on the car and grin at me like psycho clowns before they eat me? No fucking way. I'm going with you."

"But you can barely walk."

"Doesn't matter—I'll manage. I'd rather be crippled than turned into possum shit."

Todd started off at a limp, wincing through the pain. Rachel moved in to assist him but he waved her back.

"I can do this on my own."

"Bull. I got to go slow to let you keep up anyway, so I might as well help."

"Or, you could walk on ahead and I'll catch up when we get to where we need to go."

"That's stupid, Todd. Just let me help you."

"Screw that. I'm fine."

"No you're not. You got a gaping wound in the back of your leg."

"It's not that bad."

"I dressed the damn thing. I know what it looks like."

"Look, in all this time we've spent arguing, I've already taken several steps. Just leave me alone and let me walk."

Rachel sighed, half exasperated at Todd's bullheadedness and also half relieved that he still felt well enough to walk on his own *and* argue with her about it. The anger was a sign of life, and it might keep him from wearing out. She contemplated antagonizing him a bit more, but didn't. He had been through enough already.

They walked quietly up the road for a few minutes. The lack of sunrays penetrating the lofty grove made the crisp autumn day a little cooler. Todd was glad for the slight chill in the air, and even wished the temperature was a little lower like it usually was in October. He felt hot otherwise, like he couldn't stop sweating. His vision kept blurring in and out at times, and there were moments when he just wanted to punch something. He wasn't one to give in to violent impulses, but he thought maybe the entire frustration of the situation around them was getting to him—or maybe it was just life, altogether. He already had no parents, and Brandon was like a brother to him and now he was dead, too. After that, he was forced out of his home by a bunch of deranged possums with a hankering for human flesh. Now, the car they had left in was out of commission because his stupid-ass sister didn't gas it up. That was enough to piss anyone off.

On they walked until the end of the road was nearly in sight. On their right, the expanse of woods disappeared and gave way to a large open field with more trees off in the distance. Ahead, the road curved out of sight, leading into another long stretch of tree-swallowed road.

"Down there the road changes," Rachel said. "I think it turns to Martin Lane. That leads right into town. But, it's tight and we might get hit if we're not careful."

"Hit by what, Rachel? Nobody's out driving today. It's like a ghost town out here."

"Well, maybe they're staying home because of the reports about people dying and stuff."

"Or there might be another reason."

"Like what?"

"What if we get to town and nothing's left? What if we get there and the possums killed everybody?"

She scoffed, although the same fear dwelled within her. It wasn't just the hideous attacks back at their house, but the quiet that seemed to have descended over the city, not just out there on that lonely road, but the whole time they were driving. She hadn't seen anyone else, and that was unusual—unusual and eerie.

"I doubt that," she said, unsure if she was trying to convince Todd or herself.

"Why? Why couldn't it happen?"

"What about the police, and all the hunters and other men with guns that live around here?"

"What about them?"

"I'm sure they'd take care of things."

"Maybe—hopefully. But, what if there are too many possums? What if they just can't get the job done? We might be walking into something even worse than what happened at our house."

"Don't be so grim, Todd."

"Don't be so stupid, Rachel! Stop acting like there's nothing wrong. These fucking things killed Brandon!" Todd stopped in the road at the last statement, and said it with such force that Rachel stopped, too.

When she turned around to look at him, he asked, "Doesn't that mean anything to you?"

Rachel stared at him for a long moment, feeling the pain of his question radiate in her heart. "Yes, Todd. It means quite a lot to me."

"Then act like it!"

"How the hell could you say that? I cried my eyes out this morning for him."

"Now you're acting like nothing is going on!"

"That's because I'm trying to make sure you get to a doctor safely."

"I'll be fine. That doesn't mean you should act like nothing bad happened to Brandon."

"Believe me, Todd, I'm not. I'm carrying around that pain like a god-damn knife sticking in my heart. Every step I take, I feel it twisting. I miss

Brandon more than you can imagine. I loved him. But, you're my fucking brother and I love you more and right now, I am worried about *you*. I'll never forget Brandon, but he's dead and can't be saved. You can, and I'm not going to stop until you are!"

Todd was silent as he stared at his sister, tears welling up in his eyes. "Why did he have to die, Rachel?"

"I don't know. I know you loved him. He loved you, too. You were like brothers, and don't think all of this isn't fucking killing me slowly. I've been slowly dying since mom and dad died."

Todd's tears exploded and he leaned into Rachel; she embraced him as he cried on her shoulder. His tears breaking made her tears pour forth. She cried into his chest. They stood in the middle of the road, as one force, lamenting their broken lives—lives filled with mental anguish and endless heartache; lives arrested by tragedy and thrown into an abysmal pit with seemingly no way to climb out—this is how they lived every day, but they always pressed on. They always stood strong.

Todd pulled away from her softly. "Our lives are fucked up, Rachel."

She let go and backed away, too. Wiping her eyes, she said, "I know. They are really fucked up. But, we're going to keep moving, like we always do. Although this incident today is the craziest, most fucked up shit we've ever been through, we're still going to make it. Alright? You and me, like always."

Todd brushed away the last of his tears and breathed a small laugh. "That's right. We always make it through."

"Always."

"And we'll make it through this."

Rachel smiled and said, "You better believe it. Now, let's go."

They continued on, nearing the bend in the road. This section of the street was much darker as the tree branches became thicker and more laden with leaves. Evening would be coming on soon, so they wanted to hurry and get around the curve just in case a car did come. They could see the path from where they walked and it didn't look too inviting—dark, tight, and dangerous. They stopped about fifteen feet from the turn. The way the road curved sharply beneath the large trees, with their branches stretching out to touch one another from both sides of the road, made the curve look like a portal to somewhere sinister.

"I don't really like the way that looks," Todd said.

"Me neither. It gives me the creeps."

"Maybe we should go back the other way."

"You think you could do that on your leg?"

"Probably."

"I don't know, though. It seems kind of stupid if we do."

"That road is really narrow. We'd practically have to walk down the middle the whole way, and it will be dark, soon. If anyone's driving on it, we'd get hit. If there are possums down there, we'd have no chance to get away."

"We wouldn't have a chance, anyway."

"I know. But, it just feels like less of a chance going down there."

"I guess we can turn back. How's your leg?"

"It hurts, but not as bad as it did when we first got out of the car."

"Then let's go back."

When they turned to head back, they both spied something moving far away in the field before them.

"What is that?" Todd asked.

A large sheet of grayish shapes was gathered in the field several yards ahead. At first, they couldn't figure out what it was, but it looked like it had ripples going through it, like the breeze billowing through a blanket. There were no trees above the mass, so they were not shadows. But, the long walk along the shady road had settled their eyes to dimness, so peering across the evening-sun-drenched field confused their vision for a moment. They now had to accustom their eyesight to that last blast of rays that glows before evening rolls into the sky and closes its hand around the light.

"I don't know," Rachel said and walked to the edge of the field.

It took a few seconds for their eyes to adjust. Rachel had massive astigmatism and wasn't wearing her glasses, so the shapes were impossible for her to define. Todd, however, had 20/20 vision and could see them perfectly.

"Oh shit," he said.

Rachel felt her heart go numb. "What is it?"

"It's a whole bunch of possums."

"Oh shit," she echoed. "Do they see us?"

Todd shook his head. "No. But, they're doing something really weird."

"What are they doing?"

"Walking around in circles."

There looked to be nearly a hundred possums out in the field, each one individually spinning slowly around. Around and around they went, seemingly without purpose, twirling under the fading daylight. Every single one of them, except one, and Todd could see it clearly, standing in the middle of them all, glaring over at him and Rachel.

"Wait...," he said, but trailed off.

"What?"

"Damn."

"What?" she repeated.

"There's one out there that's as big as a dog."

Rachel swallowed. "What kind of dog?"

"A big dog."

"Like Bucky was?"

"Bigger."

"Then it can't be a possum."

Bucky was a cocker spaniel Todd had when he was a kid. He weighed about thirty pounds at his heaviest. Even at a distance, Todd could tell that the possum he was looking at was much bigger than Bucky had been. Unlike the others, this one was not spinning. It was looking right at him and Rachel with big dark eyes that could not be missed even from that far away. If the smaller possum that had gripped his leg earlier could do what it did, he could not—did not want to—even imagine what damage this beast was capable of inflicting. He feared, though, that he might soon find out. As the other possums walked in their circles all about the field, this one simply stared intently at what Todd believed it perceived as its next meal.

"Rachel, we better get moving."

"Why?" The anxiety in her voice was clear.

"Because that big one is just staring at us."

"What are the others doing?"

"Still spinning around."

"Okay, let's start walking."

When they turned away, they were both halted by a sound that made them both go cold. Out in the field, a deep, rumbling squeal rose up into the air.

With her eyes wide, Rachel asked, "What the hell was that?"

Todd turned to look across the field again, and saw the large possum standing on its hind legs, almost like it was barking at the sky. The possums twirling around it stopped and looked at their leader, then slowly began to turn their attention to Rachel and Todd. When the large possum lowered itself back to the ground, it issued a long, low growl that traveled across the quiet evening and reached the Owenses ears, causing their bodies to break out in goose-pimples. When it was done, the smaller possums started running for the road.

"Oh shit," Todd said. "They're coming!"

Rachel yelped and started running back towards the car, but Todd yelled for her to stop.

"They'll cut us off if we run that way! We have to go this way!" Todd motioned towards the narrow bend in the road, knowing that was their only chance.

"But, they'll catch us if we go down there!"

"Maybe we can get in the woods and hide."

Overhead, evening was almost over and the sun would soon be down. Todd hoped maybe they wouldn't be seen running down the road. The possums were slow, and the Owens siblings had an incredible head start, but with his leg injured, he didn't know if he could get away fast enough.

Rachel joined him and they ran down the bending road, vanishing under the roof of the woods. All down the road, the leaves touched on each side, creating a tunnel of trees. Brown autumn leaves scattered along the road crunched beneath their feet. Slight radiance from the last bit of the day overhead, and small house lights from far, far back in the woods, fused to provide a dim glow to guide their way. From what both of them could see, the road was long and without a stop anywhere along the way. All they could do was run and hope the possums never caught them.

They ran for several minutes before they finally heard the leaves crunching way behind them. The squeals and snorts were faint on the night air. Todd looked back but could see nothing. It was full-blown night now and only a small amount of moonlight penetrated the leaves overhead. All was dark. But, his eyes had adjusted to the pitch, and he was able see something off the road to the right of him.

"Rachel!"

"Yeah?"

"There's a shed."

"What?"

"A shed, off the road just a few feet away. Maybe we can hide in it."

"I'd say it's our only shot."

Todd veered to the right and headed for the shed. Rachel followed beside him. It was long, tall, and made of rusty metal. When they reached it, they could see it was old and ramshackle, and there was no door. If they hid in there, they would be found.

"Shit, now what?" Todd asked.

"Can we climb on top of it?"

Todd looked at her and nodded. "It doesn't look too sturdy, but it's all we can do, right now."

The chilling sounds of their pursuers grew nearer, and the crunching of the leaves got louder. They were running out of time. Todd limped around to the side of the building and saw a barrel.

"We can climb up there on this."

"Is it tall enough?"

"I'll lift you up then you can pull me."

"No. Your leg's bad. You go up first."

"I can't climb without help. Are you able to lift me?" he asked.

Rachel sized Todd up. She wasn't a weakling by any means, but neither was she very strong; Todd was kind of big. She wasn't sure if she could or couldn't lift him, but she doubted that she'd be able to. She shook her head and replied, "No. I don't think so."

"Me neither. This is the only way."

Knowing time was short and Todd was right, Rachel surrendered and got up on the barrel. Todd clasped his hands together and held them up for her. "Reach up, grab the roof, and then step on my hands and I'll push you up. I'm strong enough to do it."

Rachel did as Todd asked and she was soon pulling herself up onto the roof. Once atop the shabby shed, she lay on her front, positioned herself so she was facing her brother, and held out her hands.

"Your turn."

Todd was already fighting his way up onto the barrel, which wobbled beneath his weight. The pain in his leg was overpowering and he feared he wouldn't make it.

"Come on, Todd!"

"I don't know if I can!"

The possums could be heard and smelled as they drew near. In would be less than a minute before they were swarming the area. Neither Rachel nor Todd could believe this was happening. As Todd watched the barrel wobble beneath his weight, and as Rachel listened to the ornery creatures coming as she reached for her brother, both of them thought this was complete bullshit. How the hell did something like this even happen?

Frantically, she said, "Hurry Todd! You can make it. You've come this far!"

Todd made one last push with his right leg and felt like his calf might explode, but he managed to get all the way onto the barrel. He threw his hand up for Rachel to grab, but lost his balance as the barrel tilted to the right, wobbled, then tilted some more, causing his body to lean that way, which put more weight on the right side of the barrel. It did not right itself and kept tilting. Todd reached out his hand again but Rachel was now out of reach. Soon, they were both watching the other pull away as Todd fell back into the darkness. He hit the ground a second later. Rachel screamed his name just as the possums came into view. Her shriek drew their attention and they turned towards the shed. Todd quickly grabbed the barrel and pulled it on top of his prone body.

The moon had shifted in the sky, directly overhead, and shone down on the possums. Their glittering eyes now hovered at the edge of the road. Todd hoped that if he lay still enough, they'd never know he was under the barrel. But, when the big one came to the front of the crowd and looked directly at him, he knew he was royally fucked.

The creature squealed again, a sound almost like glee, and the others began to step slowly from the road.

Rachel considered climbing down to help her brother, but thought if she did, she would draw attention to him. She, too, hoped they didn't know he was there. But, they were making their way towards him. He lay still, silent, and looked unafraid. She was not going to let him die.

She started banging on the roof. "Up here! We're up here! Come and get us!"

It worked; they turned their attention to her—even the big one. They went to the base of the shed and started scratching at it, scrambling to climb upon it. Many of them walked inside to look for a way up, but they could not find one. Rachel kept pounding on the roof, hoping to keep them occupied.

After a couple of minutes, several of them lost interest in her, though others had begun forming a wall at the base in hopes of scaling the shed. They were about three feet up the wall and growing higher by the minute. Soon, they would be up there with her.

Others had begun to walk around the shed, some passing Todd where he lay beneath the barrel. Many still hung out in the road, including the big one, which seemed confused as to what was going on. It was looking around, looking up, looking for something that wasn't there. It sniffed and choked and hacked and squealed, but did not look in Todd's direction.

Not until something fell out of the tree above Todd and hit the barrel right in front of his face. Fearing it was a possum, he yelled, "Oh shit!" and instinctively shoved the barrel away, rolling it over several possums nearby.

He never knew that what had fallen off the tree was simply an old bird's nest abandoned long ago. But, now the big possum knew where he was, and so did the others, and they all decided they had found themselves an easier meal than the one that was high above them.

Within seconds, they were coming for him. Todd searched the ground for a weapon but could not find one. He knew it was over. He was about to end up like Julie and Ralph.

Rachel swung her legs over the side of the roof and dropped to the ground in front of her brother, ready to kick, scratch, and claw if she had to. She stood in front of him, not really knowing what she would do, but she was ready to die fighting.

As they prepared for certain grisly death, it looked like the moon overhead began to glow brighter on the street. The light grew and grew, getting brighter and brighter, until they both realized it was not the moon at all. Before it registered what they were seeing, something emerged from the darkness and slammed against the large possum, sending it somewhere off into the night. Rachel screamed really loud and heard another screech to match it, with a lot of bumps and squeals accompanying it.

"It's a car!" she said.

Voices began to shout as gunshots rang out in the night. All the possums turned towards the commotion. A few small circles of light began dancing around in the dark as more shots were fired and the raised voices spoke. The possums squealed and hissed, but it was no use. Whoever had taken them by surprise was able to push them back. Two loud explosions rattled the air around them and the possums surrounding Rachel and Todd fled into the woods on the other side of the street. In the span of a few minutes, the street had gone from a possum warpath to as silent as a soft winter snowfall.

"Who is that?" Todd asked.

"I don't know. Let's go see."

They walked to the edge of the grass and stepped out onto the road. Two figures were walking around the car, passing back and forth in front of the headlights. It looked to be a woman and a man. The woman was plain dressed and the man looked to be a police officer. They were looking around and underneath the car, shining flashlights around towards the trees and up the road. They spoke back and forth to each other but Rachel and Todd could not make out their words.

"Hey!" Rachel yelled.

The people halted and looked their way.

"Someone out there?" the man called.

The woman held up a very powerful flashlight and said, "I see them, by the road."

The cop recognized them right away. "Rachel? Todd? Are you two okay?"

Though he wasn't on the force at the time it happened, Officer Denton remembered them from their past tragedy. But, neither Rachel nor Todd knew who he was. Bardstown didn't have many cops, but the Owens siblings never had any run-ins with the law, so they didn't often meet members of the force. To them, he was just another officer.

"Yes," Rachel answered, not really caring if she didn't know who he was. "I mean, Todd's been bitten by a possum, and he's getting pretty sick."

Denton and Selma were walking up to them. Denton asked, "So, you all were attacked, too?"

"Yes. If you hadn't come along, we'd be possum food," Todd told him.

"How bad is your wound, son?"

"It was bleeding pretty bad earlier. It aches and burns. But, I think I'll be fine if I get to a doctor."

Rachel said, "We were heading into town when my car ran out of gas. How is everything there? Have the possums attacked there, too?"

"I don't know. We're on our way there, now. This is Selma Donaldson. Her home was overrun with possums earlier."

Selma offered a weak wave but didn't say anything.

"Ours was, too. That's why we're out here, now," Rachel said. "Have you heard about any other attacks?"

"I heard a little bit over the radio earlier. I think there's been a few more. But, dispatch has gone silent, which worries me. I'm not even getting other officers over the radio."

Rachel and Todd looked at each other, worried, but didn't say anything. Neither of them wanted to say what they were thinking.

"Look, if you two are going to town, you might as well ride with us. There's no way in Hell I'm going to leave you all out here. Do you need help walking back to the car, Todd?"

"No, sir. I can manage."

"Let's go, then," Selma said. "I don't like being out here on this street. They might come back."

"I'm with you on that," Rachel said.

The four of them returned to the car, and Rachel and Todd got in the back. Officer Denton made sure to check the interior for any possums before getting in since, in the heat of the moment, he and Selma had both left their doors open.

As they were taking off, he asked Selma, "Did you see the size of that thing I hit? It was huge."

"Yeah—there's no way that was a possum."

Rachel and Todd shared another look but kept quiet.

It *was* a possum. *It* was intelligent—and they didn't want to talk about *It,* anymore.

CHAPTER FOURTEEN

The convoy of one van and two trucks traveled down the highway, heading into town. Tommy drove the lead van with Tony in the passenger seat beside him and Greta, Cara, and Tyler in the back. Kyle and Jessica were in Kyle's truck in the middle, and Clyde and Susie brought up the rear. Kyle's truck was an F-150; ugly grey with bad shocks. Clyde drove a sleek, black, Nissan Titan that rumbled like a school bus. So far, they hadn't seen anymore possums and they hoped that maybe they had eradicated the last of them, though, for the most part, they doubted it.

The gigantic possum lay dead in the bed of Kyle's truck. Clyde had volunteered to take it, but Kyle admitted that his truck was a lot shittier and decided he didn't really care if the creature's corpse bled all over his dirty truck bed. As they hoisted it in, they remarked how heavy it was. They estimated close to fifty pounds, and it was nearing three feet in length. None of them had ever seen a possum quite like that, especially with a lower jaw that stuck out a little more than the upper, revealing long, thick, sharp teeth that looked like they could chew through just about anything.

The sheer size and savage appearance of the bloody beast was disconcerting enough. But, Clyde knew there had been more than one, and only one had been found among the dead. The others were out there somewhere, so the fact that they hadn't seen anymore possums worried him more than it eased his spirit.

"You think it's over?" Susie asked.

Clyde looked at her and said, "I hope so."

"But, you don't think it is?"

He was silent for a few seconds before shaking his head. "No—I don't."

Susie sighed and looked out the window. The dashboard lights reflected her face against the glass; in the window's reflection, she saw Clyde turn and look at her without speaking. She pretended not to notice and let it go.

They were both scared. Susie was scared of the possums and Clyde was scared he wouldn't be able to protect her from them. Back in the van, he had almost lost her. The creatures were seconds from attacking. If they would have descended, each of the four of them would have died. Tony wouldn't have been able to stop that. Thank God he had arrived when he did. If he would have been a minute later they would all be slaughtered skeletons decaying in the van.

Susie was Clyde's world, and he would rather die than have her suffer; he would rather die than be without her. Coming that close to the end only reinforced that truth that he already knew. If she was going, he was going, too. But, he would give everything he had to protect her, even if he had to pound every possum to death with his bare hands. If that's what it took, he'd do it, or he would die with his fists full of their blood.

As Susie watched the darkness pass, she pictured the possums rushing through the night, finding animals and people to snack on. She couldn't imagine what it would be like to suffer such a fate, but she had come so close to finding out. Clyde had lain upon her in the van as she looked over his shoulder and saw the animals gathering by the window above them; he had been willing to experience the agony for the small glimmer of hope that she would survive. She wouldn't have, though; she was certain of that. Undoubtedly, to her, Clyde had known it, too. But his love for her was strong enough for him to risk it. In her heart, she knew that if the possums were to kill her, they'd have to kill him, and that brought her some comfort.

Jessica was looking through the back window at the dead animal in the bed of Kyle's truck. Despite the full dark outside, there were enough orange streetlights along the highway to cast sufficient light to enable her to view the monster. It fascinated and frightened her to see a possum of that size. All her life she had been around these animals and never saw anything like this.

"It looks almost prehistoric," she commented.

"What's that?" Kyle asked.

"The possum—it looks prehistoric, like a discovery on National Geographic, or something."

"Well, it's not a dinosaur, I can tell you that. But, you're right: it's an ugly sucker."

"How did it get so big?"

"Don't know. I've never seen anything like it. Maybe it's a different breed that lives up in the hills."

"Maybe so," she said and kept staring at it. "It scares me, though."

"I don't blame you there, but it's dead now—nothing to be scared of."

"There were more."

"There were a lot more, but they're all dead. Tony and his people killed them all."

"No—there were more of the big ones. I saw them outside the van. But, I didn't see any more of them dead."

"Well, I'm sure they were dead somewhere, you probably just didn't see them. But don't worry about it. If they are out there, we'll kill them, too."

"I suppose so."

After a few more seconds of her gazing at the incredible kill, Kyle said, "Turn around and quit looking at it. You're just going to keep on scaring yourself."

Jessica tore her eyes away and sat quietly in the passenger seat. Even though it was dead, it unnerved her to turn her back on it. What if it wasn't dead? Surely it was. Even if it wasn't—even if it was playing possum—it couldn't attack her through the glass. Could it?

An even worse thought invaded her mind: What if this was the possum that killed Jaime? The notion sent a shudder all through her body that climaxed as a mighty swell behind her eyes. She wanted to cry but choked it back. No time for that now.

She kept throwing quick glances over her shoulder, fearing she might see the creature's ugly, bloody face in the window behind her. Why in the hell did they have to bring that damn thing? What good could it possibly do carting that carcass around? She wished Kyle would just pull over and throw it out on the side of the highway.

Cara sat against the door at the back of the van, sharpening her hunting knife, which she had already used to kill several possums. Tyler watched her, feeling safe having her around. She was tough—a lot tougher than him. Her blonde hair was stained with blood, and she had small crimson flecks on her face and arms. Tyler was glad they found her; she had nerves of steel and reflexes like lightning. Volleyball players must be strong. He never really watched or played the sport, but if Cara was an example of their physical abilities, then Tyler felt that was a sport that never got its due credit.

One thing he did know was that if they ran into anymore possums, he wanted to stay next to Cara. He saw her fight, and she really knew what she was doing. She was faster than Tony or Tommy, and was maybe almost as strong. Any possums that got near her during a fight died almost instantly. She was so quick on her feet, and so sharp with that blade, that they couldn't even swarm her. Tyler was amazed at the way she would side-step, backpedal, and skip around the creatures as they banded together; if any got too close, she would swipe at them with her knife and cut them down like a cat. They could never corner or surround her because she was so damn quick and agile. None of his guy friends could fight that well, and he'd seen plenty of them get into squabs. He was definitely staying as close to her as he could.

"You sure know how to fight," he said to her.

She looked at him with her cold blue eyes, brushed her golden hair away from her face and said, "You can either fight or die."

"That's true. I'm glad I'm fighting next to you."

She smiled. "Thanks. I'm just good with a knife, is all. I wish I had my bow. I can bring a deer down at almost a hundred yards. Not super-impressive these days, I know, but it's not bad."

"I think it's pretty impressive. I couldn't bring one down at a hundred feet."

Cara laughed. "Wimp."

Tyler smiled. "Yeah. I guess so."

"Anyway, as long as Greta has her gun, I'd say we're pretty safe. I've never seen anyone shoot like that," she said.

"I took shooting lessons for a while," Greta replied.

"Shooting lessons don't make you that good," Cara told her. "My dad is a hell of a shot, but not like you."

"Guess I have a natural ability."

"I paid for the lessons," Tony chimed in.

"A wise investment," Cara said.

"Yeah, she sure saved our asses a few times," Tommy added.

"Well, hopefully I won't have to anymore. Maybe it's over."

"We'll find out, soon," Tony said as the lights of the town center grew brighter in the distance.

As they drove along, they saw something moving in the breakdown lane. The shape was hard to define in the darkness, but the passing headlights flashed across the figure and they could see it was a person.

"Looks like someone's out walking," Tommy said.

"Pull over and see if they need help," Greta told him.

As they drew closer to the walker, the lights revealed them much clearer. Tommy pulled over first, and Kyle and Clyde passed them up before pulling over themselves.

"What the hell is that?" Tommy asked.

"Looks like a British knight, or Ned Kelly and his stupid iron mask," Tyler said.

At first glance, the figure was quite comical. Whomever it was had on a large rectangular helmet and thick dark coveralls. Big padded gloves covered its hands and there was a utility belt strapped across its waist, with several different tools dangling from it. Tony knew right away who it was.

"That's Herbert McElroy," he said, then opened the door and got out.

Herbert stopped and stared at the van. The reflection of the headlights on the helmet's plastic facemask made it hard for either man to see the other's face. But, Tony didn't need to see the man's face to know who he was. There was only one man in Bardstown that would gear up like that to face a hoard of crazy possums—and that was Herbert.

"Herbert! It's Tony."

"Harris?" his muffled voice replied.

"Yep."

Herbert took his helmet off and said, "You know what's going on around here?"

"I sure do."

"You been attacked?"

Tony walked up to him. "Sure have. They killed a lot of good people. You?"

Herbert nodded slightly. "Steve and Gene."

Tony looked at the ground for a second, then met Herbert's eyes again and said, "I'm sorry. They were good men. They got a lot of my good friends, too. Clyde Jefferson is with us, and they almost wiped out his entire bonfire party. I think they've been killing all over the city."

"I heard that on the radio before they attacked. I've been trapped in my shed most of the day. I almost got attacked by some more after I decided to leave, but they played dead on me when I went after them with my machete."

Tony chuckled. "Guess even they knew better than to mess with Herbert McElroy."

Herbert smiled. "They do seem smarter than the average possum."

"Well, we're going into town to try and make sense of all this. I'm guessing you're doing the same."

"Yep."

"Then jump on in and ride with us. We could use another fighter."

"Sounds good to me. Hey, Greta's okay, right?"

"I wouldn't be out here if she wasn't."

"Good—we'll need her in case we run into anymore of these little fuckers. She's a hell of a shot."

Tony rolled his eyes. "Yeah, I know. I keep on hearing about it."

"You always will."

"I know. But, I paid for the lessons."

Herbert chuckled. "I know you did."

"Well, it was a wise investment." Tony returned the smile.

The two men walked back to the van and got in. When the vehicle pulled back onto the highway, the two trucks fell in behind them and they continued rolling into town.

CHAPTER FIFTEEN

It's so dark.
Why can't I breathe?
Where am I?

Ingrid didn't realize she had drifted off to sleep in the trunk of Jeremiah's car. The dark interior was stuffy and she was beginning to feel claustrophobic. Her breathing became shallow; she felt like she passed out from the heat inside that aluminum tomb. It was supposed to be autumn. Why was it so hot? That damned Kentucky weather was never consistent.

But it wasn't the weather. It was the circumstance. Ingrid was trapped in a box surrounded by her death. Not just her own personal death, but the death of everything that was her: mom was gone, and now Jeremiah. What did she have left? Why did she even bother hiding from the possums? She might as well just rise out of this trunk and hand herself over to their hunger. There was nothing left for her now. No reason to keep breathing. Maybe it wasn't the heat suffocating her, but the acknowledgement of the unnecessary continuance of her existence. Perhaps her body was wisely giving up.

Let's go...nothing to see here, it was saying—and so correct it was. Fuck it—time to move on. This will be the first day of the end of her life.

But, on second thought, screw that! These motherfuckers killed her mom and brother. Why should they be permitted to have her, too? If there was a reason to keep breathing, it would be to bring about their destruction—getting revenge for them tearing away her last remaining loved ones. She needed to keep away from their jaws; she needed to stay

179

alive, not out of fear of death, but for need of vengeance. Death was acceptable; but not until her mission to take out as many of these assholes as she could was complete. If she were to die succeeding at that task, then a glorious fall it would surely be.

They were still out there—she could hear them feasting on what remained of Bobby and her brother. She tried to shut those sounds out because it was like they were gnawing on her heart each time she heard them slobbering on flesh. Out on the road, their grunts and snorts carried on the still night air. She feared she might be trapped in the trunk until she died, and would thus miss her chance at reprisal.

Just go away! There's nothing left for you here!

Did they know she was still in there? Is she what they were waiting for?

No way! That's impossible.

Why did they have to hang around then? Couldn't they go find dessert elsewhere? Thankfully, the possums inside the car had given up trying to claw through the seat to get at her. They never quite tore all the way through, but she had heard fabric ripping and really began to fear that they might find their way to her. Good thing they didn't because she had lain unconscious for a span of time she didn't know. If they had spilled into the trunk, she never would have had the chance to defend herself.

Maybe there weren't many of them still hanging around. There was a tire iron in the trunk with her. If there were only a few possums remaining, she might be able to kill them and get away and find the rest. She decided to risk a peek and see what the street looked like.

Her fingers searched the underside of the trunk for the lever. Once she found it, she tinkered with it until it popped and the lid cracked open. Before raising it to look out, she waited and listened for any signs of attack. She expected that any second, possums would begin hurling themselves onto the trunk, trying to dig their way inside. In case that happened, she wanted to be ready, so she felt around for the tire iron and brought it up to her face.

"You can do this, Ingrid," she whispered to herself as she planted her palm on the trunk above her head.

She pushed the trunk open a centimeter at a time until she could squeeze her eye to the crack and glimpse the roadway. When the area around the car became visible, her stomach dropped. Possums still lined the road as far as she could see. Even though her line of sight did not reach a great distance, she could see far enough to know that there was no way she could clear the road with just a tire iron.

For a second, she considered the possibility of escaping back into the car and driving away. As gruesome as the thought was, she figured the little monsters had probably devoured the parts of Bobby and her brother that they would deem edible. Maybe they had mostly departed and only a few stragglers were still hanging around, lapping up the last drops of blood that hadn't congealed to the seats.

It might be a smart plan. But, it might be a fatal one. Would she be fast enough to move from the trunk to the driver's seat, move Jeremiah out of the way, and get the car moving before more possums poured in on her from the broken windshield? And, if she was fast enough, would the car even start? It had taken a pretty severe blow and wouldn't start back up before, what were the chances of it operating now?

No. The plan was too risky and not likely. She was stuck in the trunk until the possums moved on. Until then, all she could do is lie there and be thankful that they seemed to have forgotten about her. Surely, they wouldn't hang around the car forever.

She let the trunk lid lower back down and pulled the little lever until it clicked shut again.

She waited, for more countless minutes, gripping the tire iron and listening to the possums outside.

She waited, lying on her stomach, smelling the carpet inside the trunk, feeling it scrape against her skin each time she moved.

She waited, there in the dark, trying to push the image of her brother being maimed to death by flesh-eating possums out of her mind.

She waited, wondering if she'd ever get out.

She waited, for her moment of escape.

She waited, for possible death.

She waited, until she fell back to sleep.

CHAPTER SIXTEEN

Herbert wiped the remaining blood off of his hammer, sticky from smashing in the head of the last large possum on the street. The group had run into a small pocket of them blocking a side road they needed to turn on from the highway. Major roadwork had blocked the main road into town; they had considered going around the work, but the road was too jacked up to drive down, so they were forced down a more remote path. The problem was they had to drive over the possums, and there were a few of the larger ones among the group.

Clyde and Kyle were able to fire off a few shots, but it was too packed and too dark for them to risk taking too many shots and wasting the bullets, or hitting someone else in the party. Greta was the only one in the group who was a good enough shot to do any real damage. She managed to take out a few, but in the end, Herbert had to jump into the fray and lay waste to the creatures.

His machete did a great deal of damage for a few minutes, but it became too bulky as the possums closed in on him. At first, Tony, Clyde, and Cara were coming forward to help him, but he told them to back off because he had it under control.

"I got the suit. They can't bite me," he'd said.

He then broke out the hammer and went to work. He didn't use his blowtorch due to the space being somewhat enclosed and heavy on foliage. Though a slight rain had fallen earlier, he didn't want to risk setting the small wooded area ablaze. He managed to clear the road. Several of the possums ran, knowing they were facing a formidable foe.

Those that stayed till their demise were quickly kicked into the roadside ditch before the procession moved on.

Clyde's Titan was now leading the cavalcade down the long stretch of dark road. Down there, there were no streetlights, and the moon was too far on the other side of the sky to make a difference. The headlights of his truck were big and bright, but they seemed to somehow die against the dense darkness ahead. Their radius of illumination did not stretch far, and Clyde had to be vigilant for anything that might cause a hitch in their journey.

"That guy's a maniac," Susie said.

"Herbert?"

"Yeah."

"He's got to be, right now. We all got to be. These things out here are vicious. If he didn't go berserk back there, we might all be dead, or stuck, trying to find another way into town."

"We could have just run over all of them."

"Man, there were some big suckers out there. They might have hung one of us up. Down this narrow road, if someone gets hung up, everybody behind them gets hung up, and the rest of the possums would swarm. You know what they can do to a vehicle. We had to do what we had to do."

"I know, but he scares me."

Clyde chuckled. "Old Herbert scares everybody, girl. Don't feel bad."

Two trucks and a van made for a tight squeeze down the narrow road. It curved a couple of times, so sharp that the large vehicles had to slow nearly to a stop to make it without sliding into the ditch. They passed a large farm, heading east. The moon was to the northwest, full and bright, shining just above the tip of a silo beyond the three-story farmhouse in the middle of the field. In Kyle's truck, Jessica noticed the dark shapes moving along the farm.

"I think there are some over there," she said.

Kyle looked and saw them, too. There weren't many, but enough to have killed anyone caught out in the field. The way they were gathered in one section far from the house made him fear that was indeed what had happened.

"Hopefully they stay over there," he said, and they did. He looked in the rearview mirror as they passed. None had followed.

They drove on, with the woods to their left and the last section of the farm to their right. They left the house, the moon, and the silo behind them, towering above the hungry possums in the dark. The lights at the center of town could be glimpsed sparkling through the trees a few miles away as they took the last curve in the road that sent them northeast. When the convoy emerged from the trees onto a stretch of road that was a little more open, with only small sections of woodlands scattered along it, they saw a large mass of possums lumped together up ahead.

"More possums," Clyde said. "I know Tommy's got to see that."

He slowed the Titan to a stop several yards away from the swarm. Tommy pulled the van up next to him and Kyle stopped behind them.

"You see that?" Clyde asked Tommy.

"Sure do."

"Guess we need to take them out."

"Damn right we do."

"It looks like they're gathered around a car," Susie said.

Beside Tommy, Tony confirmed, "They are."

"I bet they got somebody," Tommy added.

"Well, let's go get *them*," said Tony.

"Kill your headlights," Clyde said. "We'll try and sneak up on these fuckers."

The lamps on the Titan and the van went out.

Behind them, Jessica said to Kyle, "Turn your lights off."

Kyle did so and all went dark along the street. This time, the sky above them was clear with no thick branches hanging overhead; there was enough moonlight to catch the animal silhouettes moving in the road.

Clyde rolled the Titan slowly ahead and stopped about a hundred feet from the swarm. He noticed the car was up against a streetlight. It looked to be the only light on the street, and it was out. There were no other lights to be seen.

Clyde stepped out and said to Susie, "Stay in here."

The van doors opened and closed behind him. Greta, Cara, and Tony were the first to emerge and stand beside him. Tommy joined them a few seconds later with Tyler behind him. Herbert came staggering out last in his bulky gear.

"Stay with the car, Tommy," Tony said.

"Hell no," was his brother's reply.

"Somebody's got to keep it running just in case."

"Let Tyler do it," Greta said.

Tony looked at her questioningly, but she said, "No offense to Tyler, but he can't shoot or fight. But, he can drive."

"She's right," Tyler said. "I'll man the van."

"But you did pretty well back at our house," Tony said

"I don't know what I was doing. I just went nuts. I got lucky. I'll stay with the van."

Tyler returned to the van—a little too eagerly for Tony's liking—and got behind the wheel. He didn't turn it back on out of fear of rousing the possums.

Kyle came up beside them. He had left Jessica in the truck. Neither she nor Susie could shoot, but like Tyler, they could watch the vehicles. Kyle had his shotgun ready. Everyone was armed with their weapon of choice. Cara didn't have a gun anymore, so she hung back. But, if the fight got close, she was ready to kill.

"Anybody got an extra piece?" Herbert asked.

Nobody did.

"I'll walk behind you guys. If you run out of bullets, I'll start splitting skulls."

"Fair enough," Tony said.

"I'll walk with you," Cara told him.

"Be my guest."

Greta, Clyde, Tony, Tommy, and Kyle all formed a line and walked slowly towards the possums; Cara and Herbert stayed just a few steps behind. When the five in front were close enough to start shooting, they aimed their guns.

"Wait," Cara said.

They waited, and Tony asked," What?"

"What if somebody's in the car?"

"Then they're probably dead."

"They might not be. They might be locked inside, hiding from the possums."

"She's got a point, Tony," Greta said.

"What can we do then? They're all gathered around the vehicle?"

Before anyone could answer, Herbert ran around the group, off to the side, lifted off his helmet, and started yelling, "Hey! Over here you assholes! Yeah, that's it. Right here. Come and get it, you fucks!"

All of the possums by the car turned their attention to Herbert, who was several feet to the left of Greta and the gang. Another series of those deep, wild barks sounded in the direction of the car. Hearing them again gave Clyde chills.

Once the barks were over, the possums began migrating towards Herbert. He looked at his allies and said, "Fire away."

He slid his helmet back on and went to rejoin the group.

"They're kind of hard to see," Tony said.

"You got your spotlight, Kyle?" Clyde asked.

"It's in the truck, man," Kyle replied.

"I got my Maglite," Herbert said and pulled it out and turned it on.

The beam was strong, but did not reach far enough to cast sufficient light upon the attackers.

"That's not enough," Clyde said.

The Titan's headlights suddenly came on and the entire group of possums was bathed in the bright, white lights, setting their angry eyes aglow.

"How's that, baby?" Susie yelled from inside the truck.

Greta smiled at Clyde and said, "What would you all do without us?"

"You'll never hear the end of that, Clyde," Tony said.

"Oh well," Clyde said and fired the first shot, taking down one fat possum.

The others opened up fire and the possums went down one by one. Some broke away and ran off into the dark, but most were gunned down, including another one of the large ones. The gunfire went on for a few minutes, until most of them had run out of ammo.

One of the large possums had broken away into the trees and tried to flank the party, but Cara caught it sneaking up behind them. As it made its way for Tommy, Cara stepped in to intercept it, knelt on the ground, held out her knife and waited. The creature made a movement to jump, but Cara sprang forward with her arm outstretched, thrusting the blade before her, and rammed it straight into the massive marsupial's right eye, all the way to the brain. The force with which she drove herself against it

186

overpowered its body and sent its corpse crashing to the ground in front of her. She stood over her kill and wiped the blade along her shirt.

"Impressive," Herbert said. "I think we might be related."

Cara smiled. "Except I don't need all that armor."

Herbert chuckled and nodded. "Fair enough, girl."

The party walked ahead to survey the scene. All the possums were dead, unless there were some still in the car. Herbert approached the front of the vehicle, pulled out his machete, and turned the Maglite back on. He pointed the flashlight at the car, looked inside, and grimaced.

"Man, looks like two dudes got ate up over here." He shined the light on the shattered windshield, then up at the streetlight. "The streetlamp fell and busted the windshield when they hit the pole. I bet that's how the possums got in."

"I guess no one survived this one, then," Kyle said.

"Guess not—no possums left alive, either," Tony said. "Let's move on."

They returned to their vehicles—Tyler giving the van driver's seat back to Tommy—started them up, and began to drive off. The Titan passed first, then the van. As Kyle's truck drove away, Jessica saw the trunk of the crashed car fly open. She turned in her seat and rolled down the window.

"What's going on?" Kyle asked.

"Slow down!"

She leaned her head out the window and thought she saw someone getting out of the trunk of the car.

"Stop for a second."

With her head still out the window, Jessica thought she heard a woman's voice calling after them.

"There's someone back there!"

"Really?"

"Yes! Yes! Go back!"

Kyle flicked his headlights over and over to get the van's attention. It worked. Tommy stopped and flicked his lights at Clyde, who stopped the Titan when he noticed the van falling behind. Both Tommy and Clyde put their vehicles in reverse and stopped near Kyle.

Kyle leaned out the window and yelled, "There's somebody back there! I'm going to get them."

He backed up quickly, all the way to the car, and stopped when he saw a woman with reddish-black hair standing in the road. She approached the driver's side window.

"You okay?" he asked.

"I am now," Ingrid said. "I've been trapped in that trunk all day."

"Oh...so you knew those guys back there?"

"I did. One was my brother, Jeremiah. Our mother was killed this morning in our front yard."

"Barbara Jones?"

"Yeah."

"I heard about that on the radio. I'm sorry."

"Can't do anything about it now. Do you mind giving me a lift?"

"Not at all. Get in beside Jessica. My name's Kyle."

"Thank you. I'm Ingrid."

"Pleased to meet you, even if the circumstances are shitty."

Ingrid went around the back of the truck towards the passenger side, and as she passed, she glanced into the bed and saw the hideous creature dead on the metal. She winced and continued on.

When she climbed in with Jessica scooting to the middle, she said, "Is that one of the possums in the bed back there?"

"Sure is." Kyle flicked his lights at the others, signaling them to move on.

"I've never seen a possum that big before."

"Nobody has," Kyle replied, moving along behind the van. "Some of them are huge. I can't tell you where they came from or why they got so big, though."

"They're disgusting," Jessica said.

"That they are," Ingrid agreed and looked out the window.

"We're going into town. You got anywhere to be?"

"Nope. We were just trying to get away from them when we left our house, after they attacked us."

"They attacked us at a bonfire—killed all our friends, Jessica's sister, too. We're just going into town to see what's happening. Hopefully, we'll get some answers."

Ingrid shook her head and leaned back in her seat. She didn't need to know. She didn't want to know. She just wanted the nightmare to end, if that were possible. Somehow, she doubted she'd ever wake from it. If she did, she wanted her revenge, first.

CHAPTER SEVENTEEN

C hip's wound bled like a fresh bullet hole for quite a while. He went to the town doctor and her receptionist told him that she had gone to lunch and never come back. If Chip had half a brain to think beyond his own needs, he might have realized that was very odd behavior. For an alleged news journalist, he was sometimes not very perceptive.

The immediate care center wasn't far from the doctor's office, so he made the trip over there. As soon as he walked in, he was shocked by the amount of people waiting in the emergency room. The room was passed capacity and folks were standing up all over the place. Many of them had bloody bandages stuck to or wrapped around some part of their bodies.

"What's the issue?" the slim young man behind the counter asked.

"Possum bit my leg and arm."

The lad raised his eyebrows. "Another one?"

"Has this been happening a lot?"

"Just about everyone in here was bitten by a possum. It's really strange. I wonder if it's possums that killed those people."

"I'd be willing to bet on it," Chip said and signed in.

After a couple of hours, Chip got checked and the doctor told him there was a slight infection but nothing to be concerned about. She cleaned and dressed the wound, wrote him a prescription for an antibiotic and painkiller then sent him on his way.

Now, he was loading the van and getting ready to follow a story involving gunshots fired on some back roads and a possum infestation somewhere in town. He took the painkiller but it didn't help much, and he

190

didn't know if the antibiotic was doing any good, yet. But, he felt feverish and achy but also very robust and jumpy—like he was caught in the grips of an anxiety attack, which he'd never had before. People were really starting to get on his nerves—which wasn't new for him—and he felt like punching the cameraman because he wasn't moving fast enough.

"Come on, Chuck!" he yelled as the lanky cameraman heaved the big handheld into the back of the van.

"Where the fuck is the driver?" Chip snapped, but the driver was already behind the wheel.

"I'm right here, Chip," he said.

Chip turned away and ignored him.

Bunch of assholes.

One of the crew members brushed past him and accidentally bumped his hand, and it nearly sent Chip into a rage.

"Why don't you watch what you're doing, dickface?"

The crewman—a short, gangly fellow with shabby hair and bug eyes—looked at him with his mouth in a circle.

"Don't look at me like that, you freakish bastard. Watch where you're going next time, and if you ever bump my hand again, I'll stick yours so far up your ass you'll be able to jerk-off your tonsils."

The crewman's mouth moved soundlessly and it took Chip all the restraint he possessed to not repeatedly knee him in the balls until he died.

"Get in the van before I shit in my hand and stuff it in your mouth!" Not even Chip knew where that insane threat came from.

Once the crewman decided that he wanted to endure no more of Chip's strange and unusual verbal abuse and threats, he scurried off into the van. Chip climbed into the passenger seat and asked, "Everybody in?"

A bunch of weak responses issued from the back caused Chip to turn angrily in his seat. "What the hell did you dickless twits say?"

They responded louder and in the affirmative.

"Good—and if not, then those who didn't make it are missing the bus. Fuck 'em. Get moving to wherever this damn shooting was heard."

The driver backed out of the news station parking lot and sped off down the road. Chip looked in the back and saw Chuck the cameraman, Harold the sound guy, and that mealy-mouthed little prick that had bumped his hand. He believed his name was Tanner, or some pansy-ass name like that. He wanted to bash the chump's head in with the camera and he didn't even know why. The guy had never affronted him. In fact, Chip hired him because he liked his spunk and his wit. But now, he just wanted to stuff razorblades up his ass and in his cock-hole and watch him bleed out.

Where's all this violence coming from? I'm not a violent man. In fact, I know I'm a complete wimp.

Chip had never been in a fight in his entire life. He was always too afraid of getting hurt or having his face messed up. A friend of his in high school compared him to some vain British character from an old boxing game for Super Nintendo—the Narcissist, or Prince Vanity, or something dumb like that—that became enraged if you managed to actually hit him in the face. Chip didn't know about all that, but he knew that getting hit by another human being was not his idea of a good time. Not only that, people rarely made him mad because his supercilious nature prohibited him from being affected by the opinions of others.

So, why now? Why all this anger and sudden propensity towards violence? It was rather alarming; and, what was more unnerving was that he actually realized it wasn't right, but he could do nothing to stop it.

The news van hit a bump in the road, jarring Chip's body and making his teeth clack together. He yelled at the driver, "What the fuck are you doing? Where did you learn to drive, fuck-nuts? The Amazon Jungle?"

"There was a pothole. I didn't see it."

"Well, next time, see it! Or I'll pothole your damn skull!"

The men in the back were nervous. Chuck, who had known Chip the longest, said, "You alright, Chip?"

Chip whirled around madly. "Yes, I'm alright! Are *you* alright?"

"I'm fine."

"Not for long if you don't shut that hole in your face!"

Watching Chip's face distort in anger, Chuck was suddenly reminded of the very angry man from the film, *Titanic,* who had threatened to throw Kathy Bates off the lifeboat if she didn't sit down and keep quiet. Chip looked like he might throw Chuck from the van if he asked him another question, so he didn't say anything else.

After a few more miles of feeling like he was going to blow, Chip started shaking his leg and tapping his fingers on the dashboard. The driver looked at him and asked, "Are you alright, Chip?"

"If any of you pencil-dick, eraser-nuts, motherfuckers asks me that again, I'm going to eat your fucking eyeballs right out of their sockets. Do you understand?"

The driver then got angry. "Look man, you need to chill. You've been hurling threats and insults at us since you got back from the hospital. There's no need for that bullshit."

The fever that had been creeping around inside Chip's head suddenly seized control of him as he listened to this lowly van driver scold him. The heat grabbed hold of his neck, tightening it up, and travelled down his spine. When it reached the base, it exploded in a ball of fire, raging through his stomach, rushing through his veins, and pounding in his heart. His next actions were beyond his control. A primal scream escaped his lips and he threw himself at the driver, grabbing him by his flabby throat and leaning in towards his face with his mouth open.

The men in the back screamed as Chip bit down on the driver's right eye socket, squeezing the eye right out and smashing it between his teeth. The van swerved as he felt the jelly-like substance ooze onto his tongue. The sensation made him want more. He chomped down on the left eye just as the van bashed against something hard and stopped moving, knocking him off the driver, who was knocked out cold after hitting his head on the windshield.

Chip rose up and looked at the men in the back with the driver's left eye dangling from his mouth; he breathed so hard that spittle exploded from between his lips.

"What the fuck man!" Harold screamed.

Chip lunged into the back of the van, landing on the sound guy, clutching and tearing at his throat until blood was spraying all over the interior. Chuck grabbed Chip around the neck, but Chip grabbed his fingers and broke three of them one-by-one. Chuck yelled and let go. Then, there was mealy-mouth—he was looking at Chip in a horror-stricken state that the newsman would have found comical if he wasn't in the grips of some frightening fury.

He roared at the man and went after him. The man tried to back out of the van but Chip grabbed the back of his leg, pushed up his pants leg, and began digging his fingernails into the meat. The man wailed and rolled over. His feet flew out to kick Chip away, but Chip was impervious to the impact at the moment and flung himself on top of the man and started bashing his face in with his fists. The skin of his hands cracked and broke, and he felt bones move inside them, but he kept pounding until the man's face was mush.

Chip's fists sufficed so well as tenderizers that there were facial chunks smeared on his knuckles. He stopped pounding for a second and examined his hands. Seeing the pieces of mealy-mouth's meat dangling from his fingers, he became hungry. It began as a soft rumble in his gut and in seconds was a raging voracity. He began licking and chewing the chunks from his hands, relishing the rewards of his newfound barbarianism.

Chuck sat back against the wall of the van, watching in terror as Chip eagerly licked away the remains of mealy-mouth's face that were squashed on his hands. Once he had devoured it all, he gazed down at his victim's battered cranium and, breathing heavily, put his face in the pulpy mess of the man's former head and started eating what was left.

Chuck was aghast at this display of inhumanity before him. The sight and sounds made by Chip's animalistic feasting twisted his guts like a wringer. Chuck gagged and wretched, and then threw up against the wall and carpet in the back of the van. When he was done, he looked up and saw that Chip had turned his way.

Chuck wiped the vomit from his lips. "Look Chip, calm down. You're not yourself."

Chip wiped the blood from his chin, still breathing heavily, and said, "I am myself. I am me. I am Chip."

"What the fuck are you talking about?"

"I am going to eat you."

Chuck held up his left hand, his right hand going for the camera. "No, man. You're not going to do that. You're not some fucking zombie."

"No! I am not a zombie! Not anymore! I am free!" he called, rising up on his knees and shaking his fists in the air.

After Chip uttered that odd declaration, Chuck lifted the camera and jammed it into Chip's face, knocking him back. The impact split the skin

194

on his forehead and busted his nose. Blood now gushed down his face, but Chip was still in primal form, and he simply leapt up and grabbed at Chuck.

The cameraman started punching, but it did no good. Chip kept coming. It did not take him long to force the skinny man down and take a bite of his face, right beside the nose. Chuck screamed and Chip bit down again, this time tearing away part of Chuck's right cheek. He then went for the throat, digging his teeth into Chuck's Adam's apple and ripping it completely out. Chuck's scream was choked off as blood spurted and flowed from the wound. Chip savored the taste of the blood and started eating his old friend.

Minutes passed into nearly an hour as Chip went from body to body, eating the parts he most desired. The driver woke up when Chip crawled up behind him, from the back, and bit down on the right side of his neck. The driver screamed, but only for a few seconds, for death soon took him as it had the others.

It seemed there was no satiating the churning vortex within Chip's belly and so he ate and ate. The kill felt so good. Watching these men die made him feel like a king, like a warrior, and devouring them made him feel liberated from some ages-long oppression. When he opened the van doors and climbed out, he felt like the world was his. The fever was gone and he felt stronger than ever.

Looking around, he saw that the van had smashed into a parked car in someone's driveway on an unlit dead-end street. He wanted to eat some more people, or animals—he didn't care which—and so he began walking into town because he knew that was the place to hunt.

He thought about what Chuck had said, about him being a zombie. Chip wanted to eat flesh, but he wasn't dead, and he was completely lucid. His mind was alive and aware and remembered everything about his life. He didn't harbor some mindless urge to murder—not at all. He knew he was anchorman Chip James; he knew he had just killed and eaten members of his crew, and that an act of that nature was something that would land him either in prison or a mental facility. He remembered being bitten by the possum, and he recalled everything bizarre that had happened that day. Now, he just wanted to slaughter the living and devour their remains. He didn't know why, and he didn't care. It just felt like that was what he was supposed to do—what he needed to do.

There was a large guardrail at the end of the street to keep cars from passing into the next neighborhood. Why that was even there, he didn't know. There was nothing but another clip of road on the other side. The rail separated a more well-to-do neighborhood from a working class one and he thought that might have something to do with it. The snobs couldn't have the laborers coming in and infecting their neighborhoods with their work ethic and social values. Chip understood. He didn't like people that were less than him, either.

After crossing the guardrail, he turned a corner and came across a large band of animals moving around in the dark. He stopped mere feet from their gathering and watched as they ate a group of dead people. At first he was scared, remembering what that possum had done to him earlier at the home of Rachel Owens. But, as he watched them eat the flesh and the innards of these freshly eviscerated corpses, he felt like he understood their previous attack on him. It was nothing personal, but a duty and necessity.

The fear was soon replaced by hunger. He stepped over to the crowd and many of them looked up at him. He thought they would attack, but they only stared. After a few seconds, they went back to eating. Deciding he could no longer take the torment of watching them dine on what he too craved, he walked past several of them, to the nearest body, and knelt on the ground beside them.

They were everywhere, all around him, and could have easily destroyed him. He waited for them to do so. But, they never did. They didn't acknowledge him further. Once he decided he was safe from their assault, he dug his face into the open belly and started lapping and chewing up the offering laid there before him.

CHAPTER EIGHTEEN

The night was now dark—as dark as it could possibly be. This was when they were at their best. Together, they made their way down the pitch black roads, through the deepest woods, and the tallest grassy fields. They hungered—searched for sustenance. No longer sated by the plants, the insects, or the food humans laid out for other animals; they craved flesh. Years of omnivorous living had weakened their kind. It had been an adaptive move to survive. Their place on the food chain had dwindled through the ages. Once proud predators, they were now relegated to hiding under homes and in dark places, playing dead when threatened. No more. The masters had returned. They were calling to them. Humans would no longer dominate the land.

Now, there was rage. Something beyond the need to rise back up the food chain. This was different. This was fury. There was something in their veins that hadn't been there before, not even in the earliest days of their kind's existence.

The need went beyond mere hunger or thirst. There was a longing to kill, to maim, and to feel the breaking of flesh beneath the teeth. There was a need to smell fear. No longer would they be subjected to releasing their bodily waste as a means to ward off predators. No longer would they be the prey. The old days were on the rise again. They had never been kings, but they were once greater than this, and soon they would be again. The masters would see to it.

Along they went, biting and chewing their way through any human or animal that got in their way. But, they hated the humans most. The need to kill *them* was strongest. There was some connection now between them and man that was not there before. This was new, like the rage.

Barks in the distant night heralded the arrival of their new, but old, leaders. Their queens and kings had risen and returned. Where there was death and nothingness, there was now life. There was now strength. There was a new tide.

Intellect in their breed had long been overlooked, though they were far sharper than credited. Smarter, they were, than the smaller animals that raced through the fields. Stronger, they were, than those who resided in the trees and the meadows. Even the long, slimy, creatures that moved with ease along the ground, striking fear into the hearts of men, could not match them. Yes—some had bites that were deadly, slowly bringing humans and other animals to death, but these bites did not affect their breed. Bites from the dirt riders were of no consequence to them. Their poison died in the veins of the great and mighty possum.

Now, they would all know fear. Possums were no longer going to hide in the shadows and wait to be defeated beneath man's mighty machines. They would no longer fall prey to the powerful thunder sticks with which they brought down other animals. They would no longer die in the mouths and beneath the paws of those other animals—not now that the masters had arrived. Their old predators, long gone, could no longer stand in their way. Lost in time those were, yet the possum had endured. Soon, their kind would rightfully reign over the kingdom.

In the heart of the territory they were now conquering, every possum in the land converged. They emerged from the shadows of the woods. They walked down the empty roads. They crawled from beneath many buildings. They rose from the tunnels under the land. Out they came, in numbers they didn't know they possessed, hundreds upon hundreds, into the center of the land, where the night sky was made brightest by man's tall torches, where the people were present, where they could feast.

Down from the distant hills, the masters came, calling to them all. Filled with the glory of the past days and the rage born in these new ones, they knew it was truly time to conquer and kill.

The possums of Bardstown gathered and marched through the night, prepared for their war to gain preeminence.

CHAPTER NINETEEN

The town lights were now visible up the road. Clyde, Tommy, and Kyle had entered the district from the southwest, heading northeast through the back roads. They turned onto the main road heading towards the roundabout—Clyde first, then Tommy, and then Kyle. None of them was entirely sure what they were going to do once there, but Tony's plan was to round up a team, hunt the possums down, and exterminate them. Once they entered the town square, they all realized that wasn't going to happen.

The main section of the city was in chaos, every bit as bad, or worse, than any of the back roads and neighborhoods where they had been. People were dead all over the square: on the sidewalks, on the stoops of businesses, and out in the street. Possums dined on a smorgasbord of dead and dying humans. There were still some small groups of people or individuals making a stand, and many dead possums lay about the roads, but the defensive was to no avail. All over the square, man was brought down.

A lot of shop doors were wide open, windows broken in others, possums raiding the buildings that still had lights burning. There were a couple of businesses on fire; someone had even smashed into a fire hydrant on the side of the road and it was blowing up like a geyser. It looked like a full-scale riot had erupted in town.

"This isn't good," Tommy said to Tony.

"No, it sure isn't," Tony agreed.

"We got much ammo left?" Tyler asked.

"Not really," Greta said. "We got enough for maybe one more good fight."

"Well, there are probably at least ten good fights left out here," Tony said.

Clyde navigated the carnage slowly, trying his best not to defile any human corpses with his tires, but it was impossible not to. He felt the truck roll over the dead, heard the bones cracking underneath. Those in the van watched from behind as limbs were crushed and severed from the bodies, twisted and mangled by the truck's wheels, and as internal organs exploded from their orifices; some of the bodies burst apart, spraying gore. All but Tommy turned away, because he was the unfortunate one who had to keep his eye on the road. He wanted to stop but knew he couldn't, so he pulled up slowly behind the Titan, ignoring the horror and following its path.

"Man, this shit is crazy," Clyde said to Susie. "I can't believe what I'm seeing."

"What are we going to do?"

"I don't know. Leave town altogether, I guess."

Clyde bounced over some broken items in the street and then squeezed between two broken down cars—one against the left side of the street and the other right in the middle. He had to gun the brakes a few times to get around it, and when he finally broke free, he zoomed out a little too quickly. The van followed suit, and was able to get through a little easier. Kyle, seeing the congestion that lay ahead, veered to the right of the car in the middle of the road and headed towards the roundabout.

"What are you doing?" Jessica asked.

"I'm getting the hell out of here. Look around us, this place has had it."

"Wait; hold on, Kyle, calm down. You're not thinking clearly. We need to stick with the others. We don't want to get separated. Don't you agree, Ingrid?"

She turned pleadingly to Ingrid, but Ingrid really had no preference. She really didn't care. They could stay and fight or ride off to die in the dark. It made no difference to her.

"It's up to you all," she said.

"But, don't you think it would be smarter if we all stuck together?"

"There would probably be a better chance of survival, but not much. There are so many of them, they'd run us all down."

"She's right, Jessica. We got to get out of here. If Clyde and Tommy are smart, they'll follow us."

Kyle drove around the courthouse at the roundabout and headed away from downtown, further along Stephen Foster Avenue. It was the most lighted path, and it would lead to the expressway. Kyle was heading out of the city altogether.

"Where are we going?"

"I'll ride to Shepherdsville. Maybe the Bullitt County sheriffs can help us. That should be far enough away from this mess."

Jessica took her cell phone out and dialed Susie's number. Susie picked up after three rings.

"Where are you guys going?" Susie asked.

"Shepherdsville—you guys should come, too."

"Where are they going?" Clyde asked.

"Shepherdsville."

Clyde looked around at the square and said, "Sounds good to me."

"We're coming, too," Susie told Jessica.

"Okay. Hurry up!" Jessica ended the call. "Susie and Clyde are coming, too."

Kyle eased up. "Good. See? I told you shit was too fucked up around here."

Ingrid looked at Jessica. "Why don't you just use your cell to call the police?"

"I already tried. They aren't answering anywhere in the county."

Clyde rolled down the window and waved for the van to follow him, and then pointed off towards the roundabout where Kyle went, then waved again.

"What does that mean?" Tommy asked.

"I think he wants us to follow him," Tony replied.

"Are we going to?"

"I don't know," Tony hesitated.

Greta leaned towards the front and put her face between them and said, "Baby, there's nothing to save here. You saw what they did to all those men back at the house. There are just too many out here and no one left to help us fight them. Let's follow Clyde and get the hell out of here."

Tony nodded and said, "Agreed. Follow Clyde, Tommy."

Tommy honked to let Clyde know he understood. Clyde then began to take off, but a fat swell of possums got beneath him, jamming up the wheels of the truck. Some of the possums bit the dust, spraying up blood and chunks of internal organs that landed on the hood of the truck. There were enough to get him stuck for a second. He gunned his engine and was eventually able to break free. The van got caught up behind him, but was able to get out pretty quickly. But, somewhere between that stall and the courthouse at the roundabout, Clyde had picked up a lot of speed trying to get out of town, and Tommy did the same behind him. When they got near the center of the circle, something large, round, and black that Clyde didn't see at first came into view too late for him to swerve and miss it. The hefty object got caught up in his wheel and jammed the tire, breaking the CV axel and causing the truck to turn and slam into a large stone monument next to the courthouse.

This happened so quickly that Tommy had little time to react. All he could do was stomp on the breaks and turn the steering wheel to try and avoid Clyde's Titan. None of this did anything to keep the van from wrecking into the truck. When Tommy had turned the wheel, his side of the van smashed into Clyde's side of the truck. Luckily for Clyde, the impact of his truck hitting the monument pushed him and Susie closer to the passenger side, so when the driver's door caved in, Clyde was not there to feel the effect. Tommy, on the other hand, took a hard knock to the skull, breaking the window and lacerating his head. When his head ricocheted off the window, it snapped back into Tony's, who had slammed up against his brother.

In the back of the van, the door popped open and Tyler fell out. Cara was knocked against the wall of the back driver's side, and Greta was sent rolling backwards towards the doors, but stopped midway through. Herbert didn't go very far. He was up against the passenger side wall in the back when it happened, and only banged up against the wall a couple of times.

Tyler rolled onto his back and sat up, looking around at the square. He spotted a large group of possums, some of them quite big, looking at them from about fifty feet away.

"Hey you guys. We've been spotted."

Clyde heard him and looked towards the square and saw the animals watching them.

"Open the door," he told Susie. "We're going to have to run."

Susie opened the door and got out; Clyde followed behind her. Just as he came around to the van, Herbert was helping Tyler to his feet and Cara was sliding out with Greta behind her. Tony and Tommy were pretty well banged up in the front and Greta went to help her husband.

"Somebody might want to get the guns," Tyler said.

"Greta?" Clyde called. "Get the guns. We're about to have company— and a few of them are those big motherfuckers."

"Hold on," Greta said. "I'm trying to help Tony and Tommy."

Just then, two of the large possums stood up and started barking, reminding Clyde of the Velociraptors from *Jurassic Park*. He knew what that meant and started to get jittery, with Susie biting her lip next to him and grabbing his elbow.

"Come on, Greta! They're coming."

Greta looked back and saw the possums begin to creep towards them. "Oh shit!" she said. "Come on, Tony."

The possums were lumbering across the square—seventy to a hundred of them—several were large, a few of them *very* large, and all of them snorting and snarling, caked in blood, with their dilated eyes glowing in the shimmering streetlights. If the humans had their weapons in full force, they could make a stand, but no one had any ammo left besides Greta and Clyde, and neither of them had very much.

"Greta?" Clyde said. "Tell me where the ammo is and I'll get it."

"There's not enough left to fight all of them. We're going to have to run."

"Where the hell are we going to go?" Tyler asked.

Cara pointed down the street towards a large stone building. "The County History Museum."

"Sounds good," Clyde said. "Let's go. Greta, come on!"

"You guys go; we'll be along in a second."

"No way!"

"Listen to her, Clyde!" Tony said groggily, feeling the effects from knocking skulls with his brother. "No sense in you guys hanging around."

"I ain't leaving y'all."

"Get the others to the museum. You're the only one with any bullets left other than me," Greta told him.

Clyde nodded and relented. "Come on you all." He started jogging towards the two-story stone building down the street.

Herbert hung back and said, "I ain't running."

Clyde stopped. "Come on, Herbert. Don't go all psycho right now. Save that shit for later."

Greta managed to get Tony out of the car. His head was bleeding and he was barely conscious. His head had hit Tommy's pretty hard. Tommy was disoriented and Greta tried to wake him up.

She leaned in and shook him hard. "Come on, Tommy."

"What's going on?" he mumbled and looked at her, blood running down his face.

Tony was awake, but leaning on Greta. She looked at Tommy and said, "We're about to get ripped apart. Get out and let's go."

Tommy's eyes widened and he started to look around. When he finally realized where he was, he nodded and started to wiggle free from the car. When he tried to pull his right leg up, he yelled in pain.

"Shit!"

"What?"

"I think my leg's broken, and it's stuck."

Greta looked at his leg, saw it was twisted at an unnatural angle, and smashed between the door and the seat. In that very second, she knew Tommy could not be moved from that spot.

"Oh shit."

Tommy sighed. "Yep. I think I'll be staying here for a while."

Greta's eyes began to water. Tony woke up a little more and said, "Fuck that, get out of the van!"

His speech was a little slurred, but he was coming back around. He reached in for Tommy's hand and tried to pull him out.

"Come on, bro!" he said with more force.

Tommy pulled away. "My leg is fucked, man. I ain't going anywhere. How about you two just take off for the museum and lead the possums away from me? Does that sound like a good plan?"

Greta looked behind her. The possums were almost upon them and edging closer. Herbert, like the maniac he was, was walking right towards them.

"Come on, you little bastards," he said as he pulled out his machete. "I'm ready to dance!"

The others were almost to the museum. They were well ahead of any possums—mainly because the majority of the animals were now heading towards Greta and the wreck at the roundabout. The madman in the helmet and coveralls stood in the street, several feet from the crashed vehicles, and was taunting the possums. His brazen challenges seemed to stall them momentarily; Greta thought, for a second, they may have been studying him, trying to figure out what they were up against.

No damn way! They aren't that smart.

Tommy wouldn't budge despite how hard Tony tried to pull him. Eventually, Tony gave up when Tommy yelled at him to stop.

"I can't leave you, brother!" Tony was on the verge of tears.

"You got to, bro. Just give me the gun and lead the fuckers away. They may not even notice me. You know I mean?"

"Yeah," Tony said weakly and without much hope.

"So, we have a deal?"

Tony nodded. "Give him the gun, Greta."

She turned back to look at Tony, then Tommy, and handed her brother-in-law the gun. "There are only a few shots left."

Tommy took it and nodded. "If I have to use them, I'll make them count. Now go!"

Greta lead Tony from the van, he stumbled at first but was able to gain his footing. When he did, he stopped and looked back at the van.

"We didn't close the doors!"

Greta glanced over her shoulder and saw the possums were too near for them to return and shut the van doors.

"Don't look back," she told him.

Ignoring her, he yelled, "Love you brother!"

"Yeah, yeah—I know," Tommy yelled back. "But, I love you, too."

"Stop yelling at Tommy," Greta told Tony. "When he yells back, he'll draw their attention. We need to draw them away from him."

"I think Herbert's doing a pretty good job of that."

Herbert stood several yards away, still brandishing his machete. "What are you assholes waiting for, huh? An invitation?"

The possums continued to look at him quizzically.

"Well, here it is." He held out his machete. "I cordially invite you all to come get fucked!"

Amid the ruckus around the square—the fire alarms, smoke detectors, fire hydrant water shooting into the air, random car alarms, dogs barking in the distance, and the moans of the dying folk on the ground—those familiar barks rang out from somewhere behind the courthouse, catching everyone's attention.

Herbert lowered his machete to listen. Greta and Tony stopped halfway to the museum. Clyde and the others stopped mere feet from the sidewalk in front of the large stone building. In the van, Tommy sunk low in the seat, not wanting to be seen by whatever was making the bone-chilling noise.

Soon, the collective sound of those familiar snorts, hisses, growls, and snarls began to swallow the night, drowning out all other sounds. Claws began to scrape and skitter in unison from around the courthouse just before hundreds more possums came into view.

"Oh fuck," Herbert said.

He tucked his machete back into its holder and took off towards the museum, but found his path blocked by possums. When he looked back towards the courthouse, he saw the new swarm had melded with the other swarm and formed a tide so large that nothing short of the National Guard could stave off their surge. So, he ran into the dark, away from Stephen Foster Avenue, away from the roundabout, and away from the museum. He bolted into the shadows of the empty buildings with psychotic possums on his tail. As he vanished into the shade, several caught up to him and were biting on his pants, clinging to his sleeves, but they could not bring him down. He dashed down the road and vacated the square with several possums clinging to his clothes.

"Can you run?" Greta asked Tony.

"Yes," he said and they began to run towards the museum.

"Come on you guys!" Clyde yelled.

He and the others had mounted the sidewalk and were headed towards the museum just a few feet away. As they passed an alley between that building and another, a couple dozen possums raced from the darkness, separating Clyde and Susie from Cara and Tyler. Clyde and Susie backed away towards the museum and Clyde took a few shots, emptying what was left in the gun: three shots, but only one dead possum. Cara and Tyler took off across the street, Cara leaving Tyler in the dust.

A few possums turned towards Clyde and Susie; they took off down the sidewalk and up through the museum courtyard then banged against the front door with the possums nearly at their heels.

"Anybody there? Let us in!"

Clyde saw someone inside, heading for the door. It was a woman with teal hair and black glasses flanked by a man in a dark robe. The possums were almost upon them, and he pounded the door harder.

"Come on, come on!"

The figure opened the door and Clyde and Susie practically fell inside. Clyde shut the door and asked, "Either of you got a gun?"

"Yes," the young lady said and held up a snub nose revolver.

"Can you shoot?"

"Not very well."

He took the gun from her and opened the door.

"Hey!" she said.

The possums were on the porch and Clyde's shots did not miss. Heads exploded, faces burst open, and bodies were riddled with holes as each one fell dead before Greta and Tony came up to the porch. They slid right past Clyde and the door slammed shut.

Just after they stepped inside, they heard Greta's pistol going off over by the courthouse. Tony blocked it out and choked back his tears because he knew, at that moment, that he would never see his brother alive again.

He was correct. Possums had swarmed the van. Tommy managed to kill a few before his bullets ran out. He broke one's neck before one of the big ones got him by the throat and tore the flesh from it. He was dead by the time they had torn his belly open.

Jacob Floyd

CHAPTER TWENTY

Cara ran as hard as she could with Tyler struggling to keep up. Even though she was several feet in front of him, she could still hear him panting. She made up her mind that she wasn't going to slow down; if Tyler couldn't keep up, then oh well. She never asked him to come with her, anyway.

Tyler was falling further behind but he didn't expect Cara to wait for him. When the possums had come out of the alley, he just ran in the direction that seemed like the best chance for an escape. If he kept up with Cara, then cool; if he lost her, so be it. Even though she could fight, he couldn't worry about all that. He just had to keep running, and he did, watching her pull further away.

They made it out of the square and down one of the side streets. Cara ran past a few houses and turned left through someone's yard. Tyler followed her a few seconds behind. They raced between houses, across open yards, and into the woods. Some possums had followed for a while, but neither Cara nor Tyler heard any behind them anymore. Tyler hoped they had managed to lose them.

Cara disappeared into the woods several yards ahead of him. When he finally broke through the trees, he stopped to breathe and listen. He heard Cara's breathing not too far away. He reached into the pocket of his coveralls and pulled out a flashlight. It wasn't a very big one, but it gave off quite a shine. When he spotted her a few yards away, her eyes flashed angrily and she said, "Turn that fucking light off, idiot!"

He did as told and walked over to where she stood. "What the hell's the matter with you?" he asked.

"You want them to see us?" she snapped.

"They can probably sense us in the dark. They're nocturnal," he replied.

"I don't give a shit. They don't act like normal possums, so we can't be too sure."

"So, what do we do now?"

"I guess we try to find our way back into town. If we stay out here, they'll find us sooner or later."

"That plan's as good as any. You got your knife?"

"Yeah. Do you have anything?"

"I got my work knife."

"What kind of knife is it?"

"A pocket knife."

"That ain't much."

"It'll have to do."

"Yeah, well, just don't slow me down, okay? If there's a fight, don't get in my way."

Tyler nodded. "Got it."

They started walking, trying as best they could to keep quiet. Cara succeeded at this but Tyler did not because he still wore his heavy work boots. They crunched leaves and snapped branches and twigs with almost every step. Each sound, to Cara, seemed amplified twice as loud as the last. She really just wanted to duck off and lose him in the darkness, but she wasn't *that* cold. Tyler was weak and he needed somebody with him. She wouldn't risk her own life anymore than she had to, but she wouldn't just abandon him in the middle of the woods with wild-eyed possums on their trail—not purposely, anyway. If they had to run, as before, she would not wait for him, but she wouldn't just take off and leave him for no good reason.

The path in front of her suddenly lit up and she could see her shadow cast along the ground. Her heart jumped and she spun around. Tyler was holding his flashlight out, the rounded bulb of it burning her retinas. She quickly smacked it out of his hand and reconsidered her magnanimous decision not to abandon him. It hit the ground and sounded like the lid popped off. The light went off as the top batteries sprung out onto the ground.

"What did you do that for?" Tyler asked.

"Because, you moron, we don't need to draw attention to ourselves! I already told you that!"

"Do you actually think these possums are smart enough to track us by a flashlight beam?"

"I don't know if they are or not. Before today, I thought they didn't eat people. But, they're doing that shit now, and if they're doing that I'm willing to believe they can do a lot of crazy shit. So, I'm not taking any chances."

Cara resumed walking and Tyler followed. Their steps were slow and cautious, seeking silence and vigilance.

"I guess that makes sense. I just never would have thought possums would do this."

"*O*possums, actually," Cara said.

"What?"

"In North America, they're called opossums, not just possums. That's what they call them in the east."

"Oh—well excuse me. It's the same thing."

"No, actually they're not. They are two completely different breeds."

"Like I care."

"You should. Ignorance is a pitiable quality."

"I don't know if it matters at this point. All that matters is that they *are* eating people. But, just for you, if I survive this, I promise to educate myself extensively on the history of both the possum and *o*possum."

A few more steps and they heard a deep growl nearby in the woods. Cara held up her knife, ready for an attack. Tyler got his out too, hoping that he'd be able to kill at least one possum—or opossum—before he was taken down. He didn't think he had another Hulk moment left in him like he had at Greta and Tony's, but that didn't mean he wouldn't try.

"Now would be a good time to turn your flashlight on," Cara said.

"I left it on the ground where you knocked it out of my hand."

Cara was silent for a few seconds, holding down her bubbling fury. "Why?"

"Because you have such an issue with me using it."

"What?"

"You kept telling me to put it away, so I just left it."

"Are you really pouting at a time like this, you big baby?"

"No! I'm just saying…"

"Well, don't *say* anything!"

The growling continued, but Cara noticed that it didn't sound like the possums. It actually sounded like a large dog. When the growl turned to a yelp, a vicious snarl, and then the sounds of hissing and more growling, Cara then realized that there were animals fighting somewhere in the woods. She took out her cell phone, hoping it would put off enough light to see by.

Its glow was bright, but narrow, and it revealed what looked like a large brown dog embroiled in a brawl with a large possum. She saw the creatures rolling around, lunging at each other, and then darting back and forth between the trees. The battle was tough to follow due to the small radius of light, so Cara had to keep moving the phone as the animals often jumped and rolled into the darkness. The dog was pretty big, like a Labrador. But, it wasn't much bigger than the possum, and its mouth was much smaller. They snapped at one another, the possum getting the better of that exchange. But the dog, with its longer arms and bulkier body, latched onto the creature and wrestled it to the ground. He bit his big jaws into the possum, which squealed and thrashed and bit back, drawing blood from somewhere on the dog's shoulder. They wrestled for many seconds until the snarls of more possums could be heard in the distance.

"Oh shit," Tyler said. "What's that?"

The possum barks floated on the air. The skin on the back of Cara's neck tingled as she listened.

"I think that's the big ones," she said.

"How many are there?"

"I don't know, but it sounds like a lot."

The Labrador let go of the possum and backed away with a threatening growl. The possum stood, wobbled, and raised up on its hind legs and barked. When the call was answered by several similar barks, the dog retreated into the woods.

Mere seconds after the dog vanished, nine more large possums came thundering into view. As soon as Cara saw them, she dropped her phone in fear and ran away. Tyler, having seen the possums almost at his feet before the light went out, ran the opposite way, back towards where he and Cara came from. As bad as it made him feel, he'd hoped the possums had decided to pursue her instead of him. She had a better chance of surviving an attack.

He didn't make it very far, because as he retraced the course they had previously come, he had done so with much more accuracy than he intended. As he came to where the two of them had stopped earlier, he stepped on something that rolled beneath his feet and made him slip. When he hit the ground, his hand fell upon the flashlight, and he recognized it instantly.

Cold fear rushed through him as he picked it up and felt for the batteries. Two were missing so his hand began to blindly search the ground. He found the lid first, then one battery. He heard only leaves in the trees moving softly above him. That and the fact that he hadn't been ripped to shreds yet told him that the possums had tracked Cara after all. He hoped she made it—he liked her, but not more than he liked himself.

After a couple of minutes of searching, Tyler found the last battery. He pushed them inside the flashlight, tried to apply the lid but couldn't get it down all the way.

"Shit!" he yelled, then immediately felt stupid for doing so.

He fumbled with the batteries some more, listening to the darkness around him, and still did not hear the creatures. He did began to smell a foul odor, like wet metal and moldy clothes, but figured it was just the nasty smell of the autumn forest. If it were them, then he would no doubt be feeling the vicious sting of their teeth at that very moment. Even if they weren't near, they might be soon; and, if not that pack of mutant possums, he had no doubt another swarm of relatively normal possums would come soldiering through sooner or later. His panic was at an all-time high knowing how close he was to obliteration.

He got the batteries back into the flashlight—hoping his guesswork was successful and they were in properly—then slid the lid on and began to turn it. The spring inside pressed the batteries down like it was supposed to and the flashlight clicked together. Right after it did, he heard a stick crunch behind him and felt his neck begin to sizzle with fear.

He thought he heard breathing and froze, afraid to even blink.

Breathing.
Crunch.
Snap.
Breathing.
He swallowed. "Cara? Is that you?"

The only replies were the soft smashing of leaves against grass in the darkness, and the slight breaking of tiny sticks that had fallen from larger branches. Tyler began to shake; his jockeys became saturated by his urine. He pressed his thumb against the button on the flashlight and hesitated.

Maybe it would be better to die blindly.

But, the pesky human instinct that was the need-to-know drove his thumb to press the button. He was holding the flashlight down, so when it came on, the beam was shining on the ground and all he could see were the dead leaves and grass upon the cracked forest floor in front of his knees.

When he raised the flashlight up, he was staring into the face of terror and death. Before him, three possum faces, larger than his own, stared back at him from a few feet away. His heart almost stopped. He swung the flashlight around and saw three more next to them. He decided to turn and run, but there were four more behind him. They had closed a circle around him, and as he spun, all he saw were ten bloody faces with huge black eyes looking at him. Their dirty bottom teeth rose from the protruding lower jaws like long, rusty sabers.

Tyler tried to stand up and run, but his legs were unable to life him; fear had locked them in place. When the first possum opened its mouth and squealed, revealing a giant mouth stained with blood and speckled with bits of flesh in its teeth, the others around him began to do the same. The harrowing sight of ten giant, screaming possums surrounded him. There was no way out.

"Fuck it," Tyler said and clicked off the flashlight.

He then leaned forward, put his face to the ground, and screamed in agony as he felt the first set of teeth pierce his coveralls and tear into his body. As the others joined in, ripping with their claws and pulling meat away in their jaws, Tyler wailed until the blood and bile clogged his throat. Seconds later, he fell completely silent as he rode the agony straight into death.

Cara heard him screaming but she didn't stop running. Several possums were on her tail. There was only a single large one among them, but there looked to be a few dozen smaller ones scattered about in pursuit. She felt bad for Tyler, but he had been dead weight, and his stupidity with the flashlight and his lumbering footsteps had no doubt given them away and brought this attack upon them. Why should she die for his incompetence?

The woods had grown sparse and the moon gave her plenty of light by which to see. She could smell water and knew that a creek would be coming up soon. Her plan of action was already set: no matter how wide the gap, she was jumping as soon as she reached the edge. She had a damn good vertical and long jump, and she was a strong swimmer, so she had no doubt the creek would prove a perfect escape for her.

The only problem was it was still a ways off and these possums were coming at her from all angles. They had no chance against her in a straight run, even though they seemed to be fueled by some rush of adrenaline that made them much faster than the average possum—the larger ones being especially swift. But, there were so many and they were cutting off her path, emerging from different corners of the darkness. Eventually, they had measured her course so well that she was barely running a foot in front of them.

She ran like that for a few minutes, never losing her stride. She even managed to successfully jump a fat, fallen tree branch without missing a beat. She had covered a lot of ground in a couple of minutes and now the creek was coming at her fast. She could see the moon's reflection rippling across the water. It was only seconds away. She could jump it, it wasn't that wide.

It's getting closer.
The possums growled.
Here it comes.
The possums snarled.
No hesitation.
They were at her heels.
Here it is.
So were they.
Do or die, Cara!

And she jumped.

Cara sailed into the air with all the force she had. She watched the creek slide away beneath her as the other side drew closer. Her flight hit its apex a little less than midway across, and she began to descend. Judging by the distance, she thought she might not make the other side cleanly. No matter—she would hang on and climb or swim a little ways downstream and find a good spot to scale the bank.

Possums fell into the water below her. She heard them splash, one after the other. She was aware that they could swim almost as well as they could climb. If she hit the water, she might have a new problem to contend with.

Cara's body came down and slammed against the bank on the other side. Her fingers gripped the ground above her but without much strength. She still held her knife in her right hand, hindering her hold on the bank. Her feet hit the water; the dirt beneath her hands broke and she slid down the bank wall and was soon submerged in the creek.

After her plummet down the bank wall, she tried to look around underwater, but it was completely black. Her weight didn't take her all the way to the bottom but she knew it couldn't be very deep. There was only a slight current, so she kicked her way to the top. When she did, she came face-to-face with several possums that were floating in the water around her, in the same manner the skulls of the dead bobbed around JoBeth Williams in *Poltergeist*. They hissed and spat water in her face. Their little paws began to flap against the water as they swam towards her.

Still clutching the knife in her hand, having held onto it like a lifeline during her entire flight, she raised it above the water and struck out at the closest possum, slashing its face and causing it to back away. She then thrust at the next one, stabbing it in the mouth. Another was coming around beside her and she quickly swiped at it, cutting a long tear in the side of its neck. One jumped on her from behind, but did not make purchase with its teeth. Cara reached back and thrust the knife down towards the possum and felt the blade slide into its body. The creature then screamed and fell off of her. The water around her was clear. All other possums were a good distance away, so she began to swim downstream.

The bank was too high above her to reach. She swam about fifteen feet before she found a large tree root sticking out of the ground and hanging over the water. As she passed it, she reached up and grabbed it, pulled herself up, and hoisted her wet body onto the land with a hard smack against the soil. She then lay on her back for a few seconds to catch her breath. The possums in the creek kept swimming. On the other side of the water, many were watching her. She sat up and stared back.

"You sure are some smart opossums, aren't you?"

They suddenly became agitated and started running in circles, dashing back and forth along the bank, squealing and shrieking. The behavior was quite strange, and it made Cara feel uneasy. What was it that had them all in such an uproar? Then, her back went rigid when she heard the threatening growl behind her a few seconds later.

She turned her head slowly, afraid to see what might be there. She hoped it might be the Labrador from earlier, but somehow she doubted it. When she twisted her head around enough to see, she looked upon a possum that was even bigger than the one that had previously been battling the dog. This one looked like it would have won that fight. Its head was massive, its body long and fat, and its claws were like small kitchen knives ready to carve a fresh, meaty dinner.

When the thing's glowing eyes met hers, it growled even deeper, even stronger, and clawed at the ground like a bull about to charge. Cara swallowed her fear and gripped the knife.

"What are you?" she said.

It growled again and hissed.

Slowly, Cara rose to meet it. Her wet sleeveless-tee shirt and gym shorts clung to her skin, making her feel cold and shivery, but she did not let that distract her. Her blonde hair was soaked, matted to her forehead, and clotted with dirt and debris from the creek. Like the warrior her appearance made her seem, she lifted her knife and lowered her voice.

"Don't make me kill you."

The possum stood on its hind legs and barked three times, then growled. It was covered in blood and dirt and smelled like death. Cara knew no mercy would come from it, so she planned to grant none in return. She sized her opponent up, trying to figure the best strategy to fight it. There was no way she could wrestle the creature. Its jaws were too long and its claws too sharp. She could not stand against that. She had to let it make the first move, and it did.

The possum ran at her, and she waited for just the right second and jumped over it, just like she would have jumped to spike a volleyball onto her opponents—something her tall frame specialized in. She landed and turned just in time. The possum was coming at her again—such a fast creature. This time she side-stepped its approach. It pivoted on all fours, sliding in the dirt, and charged her again. Cara backed up against a tree to gain her balance. The possum leapt hard into the air, heading right for her chest. She moved aside and it smashed face-first into the tree behind her. When it fell, it rolled on its side. Cara ran forward with the knife held above her head and fell towards the prone possum, bringing the weapon down. The possum, sensing her proximity, rolled away, but the knife caught its tail and it screamed. On the other side of the bank, the smaller possums answered with frantic squeals.

Cara yanked the knife free and started backing away. The possum rolled onto its feet and growled again. It rushed her angrily, its fat, furry body shaking back and forth with each wobbling step. Cara kept backing up, closer to the creek.

"Come and get me, you bastard!" she screamed.

The possum leapt for her one more time in a blind rage and Cara dropped to the ground. The maniacal animal flew over her and landed with a heavy splash into the creek.

She rose to all fours, looked into the creek, and saw the possum glaring at her as it slowly drifted away. When it barked, all the possums on the other bank descended into the water with it. Cara didn't wait to see what their plan was; she jumped to her feet and took off, escaping as quickly as her powerful legs would take her.

CHAPTER TWENTY-ONE

Kyle wasn't sure what he was going to do when he got to Shepherdsville. He wasn't too familiar with the city, having only been there once to take a local history and haunts tour with some friends. But, he remembered the starting point was by the police station and figured that would be the best place to go.

Jessica and Ingrid were both silent. Since Clyde and Tommy never followed, Jessica got really nervous and even mad at Kyle for not going back for them. Ingrid said nothing, despite Jessica's constant search for her support. Ingrid didn't care; her mother and brother were dead, what happened to the rest of them meant nothing to her. She wasn't even sure she cared what happened to herself.

When Ingrid refused to side with Jessica, she got a little huffy. Jessica wanted to tell her off and remind her that if not for her, no one would have seen her get out of the trunk of that car she had been trapped in. She wanted to tell Ingrid she could get out and walk, but the woman had some impressive muscles and a really hard demeanor, so Jessica decided to keep her displeasure to herself. There was also hollowness in her eyes, like she had nothing to live for; Jessica assumed that a woman like that probably wouldn't hesitate to beat her nearly to death.

Not that her words would have bothered Ingrid anyway. Ingrid wasn't even sure why she climbed out of the trunk in the first place. She heard the entire shootout take place. She knew people were out there, but she just lay there, debating on whether or not she even cared enough to open the trunk and climb out. The possums were dead all around her, which would

219

have given her the opportunity to escape and go it alone, but it also took away her need for vengeance upon those that had eaten her brother. Undoubtedly, those responsible for his death were among the possums slaughtered in the street. But, there were likely more out there and maybe they were related to those possums, or maybe even some that had dined on Jeremiah had moved on and not been present when the cavalry came. She might still have unfinished business. However, being around people was not something she was sure she wanted to do. But, as she waited in the trunk for the party to roll away, a little voice told her to get out and go with them.

The voice had sounded like Jeremiah's, and so she had asked, "Is that you, little brother?"

Of course, it wasn't. Little brother was dead in the front seat right next to his perverted friend. Poor old Bobby: he wasn't a bad guy. He didn't deserve such a nasty end.

Kyle came to the end of Stephen Foster Avenue and turned the corner; when he did, his truck ran over something jagged and made of wood. A sharp piece jabbed into his tire and sank in, gouging a massive hole in it. It only took a few more feet before the thing blew and sent the truck careening all over the road.

Jessica screamed as Kyle turned the wheel to steady the vehicle. It did no good. He hit fallen trash cans, a parked car, and then the curb—which he hit so hard the impact knocked the front-passenger wheel off.

The car bounced, rattled, and parked itself partially on the street and the sidewalk. Jessica had bounced back and forth off of Ingrid and Kyle like a pinball. Ingrid, who had held onto the roof and pressed her feet hard against the floor to keep her balance, had her door open the second they stopped and she was already on the sidewalk looking at the tire.

"We're not going anywhere, champ. That whole wheel is gone."

"What was that in the road back there?" Kyle asked, rubbing his forehead where it had hit the window next to him.

"It looked like a busted up chair, and you could have seen it a mile away. What the hell is wrong with you?" Ingrid asked.

"I don't know. I didn't see it."

"Well, good job. Now, we're stuck."

"Hey, watch your mouth, bitch," Jessica said, finally letting that anger boil over. "We didn't have to pick you up."

Ingrid, unperturbed by Jessica's words, said, "No, you didn't. I should have just stayed in the trunk."

"You know what? Fuck you!" Jessica started to get out of the car, but Kyle grabbed her wrist.

"Leave her alone. She lost her family."

Jessica looked at Kyle. "So fucking what? I lost my sister. A lot of people lost their family. She's not fucking special." She turned back to Ingrid. "You ungrateful cunt!"

Ingrid chuckled and shook her head. She thought about punching Jessica square in the mouth, but then decided not to. Soft, spoiled women like her couldn't handle adversity and she was just breaking in the face of it. Ingrid couldn't hold it against her: she was most likely the type that had guys do everything for her most of her life—daddy, brother, boyfriends, horny morons at school, this goofy idiot in the truck—no doubt she made them all dance to her tune. Reality was her worst enemy and Ingrid didn't have the time or desire to deal with her. So, although Jessica kept cussing at her, Ingrid looked around the street at the carnage that lay about the roadside.

It was a residential street, and the weekly garbage run had been scattered about. Houses were dark and silent, even the ones with open doors. Taking a closer look at the mayhem, she saw still forms lying in ditches and yards, even some on porches. This street had been attacked—no doubt about that. The only question was how long ago had it happened?

It didn't take long for that question to be answered. She soon heard the familiar snarls behind her. When she looked around, she saw the animals emerging from the bushes, climbing down the trees, and exiting the homes. The siege had been recent, and the assailants were coming to investigate the crash—and probably Jessica's big angry mouth.

Ingrid glanced behind her, in the direction of town, and saw nothing blocking her path. It would be a long run down the avenue, but not impossible to make. She was in good shape. She could outrun them.

She turned back to Jessica and Kyle and, interrupting Jessica's adolescent, expletive-laden tirade, said, "You guys might want to get out of here. I'm going back to town. Good luck and thanks for the ride."

She ran from the truck back towards town. When she reached the corner, she saw a men's Fuji bike lying on the ground and absconded with it.

"Where the fuck are you going, you whore?" Jessica screamed.

Kyle nudged her. "Look."

She turned and they looked out the windshield as the possums came towards them.

"Oh shit," Jessica exclaimed.

"Yep."

"You have any shells left?"

"Yes, I do. Get out of the truck and start running towards town. We've got to get back there. I'll cover you."

The streetlights lining the road were bright and lit the entire block. Kyle could easily pick some of the possums off. He looked for large clumps of them and fired, the echo of his shotgun booming through the wasted street. Shot after shot, he took them down before they could reach him. Though his aim was impeccable, he ran out of ammo before removing the threat; there were just too many possums to contend with. He simply did not have enough shells left to kill them all. He pulled out the last he had and his hands trembled as loaded them in.

Jessica, having elected to stay with Kyle instead of run as he had suggested, backed away as he took his final shots. Though it appeared he made good on just about all of them, it didn't do nearly enough damage. For every possum he killed it seemed three more emerged to join the march. There wasn't much else they could do now but run.

Kyle threw down the shotgun and said, "Run!"

The possums weren't far behind, and Kyle ran around the bed of his truck to catch up to Jessica. When he did, he passed right under a tree. There was a low-lying branch that rested only a few feet above his head, and a younger possum dropped down by its tail and reached for his face. Its claws dug into his cheeks, causing him to stop. The possum released the branch and fell on Kyle's face and started chewing, gouging his cheek, tearing off the tip of his nose, and scratching deep grooves into his face and neck. The other possums caught up and went for his legs. It didn't take long before Kyle was dead and bleeding beneath the mass.

Jessica ran down the street screaming. Many of the possums that weren't feeding on Kyle pursued her. She was not fast nor was she strong-willed. Her mouth gaped open as wide as it could as she wailed in terror, her feet loudly slapping the concrete and her brown hair flowing like a scarf behind her. Some of the possums that had been up in the trees ran along the branches overhead, leaping out onto the power lines, running nimbly on them to keep up with her. She didn't get much further, not even to the end of the street, when three smaller possums jumped off the power lines and landed right on top of her, simultaneously biting down on her neck, her right shoulder, and back.

Jessica fell in the middle of the street and bawled as possums rained down on her. Soon, she lay beneath more than a dozen that were eating her alive.

Ingrid peddled on, as hard and fast as she could. She was already long out of earshot when Jessica had become possum food, so she never heard her scream. She never thought the woman had a chance anyway.

Possums had taken notice of Ingrid several minutes ago, and she pumped her powerful legs. The bike zoomed down the road and the center of town was coming back into view in just a few minutes. She glided towards the courthouse and heard gunshots. When she swung around the roundabout, she didn't see anyone out in the square. When she looked towards the front of the courthouse, she saw the van and truck crashed against a stone monument. Possums were swarming the van and she wondered if any of the others were inside.

The bike sailed past the possums. There were more running off down a side street, seemingly in pursuit of something unseen. The businesses were dark, except for the museum. She saw lights on inside as she rode upon it. Maybe someone was in there. If not, she could just ride on.

When she came upon the building, she saw a few dead possums in the yard. Surely, someone was there. Fleeing on the bike from the creatures brought her back to life a little bit, and now with a sliver of instinct to survive reignited within her, she stopped at the curb, looked behind her, saw no other possums, and let the bike drop to the ground. She then ran to the door and started pounding on it.

There were many shapes inside, and a man in a cloak of some sort opened the door for her. Without a word, he let her pass by him. When he did, she saw he was a priest and thought, *Of course. Isn't the world ending?*

She came into the living room and saw others were inside.

"You made it just in time," the priest said.

"Thanks, father," she said.

"Just call me Carlos. This was to be my first day on the job."

Ingrid could see that he was young. His face was smooth and his eyes were eager. She thought he must have believed he was there for a purpose, like some epic Biblical shit was going down.

"Thank you for letting me in."

Carlos motioned to a teal-haired woman behind him. "It is she who opened this place up as a sanctuary. She is the caretaker of the museum and lives upstairs. She also let these other folks in."

Greta, Tony, Clyde, and Susie were sitting in what was called the Pioneer Room, just beyond the living room. Ingrid and Greta recognized each other and they nodded to one another.

"I'm sorry about your mother," Greta said.

"Thank you."

Ingrid had never seen the others, but she deduced that the dark-haired man next to Greta was her husband, Tony, who ran the local garage. Her mother had always spoken kindly of him as well, stating that he was a good husband, a hardworking man, and a pillar of the community. She had no clue who the other two were. She assumed all of them had been the others riding with Kyle.

"Are you the people who were in the van and the black truck?"

Clyde nodded. "Yeah."

"I'm the woman from the trunk of the car."

"Oh God," Greta said, putting her hands over her mouth. "Tell me that wasn't your brother?"

Ingrid swallowed hard and nodded. Greta turned her head to hide her tears.

"What happened to Jessica and Kyle?" Clyde asked, ignoring the brief conversation.

Ingrid shrugged. "Kyle's truck blew a tire and the wheel fell off. The street we were on was overrun with possums, so I grabbed a bike and peddled back to town."

"What did he do?"

"I don't know. I heard some gunshots going off as I rode away. That's all I know."

Clyde shifted his weight and cocked his head slightly to the side. "So, you just left them?"

Ingrid nodded.

"They picked you up and you just left them?"

"I did what I had to do. I saw the possums before they did and let them know. They sat in the truck. I wasn't staying around."

"The woman did what she could, Clyde," Tony said.

Clyde eased up and took a seat. The teal-haired woman looked at her and said, "My name is Denise. Everyone is welcome to stay here until help comes. The building is made of concrete and stone. The possums won't be able to dig their way in."

"Are the doors made of stone?" Ingrid asked.

"No."

"Then they can get in."

"We'll just have to remain vigilant."

Ingrid nodded. Denise offered her a drink and a seat in the living room. She took both and lay back on a comfortable easy chair and closed her eyes, hoping she'd wake up to something other than this.

CHAPTER TWENTY-TWO

Officer Denton stepped on the gas as the lights of town came into view. They were moving in from the northwest. Instead of driving down Stephen Foster Avenue, Denton had opted to take some side roads around the commercial and historic districts.

"Is there an immediate care center we can get Todd to?" Rachel asked.

Denton checked the clock. It was coming up on eleven. "The immediate care center is closed. But, the ER next to it will be open. After we stop by the station and get some details on this madness, I'll drop you guys off there."

"Can't we go to the ER first? He's getting worse."

Todd had grown pale and was sweating profusely. He was getting very irritable, too. Several times during the car ride he snapped at Rachel. It was never anything too dramatic, but it was very uncharacteristic. Todd had always been a smart-ass, but he was never nasty. Now, he was just being unkind. She didn't like it. They had been through too much already, including near death, and he needed to stay strong, not just for himself, but for her, too.

"The station is just a few streets over. After I stop there, I'll take you to the ER."

"Just let it go, Rachel. Don't be rude. They didn't have to pick us up. Don't be ungrateful," Todd chided her.

"I'm not being ungrateful, Todd. I want you to get better. Stop being so mean!"

"I'll be fine, god-damnit. Stop harping on it."

Selma glanced back at Todd, who looked very sick. At first, she wanted to tell him to watch his mouth, but then thought better of it. The kid lost everything except for his sister—which, in Selma's opinion, meant he should probably be kinder to her—and he must have been grieving. He was just a kid closing in on his teenage years and everything had crashed down around him. Emotional scarring was probably unavoidable. Besides, it wasn't her place to intervene. Rachel was a grown woman and Todd was her younger brother. She could handle it in her own fashion.

Denton ignored their banter. All he wanted to do was get some reinforcements. The boys at the station were not answering his calls, and he feared the worst.

They took a couple of turns and headed into an open street where there were a few businesses, a small park, and the police station, which wasn't exactly grand. It was a brick building with a gravel lot, two-stories, and a few rooms. When Denton pulled up to it, he saw the glass doors were busted. A few police cruisers were parked outside, and so were the dispatchers' vehicles. A sick feeling formed in his gut as he skidded to a halt right there in the street.

When he jumped out of the car and ran for the station, Selma opened her door and got out to follow. Rachel wanted to remain in the car with Todd, but he insisted on getting out so he could see what was going on.

As they approached the station, Todd seeming a little worse for wear, gunshots were fired inside. Selma came dashing out and said, "Get back to the car! They're everywhere!"

Denton fired some more shots and backed out. When he had walked in, the station looked like a nightmare. The walls and floors were stained with blood, and the half-eaten corpses of dispatchers and cops lay scattered. A lot of possums had been killed, too, but there were so many more dining on his fellow officers that it was clear which side had emerged from the battle victorious.

"Get back to the car!" he yelled as he backed out to the street and fired a few more shots before his gun clicked.

Once he got to the car, he was going to get some more ammo and decimate those little bastards. After they had left Capt. Dean's body back at home, Selma had rounded up as much of his arsenal as she and Denton

227

could carry just in case they had to fight. One bag was in the passenger side floorboard and a bigger one was in the trunk.

"Selma! Get in the trunk and get some more weapons!"

Selma nodded and ran to the trunk, but stopped before she could open it. A herd of possums was running towards them, too close and too swiftly for her to open the trunk and get the bag out in time.

"Get in the car!" she screamed. "They're here!"

Several more possums came running from the square and climbed up the other side of the car. Selma screamed again. Denton turned and saw what was going on. Possums were closing in on them, and all of his shooting had riled up the others in the station.

He looked towards the square and said, "Cut across the square and head down the alley next to the museum!"

"Can you run, Todd?" Rachel asked.

"I don't have a choice," he said and took off running.

Rachel was glad to see he was moving pretty well, only a slight hobble as he ran beside Selma. Rachel was in the back, a few steps behind them, and Denton was a couple of feet ahead.

They dashed from the darkness of the street out into the bright lights of the square. There were a few living possums, but not many. Most were gathered by a couple of vehicles that looked to have crashed near the courthouse. There were, however, several dead possums alongside a lot of dead humans. None of them could believe the scourge had gotten this far.

"What the hell is happening?" Rachel screamed and Selma looked back at her.

"I don't know, sweetheart, but it sure is bad."

"No fucking shit!" Todd yelled.

They ran across the square, heading towards the alley. Denton yelled over his shoulder, "Come on!"

"Where the hell are we going?" Todd shouted.

"Down the alley and a few streets over. I got a buddy who lives not far from here. We'll see if we can hole up at his place."

"What if he's dead, too?" Selma asked.

"I don't know then!"

Their voices carried on the air, and as they neared the museum, the front door opened and Denise stepped out onto the porch and waved them in.

"Come on in here!" she said nervously. "They're right behind you!"

Selma looked back and saw a line of possums a couple of feet behind Rachel, who was wearing out quickly. If they didn't make it to safety soon, she would be dead, and the rest of them would no doubt follow soon after. Without speaking a word, they had all decided the museum was a better plan.

The four of them mounted the sidewalk and cut through the museum's yard, heading straight for the door. Denise stepped aside to let them pass. Clyde was standing nearby with the snub nose.

"Just slam the door when they get in."

As soon as Rachel had entered, Carlos, who stood behind the door, slammed it shut. Everyone had made it in safely, including six possums that trailed in behind them.

CHAPTER TWENTY-THREE

The six possums, all of average size, spread out as they ran in. Clyde readied the snub nose while Ingrid snatched up a bat that Carlos had left lying against the western wall of the living room. Greta, who had been given a shotgun by Denise, stood in the Pioneer Room—which held exhibits of Nelson County's earliest days—waiting for one of the possums to run into the open so she could blow it away. Tony took a cold poker from the retired fireplace and stood beside his wife. Denton, now out of ammunition, pulled out his tazer and can of pepper spray. Susie hid behind an exhibit in the Pioneer Room while Selma smashed herself into a corner of the living room, pulling a chair in front of her. Rachel escorted Todd to the Pioneer Room, and seated him in a chair behind Greta and Tony.

Clyde fired at a possum that darted across the living room and missed, puncturing the bottom of the front door. He fired again and nailed the animal right between the eyes. Denton tazed one and then stomped on its head. Greta waited patiently for any possums to come her way.

Four possums remained, and they were dashing about under tables, exhibits, and chairs. Clyde fired another unsuccessful shot that simply put a small hole in the wooden floor that lay over the stone. One possum came at Ingrid and she swung the bat at it and missed. The threat was quite clear to the possum and it retreated. But, she would not let it go so easily. She chased it into a corner and made good on her next swing, cracking it right across the face and putting its lights out permanently.

Two possums broke from the living room into the Pioneer Room and Greta aimed and fired, splitting one in half. The other tried to run behind an exhibit, but was cut short by a slug shattering its entire head.

In the front room, Clyde took aim and fired at the final possum and didn't miss this time. He shot it right in the side as it turned towards Selma. It skidded along the floor and slammed into the wall, trailing blood behind it. Once it stopped moving, everyone became still for a few seconds.

"Is that it?" Susie asked.

"I think so," Clyde said.

"That's it," Greta confirmed with a sigh.

Next to her, Tony threw down the poker he never had to use. He walked over to Officer Denton and said, "Officer Denton, good to see you, under the circumstances."

"Hello, Tony. I'm glad you made it through all of this. Where's Tommy?"

Tony sucked in a deep breath and said, "In the van crashed against the courthouse outside."

Denton, understanding, breathed deeply as well and said, "I'm sorry, Tony."

Tony nodded slightly and looked at the floor, watching Denton's dirty black shoes become a tad blurry. The officer then clasped him on the shoulder and gave it a slight squeeze.

"Where are the other officers?" Clyde asked.

Denton turned to him. "Dead."

"What?" Tony said, looking back up at Denton and quickly wiping his watery eyes.

"We just came from the station. The whole place is a wreck. Several officers are dead in there—the dispatchers, too. There are still a few other officers missing in action. I assume they are dead, as well. A lot of dead possums over there, but a lot more live ones, and they chased us out. We had to abandon my car, and all of our guns are in there."

"There were a few cops killed at my place, earlier," Ingrid said. "One of them was Officer Jackson."

Denton looked at her. "That would probably account for the rest then. Jackson was a good man."

"He seemed like it."

"Damn. What's going on out there?" Clyde asked.

"I don't know. It's insane. I've never seen anything like it. It looks like they're all over town, killing people and eating them."

"So what the hell are we going to do?" Susie asked.

"Has anybody tried calling for help?" Denton asked.

Carlos stood up. "I did and no one believed me. I called surrounding towns and counties and they treated it like a prank."

"I don't blame them." Denton said. "Maybe if I call, they'll listen. My cell is back in the car. Anyone else got one?"

No one else had theirs. They were either dead or lost.

"What about you, Denise?" Denton had known the caretaker ever since she took over the museum.

"I dropped it when I came in earlier. I was coming back from lunch and possums tried to attack me when I left my car. I had it out to make a call and they scared me so bad, I jumped and it fell right between them. They looked so terrifying that I wasn't about to reach down there and get it."

Todd was shaking and groaning slightly. Rachel touched his forehead; it was extremely hot.

"My brother needs help. He got bit earlier and he's been really sick ever since. I need to get him to the ER."

Carlos, eyes wide, said, "How long ago was he bitten?"

"I don't know—several hours."

"Where at?"

"In our backyard."

"No, I mean where at on his body?"

"Oh – the back of the leg. It wasn't too bad, but it bled enough."

Carlos considered this for a moment and nodded. "I don't think we can get him to the ER, right now. Even if we could, I imagine it is not a safe place to be—just trust me on that. Maybe we can use some first aid stuff to help him out for now. Denise, do you have anything that can help?"

"I have some stuff upstairs in my bathroom. I can clean the wound and give it a fresh wrap. I have Tylenol for fever, too."

"That'll have to do for now," Carlos said.

"Okay, I'll go get it."

"No!" Rachel said. "That won't do for now! He is *sick* and he needs help! I have to get him to the ER!"

"Young lady, please listen to me," Carlos said coming to her. "I was at the ER a few hours ago. It's not safe. I fled from there and ended up here."

Rachel's eyes were tearing up and she shook her head. "No. That's not possible."

"It is."

"So, the possums were there, too?"

"Well, yes. But, that wasn't the main problem."

Everyone looked at Carlos.

"What do you mean?" Rachel asked.

"Nothing, dear – just trust me when I tell you that the ER is not a viable sanctuary at this time."

Clyde then spoke up. "Nah, man – what the hell do you mean that possums weren't the main problem? They seem to be the only problem, right now."

"There's something strange at work here. I don't know what it is."

"No time for mystery, Carlos," Tony said. "What the hell are you talking about?"

Before Carlos could say another word, there was a loud bang against the front door. Everyone turned to see what had caused it, though they all knew the answer already. But, what they didn't know was that when Clyde had accidentally shot the front door, it had blown a possum-sized hole right in it, and sent several cracks through the wood, considerably weakening the door. Now, one big-headed possum had managed to force its way through, and it was making the hole bigger as it pressed in.

Selma had flashbacks of her basement door shattering, which flooded her mind with even more horrible recent memories, and backed away quickly.

"They'll break through that door!" she said.

Just as she said that, the door splintered in and several possums burst through into the room.

Denise yelled, "Everyone, follow me!"

She led them through the Pioneer Room, down a hallway, past other exhibit rooms, to a large iron door that was partially open. She slung it wide and stepped aside to let them all pass. Once everyone was through the doorway, she shut the door hard, and slid the surface bolt in place, shutting their pursuers out.

The all stood in a cold, bare corridor that lead back to an old stone section of the building. The possums that had gotten in were now slamming against the door. But, it was so heavy and solid that it didn't budge.

"We should be safe back here," Denise said, and flicked a switch that turned on several fluorescent lights above them.

CHAPTER TWENTY-FOUR

The Nelson County History Museum in Bardstown, Kentucky was an impressive, two-story building made entirely out of limestone and sandstone (and some concrete added through the years) with walls that were more than two-feet thick. Construction of the building began sometime in the late 1700s and concluded officially in the early 1800s. For more than a hundred years, it was the county courthouse. Many big cases were held there, and at one point, a section for holding cells was built onto the rear of the building. This is where people were held during trials. If they were found guilty, they would be sentenced and transferred to a more permanent facility. When the current courthouse was built in the early 1900s, the old courthouse was shut down and stood vacant for many decades. In the late 1970s, the building was slated to be torn down, but a group of county historians purchased the building before it was demolished and left it empty for a few years, much to the displeasure of Nelson County's powers that be. Once the county legislature leaned on them with threats of declaration of abandonment to be subsequently followed by the structure being condemned, they got some financial backing and turned it into the museum.

Over the years, the rooms inside the front section of the building had been used for different exhibits and events that bore significance to Nelson County history; the back, however, had always remained as close to its original form as possible since it was the museum's biggest draw. People were fascinated by old-fashioned jails.

The holding area of the former courthouse was like a fortress, with the thick stone walls and heavy iron door. Not even the persistent and savage possums could break their way inside. They might have gained full run of the rest of the building during the course of their recent invasion, but they would not dig their way into the back.

Because of this, Denise, Carlos, Greta, Tony, Clyde, Susie, Ingrid, Rachel, Todd, Selma, and Officer Denton sat huddled in the four cells that lined the rear corridor. Rachel had taken Todd into the cell in the far left corner of the block, and Ingrid had taken the one across from them, where she sat alone and brooded for a while. Selma, sensing her loneliness, and relating to it, decided to join her for mostly silent company.

Selma came to the threshold of the cell and looked at the dejected figure slumped on the cot. Ingrid was beyond despondent. She had lost her mother and brother in one day, to even call her mournful was a subtlety. Inside, the young lady was destroyed, and that state of devastation showed on the outside. Selma knew how she felt, but doubted she could understand the full impact the events had on Ingrid. Yes, she had loved her father, and he had meant the world to her, but he was elderly and had lived a good, full life. His passing had been a possibility she had begun thinking about, with much sadness, a lot more lately. While it crushed her that he had died in such a gruesome fashion, she could at least take some pride in the fact that he went down fighting. He had literally taken his enemy down with him. Ingrid was young and her brother had been young. Their mother was no spring chicken, but she was far from her twilight years. Piling that upon the loss of her father at an early age, Ingrid's life was in shambles in ways that Selma could not imagine. Ingrid's position was, in some ways, very similar to that of Rachel and Todd's; but, even as grim as their lives had become, they still had each other. Who did Ingrid have? The very thought of being alone in the world the way Ingrid was, with the ghastly deaths her loved ones had suffered forever burned into her memory, filled Selma with a pity and sadness that threatened to strangle her heart with hateful hands.

There was nothing she could do for the poor soul except try to be a friend.

"You mind if I sit with you?" she asked.

"No, go ahead."

"I promise not to bother you with idle conversation. I just don't feel like listening to the warlords in the next cell devise their battle plans and philosophize about our current predicament."

Ingrid let a partial smile appear on her face. "Me neither."

Selma's soft, caring voice did slightly ease Ingrid's pain. Though she was no fool and knew that Selma took pity on her for her situation, there was nothing condescending or phony about her approach. She genuinely cared, and she wanted to let Ingrid know, in some way, those feelings. Ingrid could sense it, and she liked Selma instantly for her kind heart. In some ways, it reminded her of her mom.

There were four cots in each room: two attached to each of the side walls. Ingrid sat on the right wall and Selma on the left, and they did not speak for several minutes, until Greta wandered in.

"Care if I join you all?"

"It's up to Ingrid. She was here first."

"I don't mind."

Greta sat next to Ingrid. "I don't want to talk about possums anymore."

"That's what I said," Selma replied.

Ingrid shrugged. "I don't want to really talk about anything anymore. But, I don't think we're going to be escaping the topic of possums anytime soon."

The other women nodded silently and let their bodies sag on the uncomfortable cots.

"I can't believe people actually used to sleep in here," Selma said.

"Well, they *were* prisoners," Greta said.

Ingrid looked at them both and said, "So are we."

The other two women nodded and all three remained silent for the next few minutes.

"You're going to be okay." Rachel felt Todd's head again; it was slightly cooler than before. "I think your fever is diminishing."

"I'm starting to feel better, just tired. It's weird, though. I feel exhausted like I want to sleep, but I also feel like I could run out there and start killing those damn possums. I'm still really sweaty, though; and, I feel hot and cold at the same time."

"That's the fever. But maybe the infection isn't that bad, if you're feeling energized. Maybe there is no infection."

"I don't know. If I got a fever then there's an infection, I think. I guess we'll see when I get out of here. I think I'll just stretch out for a minute and rest."

"Okay, I'll move over there."

Todd stretched out on the bunk hanging from the right wall and Rachel moved over to the left one. She decided she needed a rest, as well. She lay back on the cot, closed her eyes, and dozed off pretty quickly.

Officer Denton, Tony, Clyde, and Carlos sat in the first cell on the right, discussing the situation, trying to figure out how to escape. Denise and Susie were in the cell across from them, lying down. It had been a tiring day for them both. Denise preferred to head up the stairs at the end of the corridor to her quarters, but decided to stay with Susie. A part of her didn't want to be alone, but she also didn't want to worry about the chaos at hand for the time being. They were safe there, for now, and someone was bound to come for them soon. This much she had expressed to Susie when the young lady had showed her concern.

"What if they don't?" Susie said.

"They will, eventually. But, if it takes a while, this place is pretty well stocked. I got a lot of stuff upstairs."

"What if the possums get in?"

"They won't. That door is heavy iron, over a foot thick. They won't be able to chew their way through that. Besides, I imagine they won't hang around long once they realize there's no food for them here."

"But, what if they stick around because they can smell us? Like zombies?"

Denise shrugged. "I don't know. I don't think that will happen."

"I sure hope not."

Back in the cell where the men were strategizing and theorizing, each one told his chapter of the story: Denton explained to them what he had seen over at Selma's, and told them about Capt. Dean's killing field; Clyde described the incident at his bonfire, and how his girlfriend's best friend had lost her sister, and how she and Kyle might be dead, now; Tony relayed his side of the story in full, prior to meeting up with Clyde, and then after, in order to fill Denton in.

Carlos kept quiet and listened, glad that the others had forgotten what he said to Rachel before the possums invaded. That was a secret he wanted to keep to himself. Not for any malicious purposes, but because he didn't want to add more worry on an already dire situation. It was already baffling enough that the possums had even orchestrated such a brutal uprising. They were wily and unpredictable and that made it hard for the humans to plan their next move. If Carlos added what he knew to the pot, it would only make matters much more difficult. They had to combat the possum issue currently at hand and worry about other threats when they came face to face with them.

"If anyone still had a way to communicate with the outside world, we might be able to figure something out," Denton said.

"They'd probably still think it was a prank," Tony said.

"Not if I told them I was an officer."

"They'd probably just think you were lying."

"What if they don't?" Clyde asked. "They got a phone here, don't they? We could try."

"It doesn't work. Phone lines are down," Carlos said.

"Damn, man!" Clyde slammed his palm down on the cot he leaned against. "What the fuck is going on, man? Why are we held up in here? They're just fucking possums."

"Yeah, but there are a lot of them," Tony reminded him. "And some are huge."

Susie and Denise heard the commotion from their cell and quickly rushed over to see what was going on.

"Is everything okay?" Denise asked.

Susie walked right up to Clyde and slid her arm around his waist. He put his around her shoulders.

"You okay, baby?"

He smiled down at her. "About as good as any of us can be, I guess. We're just trying to figure out what's happening, why these possums are acting all crazy."

"I think it's a form of rabies, or some kind of infection," Denise said.

"Rabies ain't going to make possums act like that," Tony said.

Denise shrugged. "It could be a different type, maybe one we don't know much about."

"I doubt it," Tony said. "Possums don't get rabies very often. Their body temperatures are too low."

"They're called *o*possums, by the way, and I said it could be a type we're not familiar with."

"I don't care what letter you put in front of their name, they don't usually get rabies. It's extremely rare for just one to get it, let alone hundreds, or even thousands. Even if they did, it wouldn't make them act like that."

"And it wouldn't explain those big-ass possums, neither, unless it's a type of rabies that causes mutations," Clyde added. "Those big ones are huge, and they're smart. I saw them before Tony and Greta and them saved us at my place. They were watching us, and I swear one tried to talk."

"That's crazy," Denton said.

"No it ain't man. I saw it."

"He's not lying. We killed one of those big ones," Tony confirmed.

"I've seen the big ones. Selma's dad was killed by one, and I've heard them bark. But, I don't think they're so intelligent that they have a plan of action."

Susie came to her man's defense. "Look at what they've done to the entire town. They're smart. I'm telling you."

"How did they get that way, though?" Denton asked.

Denise said, "Opossums are smart creatures, anyway."

"Smart enough to lead a siege on an entire town?" Denton scoffed.

"You know there are some weird buildings up in the hills a few miles west of town," Susie said. "What if there is some undercover government shit going on? Like experiments and stuff?"

Denton laughed. "I don't think there's a conspiracy at hand. What could they possibly want to experiment on possums for? And what could they be doing to turn them into this?"

"Could be evolution," Tony said.

"Or the government," Susie insisted and looked up at Clyde.

"I don't see why not," he said. "I mean, I don't think there are too many explanations that would seem far-fetched at this point."

"Clyde has a point," Denise said.

"So does Tony," said Denton. "What if they've evolved into some sort of crazed predator? A bunch of them live up in those hills; maybe they've changed over time."

"Then why isn't it happening elsewhere?" Denise asked.

"How do we know it's not?" Tony replied. "Have you had any contact with the outside world about this?"

"I was checking on the Internet before my laptop died. I didn't see any news stories about it."

"You're still getting Wi-Fi in here?" Clyde asked.

"Barely—the connection's always sucked; and, we wouldn't get any back here, anyway. I can rarely get it to work upstairs."

"I'll tell you all what is happening," Carlos spoke up.

They all looked at him, as if he actually had the answer.

"It's a judgment of sorts."

"Oh God," Clyde said. "Here we go."

"No, I'm serious. This is some sort of punishment. Or, it's some sort of change in the world that God has deemed necessary."

"Yeah, Egypt gets the locusts and Bardstown gets the possums. Whatever, man," Clyde mocked.

Susie and Denton laughed along with him, but no one else did.

"Laugh if you wish, Clyde," Carlos said. "But there is something beyond our reasoning happening outside these walls—something we can't explain."

"Just because we can't explain it doesn't mean someone else can't."

"Come on, Clyde, back off," Tony said. "Who are we to say he's wrong? Do you have an explanation?"

"Man, I like the government idea, or even evolution. Hell, rabies makes more sense to me than that Biblical shit."

"Why don't you chill, Clyde," Denise snapped. "No reason to mock someone's faith just because you don't have any."

"Look, I'm sorry if I offended anyone," he said. "I got faith, just not in that religious jive. I got faith in me, in my girl, and all of you. I got faith in what I can see. I got faith that we can get through this on our own. We don't need to ask a dude we can't see for help."

"Well, whether you can see Him or not, He will see us through this," Carlos said.

"Whatever, man. You do you."

Tony held out his hand and stepped in the middle of the cell and said, "Look, I don't know about rabies or government experiments, or evolution or religion, or any of that shit. I'm no scientist, or holy man, or veterinarian, or political major, so I don't know what the hell is going on. All I know is that people have died and the town has been ripped apart. I don't care about figuring out what has caused this anymore. All I care about is surviving it and getting the hell out of here."

"I'm with that," Clyde said.

"Me, too," Denton added.

The others nodded in agreement.

"So, how do you plan on getting out of here?" Carlos asked.

Before Tony could answer, everyone's attention was stolen by a loud scream coming from somewhere down the corridor.

"What the hell was that?" Clyde asked.

CHAPTER TWENTY-FIVE

A few minutes after dozing off, Rachel woke to the sound of Todd struggling on his cot. She turned her head and watched him move to the edge, swing his legs over, and lean his head down with his hands folded together.

"You okay, Todd?" she asked after watching him sit that way for a few seconds.

"Shut up, Rachel," he said without looking up.

"No need to be rude, Todd."

"Yeah, and there's no need to keep asking me the same fucking question over and over," he snapped, lifting his head and glaring at her, his voice rising as he spoke.

Rachel was startled by his sudden outburst. She rose up in bed and sat back on her hands. "What the hell is your problem?"

"I don't know, Rachel. Maybe the possum bite in my fucking leg is the problem. Maybe everybody I fucking care about being dead is the problem."

Todd felt his heart began to hammer in his chest. His legs started to shake; his hands had involuntarily separated and kept clenching into fists. Rachel watched nervously as his jaw muscles flexed.

She swallowed hard. "Well, I'm still here."

"Big fucking deal. What good is that?"

Rachel felt like a sword had pierced her heart. Did he really just say what she thought he said? Her eyes filled with tears and a couple dripped down her cheeks. "That's the most hurtful thing you've ever said to me, Todd."

"Well, just be glad they're only words, Rachel."

"What's that supposed to mean?" She moved to the edge of her cot with her feet resting on the floor.

"It means if you keep talking, I'm going to beat the hell out of you."

Rachel put her hand on her chest and felt her breath stop. Todd had *never* threatened her with violence. She then said, "Todd, you're scaring me. What's wrong with you?"

Todd leapt to his feet and pointed at her, causing her to jump back. "I told you to stop asking me the same god-damn questions all the time."

His voice was not loud, but calm and dripping with malice. His eyes seemed to shine with some strange hysteria. Rachel backed up on her cot again, pressing herself against the wall with her legs curled up. Tears were flowing down her face, dripping off her quivering lips. After everything that had happened to them this day, how could he act like this? She understood he dealt with sorrow differently than she did—it came back to that fact that she cried and he didn't—but, there was no call for this. He had no right to take it out on her.

"Stop it, Todd. I'm sorry for whatever I did to piss you off. I love you. All I've wanted to do today was get you to the hospital. I just want to help you."

"Help me? What have you ever done to help me, you selfish bitch?"

"Oh my God, Todd, please stop."

"Don't fucking tell me to stop. If you tell me to stop one more time, I swear to God I'll kill you."

Rachel said nothing else, she only sobbed into her hands. This enraged Todd further.

"Stop it, Rachel. Stop fucking crying. That's all you do is fucking cry and I'm fucking sick of hearing the shit."

Now with the fear of her little brother looming over her, Rachel tried to choke back the tears but couldn't. She pressed her hands over her mouth and tried not to look at this strange lunatic who used to be her sibling.

"God-damnit, Rachel! I said stop!"

"I can't, Todd! I'm sorry. Just leave me alone."

Todd looked down at her, watching the tears streak down her face. All he wanted to do was hurt her.

"I'm so tired of looking at you. You know that?"

"What?"

"Ever since mom and dad died, I've had to do nothing but look at your ugly face. It's your fault Brandon died."

"What? How can you say that?"

"Because it's true."

"He got attacked by possums. I wasn't even there!"

"And he wouldn't have been there either if you could have just driven yourself to work like a normal person."

"He wanted to drive me!"

"You could have let him stay the night. Why didn't you?"

"Todd, stop this…"

"I said not to tell me that again! You know what? I wish you would have been in that fire instead of mom and dad."

Rachel was about to puke. She couldn't believe what she was hearing. The sadness was like a drill twisting through her heart. Her entire life with Todd passed through her mind, and she thought about how hard she'd always tried to help him. She thought about how she risked her life to keep him safe when the possums came. His words were a spear thrust deep into the core of her soul, but that pain soon turned to anger. Now, as he stood above her, lashing out at her as she cried, she saw him less as a little brother and more as one of those vultures empowering themselves with her misery. It was too much for her to handle right now, and she wasn't going to take it.

"You know what, Todd? I've done everything I can for you ever since mom and dad died. I've done everything I could to help you tonight. I almost died helping you. So, if you're so god-damn angry at me and you hate me so much, just fuck off. Fuck you for saying such shitty things to me, you asshole!"

Todd's face turned bright red as he lunged for Rachel. She screamed and tried to back away but he fell on the bed and grabbed her by the throat. She swung at him, punching him on the arms and the face, but he kept moving towards her.

His claws dug deep into her neck, drawing blood. She leaned back and tried to kick him, but the angle would not allow it. Todd's fingers slipped from her neck and she tried to slide away, but he reached out for her and grabbed hold of her hair. Rachel tried to fight his grip as he drug her back towards his face. His mouth was open and he breathed heavily; the look in his eyes was crazed, enraged. She raised her hands and began slapping at him, and Todd finally snapped.

All he wanted to do was tear a chunk out of her neck and drink her blood, but she kept backing away. Tired of her resistance, Todd grabbed her head as tight as he could between his hands and threw his entire weight forward, bashing her head against the stone wall.

Rachel's vision shot full of white and blue sparks before dimming out. It felt like someone had taken a hammer to the back of her skull. Todd pulled her head forward again and smashed it against the wall once more. Everything went dark and blurry for her.

The others came into the room just after Todd slammed Rachel's head against the wall for the second time. A large splatter of her blood shone on the stone. They lingered in the doorway, shocked by the spectacle. Tony was the first to move.

"What are you doing, Todd?"

He moved towards the bed to pull Todd away just as he was closing his fingers around Rachel's windpipe. Tony grabbed the back of the boy's shirt and pulled as Todd's nails dug into his sister's flesh. Rachel was gagging as blood seeped from the wounds. His fingers tightened and he dug into her trachea for the final yank.

Rachel, struggling to breathe, looked into her brother's eyes and saw only rage and madness there. He was going to rip her throat out and she could do nothing about it. Even Tony pulling on his shirt from behind could not dislodge his iron grip. The fury that had engulfed her brother seemed to make him twice as strong as he normally was. She pulled at his arm with both hands but could not break the hold.

But Clyde could.

His hand suddenly shot into Rachel's line of sight and clasped around Todd's wrist, squeezing it as hard as he could. The pain shot through Todd's arm and he let go, releasing Rachel from her coming death and enabling her to breathe again.

With the hold now broken, Tony yanked Todd off the cot and cast him to the floor at Clyde's feet.

"What the fuck are you doing, man?" Clyde yelled.

Todd stood up and shoved him against the wall with surprising strength. Susie screamed and slapped Todd; he grabbed her wrist, bit down on her arm, and tore off a chunk of her forearm. Clyde made an unintelligible scream and grabbed for Todd, but the kid dodged him and headed for the iron door.

"Don't let him open that door!" Carlos yelled, but it was too late. Todd was already pulling back the bolt.

Tony looked around and saw an exit sign to his right and a small metal door beneath it—not an original part of the building, but cut out years later for safety reasons. He knew there were a lot of possums inside the museum, so he quickly deduced that not many would be left outside. He knew that wasn't an iron-clad conclusion, but with the cellblock door already starting to swing open, and the cell doors too old and unpredictable for anyone to hide back there (not to mention that the smaller possums could possibly squeeze between the bars), it was the only decision he could see that carried an opportunity for survival.

So he looked at the others and yelled, "This way!"

Greta, Ingrid, Selma, and Denton followed behind him as he pushed the crash bar and fled into the night. As soon as Denise saw Todd begin to unlock the door, she helped Rachel groggily rise from the cot and took off for the stairs leading up to her apartment, dragging the young dazed woman behind her. She called for the others to join her, but only Carlos heard her. He followed her and Rachel, not wanting to risk going outside. The two women were already at the top of the stairs by the time he reached the bottom. The possums were almost to him as Denise fumbled with her keys, cursing herself for locking the apartment every time she left it.

Rachel, wobbly and still rubbing her throat and the back of her head, and partially in shock from her brother's attack, muttered, "They're coming."

"Hurry up, Denise!" Carlos urged more emphatically, clanging up the stairs.

There were over twenty keys on Denise's keychain, so it took her a second to find the correct one. Once she did, she jammed it into the lock and turned it, pushing the door open and stepping inside. Rachel stumbled in behind her and fell to the floor. Carlos was almost to the top when two possums grabbed his cloak. A few more were skittering up his back. Denise stood there with the door open and a terror-stricken look on her face. Carlos cried out when he felt the teeth dig into the back of his neck.

Denise stepped forward and reached for his hand, but he waved her off and yelled, "I'm not going to make it! Close the door!"

"No!"

Carlos reached the top and knew that if he entered, he'd bring a host of possums with him. He also knew the terrible secret about the possum bites, and cursed himself for not having told the others.

"I've been bitten. I'm as good as dead," he declared, trying to pull the possums off of him.

"What do you mean?"

He was bitten again and screamed, "Their bite is poison!"

More possums were coming. Time was up. He leaned forward and pushed Denise back into her apartment and then grabbed the outer doorknob and pulled the door shut to keep her and Rachel safe. A lot of angry teeth then began digging into the back of his legs and ankles. He lost his footing and fell backwards, slamming against the steps and rolling to the ground.

Lucky for him, he was already dead when the possums began to eat him.

Inside, Denise locked the door and looked at Rachel where she lay on the floor clutching her throat, rubbing the back of her head, and softly crying.

"Did you hear what he said?" she asked.

Rachel cleared her throat and said, "He said their bite is poison."

"I wonder what that means."

Rachel sighed and said, "I think I have a pretty good idea."

"You do?"

Rachel gulped and nodded.

"What?" Denise asked.

Rachel looked at her and said, "You're going to want to barricade that door."

When the emergency exit opened, with no alarm sounding, Clyde grabbed Susie and started dragging her towards the outside. When they got a few feet into the yard, Susie tripped on a large rock embedded in the ground, slipping from Clyde's grasp and hitting the dirt. The possums swarmed her instantly—teeth and claws working furiously—and she began to scream.

"Susie!" Clyde roared.

Without thinking, Clyde ran to her and started kicking and stomping on the possums. Many were biting his legs but he didn't care. He reached down, pulled them away, and tossed them in different directions. He dropped to ground and started knocking and yanking them off of Susie, causing them to pull deeper holes into her flesh. Some bit his hands, tearing the skin away, but he just flung them aside.

Though he fought well for a few seconds, Susie died screaming and soaked in blood right in front of him. With his face full of tears and his body filled with rage, he started grabbing possums and twisting their necks, oblivious to the teeth and claws that occasionally dug into his body. He smashed them with his fists, punched them, and knocked them aside. He even stood back up with some clinging to his elbows and back and started kicking and stomping again and again and again. Though many more grabbed his body, his rage did not abate. Within less than a minute, blood was gushing from the many wounds in his frame, but he had managed to successfully get all the possums off of him.

They stood away, looking up at him. He breathed heavily, dripping blood, surrounded by many of their dead, and said, "That's right. You'd better back the fuck up."

Clyde thought he'd scared them off, but he was wrong. He didn't know three large possums had crept up behind him. The lesser possums had retreated before their masters. When the first one bit into his leg, he felt a hot pain burn through his blood that almost blinded him. When the second one rose up and bit him on the lower back, he collapsed to the ground.

The third one barked and the feast began.

The side door led into the backyard, which was surrounded by a ten-foot chain-link fence. Tony and Greta turned right upon exiting and headed for the gate at the back of the yard, which was unlocked, thankfully. Tony flipped the handle and shoved it open and waited for Greta. When she passed, he closed the gate behind him. There weren't too many possums following them, and the few that were had stopped at the gate. They turned around and went after Ingrid, Denton, and Selma, who turned left at the exit and headed towards the other side of the yard.

Ingrid reached the fence first, and with one jump and a pull, she was straddling the top. Denton was running behind Selma, trying to keep between her and the possums.

When they approached the fence, he said, "Start climbing, Selma. I'll help you."

"I can make it. Don't risk yourself for me."

"I won't let your father's death be for nothing. Now start climbing."

Ingrid held out her hand. "You better hurry up."

Selma protested no further and climbed upon the fence; she reached for Ingrid's hand and was yanked hard up and over the fence. Denton started climbing and a possum attached itself to his shoe. Its teeth didn't break through, but it made it hard for him to climb. Ingrid jumped down on the other side with Selma and waited. Denton was coming up and another possum grabbed his other shoe, this time hanging on by the heel. He tried to use his legs to climb, but the presence of the possums made it difficult. As he neared the top of the fence, he was using only his arms to pull himself up. When he reached the top, he tried to throw his legs over, but the possums hanging onto his feet threw off his balance and he spilled headfirst over the top.

"Shit!" he cried.

When he landed, he hit the ground face-first with his body landing upright, causing all of his weight to come down on his head. He toppled onto his back but his head didn't move, and his neck snapped in half.

No!" Selma screamed.

The two possums that had been clinging to his feet now crawled upon his torso and began digging in. Many others were coming from around the building to join them. Those that were in the backyard started trying to dig out under the fence. This reprieve would not last long.

Ingrid grabbed Selma's hand. "You'd better get moving, lady."

They ran from the front yard to the alley beside the museum, away from the oncoming possums. As soon as they hit the street, they turned right and ran down the road before cutting through some dark yards towards a farm house.

On they ran with possums in pursuit. They fled into a vast, wide open field. At one end there was a shed with an opened door. Selma was falling behind and Ingrid knew she wouldn't make it if they kept running like this. Of all the people she had met that evening, Selma was the only one she really felt for. The woman had sad eyes and a nice demeanor. She had also been the best comfort to Ingrid and she really didn't want to see her die. As she had observed before, the woman reminded her too much of her mother. That's why she'd actually stayed atop the fence to help her over. Anyone else, other than Greta, she would have left behind.

Then she had an idea.

Suddenly, Ingrid veered left and ran towards the shed. Selma noticed her and said, "What the hell are you doing?"

"Just keep going towards the woods. I'll catch up to you."

Selma saw the possums coming, and they weren't far behind, so she did as Ingrid said. Selma wanted to help her but knew she would only slow Ingrid down. Maybe if she ran, the possums would follow her and spare Ingrid. If not, Ingrid might actually lead the possums to their demise. She seemed more than capable of the feat.

Ingrid was glad Selma didn't come after her—but surprised. Her plan was flimsy at best and she knew it didn't make a lot of sense. But, in the heat of this hell, rationale wasn't at the forefront of her thought. Now, all she needed to do was get the possums to follow her instead of Selma.

She screamed as loud as she could. She didn't say anything, just loosed a primal roar that, for a minute, made her soul feel relieved of its immense and ever-present misery. It felt so good that she did it again, without really hearing or realizing it. Her feet pushed harder and her body moved faster. She howled continuously as she ran through the field, going numb to the world around her. When the tide of unrestrained wrath drained from her spirit, she was not far from the shed and hoped her distraction had worked. She looked behind her and saw that every possum in the vicinity had turned her away. Their forms were barely visible in the moonlight, but she could see them well enough. She glanced across the field and saw Selma's dark form was almost to the trees without any possums in pursuit. Ingrid smiled in triumph.

Bring it on then, fuckers.

As she came upon the shed, the possums were right behind her. There was a dim orange bulb glowing inside. The structure was not large, but long and loaded with tools. As soon as she entered, she picked up a billhook that was lying on a wooden counter along the wall and turned around to greet her attackers. She barely had time to take in a breath before they fell upon her. She sliced through the entire first wave as they entered—driving the black blade into the heads and bodies of the creatures left and right—covering herself in their blood. More were coming, some that were large, and she set the billhook back on the counter and looked for a weapon with a better reach.

To her left, she spied a scythe hanging on some nails. She pulled it from the wall, swung around, and started cutting down possums as they entered. Ingrid was strong and she wielded the weapon with quickness and precision. A couple of possums managed to dodge her attack, but not for long, as they ended up momentarily impaled on the wicked blade.

When the first of the larger possums entered, Ingrid managed to gouge its neck with the scythe and it rolled over and died. But, a second one slammed right into her legs, knocking her against the counter and casting her to the floor.

A voice inside her head said, *Fight, Ingrid. Fight!*

Jeremiah? Is that you again?

She rose up on her rear and sat back against something cold and hard; she thrust the scythe at the possum, hitting its neck with the upper side of the blade, and pushed it back. She then brought the tip around and drove it into the animal's shoulder. The scythe was too long for this short range combat, so she tossed it at the creature and reached up for the billhook again.

Her fingers gripped the handle, but it was too late. The big possum bit her right under the arm and grabbed hold. She screamed and tried to elbow it in the head, but its grasp was too tight and every movement caused its bite to rip and tear at her muscles. She swiped her other hand along the ground beside her and happened to feel something sharp. It was a sickle

252

and she brought it up into the temple of the possum. The bite under her arm clamped down harder at first, causing her to scream some more, and then loosened as the possum went slack and fell to the floor.

Several other possums were entering the shed; they reached her legs and started biting. She kicked at them, knocking them away. She punched a few that got too close and managed to keep them off her upper body. But, the wound under her arm was gushing blood and she felt her legs begin to tingle as she grew weaker. This was a bad plan from the start, and now it was proving fatal. She just hoped that Selma had gotten away, because after the possums were done with her, they'd no doubt track the poor, slow woman down.

Behind you, Ingrid, spoke the voice in her head again.

She turned her head and saw she was lying against a tank with a flammable liquid placard attached to it.

You know what to do.

Ingrid swallowed. There was no way to fight all the possums off and survive, but she could make a huge dent in their ranks and keep them from going after Selma. She went into her pocket and pulled out her lighter, then lifted her arm and turned the tank on. Liquid began to spray out behind her.

"Come on, you motherfuckers!" she screamed.

She waited for the rest of the possums to enter the shed. Many were biting all over her legs and had worked their way up her body. She lifted her arm into the air as they scaled her and dug in their teeth. Holding the lighter aloft, and feeling the possums tearing into her, she winced and said, "See you in a second little brother."

The possums covered her upper body all the way to her head. With the last bit of toughness she had in her, she fought through the pain and her hand sailed above the swarm and her thumb flicked the lighter, bringing the flame into the liquid. The fireball erupted and, within seconds, the entire shed was obliterated. The explosion blew many possums into the air and killed every last one of them.

Selma couldn't run anymore. She had stopped to rest many yards away from the shed. When the blast erupted, she jumped and put her arms over her head. In a few seconds, flaming possum parts were raining down around her, making sloppy smacking sounds as they landed in the grass. She screamed and ran into the woods, mourning Ingrid but not looking back.

CHAPTER TWENTY-SIX

Greta and Tony were running through the dark towards East Flaget St. The vehicles that had been left at their house by the men who died fighting there lined their front yard. Bill (God rest his soul) drove a Chevy Blazer—or did when he was still breathing—and Tony intended to find his corpse, dig out the keys, and get Greta and him the hell out of town.

They turned onto East Flaget and their house came into view. No possums could be seen behind them, but they ran as if the creatures were nipping at their heels. The night hung like doom above them; their street was as silent as the grave. They ran through their yard and towards the back, trying to ignore the corpses of their fallen friends. There would be time to mourn them but it would not be tonight. Bill's shredded body lay beneath the motion light, and Tony fished the keys out his coat pocket.

"Got the keys, now let's get the hell out of here."

"What about the animals?"

"They're probably dead, honey."

"Can we at least check to see if they're here?"

"Yeah, sure. I can grab some weapons."

"You look in the house for Hitch and Romero; they could have gotten back in through an open window, but watch out for possums, too. I'll check around the garage for Tippi."

"Okay."

Tony ran to the house and Greta went to the garage. She called for her dog and received no answer. She stepped further in and saw no sign of her.

Lowering herself to the ground, she crawled beneath a broken down Cobalt that had been in the garage for several weeks and still didn't see her. Tippi usually liked to crawl under shelves or cars in the garage when she couldn't get back into the house, but she wasn't here, and that made Greta nervous. When she was about halfway under the car, she heard a low growl behind her. It was a sound she knew well. When the bark followed, she knew what was coming, and it wasn't her beloved Tippi.

Quickly, she pushed herself all the way under the car, not sure if it was a wise move. Once squeezed all the way to the other side, she turned her head and looked straight into the black eyes of one of the master possums.

Its breath was heavy and its eyes cold; its countenance was that of a creature ready to kill. Greta could smell the sickening scent of blood wafting from its partially-opened mouth. It stared into her eyes as if it was trying to tell her something—no doubt it would have been a threat of some kind. As she returned its glare, she expected it to lunge for her any second, but it didn't. It just sat there, its sides pulsating from heavy breathing.

The tension beneath the car was smothering. As she looked in the master possum's face, she realized that this was no wild animal. All the speculation the men had gone through earlier was not idle. Clyde had insisted the creatures were highly intelligent and had a plan, but a few of the others scoffed at the idea. Now, Greta knew they were foolish to do so. Clyde had been correct—these things' movements were calculated. They progressed with purpose; their actions were not of base instinct but of volition. Whatever the monster there with her now was planning, she wished it would come on and make its move.

"Go away!" she yelled.

The creature hissed and started to shuffle under the car. Greta tried to think quickly. In such a tight spot, with her arms mostly pinned and her face exposed, she stood no chance of survival.

The slobbering creature had blood all over its face, and it crept closer. It stopped just a few feet in front of her, growled and shuffled its paws. She felt the tears coming but held them back. If this creature understood emotions, she would not give it the satisfaction of seeing fear or sadness on her face before she died.

"You can go to Hell," she told it.

The possum opened its mouth wide and released a long, foul, saliva-spraying hiss and sprung forward. Greta braced herself for the pain of the coming death. Her life did not flash before her eyes; there was only darkness, and numbness, knowing she was about to suffer greatly before her passing. There was terror—the kind that sent ice racing through your veins and waste spilling through your guts. Her throat was not very exposed, which meant the beast would have to gnaw through her face, which would be wildly unpleasant. As weird of a last thought as it was, she wished her throat was more open to the possum's jaws.

She waited for the attack—but it didn't come. When she opened her eyes, she saw the possum struggling to move forward. It suddenly squealed in her face as it was dragged out from under the car.

When the possum was removed, she saw four yellow legs standing beyond the car. The possum was slung around and tossed aside. Then, the creature that had saved her lowered itself to the ground, and Greta saw Tippi's head with her lips pulled back in a menacing growl.

"Tippi!" she cried.

Tippi sprung at the possum, clamped her mouth around the back of its neck and bit down. Blood oozed out instantly and the creature tried to back away from the hold but could not. Its face was pressed to the garage floor and Tippi was not letting up. The possum wriggled its head around in hopes of squirming free, but the Lab would not allow it. Tippi thrust her front paws forward to pin the possum down and bit as hard as she could, snapping its neck bones in a multitude of tiny crackling sounds. The possum shrieked and kicked for a few seconds before collapsing on the floor. When Greta was sure it was dead, she crawled out to pet her dog.

"Good girl," she said and Tippi licked her hand, leaving smears of possum blood along it.

Tony came into the garage and smiled when he saw Tippi. "Glad you're okay girl." He saw the dead possum and asked, "She do that?"

"She saved my life."

"I knew she was a wise investment. Look, I didn't have time to find any weapons; but, we got to get going. I heard possums coming down the road. They'll be here soon."

Greta looked past Tony and saw the possum shadows along the ground coming closer to the garage door and said, "They're here, now."

The sounds were rising up in unison, like a bestial war cry in the wild. They were near and there was no escaping them. Tippi growled when they came into view and crowded the doorway. With her hackles rising, she was ready for another brawl. Slowly, the beasts poured in, taking their time, as if measuring their prey.

"What do we do, Tony?"

"I don't know. There's not much we can do."

"Can we get in the Cobalt?"

"The windows don't roll up."

More possums entered the garage, with many more piling up behind them. Greta looked around for a way out, or a place to hide, or a decent weapon with which she could make a stand. There was a work bench a few feet from Tony with several tools resting on it, but they were surrounded and possums blocked the way, so she could not reach it. All the windows were open but most of them were also beyond the sea of marsupials. There was one behind her, but it was also on the other side of the car. If they made a break for it, they would be dinner before they could jump through.

"There's no way out," she said.

"No, there isn't," Tony agreed.

Something leapt onto the windowsill behind her and shrieked like an injured banshee, but it clearly wasn't a possum—it was a feline. She turned and saw Romero in the window. Hitch jumped up and stood next to him. Their backs were arched, their ears flat to their heads, and long, low feline growls rumbled in their throats.

Tony and Greta smiled and, for one second, felt a smidgeon of hope, even though they knew there wasn't a lot their beloved cats could do here but die. Greta wished they'd just jump down and run back off into the night.

But Hitch and Romero weren't the only visitors to arrive. Howls and barks that didn't belong to possums began to sound out all around the garage. More feline hisses and growls began to mix with the chorus. Suddenly, all four garage windows filled with cats as numerous dogs, large and small, from terriers to Dobermans, flanked the possums in the doorway. They all lowered themselves to the ground and growled, clearly ready to rumble.

Tony laughed nervously, almost feeling like crying. "I think every stray you ever fed around here just showed up—with their friends and family."

Greta, who *was* crying, smiled. "I knew it was a wise investment."

The possums turned their attention from the humans to face the dogs and began issuing their own threats. Greta and Tony huddled together, afraid to be caught in the middle of the melee. In a few seconds, the garage fell silent and the tension became an oppressive blanket floating over them.

Then, a stray cat leapt off one of the windows; it landed on a possum and the whole garage erupted into a wild kingdom skirmish. There were more than enough cats and dogs to match the possums. Tippi, Hitch, and Romero charged in. Tony helped Greta get on top of the Cobalt and he jumped up to join her; there they sat and watched the war, fearing not only for their own lives, but for the lives of their pets.

The donnybrook that broke loose threatened to tear the entire garage apart. Dogs tore at possums' necks and heads; cats scratched and clawed at their eyes; possums were ganging up on dogs, and chewing on cats. The free-for-all raged on in a perpetual state of pandemonium as the four-legged creatures rolled over each other in massive tangles of blood and fur. Greta and Tony could not imagine how long they'd have to huddle atop the car before they could make their move to get out of there. Finally, after what felt like an hour, most of the fight spilled out into the yard, leaving a clear enough path for them to escape through. Tony jumped down and helped Greta, and they blasted through the battle as fast as they could flee.

"Tippi, Hitch, Romero," Tony called. "Come on!"

Tippi broke away from the fray outside and ran after them. Hitch and Romero, still in the garage, ran across some shelves along the wall and jumped through the door. The strays and the possums were fighting to the death behind them as they ran for Bill's Blazer, which was parked in the middle of the yard.

Tony opened the passenger side door for Greta and she flung herself inside. He then opened the back door for the animals and they jumped in. When he got behind the wheel and took off, he backed into something large and it hung the car up.

They heard the squealing behind them, and Tippi began to bark.

"Must be one of those big fuckers," Tony said. "And I think I'm somehow stuck on it."

Before he could get loose, more possums came from down the street and swarmed the Blazer, covering the windows and piling against the doors. They started rocking it back and forth with several heavy impacts. Tony gunned the gas but couldn't move.

"We're stuck!"

The Blazer rocked even harder and came up off the ground a little. Something slammed against the passenger side window, sending a crack down the middle.

"They're going to get in," Greta said.

Tony tried to back up and move forwards, but neither worked. The Blazer rose off the ground again for a second and fell back down.

"We've got to do something," she said.

"What?"

"I don't know."

Cracks began to form in all the windows as they were pummeled by possums flinging their bodies against them, like stones being thrown by some punk kid. There was no escape. They had made it out of the garage to a freedom they thought was impossible only to be thwarted again by some fat-ass possum getting stuck under their wheel. In no time, the swarm would either dump the Blazer on its side or shatter the windows and invade. Tony wasn't going to sit there and do nothing while Greta got eaten. So, he had one last plan in his pocket.

He turned to Greta and said, "I love you, baby."

She looked at Tony and saw a weird look in his eye—one that was almost suicidal. Then, she saw his left hand on the door handle. She reached out and grabbed his wrist.

"No. You're not doing that."

"I can lead them away."

"No!"

"Better me than both of us."

"I'd rather it be both of us."

"I'm sorry, Greta. I'm not going to let you die."

"I won't let you, either. I'll get out, too."

She put her hand on her door handle, too. They both looked at each other for a second.

Greta swallowed and then smiled. "Maybe we can both make it if we run."

Another heavy thud smashed against the Blazer, causing it to wobble. Soon, it was being lifted, even higher than before. Loud barks outside alerted them to the presence of the larger possums. In a couple of seconds, the vehicle hit the ground, bouncing the occupants around.

"They're going to dump us soon, just like they did Clyde," Tony said.

"I know. We can make it."

"No. You stay here. I'll lead them away," he repeated.

"Not a chance. I'm going with you."

"No, you got to take care of the animals," he smiled.

"They can take care of themselves."

"I can't stop you, can I?"

"No."

Then we go on the count of three?"

"Okay."

"One," Tony said.

"Two," Greta added.

Both of them tugged on their door handles, unlocking the doors and opening them just a bit. The interior lights came on the door-ajar alarm jingled.

"You ready?" Tony asked.

Greta had tears in her eyes. "Yes."

Both of them clutched the handles, ready to pull them forward and fly from the car. Just before they did so, something hit the passenger window, making Greta jump. But, it wasn't a possum; it was something else that they couldn't see.

Possums began to fly off the window beside her, yanked away by some unseen force. They were soon cleared from the windshield, as well. They began to scatter around the Blazer as the new presence bashed them back. A man's muffled voice soon echoed through the night, yelling something they couldn't decipher. The figure came into view and they both squinted against the night to see who their savior was.

When they looked out the now cleared windows, they saw Herbert in his full riot gear swinging his hammer at the possums that were on the front of the car. He smashed several of them in the head and the rest jumped to the ground. He launched the hammer at one of them and it flew, spinning head over foot through the air, and hit it square in the face.

"Take that you little shit!" he yelled.

One jumped on his shoulder and he yanked it away, held it to the hood of the Blazer and went for his hacksaw. The blade cut into the possum's neck until Herbert sawed its head off. Possums jumped on the hood and ran after him, but he swung the hacksaw like a short sword and the tool's jagged teeth sent many of them to the ground to die. He swiped at them repeatedly until so many piled on his arm that he had to drop the hacksaw.

"You think that's enough, you motherfuckers?" he asked and lifted the screwdriver from his belt and started stabbing at them.

Holes were punctured in their forms. Herbert looked like a madman, down-thrusting the screwdriver into the furry creatures, hollering obscenities at them as he went. For Greta, it conjured a comical vision of Ralphie's dad in *A Christmas Story* swearing at the furnace in the basement and she actually chuckled. Tony didn't even notice because he was too transfixed on the enraged berserker before them, slashing and stabbing at a bunch of batshit possums.

Most of the offending creatures fell dead or withdrew into the night. One possum tried to jump on the hood and sneak up on Herbert, but he spun and drove the screwdriver into its face, where it stayed as the creature fell to the ground.

Three more scrambled across the hood. He whipped the mallet out from the back of his belt and brought it down in rapid succession, caving in the heads of the attackers like a maniac's version of Whac-A-Mole. Several possums grabbed his feet, so he knelt down and started bashing them all to bits. He killed seven before one possum dodged, causing Herbert to strike the road so hard that the head of the mallet broke off.

More possums swarmed around him as he stood up, so he took out his machete and brought it over his right shoulder. This time the possums didn't play dead—they *fell* dead instead as he swiped and slashed and cut into them, sending those that did not die fleeing back into the night. He pursued some of them through the yard and cut them down, his blade slicing through their bodies.

After laying many more to waste, he held his machete up like He-Man and cried, "That's right you assholes! Nobody messes with Crazy Herbert!"

More possums had surrounded the Blazer, so he ran back over there and put his machete away. He reached into the pouch where the spray can was and took it out, then lifted the mini-torch out with it.

"I've waited all night to do this," he said.

He stopped by the Blazer, lifted the butane can and turned on the torch, then said, "Tony, Greta—you two go on, now. I can handle this. I got those big ones off the back tire."

Tony rolled down the window. "Get in! Come with us."

"Hell no. I got some exterminating to do."

He then sprayed the can towards the possums, sending a long stream of fire spewing forth. Several of them lit up, including a few of the larger ones. Many of them ran, bumping into others and setting them aflame. In seconds, there were more than a dozen balls of fire running through the yard.

More possums gathered around him—so many, it looked impossible to overcome, even with his torch and all the armor. But soon, the neighborhood strays, fresh off their victory back at the garage, came running through the yard to hunt some more.

Tony didn't wait; he rolled up the window and backed out to the road. Greta took one last look at Herbert, hooting and hollering as flames flew from him like he was a mini-dragon, chasing off all the possums while the strays destroyed many more around him.

As they drove away, she heard him yell, "This one's for Gene, you sons-of-bitches! And this one is for Steve!"

Tony sped down the road, watching the fire disappear in the rearview mirror, silently wishing Herbert the best of luck, though he knew the man might not need it. If there was one person capable of surviving in a town overrun by mad, man-eating possums, it was Herbert McElroy.

The road was dark and it led out of town. Nothing now stood in their way. Greta grabbed Tony's hand and he pressed down on the pedal, leaving Bardstown and its entire possum population in the dust.

Jacob Floyd

EPILOGUE

Cara managed to navigate her way through the long dark woods without incident. After escaping the possums in Bardstown, her journey had been mostly quiet. There were a few times she heard leaves crunching and other unidentified sounds coming from somewhere around her, but she never faced another possum. Wherever the creek had taken them, it must have been far away from her.

She exited the expansive woods a couple of hours after her encounter with the gargantuan monster that assailed her by the creek. She walked down an unlit side road that wound around a deserted stretch of the county for quite some time. There were no houses, no buildings, and no streetlights, just the fields and hills and the moonlight above to guide her. She was not quite sure where she was, but she assumed she was somewhere beyond the southern edge of the city, near the hills.

She walked for what felt like hours; she walked so long that her feet bled and the moon changed positions in the sky. She saw no sign of anyone, not even once. She saw no cars, heard no voices, and didn't see any signs of possum attacks. For a long time, she feared everyone else was dead and that she would forever walk through an empty wasteland.

Am I dead and in Hell?

The panic of perpetual loneliness started to overtake her and she thought about stopping and screaming for help. Maybe the possums would come; that was beginning to look like a better fate than this endless solitude. For a few minutes, the spiders of anxiety danced their way along her skin, making her shiver. After a severe bout of the shakes, she managed to get a hold of herself and realize she was just weary from the day's events, and that she was traversing an area far away from civilization. There was no apocalypse at hand. Of course there were other people still alive in the world. These were only possums attacking the town. There was no way for them to overrun the entire state. Kentucky was full of country boys who were in love with their guns, not to mention Fort Knox was not too far away. The possums would be completely eradicated before their threat could spread too far. She stopped, took a few deep breaths, shook it off, and recommenced her wandering.

The path led to a narrow wooden bridge extended over a long, deep ditch. Cara stepped onto the bridge and looked down into the dense pitch beneath her. This was an unrecognizable location. Cara had only lived in Bardstown since her freshman year of high school, and she had never gone exploring. As long as she had been out in the night drifting—hours, she deduced, for the chirps of the morning birds were now tweeting softly in the distance—it was unlikely she was even in Bardstown, anymore. Wherever she was, this area was unknown to her.

She turned her head to gaze at the path she'd come from and considered going back, but did not know how close the possums could be. Her natural instincts told her that she had walked in the opposite direction of where the creek took the last ones she saw, but everything around her began to resemble an uncharted wilderness miles ago, so there was no way for her to be sure that her sense of direction was reliable. Besides, there could easily be more possum packs roving through the night. It seemed that one way was as good as the other.

So, it was to be the bridge and the unknown that lay beyond it.

As she cautiously crossed the bridge, she listened hard to the night. Katydids, crickets, and cicadas sang, the planks under her feet creaked, and the leaves in the converging trees ahead of her whispered, but there was no growling, no hissing, and no scratching of claws on the ground. She breathed easily despite her anxiety.

Cara neither heard nor smelled any water. Upon looking over the rails once again, the reflection of the moon she sought did not appear. That meant the chasm beneath her was dry. She wondered if any possums were down there. How many could hide in that creek bed? If they were down there, though, she would have heard them. Wouldn't she? She decided there was no sense in frightening herself. What was below was a mystery that she chose not to ponder. Getting away from this dark, empty land was her focus.

At a little more than halfway across, the bridge began to slightly slope upward. Normally, this would have presented no problem for Cara's strong, muscular legs, but the night had been strenuous, and her body ached. She found herself gripping the rails and pulling herself along, struggling to push herself up. Towards the bridge's end, the path mercifully leveled out, and she was soon striding across a clear grassy path through the woods.

The passage was long, and lead straight under the moon. She could see the open pathway ahead of her, walled in by tall pines and maples. The silence and the stillness made her uneasy. It was as if time had died and existence was caught in an endless night, the world no longer spinning on its axis, and everything had turned as quiet as outer space. Where she had been walking before was seemingly vacant, but somewhat open, which would have given her a fighting chance if possums attacked; what she now walked along was an inescapable tunnel. If possums were in the surrounding woods and they chose to close in on her, the act would equal certain death. A straight run here would not avail her, despite her speed; and, to venture off into the woods with them would be suicide. This realization spread fear through her, making her dangerously vigilant. If she could have seen her knuckles as she grasped her knife so hard, she would have seen they were as pale as bone.

On she walked, like a drifter in a dream, a wayfarer seeking an end she knew would come for her from out of the darkness. The moonlight was becoming blurry and her legs heavy; there was not much left in her tank. If possums didn't get her soon, then weariness would take her down.

A slight slope returned to the walk and Cara imagined herself traveling closer to the moon, preparing to ascend into orbit. She laughed and wondered again if the whole world really *was* dead. Her previous conclusion about that notion being an impossibility might have simply been her mind lulling her into a false security—a cruel coping mechanism that kept her from the painful reality that she really was now alone in life, like in that Vincent Price movie, based on that book she had to read in high school. In the end, she would find herself at war in a world full of possums—one woman the final hope for mankind.

That's so dumb, Cara. Snap out of it, girl.

The incline was now so steep, and her back so sore, that she found herself reaching out and planting her left palm on the ground to help her climb. Her right hand was still clutching that knife as if it were a body part, and there was no way she was letting it go.

Once she achieved the apex, she stood upon a hilltop overlooking a narrow, silent valley that led to another expanse of trees. Her heart sank as she surveyed the landscape and saw no roads, no city lights, and nothing of consequence beyond the treetops.

"God-damnit!" she cursed.

Once again, she turned around and looked behind her at a layout that was as empty and lifeless as that which was before her. There was no reason to retrace her steps; she knew it was a void back there. What lay ahead was yet unknown, which gave it a more hopeful air than that which lay behind. So, she began her descent into the valley, stepping cautiously so she didn't trip and tumble down the hillside in her tired state.

Wouldn't that be something? To fall and break her leg or stab herself with her own knife as she cascaded clumsily down the hill? Would she lie there until the possums found her, or would the carrion birds get to her first? Maybe she would just remain there until she died of starvation or dehydration, then turn black and decompose. Who would find her? This place looked like the western frontier, like in that novel, *Lonesome Dove.* There was absolutely nothing. Where the hell was she?

She entered the glen below, which was nothing but high grass and bushes. She crossed it in no time and entered the wooded area. The trees within were tall and skinny and without any low branches. Far away in the distance she saw faint lights. Her eyes had deceived her upon the hilltop: this did lead to civilization.

Lights?

Life?

People?

She broke into a run, kicking up leaves around her. If there were any creatures around, then they would hear her. But the same went for any humans, and she desperately hoped that at least one person was nearby.

The woods were dark, but easy to navigate. She tripped only once, not falling, and bumped a tree or two before reaching the other side. Once there, she stepped to the edge of the tree line and looked around.

Her heart leapt at the sound of human voices. Her eyes were tired and out of focus, so she closed them and tried to rub the weariness away. When she reopened them and squinted, her vision fixed on a section of light glowing about forty feet from where she stood.

Cara knew she was a startling sight at this point, but she exited the woods anyway and started walking up the street towards the light. The closer she got, the better her vision became. She saw a white van with three men around it parked beneath a streetlight, of which there were only a few on this strip of road. It was not a thoroughfare by any means—in fact, it was rather secluded—but it was an operable road, nonetheless.

The men were talking urgently, shining lights around the area. One man in particular seemed rather distressed. She was afraid if she came upon them suddenly, they might shoot her or do something drastic. She had no idea who these men were—they could have been thieves or killers. So, she stopped where she was and called to them.

"Hello?" she said.

Three flashlights suddenly turned on her and one man with a deep voice said, "Who's there?"

Cara raised her hands, showing her weapon. Another man said, "She has a knife! Is she one of them?"

The man who had been talking wildly said, "No, she isn't."

"How can you tell?" the other man asked.

"She wouldn't have stopped and said anything to us," he replied.

"Who are you?" the man with the deep voice said.

"My name's Cara. Do you know about the possums?"

The question was crazy and to the point, but she could think of no way to explain what had happened to her that sounded lucid. Besides, it took every last bit of reserve she possessed to keep herself from collapsing into a heap on the road, so she didn't have it in her to go into great detail. All she could hope for was that these men knew what was going on and didn't think she was deranged.

The men were silent for a second before they began whispering to one another. Cara held her breath, afraid of what conclusion they might reach regarding her psychotic appearance. When they were finished with their deliberation, the urgent man spoke. "Yes, we know about the possums. What do you know about them?"

Cara breathed again, relieved, but only slightly.

"They attacked a group of my friends, and the few of us who survived ran into another group of survivors out on the road. We went with them to someone else's house, and were attacked by an even larger group of possums. Most of us were killed. We went into town, but me and another guy were separated from the group. I think he was killed in the woods a ways back. I've been walking alone for a long time."

"How long?"

Cara shrugged. "I really don't know. All night, I suppose."

"Where did you come from?" the man with the deep voice asked.

"Bardstown."

The men were silent again for a moment. Then the urgent one said, "That's a pretty good walk from here."

"I don't even know where I am. Where are we?"

"Devils Backbone."

Cara was shocked. Devils Backbone was one of the ridges that ran through Nelson County, and it was near Howardstown, about thirty miles southwest of Bardstown. She knew she had been walking for quite some time, but she had no idea she had gotten that far.

Devils Backbone was dense and hard to travel. It posed a perfect haven for large armies of killer possums. That she hadn't encountered any since Bardstown was miraculous. If the possums had made it to Devils Backbone, then the situation was even direr than she had imagined.

"Have the possums gotten this far?"

Again, the men were silent, and none of them answered. Instead, the urgent man said, "Have you been bitten?"

"No."

One flashlight shut off, then the others went out, plunging Cara back into darkness, the sudden transition momentarily blinding her. That slight twinge of panic returned for a second as she heard the men's footsteps approaching. Cara lowered her arms and turned the knife in her hand, blade pointing outwards, towards the oncoming men. She was ready to cut the first one that attacked her. As they drew near, her eyesight settled in the darkness and she could see all three men were dressed in black and two of the guys looked strong, but not big; they walked with a steady march that exuded power. The other man was of average size and normal gait. He did not seem powerful. Cara decided if one of them made a threatening move, she would cut for the nearest of the stronger looking men, then stab whomever was closest to her.

The average-sized man stopped a few feet away and motioned for the other two to halt. Despite being the least menacing, it was he who was in charge. When he spoke, she could tell it was the man with the urgent voice.

"My name is Dr. Manuel. You said your name is Cara?"

"Yes—Cara Hall."

Dr. Manuel looked at the two men beside him, then back at her and said, "Well Cara Hall, I'm quite impressed you've made it so far. These possums, you see, they're everywhere, and quite ferocious. The latter a fact of which I assume you are already aware. It's rather dangerous out here, especially for one wandering alone through the dark. Morning is almost upon us. Is there someplace we can take you to make sure you get home safely?"

Cara shook her head. "My home was overrun. Both my parents and my sister were killed."

Dr. Manuel's expression grew melancholic. This girl was so young, and she had lost everything. Such a tragedy; it pained his heart to hear this, and to also realize that her story was probably unfolding around so many people in Nelson County, and maybe beyond, thanks to the utter carelessness of someone's rash decisions.

"I am truly sorry to hear this," he said.

"It's not your fault," she said numbly.

Is it not? he thought. *Perhaps not; at least, not entirely.*

"Where were you going that brought you out here?" he said.

She shrugged. "I don't know. I was just trying to get away. Several possums chased me through the woods back in Bardstown, and I was attacked by one that looked like a mutant."

For a split second, Dr. Manuel's eyes widened, but he quickly wiped the alarm from his face. He hoped Cara hadn't noticed it. In this darkness that comes just prior to dawn, he doubted she could see much of his expression. But, no matter what his face said, his heart had started pounding and chilly dread swirled in his stomach. The two men next to him stirred, too. This was not what any of them wanted to hear.

He lightly cleared his throat and asked, "What do you mean when you say it looked like a mutant?"

"It was really big—bigger than any possum I've ever seen. It came after me, but I managed to get away."

"Were you able to kill it?"

Cara shook her head again. "No. But, some people I was with before managed to kill a few."

"A few?" This time, the doctor couldn't hide his concern.

"Yes—there are many of them out there. They are enormous and have long teeth. Why? Do you know something about them?"

Dr. Manuel took a second to contemplate his answer. Cara knew possums were attacking people, but she did not know exactly what was going on; or, at least, what had caused it. But, she was no fool, and she did not seem weak. It seemed she had survived a few attacks; judging by the splattering of blood all about her body, she was a fighter. She had made it this far, and that was surprising. Not just because of the possums, but because of the other problem that had risen—a problem his colleagues had not previously foreseen. Maybe she could help them. They could not keep the outbreak a secret at this juncture, at least not in Nelson County. So many people already knew about the possums. There was no reason to pretend the attacks weren't happening. However, there was also no need to inform her of the other threat that was no doubt gathering about the county. It was almost for certain that she and many others would come to face that problem soon enough. Undoubtedly, there were those who already had.

"We might know a little bit about them. In fact, we are actually trying to find as many of them as we can."

Cara studied the three men before her and said, "It's going to take more than you three to wipe them out."

"Our goal isn't to necessarily wipe them out—not yet. We are actually tracking them, recording their movements and behaviors. Of course, if we find them in an area where they are an imminent danger to humans, we will see that the proper action is taken. There are others besides us out here tracking them."

"Really?" she asked.

Dr. Manuel nodded, then, realizing she probably couldn't see him very well, said, "Yes."

"How long have you been looking for them?"

"A couple of days."

"They've been out here that long?"

"Not quite. You see, they didn't descend on populated areas until two days ago, and even then it was a light scattering here and there. The attacks began within the last twenty-four hours or so, we believe, and we are trying to figure out how to corral them and bring them home."

"Bring them home? What does that mean?"

Dr. Manuel sighed. "Cara, please come with us. We could use someone like you. Besides, it is our duty to see that clean civilians are taken to safety."

"What do you mean by clean?"

"I mean unbitten."

"Why only unbitten people?"

Dr. Manuel smiled nervously and said, "Perhaps that is something I can explain along the way."

Cara hesitated, not sure if she wanted to go with the doctor and his two henchmen. He seemed sincere enough, but very evasive. She sensed he was hiding something. But, did that necessarily make him malicious? Maybe he was just hiding what he knew because he didn't want to spread panic. He had been, for the most part, fairly forthcoming. Maybe this would be the safest path for her.

Just as she was about to accept his offer, something came crashing through the brush behind her. She spun and the three men turned their flashlights on to see what had made the ruckus. She expected to see large possums, but instead there were several wild-looking men emerging from the woods; each of them looked crazed: their faces and hands were bloody and rage seethed from between their gritted teeth. They walked briskly and ominously. The doctor grabbed Cara by the shoulder and she turned to face him.

"Come with us," he said, adopting his urgent voice again. "We must get into the van."

"Who are these men? What are they doing?"

"Never mind that, just come with us."

The wild men broke into a run, grunting as they moved forward. Cara looked at some of them again and saw their eyes full of hate, and could tell that their clothes were ripped and stained with blood. Their intentions became clear in an instant, and Cara retreated with Dr. Manuel and his two allies.

"Do you want me to fire on them?" one of the other men asked, jogging backwards with his gun aimed at the blood-covered maniacs.

"Not if you can help it," Dr. Manuel replied. "There are too many. We do not have enough ammo. For now, we must escape."

Several more humans—men, women, and children—exploded from the woods all around them. Cara and the men picked up the pace. They came to the van and got in: one man took the driver's seat; Dr. Manuel took the front passenger's seat; and the other man slid into the back with Cara close behind him. Once in, she closed the side door, just seconds before the freaks slammed into it. They immediately began beating on the van, rocking it hard, trying to fight their way inside.

"Start the car, Larry," Dr. Manuel said to the curly-haired henchmen who had climbed into the driver's seat.

Larry engaged the ignition and the van rumbled to life. Some of the people outside were now climbing onto the van, looking for any way to gain access.

"What the hell are they doing?" Cara asked.

"Attacking," the man in the back with her said.

"Why?"

"Because they've been bitten," he replied.

Dr. Manuel quickly glanced at the man through the rearview mirror. "There is no current need to divulge such information, Rosie."

Rosie, a smooth-faced man with long, straight, black hair, said, "Can't really hide that fact at this point, boss."

Larry gunned the gas, throwing the lunatics off the top of the van. Cara looked out the back window and saw them rolling in the street. With the light blue sky that heralds the dawn now peeking over the horizon, they sped down the road away from where Cara had emerged earlier from the woods.

After they got far enough away to feel comfortable, Dr. Manuel turned in his seat to face Cara and said, "Cara, you see, it's not just the possums we have to worry about. Let me tell you why we only take people who haven't been bitten."

TO BE CONTINUED IN:

THE POSSUMS OF OF DAWN

Jacob Floyd was born and raised in Louisville, KY where he lives with his wife Jenny, three dogs (Tarzan, Pegasus, and Snow White), and two cats (Baloo and Narnia). He and Jenny own and operate two ghost walks (Jacob Floyd's Shepherdsville History and Haunts Tour and Jacob Floyd's NuLu History and Haunts Tour) as well as Anubis Press and its imprints. Jacob also authors the blog, *Jacob Floyd's Ghosts and Monsters*, which discusses dark fiction and the paranormal.

His favorite authors are Clive Barker, Richard Laymon, James Herbert, S.E. Hinton, J.R.R. Tolkien, R.L. Stine, Charles Dickens, Edgar Allan Poe, Matsuo Basho, John Steinbeck, Toni Morrison, Allen Ginsburg, Ernest Hemingway, Emily Dickenson, Poppy Z. Brite, Robert Jordan, Elmore Leonard, Iceberg Slim, Fyodor Dostoevsky, Isaac Asimov, Dennis Lehane, Suzanne Collins, J.K Rowling, Ray Bradbury, Dean Koontz, David Domine, and Jasper Bark.

Some of his favorite films are *The Return of the Living Dead, The Crow, The Exorcist, Taxi Driver, Jeepers Creepers, The Warriors, Halloween, Dark City, The City of Lost Children, Krull, Watchmen, The Prophecy* (the first three), *The Texas Chainsaw Massacre, Crouching Tiger, Hidden Dragon, The Matrix, Hellraiser 1 & 2, Nightbreed, The Neverending Story, Rumble Fish, Underworld, Dark Knight, Pitch Black, Lost Highway, The Lost Boys, Fright Night, Nerve, The Prince of Darkness, Mulholland Drive,* both *Bladerunner* movies, *The Lord of the Rings,* the entire works of Alfred Hitchcock, and the *Godzilla* films.

He also loves the numerous horror, mystery, and sci-fi television anthologies, such as *The Twilight Zone, The Outer Limits, Tales from the Darkside, The X-Files, Monsters, Alfred Hitchcock Presents, Amazing Stories, Tales from the Crypt, The Ray Bradbury Theater, Night Gallery, Science Fiction Theatre, One Step Beyond, Tales of Tomorrow, Friday the 13th – The Series, Freddy's Nightmares, The Hitchhiker,* and many more.

You can follow Jacob on social media, as well as his and Jenny's paranormal endeavors, at the sites below:

<u>FACEBOOK</u>
Jacob Floyd, Author
The Frightening Floyds
The Frightening Floyds' Shepherdsville History and Haunts Tour
The Frightening Floyds' NuLu History and Haunts Tour
Jacob Floyd's Ghosts and Monsters
Anubis Press
Nightmare Press
The Traveling Floyds
Frightening Floyds Photography

Twitter: @AuthorJAFloyd
@AnubisPress

Instagram: authorjacobfloyd

Check out his Wordpress blog: *Jacob Floyd's Ghosts and Monsters*

You can also find his bibliography on Amazon.

Also from Anubis Press:

Haunts of Hollywood Stars and Starlets by Jacob and Jenny Floyd

Explore the dark side of Tinseltown in this collection of paranormal stories, conspiracy theories, curses, and legends about some of Hollywood's most iconic names: Marilyn Monroe, Rudolph Valentino, Charlie Chaplin, James Dean, Jean Harlow, Clark and Carole, Lucille Ball, Michael Jackson, Bela Lugosi, Lon Cheney, John Belushi, and the King himself—Elvis Presley—and many more. Join the Frightening Floyds as they take you on a terrifying journey through the city of glamour and glitz!

Available on Amazon in paperback and Kindle!

THANK YOU FOR READING.

PLEASE LEAVE A REVIEW ON
AMAZON AND/OR GOODREADS.

Made in the USA
Columbia, SC
10 September 2024

41781897R00176